Warrior

"A Kazeem of Zamboria Adventure"

A Novel By

Jaysen Christopher

authorHOUSE®

AuthorHouse™
1663 Liberty Drive
Bloomington, IN 47403
www.authorhouse.com
Phone: 1 (800) 839-8640

Published by AuthorHouse 06/22/2016

ISBN: 978-1-5246-1538-3 (sc)
ISBN: 978-1-5246-1536-9 (hc)
ISBN: 978-1-5246-1537-6 (e)

Library of Congress Control Number: 2016910199

Print information available on the last page.

Any people depicted in stock imagery provided by Thinkstock are models, and such images are being used for illustrative purposes only. Certain stock imagery © Thinkstock.

This book is printed on acid-free paper.

For Cheryl
With Love and Gratitude

CHAPTER ONE

THE YOUNG MAN was beautifully muscled. Sweat poured from his brow and trickled onto his bare chest, soaking the hollow between rock-hard slabs of muscle. He may have been young, but he knew how to handle a sword. Steel rang against steel in the hot desert air, but his concentration lagged, and he watched in dismay as the old man knocked the blade to the sand.

"Well, go on. Pick it up. We'll have another go at it."

"I don't want to." The boy retrieved his blade; it was beautifully crafted, a saber with an ivory handle carved in the shape of a wolf's head. The handle was hot to the touch. He was tired. He didn't want to practice any more.

"A real enemy wouldn't give you the choice," the old man scolded.

"You're real enough," the teenager snarled, only half joking. "With friends like you, who *needs* real enemies?"

The old man could have been fifty. He could have been a thousand. It was hard to tell. He had stone white hair cropped close to his head. Like his beard, it gleamed like silver in the fading, orange sun.

He pressed the attack.

The young man barely had time to get the blade up before the teacher was on him. This was a fierceness he'd never seen before.

And this boy, at the tender age of eighteen, was already a man killer.

Up, down, side-to-side, the old man battered his blade. The thrusts and parries were so swift, so savage, that bare defense was the only thing the lad had time for. The ringing of fine Arganian steel was like a song: clang, clang—clang-clang-clang! Again the boy's sword arm went numb. Again, the blade clattered to the ground.

The young man blinked, chest heaving, soaking wet to the waistband of his loose-fitting white pants. The old man had pressed him hard, all the way back to the rocks. He fought for breath, squinting into the rose-orange rays of the sun as it sank slowly into the jagged teeth of the Faylon Range.

"Maybe you *should* call it a day," the old man agreed. The boy hated him all the more because he was hardly even breathing hard. "If I'd been trying, you'd be dead now."

The youth rubbed numb fingers with a sun-burnt left hand. "*If* you'd been trying! By the Maker, Windor, it sure *felt* like you were trying!"

"You're not yourself, Kazeem," the old man said softly. The setting sun made his eyes look like bronze disks.

The lad picked up the blade, held it in his left hand. He sucked the fingertips of his right and winced without looking up.

"Go," the old man said with a wave. "Eat. Sleep. Slay whatever demons haunt you. I can teach you no more today." He turned and walked away.

"Where would I start?" the youth mumbled to himself and went to sit by the pool.

It was a cool oasis, dotted by date palms and a small grove of cedar. It was the only fresh water for miles, and he was glad to have it, even if they shared it with every wild animal in the area.

Kazeem ate from the pot: a stew made of rabbit and carrots and potatoes. There was a piece of unleavened bread to go with it, cheese and water, but the young man wasn't all that hungry.

Windor was right. He wasn't concentrating. That, alone, could get you killed.

He hated when Windor was right.

Kazeem sat back, hands behind him in the saw grass. Like most Zamborians he was blond, and like most Zamborians he had a broad face, tanned skin and very white teeth—the product of a dairy-rich diet. He wouldn't grow much more in height, which was five foot seven or eight, but he had that stringy muscularity common to all lean men, and the promise of more muscle with the coming of manhood.

He wiped the sweat from his chest, made a pillow of his soft cotton shirt, and closed his unusual amber-brown eyes with a sigh. A warm breeze and the scent of conifers heralded the advance of nightfall. Kazeem coughed, settled himself. The birds and the wind and the gentle trickle of the water coming out of the rocks took him away.

He didn't want to go back. He never did.

But the old man was right. If he didn't get past this, he was going to get himself killed.

*

The boy was so scared he thought he might vomit, but he wasn't going to let *them* know it. He'd lost his mother at five, his father at fourteen. He'd been on his own then, stealing, eating from dust bins, sleeping in alleys…but even that had been better than *this*.

There was a name for this place, but the other kids just called it "The Home".

To young Kazeem, fourteen year old son of Kaidin, Wrotmar, it was hell.

He'd arrived with a bad reputation, partly due to his own actions, partly because of his father. Either way, he'd been unpopular from the start.

They all had names, Kazeem was sure of that, but he hadn't paid attention. Names were only to tell people apart, and he did that by sight. Still, they all knew *his* name—wherever he went. It would take years for him to understand why, but by then it wouldn't matter.

"That's the second time this month, Kazeem," the tall one said and shoved him again. "The *second* time. We let it go at first, you know, because you were new, but now you're becoming a burden."

The shove hurt. The other boy was twice his size, the heels of his palms hard.

Kazeem's eyes watered from the pain, but he blinked fast, willing them away.

He hadn't cried when his father died. He wasn't going to cry now.

There was another shove, even harder. His chest muscles ached, his shoulders cramped. He was against the stone wall now and the three of them crowded him.

"The big fish eat the little fish, Kazeem. That's the way it works. That's the way it's *always* worked. The sooner you get that through your head, the better off you're going to be."

Kaidin wouldn't stand for this. His father would have dropped all three of them where they stood. He wished he could be that strong, or smart enough to mind his own business; either would have helped.

He steeled himself, gritted his teeth. To answer, to even acknowledge their existence, was to show weakness.

"What's the matter, boy? Cat got your tongue?" The tall one turned to the fat, pimple-faced boy beside him. "Is it just me, Abdar, or is he being unfriendly?"

"All I know is that Miko's got a broken jaw." He jutted his double chin at Kazeem. "Because of him. I say we teach him a lesson." There was hate in the red face, anger in the pale blue eyes. Sweat beaded on his forehead, and his breath was rank, like fish.

They all smelled like fish.

"We let him get away with this," the third boy agreed, "people will be walking all over us."

Kazeem knew who he was, knew the other kids called him 'Spinner'; knew he was small and wiry, like himself, but he didn't look at him. He kept his eyes, luminous and stony, on his chief tormentor. The other two would go the way he went, take their cue from him. Kazeem wanted to see it coming.

"What do you think of *that*, Kazeem?" the tall boy asked with a snarl and shoved him into the wall again.

Kazeem didn't even blink. He studied the brown eyes towering above him, saw fear flicker there like a snake's tongue. Either they were playing with him, or they were afraid of him. He had, after all, sent their friend to the infirmary. His father was, after all, Kaidin, Wrotmar.

Kazeem squinted, hiding his own fear. He was fast. He could run, but where would he hide in a prison he couldn't leave? They may have called it an orphanage, but there were bars on the windows and a gate at the arch.

"I asked you a question."

Kazeem allowed himself the luxury of a normal breath, and let it out slowly. He reminded himself that these boys were bullies, that they raped and beat and terrorized weaker, younger kids—in short, that they were cowards. He told himself that they weren't going to do anything. If they were, they would have done it by now. He decided that, no matter what, he wouldn't let them see fear.

At least he would have that.

"You planning on talking me to death?" he asked, speaking for the first time since they'd cornered him on his way back from lunch.

The tall boy actually gaped, and Kazeem knew it was over.

For now.

He pulled one of the older boy's hands off the cracked wall, pushed it aside, and walked away without looking back.

"You watch your step, Kazeem-son-of-Kaidin!" the tall boy called in a pathetic attempt to save face. "Just because your old man was some kind of a killer doesn't mean *you're* anything special! You're on *our* turf now! You remember that!"

Kazeem actually smiled as he turned the corner. He'd gotten away with it. He'd actually gotten away with it.

This time.

*

He woke with a start, bolting up, the screams of a young boy ringing in his head as two older boys held him and a third beat him...

Heart pounding, Kazeem stumbled up, trotted to the pool in the moonlight and splashed cool water on his face. Drinking a little helped the nausea, but the images were burned into his brain like a brand. He'd stopped it when he could, hurt the tormentors as much as he'd been able, but in the end, what had he done except become just like them?

Worse than them.

The water made him retch. His stomach muscles cramped at the contact. The oasis was beautiful in the moonlight. That instant of relief lingered in his mind as he gulped cool night air. He held on to the image, made it his own, made it *real*, felt the nausea slip away and stay away. He sat back on his heels, head back, seeking answers in twinkling stars that didn't even know he was alive.

"You're getting better at that."

"Damn it, Windor, where'd you come from?"

The old man shrugged. "Does it matter?"

Kazeem laughed. He dropped his chin onto his chest and shook his head slowly from side to side. "Just once I'd like a straight answer from you, old man. Just once!"

"And if you got such an answer, what would you do with it?"

The boy started to reply, actually opened his mouth, but thought better of it. This was no idle question, no joke; this was formal training and as serious as a blade.

"Nothing," he answered honestly and off the top of his head, "but I'd know the truth for what it was."

The old man turned his head. The desert was never completely dark; it was too open, too wide, seemed to hold the sun's energy in light as well as warmth. And although it got cool when the sun went down, there was always illumination. Silver moonlight, frosty and surreal, bathed the pink sand in swaths of colorless substance. Sometimes it removed tone as well as color, added depth or took it away; sometimes it crawled over boulders or dropped into gullies.

For no good reason, he shivered.

"And what would you do with this...truth?" Windor asked in a voice more sensed than heard.

"Use it to my advantage, as you've taught me."

The old man stood, ghostly and ethereal with the silver disk of the moon behind him. "Practical, as always, except that you're forgetting one thing."

"Oh yeah, what's that?"

"That truth isn't an absolute; it's a perception."

The boy thought for a time, then nodded, his face the face of one who has seen a glimpse of the true human condition. "My truth isn't necessarily your truth, is that it?"

"Excellent," the old man answered with a smile. "I do believe there's hope for you after all."

*

"Why am I here?" the boy asked the next afternoon. They had spent the day in the cave, avoiding the heat, using the time to study mathematics and philosophy.

Windor looked up from the ceramic bowl, wooden spoon halfway to his mouth. "I'm not sure I understand."

Kazeem laughed. "What part didn't you understand?"

Windor didn't share his mirth. "I didn't understand any of it."

The boy finished his afternoon meal. He put down the bowl, chewed, and wiped his mouth on a small square of muslin. "I want you to *answer* me," he said. With courage born of need, he met the stare of those steel gray eyes, and held it until he saw the opening he'd been seeking. "I want to know why you took me in, why you train *me* and no other."

"I teach only one at a time. I thought you understood that."

The teen was already shaking his head. "That's not what I meant. Is it because of my father?"

The old man sighed. Outside, the slant of the sun had changed, and there was shade at the mouth of the cave. Soon, it would be safe to venture out. "You know how your father died." It could have been either a statement, or a question.

"In combat." He could see it like it was yesterday. Three Vendarian rebels. It had taken three of them. "I was there."

"Not combat, assassination."

The revelation shouldn't have been a shock. Deep down, he'd known all along. Still, it came like a blow, like the angry jolt of icy water. He was on his feet in an instant, his dark eyes wide, his voice a hoarse whisper.

"*What?*"

"When you become a problem to the powers-that-be, they remove that problem. Such was the case with your father." He waved a hand. "Sit down. I've a story to tell you.

"I suppose you're expecting an epic tale, Byzantine in nature," Windor began, rubbing dry hands slowly together, "but that isn't what I have to tell you. There are politics, to be sure, but only that. No intrigue, no mystery—he was just unlucky enough to be on the wrong side at the wrong time. No one knows who *really* runs this government from day to day. Some say Slagja of Ankoria, others Dar-Mareion of Vendar. Still others speak of rebel bands high in the Faylon Range, with close ties to the provisional seat in Zamboor." He spread his hands, and the rasping sound ceased. He turned and faced the boy. "I'm telling you it doesn't matter, because if you wait long enough, it'll change. Your father wouldn't wait. He was too proud."

He grew silent, and the boy couldn't stand it.

"That's *it?*" he asked. "That's the story you had to tell me?"

Windor stood. He was tall for an Easterner, his face full of wrinkles, but he moved like a cat.

"No. The story's about you."

"Me?"

"It's about a boy who got the truth, just as he'd asked for, about the supposedly wise old teacher who gave it to him, knowing he would act, and not in his best interests." He held up a heavily veined hand to ward off the teen's protests. "It's about how the boy went off and got himself killed…or, worse, spent his life killing others."

"Stop it!" Kazeem was livid; his chest was heaving, and there was sweat on his brow. "You tell me that my father was murdered, allow me to believe that the people responsible are still out there, and then you tell me not to *do* anything about it! You've been out in the sun too long, old man!"

"I'm just trying to keep my promise to your father, Kazeem."

"What *are* you talking about?"

"Kaidin wanted you to choose your own way, not necessarily follow the Wrotmar path. I only *teach* the warrior class, son. I don't assign caste to our citizens."

Kazeem was shaking his head. "I've had enough, Windor. You've been training warriors for God only knows how long, you have wisdom beyond measure." His voice dripped sarcasm. "Yes, yes, I've heard it all before. I see your skills, old man, I've sensed your power, and still, you seem incapable of answering simple questions!"

"What would you ask?" The old man sighed.

"I want to know who killed my father! I want to know who ordered his death!"

"I honestly don't know," Windor replied.

"Then I'll have to find out for myself," the boy promised in a harsh whisper and stalked out into the night.

"I was afraid you would, my son," the teacher said, all alone in the empty cave, "but I had to give you that choice."

*

The teacher wasn't there to see his pupil off in the morning, but Kazeem hadn't expected him to be. The only traces of him were early, predawn footprints in the sand, winding away into the hills above the cave, disappearing among the rocks where the old man held his daily, morning rituals.

That and the bag of provisions at the mouth of the cave.

The boy smiled as he picked up the canvas bag and tugged at the drawstring. Inside were bread, cheese, salt, a whetstone, rice and various herbs. He cinched it, and tied it to the other baggage on the back of the camel. Already laden with water, bedroll and weapons, the dromedary gargled impatience.

In white robe and turban, Kazeem patted the beast and pinned a sash across the lower half of his own face. "The longest journey begins with a single step."

Kazeem wore two swords; both lashed across his back, the hilts just above his shoulders, within easy reach. He pulled on a black leather belt, and buckled it; from it hung hunting knife, whip and a small canteen.

Booted and robed, his head properly covered, with only stormy dark eyes showing, Kazeem put one foot into the stirrup and swung the other leg over.

The camel was unruly, eager to be off. The warrior-boy calmed it with a soft hand and a soothing voice.

"Easy, Shalah. Soon enough you'll be wishing we never left."

Kazeem tugged on the rawhide reins, turned to face the rocks. There was no sign of the old man. The boy was alone, as he guessed he always had been.

*

From the shade of a huge gray boulder, Windor watched the boy set out. Heat shimmered before him, coming up in angry waves from the shinning sand, but he was made of stern stuff, and it would take more than the desert to kill him.

Windor watched until the boy dwindled to a speck on the horizon. And then he watched some more.

He wiped a tear from his cheek before it had time to run the length of his face.

Windor had taught the Wrotmar for more years than he could count, for more years than he *wanted* to count.

And it never got any easier.

Letting them go was always the hard part, especially when it was dangerous, when he knew he might never see them again. The thing was, he *knew*, knew deep in his heart that this one would return.

The question was: would they have anything in common when he did?

*

The desert was a strange place, beautiful in its own way, but deadly, too. Long hours sapped strength from the body, but wreaked havoc on the mind, as well. It was an ocean of sand, a no-man's land, a punishment and redemption.

It was best to keep the mind occupied, but how to do it? And then it came to him, suddenly—misdirection. Have his thoughts remove him from the physical discomfort. Pain, he knew, was a thing of the mind, and if thoughts could be controlled, so could sensations of the flesh. It was only another form of discipline, no stranger to a youth who followed the path of the Wrotmar.

Kazeem let go, allowing his thoughts to stray the way Windor had taught him.

Starting with his feet and working up, he relinquished all feeling, allowing bones and muscles to do the job of keeping him mindlessly in place. Soon, the sound of Shalah's plodding hooves was gone, then the light, and then, finally, the heat itself. Only his body remained, keeping the camel on course, allowing his mind a higher function. It helped, but not in the way he'd intended. Kazeem may no longer have sensed his surroundings, but he found himself in a place hotter than hell, a place he couldn't escape from, at least not until he'd put it behind him once and for all.

Finding his father's killers was one thing, but there was other business that needed to be attended to if he was ever going to call himself a man. There were things he had never told anyone, not even Windor, although the old man probably knew. A man named Baaka Zhinn, the so-called administrator of the Home, had started something that only Kazeem could finish. Something that could no longer be ignored. There was also the business of Nomar and Elin, the beautiful free spirits who had once saved his life. They had been needlessly butchered in an effort to protect him, and he could no longer live with the guilt of letting their killers go unpunished. He had hated leaving Windor, the safety of the desert, the peace of mind he had had while in the old man's care, but what else could he do? Windor had taught him that the only sure way to rid yourself of demons, was to slay them.

Kazeem slowed, and eventually came to a complete stop. The sun beat down, and for the first time since he'd set out he felt the heat again, cloying, searing, *alive*. All the hate he carried was justified. He knew that. But if he gave in to it completely, sought his vengeance in every quarter, how long would it be until there was no difference between him, and those he hunted?

Kazeem thought about this long and hard. He thought about it until sweat poured from him in rivers, until he actually *stopped* sweating, and became weak and unsure. He drank some water and then something hard and cold rose up in him, filling his arms and legs with a strength he could hardly believe he possessed. These were things that needed to be done, *had* to be done, or he'd never be able to live with himself.

And God help anyone who got in his way.

CHAPTER TWO

THE CAT WAS crying in the window on the day his father died. That was the first thing he remembered. The cat was white and tan, with a slanted, eastern face, and exquisite eyes. She was sitting on the terracotta sill, mewling, as they passed. The square was crowded, the air hot and cloying. Pushcarts lined the marketplace, which extended into alleys and corners for as far as the eye could see. People milled about, talking, shouting, laughing and gesturing with their hands. It was a grand collection of color and sound, smells and sensations, a vast cross-section of humanity that was overwhelming and a little bit frightening.

Kazeem loved coming here with his father on Sixthday. They always got something good to eat, and at fourteen years old he was just beginning to admit a certain grudging admiration for the opposite sex. The girls had noticed *him* long ago, but he was too naïve to feel confident about it.

"She's *cute*, Kazeem," his father said matter-of-factly as they passed the mango cart. Kaidin's voice was well modulated—he never raised it—the thing was…it was always clear, even above the din of the crowd. "Is she the one from last week?"

Kazeem nodded. He would have been surprised to know just how alike he and his father looked at that moment. "Yes, father. One and the same."

A lot of parents brought their children to market at Weeksend. There was a food court in the center of town where one could order a meal or a beverage, but it was the huge, almost square-wide canopy that drew people here, and away from the unmerciful desert sun.

Kaidin tossed the boy a silver coin. It flashed in that self-important sunlight, tumbled end-over-end to wind up squarely in his palm. He made a fist, and looked up, smiling from ear-to-ear.

"I thought so. Go, buy her a cool drink, and learn her *name*, for the Maker's sake!"

It would be days before Kazeem realized that Kaidin's sole intent was to get rid of him, years before he finally understood that it was to protect him. His father wore the clothes of the common free man. Only the weapons he carried and the set of his eyes identified him as *Wrotmar*, the warrior class. Still, it was easy to spot him in a crowd. He wasn't a particularly big man, but he carried himself in a way that made him seem bigger than most. Kazeem tried to keep an eye on him as he headed for the tent, but hormones played a very large part in distracting him, as did shiny, unbound hair, golden skin and big, dark eyes.

Tall buildings on all four sides, the highest in all Zamboria surrounded the square. After half-part Midday, shadows began to creep into corners on one side. Men gathered in doorways to talk business and to escape the glare of the sun. Some even set up shop, placing tables in the mouths of alleys. Deals were made. Money changed hands. As Kazeem was approaching the cute girl, Kaidin moved away from the pushcarts and into one of those dark corners. He paused for a moment to watch as his son talked to the girl, and felt a pang that brought a tear to his eye. Kaidin cleared his throat and shoved such sentiment away; it was something he just couldn't afford, not if he wanted to live. Kaidin knew what was waiting for him; had, in fact, come here specifically to meet it. He had already made arrangements for someone to look after the boy in the event that something happened to him, but this was something he just wouldn't run from. Couldn't. It wasn't in his nature.

Kaidin had never been afraid of anything. Honor, integrity, the way he lived, bowing to no man, these things exemplified the man, set him apart. It would have been a simple matter to extricate himself from his current dilemma, he reflected as he loosened one of his swords in its sheath. All he needed to do was go with the prevailing wind, approach the opposition party currently in control, and swear allegiance. Simple. End of problem.

Except that he had already given his word to the other side.

It didn't matter if the other side was unworthy of his loyalty—all that mattered to Kaidin was that he had *given his word.* Nothing was more important than this. A promise was a promise. It was a bond. One didn't vow something only until it became difficult or inconvenient. The Wrotmar backed this with his very life, and if it cost him his life, so be it. His son would learn what it meant to be a *man*, to be honored, to be respected and perhaps feared.

Kaidin had been a professional soldier all his life, a killer, in fact. Still, he had never plundered, never taken a woman by force, never abused a child. He did his duty, drew his pay, brought a bit of order to a world filled with chaos. In a culture where life was a violent storm, Kaidin was the self-appointed calm eye in the midst of that storm.

He didn't do this because it was easy, he did it because it was a challenge, and he believed life meaningless without adversity to overcome. When you got right down to it, the only true measure of a man was how well he handled himself when faced with difficulty. Anyone could thrive during easy times. It was facing a test with your head held high that made the difference.

If he lived to see the sun set, he would be feared in every corner of this sun-ravaged nation. If he died, he would do so with honor, earning his son a place of respect among the elite. Kaidin didn't always feel good about bringing harm to others, not even when they deserved it, but it was better than losing the essence of who he was.

The sun was in his eyes. He squinted, turned, saw his son still talking to the girl, a girl mature enough to turn a grown man's head. The smoke from an open cooking pit took him full in the face. The odor of sizzling beef, grilled onions and blackened vegetables was wonderful. The crowd was a living thing. Colors swam before his eyes. His ears heard song, conversation and the din of commerce.

The sky was bright and clear, a brilliant blue. Facing death, Kaidin had never felt more alive.

When they made their move, Kaidin was ready for them. He fought two-handed, in the Wrotmar fashion, with a short-sword and saber. There were three of them. That, in itself, was an honor, and he rose to the occasion magnificently. They were Vendarians, the Loric Column judging from their dress: black trousers and singlets, loose-fitting cloaks and red sashes at their waists. To their credit they came at him one at a time, the first calling his name before charging. He was a big man with dark hair and wild blue eyes, and there was a scar that ran from his left brow to the right side of his chin.

Kaidin had hoped for more time to size up his opponent, but the man was upon him, curved sword raised, and the moment was gone. The Wrotmar knocked the huge blade aside with both of his own, sweeping them down and out in a great, scraping shower of sparks. He booted the man, catching him in the stomach, and turned just in time to meet the charge of the second mercenary. This one was calmer, more in control of himself, skilled. He, too, wielded a thick-bladed scimitar, whirling it around and around like a windmill.

Kaidin watched, waiting for the feint, and slid neatly to the side when it came. He slapped the man across the face with the flat of one blade, watched him spin, slam into the nearest wall and collapse in a bloody heap.

The third was quicker than the other two. He was on Kaidin before he could recover, slashing him across the top of his right arm. Tough as nails, trained by the best to ignore pain during combat, Kaidin nevertheless had all he could do to keep from dropping one blade and clutching the wound. The immediate spurt of bright arterial blood and how quickly his arm went numb, told him how bad it was. He was cut almost to the bone, but knew he had to ignore it long enough to get out of this.

He countered with his saber, teeth gritted, denying the cry that ached to explode from his lips. Sunlight glinted on fine Arganian steel, as he knocked the scimitar down; the shorter blade in his left hand did the damage, whistling through the air to slice across his foe's ribcage. Blood oozed, the sash fell, and as the man bent forward from the pain Kaidin neatly separated his head from his body.

The decapitated man shuddered for a moment, still standing as his head rolled under a table, and then he fell in a shaking, violent palsy.

Kaidin had used his right arm for the blow, and the impact was too much for him. Against training, against will, the saber clattered to the brick-paved street, and he barely had time to get the short blade up to block the second charge of the wild-eyed man. He was able to deflect the blow and trip the larger fighter, and even managed to slice his blade across the back of the man's right thigh as he passed.

But it was the man he'd slapped away who did the damage, running him through from behind. Kaidin saw the steel explode from his stomach, knew that it had entered his body from the back. Unable to help it, he went to his knees, and never even heard his sword clatter to the bricks.

*

Kazeem had never kissed a girl before—he'd always been too afraid—but this one made it easy for him. Holding hands, she led him to the back of a wagon loaded with pots and pans and ceramic jars, and pulled him up the steps behind her, their hands and lips still sticky with lemon and sugar. Still holding his hand, her head bowed, looking up at him through the longest, silkiest lashes he'd ever seen, she fell to the cot behind her and pulled him down with her.

At first he was afraid he'd hurt her, but he landed on softness he hadn't even known existed…a full roundness under-laid with fierce feminine strength that he would ever after associate with womanhood. His hands were in her hair, his dry lips on her full, moist ones. She smelled of lemons and sugar and *girl*—and suddenly he couldn't seem to catch his breath. She kissed him like the girls in his dreams kissed him and for a time, she was all that existed.

The collective gasp of the crowd, the muted shouts from outside, startled him, brought him up like a puppet on strings. He was in trouble. Surely, the girl's father was coming for him, would kill him where he sat for being with his daughter, but then he heard the tell-tale ring of true steel and he knew there was a fight going on in the square. Exasperated, the girl pulled him back. She was strong; she was older, more experienced, and knew exactly what she wanted, but the boy now had one eye open and a flutter in the pit of his stomach that had nothing to do with the doe-eyed creature beside him. Her breath was hot and sweet. Her slim girl's arms were crossed behind his neck, pulling him close. She took his hand and placed it on her cheek—softer than a dove—and his heartbeat trebled. She told him to kiss her and again he lost himself.

And then someone in the crowd called his father's name. At first he thought it imagination—if not the girl's father, why not his own? But then he heard it again and suddenly knew what was happening. He didn't know *how* he knew; he only knew that he did. Pulling himself from the girl was by far the hardest thing he'd ever done, but he wasn't in control of his own actions.

"What's *wrong?*" she whispered, honey-sweet, soft and hot.

"Shhh!"

"What is it?" She sat up braced on one elbow, a frown on her full, pouty lips.

"Didn't you *hear* that?" There was no mistaking the name, not the third time.

He burst from the wagon, the girl forgotten, his head whipping back and forth, his eyes scanning the vast throng of humanity. At first he couldn't tell, but then he saw the moving circle of shouting, cheering market-goers. Only one group of people moved as a unit like that, shifting, surging…

A mob, following a fight.

Feet pounding over dusty bricks, dodging, shifting in mid-air to avoid collisions, he ran to see what the others saw. When he got there a wall of unwashed humanity blocked his path, and all he could see inside the living circle were four bobbing heads, three bound in red silk, the other wearing the slouched, low-brimmed hat of a nomad.

Just like the one his father wore.

The silk heads moved erratically, surging one way, and then the other. And the crowd moved with them, preventing him from seeing more. Kazeem finally got smart. Instead of trying to compete, he dropped to all fours and crawled through a sea of dirty legs to the front of the circle.

He stood just in time to see his father take a man's head, saw Kaidin drop one sword, saw his father hamstring the next fighter. He was also just in time to see a third man run his father through, from behind, in the back, like a coward.

He too called his father's name, but of course he used a different one.

CHAPTER THREE

"ARE YOU *CRAZY?*" It was the girl, clutching his arm with surprising strength. "You can't go out there in front of all these people!"

Insanely, all he could think of was that he still didn't know her name.

"Let go of me!" he shouted and flung off her arm. "That's my *father!*"

"Which makes you fatherless! Where's your mother?"

"Dead. From the fever. Years ago." He wanted to cry. Couldn't. Somehow that seemed shameful.

"Then you're an *orphan?* Maker help me! Now you *really* can't go out there. If the Caliphmen find you when they come, they'll take you to the *Home!*"

The name alone sent fear sliding the length of his spine. And then the thought of his father's dead body drove that selfish thought from his mind, but he was still in shock, and the girl was able to drag him down an alley. Part of who we are is defined by what happens to us, by how we handle the fickle winds of fortune. Who we are is how well we deal with the trauma in our lives. Kazeem was at a crossroad: he could go to his father, or he could run, hide, wait until he was big enough, strong enough, to avenge him. He could be taken, or he could live to fight another day. The thought sobered him. Running didn't always make you a coward—sometimes it was the only smart thing to do. He looked around the alley. It was dim, dank and dirty like most forgotten corners. If he ran now he'd see more of this: filth and broken, unused things, but at least he'd be free, and that's what his father would have wanted.

When he looked at the pretty girl again, her lovely brown eyes cemented his decision.

"What's your name?" he asked breathlessly.

"Elin." She pronounced it *Ee-lyn*—a name as pretty as she was. "Daughter of Nomar." She bit her lip when the shrill whistle of the Caliphmen pierced the afternoon. "What's yours?"

"I am Kazeem, son of Kaidin," he answered, but his eyes weren't on hers, they were pinned on the mouth of the alley and on the throng of people gathered around his father's body.

"We can't stay here," Elin said after less than a minute of this. She tugged his sleeve. "Come on."

The boy allowed himself to be led. He was walking backward, still watching the Caliphmen in their bright yellow turbans and austere gray robes as they made their way through the crowd. They had yet to look up the alley.

"Where will I go?" he asked suddenly.

"To my father," Elin answered without hesitation. "He will give you shelter."

What that really meant was that he was about to become cheap labor, but he nodded. Beggars—not to mention orphans—can't afford to be choosy. "All right. How do we get there?"

They had reached a doorway, the back of a shop where Elin was known. She opened the door, urged him to go before her, and then closed it behind them. "We have to go through the square again."

Kazeem came to a dead stop in that hot little corridor. "In *front* of everybody?"

"We'll be all right as long as we don't see anyone you know."

"My father knew a lot of people, Elin."

"And they'll all be at the other end of the market. Two more kids on the street at this end of the square won't attract one bit of attention. Not with all *that* going on. Trust me."

Kazeem looked at her with a desperation he hadn't felt since the death of his mother. "I guess I already have, Elin."

*

The gray-haired old man was watching for them when they came out of the shop. He was sure that the boy wouldn't recognize him, but he pulled the cowl up on his robe, just the same. This was, after all, Kaidin's son.

Seeing the boy with the dusky young beauty made the old man cringe. She was only going to make his life harder, poor thing, whether she wanted to or not.

Then the old man berated himself with clenched teeth. It was his own fault, really—if he had just been on time…

And then he caught himself. The past was gone, the future out of his control due to countless unforeseens. The present was his only controllable option, and even *that* much control was an illusion. The truth of the matter was that the nature of truth was fluid—it varied from person to person, from perception to perception. The old man frowned. Who knew? Maybe he'd been right on time after all— *exactly* on time.

He sighed. Among his present options was an out-and-out abduction of the boy. He had, after all, promised the father to take care of him. He paused though, unsure. The boy was destined for things no one could even imagine. Who was he to interfere with that? The old man decided to wait, to see how this played out. He watched the girl as she led the boy by the hand along the dusty, cobble-stoned road. He bit his bottom lip in silent agony and slowly turned away. Sometimes it was better to do nothing, but you never knew. That was the hard part. You never knew.

*

"It'll feel funny meeting your father after—" It was a slip, but he wasn't *completely* witless, and managed to stop himself.

"After what?" Elin asked coyly, and licked her lips.

"After what happened to my own father," the boy lied with fear-induced inspiration. Guilt was still gnawing at him like a hungry rat in the dark, but it was too early for grief. He needed to be strong now, no matter how hard that was. "What will we tell him? About me, I mean?"

Elin smiled knowingly. "The only thing I've ever lied to my father about is how many boys I've kissed. Don't worry. I think we can tell him the truth."

Panic ran through young Kazeem of Zamboria as he suddenly grasped the enormity of the thing. He couldn't go *home*. 'Home' was a concept now, the memories he carried around in his head, the kind of person he was, the way he lived his life. He had no place of his own now. All the things that were part of who he was were forever lost to him. Change, awful, sudden change, had been forced on him with violent certainty. He was homeless in the material sense of the word. He'd never sit in his own room again, never wake up in his own bed, feel the warm sun slanting in through his window. His models, books and clothes—the life he'd shared with his father, were gone. He was a new person now, one forced into a very long tale by a very quick decision. Nothing would ever be the same, and he'd better start learning to deal with it if he planned to survive.

Kazeem swayed, as the blood seemed to rush to his head. How we think of ourselves is usually how we feel about ourselves, and he felt pretty lost at the moment.

"Hey!" She grabbed his arm, and pushed him gently back against a brick wall. She searched his eyes. "Are you all right?"

"Fine," he lied. God, how he hated the concern in her beautiful dark eyes! "I just don't want to trouble you. Maybe we should just forget this whole thing and go our separate ways."

"Don't be silly. They'd find you within the hour."

"Let me go. I'll be okay." The crowd was starting to drift back this way. People were milling about. The smoke from a pushcart selling grilled meat wrapped in unleavened bread suddenly made him queasy.

"They'll put you in the Home. I told you. I've seen it happen."

"Oh, yeah? Who'd you ever know went in there?" They started walking again, despite his protests, and his stomach felt better when they got past the food court.

"A colleague of my father's, Amad Al Scincin, lost his wife to illness two years ago. He, himself, was killed in a traffic accident a year later." Elin swallowed; fear sapped the color from her cheeks. "He had two daughters, Taylyn and Shayna. Beautiful girls. I used to play with them. Like you, they had no relatives. The Caliphmen came and took them to the Home. I *begged* my father to take them in, but the last thing he said he needed was two more daughters. Three months later, after almost constant nagging from me, we went to visit...and I almost didn't recognize them. They looked horrible, lifeless. Their stories were so—" Elin choked, held up a hand. "I can't even talk about it, but I'm sure you can guess what was happening to them. It was so bad that my father set about to adopt them, but by the time the proper papers could be drawn up, Taylyn had been sold to a rich man and Shayna had supposedly run away, never to be heard from again." Elin's dark eyes fixed on his as they passed a block of deserted tables, abandoned glasses left carelessly. "I'm sure the Home is equally unpleasant for *boys*, Kazeem."

He nodded, suffering that awful fight or flight feeling that rose up and filled him with panic. This was happening too fast. For the first time in his life he was alone and scared and had only this stranger to depend on.

"Are you sure your father will take me in?" Behind them, bloated flies buzzed lazily amid unguarded glasses of sweet liquids. What kind of god *made* things like that?

"Of course he will, silly. It's not like I'm bringing him another useless daughter!"

*

"No! Absolutely not!" Nomar of Zamboor told his daughter in no uncertain terms. He gestured with a firm hand. "This is no tradesman's daughter, young lady!

This is Kazeem, *Kaidin's* son!" He turned to the boy, dejected and sitting solemnly on a divan with glass-bead brocade. "Nothing against you, son, but this is trouble my family doesn't need."

"What 'family', Father? It's just you and me now that Mama's gone. My days are spent in school, yours at the market. If we have an hour together at supper before bed, it's a rare day."

"Don't be spiteful, child! We do what we must."

"If that's so, Father, why do you turn your back on this boy? Or don't you remember Taylyn and Shayna?"

"Maker help me. You've become your mother!"

"Mother wouldn't turn him away, and you know it!"

Nomar looked from Kazeem to Elin and back again. Slowly, recognition dawned, and he held his forehead in one hand. "Oh, God, don't tell me!"

"It's not *like* that!" Kazeem said a bit too quickly.

Nomar didn't even look at him. "Listen to me, girl," he said, lowering his hand. "We've been through this a dozen times in the past hour, and it all comes back the same: my responsibility is to you, and *only* you."

"Then help me now!"

"I *am* helping you, young lady. In fact, I have given you the courtesy of treating you like an equal, discussing this affair instead of dumping you over my knee. *I* am the parent, not you! That is an end to it!"

Despite Elin's protests, Kazeem got to his feet. "I'll go, sir," he said. "I didn't come here to cause strife between you and your daughter."

"Where are *you* going?" Nomar snapped. "I said you couldn't *remain* with us, that doesn't mean we'll turn you out unfed in the night. Tomorrow we'll find a solution to this problem." He stroked his beard, pulling the dark hairs to a point at his chin, unable or unwilling to hide a grudging smile. "Besides, despite my daughter's willful, headstrong ways, I admire her courage and sense of duty. In fact—"

A polite knock at the wagon door became an insistent banging when it wasn't immediately answered.

"Quick, lad!" Nomar hissed. "Under the cot." The older man gave him a shove. "Take a blanket, cover yourself." He turned quickly, forcing ire into his voice. "Easy, now! I'm coming." He strode to the back of their tiny home, leaned down, pushed the door open. Immediately three Caliphmen climbed aboard, their combined weight temporarily tilting the wagon, making springs creak as the floor rocked. Two went poking about, while a third addressed the father.

"You are Nomar the merchant?"

"I am. What's this all about?" He turned to the other two. "Stop that, or I'll inform the Guild first thing in the morning."

They looked at their leader, and stood there with their arms folded at a nod from him.

"Your daughter was seen today in the company of a fugitive."

"What fugitive?" Nomar's tone was scornful.

"Kazeem, Kaidin's son."

"The man who was murdered in the market today?"

"Killed in personal combat, but one in the same, yes."

"She said she spoke to the lad, but only to comfort him. She's a good girl."

The Caliphman took two steps, cupped the pretty girl's chin in his big hand, and tilted her dainty face up and into the still gently swinging circle of yellow lamplight. "Comfort, indeed," he leered while the other two snickered.

Nomar wasn't a rich man, nor was he particularly political, but he was well known to the Trade Guild and well liked. No abuse against an honest guildsman's family would be tolerated, not even by representatives of the Calipha. He gently, but firmly removed the man's hand.

"My daughter is no criminal, but *your* actions here so far are unconscionable. Nor has the child you seek committed any crime, at least none that I'm aware of."

"No one said he has," the leader of the trio said, wrapping his gray cloak about him like the wings of an insect.

"Yet you storm into my home in the night looking for him."

"To protect the lad only. The Calipha is a kindhearted man, who suffers with his constituents in their times of need."

The only thing, Nomar knew, that the Calipha ever suffered from, was a hangover, but he kept his opinions to himself. He bowed slightly, keeping his eyes on the turbaned man. "As everyone knows."

"So you have no knowledge of the boy?"

"None, I'm afraid."

"You have good cause to be afraid, tradesman."

Nomar's voice turned to gravel, and his eyes narrowed. "Is that a threat?"

The other two moved towards the door, big boots shaking the tiny wagon. The officer tapped his own chest with a finger.

"From us, never. But killers have done away with the boy's father. They are obviously cruel and evil men. The Maker alone knows what they might do if they found you alone with a young and very beautiful daughter, one on the verge of flowering womanhood."

"Get out!"

"Are you certain you known nothing of this boy, child?" the Caliphman asked Elin with abysmal politeness.

"Nothing, sir, I swear."

"Nothing out of bed," the man closest to the door mumbled, and the others chuckled.

With great self-discipline, Nomar controlled his temper. He was a strong willed man, but he wasn't foolhardy. "She knows nothing!" He stood between the men and his daughter. "As I have told you, she is a good girl."

The Caliphman touched his forehead in a flourishing gesture of farewell. "If we find, tradesman, that you have lied to us we shall come back to see just how *good* she really is." He didn't bother closing the door on the way out.

But Elin quickly latched it.

*

"Don't judge me, boy," Nomar said five minutes later as Kazeem crawled out from under the cot. "I acted in our best interests."

He put his hands on his hips and studied the children. "All right. You can stay, but only until we can find a proper home for you."

Elin's mouth dropped open in surprise.

"Oh, stop gaping, girl," her father said. "You act like you've never seen me do anything stupid before!"

CHAPTER FOUR

THE GRAY HAIRED man noted with satisfaction that the merchant and the two children kept the secret well, at least for the first two months. He watched at a distance, moving when they moved, approving of the father's first decision—to get them out of the city.

School was no problem. Only for boys was attendance a matter of law. Still, he taught them both as best he could, an hour or two each day, math, science, reading, and hoped for the best.

Again the gray haired man approved, but he was getting impatient. He was tired of riding hooded and cloaked, of urging his brown mare into the brush, but he dared not interfere, dared not use magic... not at *this* stage of the game.

*

"I can't believe how quickly the time has passed," Nomar said one morning as they sat down to breakfast.

The wagon was chocked near a gravel path on the outskirts of yet another city. They had tenting which they pulled from the wagon and staked in the ground whenever they planned on spending more than a day or two. This provided them with shade, and it was a simple matter to remove the small bench and chairs that were usually lashed to the side of the wagon.

Elin brought a pitcher of goat's milk; Kazeem handed her father the pot of flavored yogurt.

"A whole season gone." Nomar mixed grains with the yogurt in his bowl, sighed, and sat back in his chair to regard the desert. The sun had only just risen, climbing slowly above the jagged peaks of the curving Faylon Range to tint the sand with pink and rose and coral. Shadows dotted the horizon as clouds scudded by, and a gentle breeze, one that belied the heat of the coming day, lifted the tent flaps.

Nomar's sigh was repeated, but he was surprised to find it one of contentment. He had his work. He had his daughter. And now he had the son he'd always wanted. Except for a woman to share it with, what more could a man ask for?

Kazeem was a good boy. He'd be a good man, a strong one, if a bit hard on himself. Nomar studied the lad surreptitiously as he resumed his meal. The boy had eyes only for Elin, which was not unusual, and gave the man an opportunity to observe him. Sandy hair tousled by the wind, tanned skin bronzed by the sun, dark eyes flashing as he smiled at the girl of his dreams. They lived *now* as brother and sister, but they were young yet and on their best behavior. That would change, but Nomar found suddenly, and much to his surprise, that it didn't frighten him as it once had. A man could do a lot worse than Kazeem for a son-in-law, and since no father had yet been able to keep his daughter a little girl forever, it was best, he supposed, to find some sort of peace in the idea.

"What are you thinking, Father?" Elin asked sweetly, sensing without actually understanding his emotional state.

"Nothing, daughter. Only how very, very beautiful you are."

Elin blushed, the color bringing life to cheeks browned by desert living. "What will we do today?" she asked, with all the feminine skill of a young woman wishing to divert attention. "Shall we go into town and set up shop?"

"I know this place," Kazeem agreed excitedly. "We'll do well here."

"I think not," Nomar said curtly.

"Sir?"

"I think we shall take a holiday instead," the father said. "What do you think of that?"

"A holiday?" Elin asked, her dark brown eyes wide and catching the light. They were beautiful eyes, filled with life, and when she smiled, it tugged at Nomar's heart in ways he couldn't even have described.

"Why not? We'll go in, secure the wagon and go shopping. We'll have lunch in a café. Afternoon tea. Make a day of it!"

"Oh, Father, *can* we?"

"It is done, daughter."

She flung her arms around him and squeezed. "Such fun!"

"Easy, child!" Nomar said, gently removing her strong, slim hands. "I can not go if I am lame!" His eyes twinkled as he lifted the silky hair at the back of her neck and let it fall. He was looking over her shoulder when he said, "Ah, I see the goats have run off again."

"I'll get them...for you," Kazeem volunteered. He had almost said, 'Father', and not for the first time, either. He checked himself, wiping his mouth with a cloth napkin before leaving the table. Nomar had become a second father to young Kazeem, but the boy was still afraid to care. Every time he had in his admittedly short life, the people he cared about died...or were killed.

"Not this time," he mumbled, "not if I can help it."

*

The man and his daughter watched as the boy climbed over the rise and disappeared among the rocks. He stepped down into the gully and was gone.

"You were right, Elin. He's a good boy. Helping him was the right thing to do."

"I knew you'd come around. Eventually," she added with a decidedly sly grin.

The girl still stood by his chair. He had one arm around her. "Am I so easily manipulated?" he asked, searching her eyes with loving amusement.

"Just by me," she said, and kissed the top of his head.

"I swear, girl, you could charm a snake out of his skin."

"And pry the lid off a paint-pot?" She tapped his nose with a fingertip. "See, shouldn't talk about me behind my back. A girl has a way of finding things out."

"You're a woman now," Nomar said, looking up at her. Tears sprang to his eyes, and he made no attempt to wipe them away. "Or, soon will be. Tell me, do you love him?"

"I think—" Elin stood straight. "Hey, what's that?"

"What's what?" Nomar asked. He was too content to move.

The girl pointed. "That. Over there. Is it a brush fire?"

Nomar turned his head, and took a sharp breath. "Not smoke. Dust."

"Strong winds?" she asked hopefully.

"Or horses. Here, let me up." He got to his feet, moved to a higher point on some rocks to the west, and squinted.

"Shall I fetch Kazeem?" Elin asked.

Nomar thought about it. If the dust cloud represented what he thought it did, the boy was better off where he was. "Leave him be, child. Help me get ready to leave." He moved closer to the trail, shielding his eyes with his hand. There, coming along the road at the edge of the scrub brush and the desert, were at least a dozen riders.

Nomar jumped from the rocks to help his daughter, but he knew in his heart that they had already run out of time.

*

Goats usually grazed alone, but they usually didn't wander this far away from each other, either. Kazeem had to admit: there wasn't much for them to eat near the wagon, and the sand offered even less. Goats had a reputation for eating just about anything, but experience had taught him that they preferred soft grasses and tender young greens. There wasn't much of either here among the rocks, but at least the stones held the water, enough so that sparse plants were scattered among them, all but irresistible to animals on a steady diet of bagged feed.

Kazeem found the first goat about a quarter of an hour after leaving the table.

"Come on," he said, taking it by the collar, "let's go find your pal." He didn't find the other stray for another twenty minutes after that. Another ten went by while he went about catching it, chasing the pesky thing as it clattered over the stones, playing with him. He ended up grabbing it with a lunging dive after tying the first goat to a stump with a piece of twine. Making his way back with the livestock took another fifteen minutes, and he was sweating like a pig before he got even half way. The desert air didn't usually bother him, but it was humid in the draw, and there wasn't a breath of fresh air. He had to stop twice on the way back to mop his face with a small cloth.

Kazeem was surprised to discover that he was happy. He missed his father terribly, and was still shocked by his own inability to grieve, but he was happy with Nomar and Elin, just the same. As the desert sun beat down upon his bare head, Kazeem remembered the life he'd had with Kaidin. His father had loved him as a proud father loves his son—fiercely, and with unwavering loyalty—but Kazeem couldn't help being angry with him for getting himself killed. Kaidin had prepared him for life as a warrior: there were many skills Kazeem had already mastered, but he was finding now that there was more to life, more than just the logistics of taking one. He had a chance to live a normal life with Nomar and Elin, a chance he might otherwise not have gotten. And yet he missed his father, thought of him often. The pangs, when they came, were brutal, almost too intense to bear, filling him with a sense of loss and despair that was far beyond mere abandonment. That threw him, but it was also true.

His father could have put his boy ahead of his own damn pride, never gone to the market that fateful morning a lifetime ago, could have found another way to deal with the situation. A million little things reminded him a million times a day what was gone and what would never be again, and all he could do was close his eyes and grit his teeth until the pain passed. No, he wouldn't hate his father for leaving him, but he'd most likely spend years wondering why the man couldn't have at least *tried* another way.

All together it was more than an hour before he got back, tired and sweating. Kazeem tied up the goats before he realized that anything was wrong. A splash of yellow tugged at the corner of his eye when he stopped at the table for a drink of water.

He was only a kid, but he'd been bred to be a warrior, trained to be a killer. It was in his blood, in his heart, and in his mind. He grabbed a knife from the cutting board and flattened himself against the wagon. His heightened senses suddenly came into play, and he quickly fell into the role he'd been born to. It was only then that he noticed the cloud of dust moving away from them over the next hill, and realized that only swiftly ridden horses could be responsible.

Kazeem was alone, almost certainly, and yet training and instinct wouldn't allow him to break the rules. It was like a trance, not in his control, yet part of who he was. When danger threatened, his heart rate increased, respirations went up to bring strength to limbs, and adrenaline seeped into muscles and joints. His eyesight and hearing suddenly seemed unnatural. Everything was too bright, and too loud.

The splash of yellow proved to be the turban of a dead Caliphman. Kazeem found him and one other face down in the gravel near the path, slashed and bloodstained cloaks hiding the wounds that had killed them. Flies buzzed greedily about. Kazeem forced himself to ignore them, squinting into the painfully intense pre-noon sun. Where in God's name were Elin and Nomar?

The ground was a mess. Several horses had trampled it, along with booted feet. Things usually hanging from the wagon on pegs and hooks were everywhere—baskets, lamps, a spade and their spare water keg. Kazeem edged around to the back once he was satisfied that the two at his feet were dead, and saw something that staggered him. A third yellow-turbaned man was lying on his back dead with his eyes wide and staring at the sun. Nomar's thick blade was planted hilt-deep in his chest...and Nomar's bloodied big hand was still gripping the handle. Kazeem dropped to his knees in a small cloud of dust and turned the older man over. In breathless surprise the boy saw that he still lived, but his wounds were many, and a trickle of blood ran out of his mouth and down his chin. Another rivulet tracked along his face, pooling in his right ear.

"Maker, help me!" the boy cried. "Why, Nomar, why did they do this?"

"They were looking for *you*, lad. Seems we didn't fool them after all." He coughed, and frothy red sputum appeared on his lips. Kazeem knew that he didn't have long to live.

"Elin?" Kazeem croaked. His chest was heaving; he couldn't seem to catch his breath, and his head was spinning. In one split second, his entire world had been ripped away—again.

"I don't know." Nomar shook his head, inclined it painfully to his left. "That way. Two of them chased her. One got her, but she kicked him and got away. I think. Tried to...tried to stop them. Couldn't. Not with these three to deal with." Nomar closed his eyes, and a tear trickled from each. "Find her. Help her." Nomar swallowed painfully. Kazeem actually heard it. "Loves you." His breathing suddenly became rapid and shallow and awkwardly spasmodic. The big shoulders hitched and he stopped breathing all together. The bloodied left hand gripped the boy's shirt, lifted the battered body with impossible strength. Their eyes met, and a last, sighing gasp leaked from Nomar's lips in a steady hiss. "Find her..."

Kazeem was up and running, blade in hand, before the light had even left Nomar's eyes. Born to tracking, he found the trail easily, running to the top of a rocky bluff overlooking a sandy gully. There were signs of a struggle. Broken turf at the edge of the cliff told a tale of its own. Kazeem crept to the precipice and looked down, knowing full well what he'd find.

Thirty-five feet below, lying crushed and broken on the rocks, was the beautiful girl he'd hoped to someday marry. With her was yet another, filthy, gray-robed Caliphman...but this one was still alive. It was easy to understand what had happened, Kazeem thought analytically as he started down. Elin, not wanting to be taken, had thrown herself from the bluff. The bastard lying with her had been fortunate enough to land in a bush rather than the rocks a few feet away, but one leg was curled under him, broken and bleeding heavily.

A cold chill unlike anything else he'd ever felt came over Kazeem as he inched down that slope, rocks tumbling, dirt rolling and sliding beneath his boots. He kept his eyes on the man, though, who watched him descend in silent agony, unable to move because of his leg and too far from his fallen sword to do more than make half-hearted lunges in its general direction. He collapsed flat on his back as the shadow of the boy approached. His eyes were huge, his breath rapid as Kazeem bent to retrieve the man's sword. It was a magnificent weapon, forged from the finest Arganian steel; highly polished, the saber glinted fiercely in the sun. It was hot to the touch when Kazeem picked it up. The hilt was carved ivory, bone white, a silver wolf's head as a pommel stone. The sword was finely wrought, perfectly balanced, as if it had always belonged in his hands. Kazeem studied it for a long moment while the crippled soldier fumbled for a dagger. He held it in one fist close to his side and extended the other hand to ward off the boy as he approached. Kazeem took a moment to shove the big knife into his belt, and then he moved forward. Expressionless, and without a word, Kazeem chopped off the man's hand with a single swipe of the blade. The hand landed with a wet *plop* in the bushes, a bloody mist hanging in the air behind it. The Caliphman screamed, tears streaming from his eyes. He pleaded with the boy, *begged* him, told him he'd done *nothing* to the girl.

Kazeem listened, still with no expression, and then cut off the other hand. He didn't remember much of what came next, only that what had once been a man was now recognizable only as a bloody mass of ruined tissue.

Kazeem fell to his knees when he was finished. He knelt there in a breathless, shaking heap, conscious only of someone screaming. He didn't recognize it as his own voice until he became hoarse and started choking on the arid and unforgiving desert air. After an eternity that was probably only a few minutes, he somehow found the strength to get up and stumble towards Elin. He bent, cradled her head in his lap and, for the first time in his life, cried. His grief was bottomless, his despair immeasurable. So much pain, so much death, and all for nothing. When he noticed the rider on the hill opposite, sitting cloaked and hooded on the brown mare, the crying ceased. He blinked back tears, fighting a feeling that he should know the man. They stared at each other for a long moment, but then the horse and rider were gone, and young Kazeem of Zamboria was sure of one thing and one thing only.

He'd never cry again.

CHAPTER FIVE

FATHER AND DAUGHTER were both in their beds when Kazeem came out of the wagon. The floor was soaked with lamp oil, all around the bodies, and Kazeem had taken only what he could comfortably carry on one mount. The other horses, along with the goats, he had allowed to roam free in the basin. He knew he should have kept at least one spare mount, but he just didn't want to bother. From now on, the less he had to worry about, the better.

Kazeem wore white muslin, his head wrapped in red cloth, his face covered by a sash so that only his angry dark eyes could be seen. At his waist he wore the sword he had taken and nothing else.

The torch was sputtering in a holder at the foot of the stairs, and Kazeem looked at it for a long moment after pulling it free. The early morning sunlight was strong, and a warm breeze wound its way out of the draw, stirring his robes. Tossing the torch into the wagon would signal the end of this particular chapter of his life, but he was used to such things. His old life had ended the day his father took him to the market; for that matter, his old life had changed long before that, when his mother had died of the fever. Change, in its own disorienting way, seemed to be the norm for him, and would continue to be, whether he liked it or not.

Everything that had happened to him since his father's death, every thought, hope and dream, had been an illusion. Destiny was like a river, strong currents pulling you in the direction it desired, and no matter how hard you swam against those currents, it would never be enough. What you, yourself, wanted didn't matter. You'd be pulled back in the direction you were supposed to be going, the direction that had already been chosen for you. Kazeem had never been meant to be a merchant, never meant to raise happy babies with a woman he loved. Fate had decreed him a killer, and that was exactly what he had become.

The torch left his fingertips in a short, underhand arc, and bounced once. Lamp oil fed it greedily, and in seconds the entire wagon was in flames. He watched until his former home was fully engulfed, and then, gritting his teeth, led the horse into the desert. The flames continued to roar behind him, but he never looked back.

*

Kazeem, son of Kaidin, understood that fate had great plans for him. He would never be a happy shop keeper with a loving family, but he would live in many places, see far-away lands, explore great cities, and be loved by countless women.

Kazeem never planned on being back in the city of his birth, never planned on running with street urchins and stealing food to stay alive, but there were those currents to contend with again. The truth was he was not yet a full grown man. He wasn't yet a great warrior, no matter what he thought. He may have been a man killer, but to the rest of the world he was still just a kid.

The capitol city of Zamboria was his home for months after burning the wagon. He slept in alleys, begged for food, stole to stay alive—but it was better than being taken by one of the state-run orphanages. From what he'd heard, he'd be better off in jail—at least a place like that didn't pretend to be something other than what it was.

"You don't have to tell *me*, Hasir," he said one night while they were eating stolen melon. "I've heard the stories, too."

Hasir was slightly shorter than Kazeem, very lean, very dark, which made quite a contrast with the tight, short, curly blond hair. Like most Zamborians his eyes were dark, brown with an amber tint that sparkled when he was amused. He had a cleft chin and was the exact same age as his new friend. Hasir was a thief, a pickpocket, a rogue, but he had been good to Kazeem from the start, as true a friend as one could hope to find in a hellhole like this city. They had met one night shortly after Kazeem's arrival, both of them trying to steal the same pies as they sat on a sill to cool.

"Oh, yeah," the other boy said, melon juice dribbling from his chin, "Who'd *you* hear about it from?"

They were sitting, legs dangling, on a thick crossbeam twenty feet above a dark alley. Kazeem tossed a pretty chewed-out rind into the open dustbin far below. He wiped his mouth on a sleeve.

"Girl I used to know."

"*Girl*, huh?" Hasir leered. "Do tell more!"

"Oaf!" Kazeem smiled and cuffed him lightly on the back of the head.

"I'll bet she has big dark eyes and skin like satin! Come on, Kaz! You can tell me. Where is she? What's she like?"

"Dead," Kazeem mumbled, which was the last thing his friend had expected him to say.

Hasir was many things, but he wasn't stupid. He recognized genuine pain when he saw it. "Maker save us! How?"

Kazeem wasn't stupid either. If he started telling people things like that—even his friends—he might just as well walk into the nearest precinct office and admit to killing a Caliphman. "She's just dead, man, doesn't matter how." He sliced another half-moon of melon. "The thing is: she knew these two girls who went in there." He chewed, swallowed. "Wasn't very pretty what happened to them."

"All the more reason to lie low."

"You saying you don't want to go through with this?" Kazeem asked, eyeing him carefully.

"Look, we can still break into one of the shops, steal some real money for a change. I'm all for *that*, Kazeem. All I'm saying is we need to be careful. I don't want to end up in no Home, and neither do you."

"You're right, Hasir, but I also don't want to spend my entire life living from one food-theft to another. If we can make just one big

score, we can call our own shots for a while, that's all I'm saying."
Kazeem became animated suddenly, pushing his rather long, straight
blond hair up and out of his strange amber eyes. "Look around you,
Hasir! Most of the kids in this shithole are doomed to walk the
streets, girls *and* boys, even the ones with parents! Others are sent
to the diamond mines at Saltare." He snorted. "Everyone else is in
the damn Home."

"If you hate it so much here, why don't you go back to where you
came from? No offense, man, but like the rest of us you had to have
come from *some*where."

Kazeem almost said, *this is it*, but caught himself in time. The
truth of the matter was that you needed to be in a city to live the
life they were living. You couldn't pull it off out in the desert or in
a small village where everyone knew everybody else. Maker knew,
he'd tried. Otherwise, he'd never have come back. "Let's just say I
wore out my welcome at my last address."

"One big take, huh?" Hasir was already weighing the pros and
cons. Being a thief at heart, a single, large score appealed to him.

"Maybe someday, huh?" Kazeem said and shifted his weight,
allowing his legs to dangle once more. He'd pushed this thing about
as far as it would go. Maybe it *was* a bad idea, after all. They were
eating, weren't they?

Down below, an alley cat vaulted to the top of the dustbin in one
graceful leap and sat there, tail swishing, waiting for dinner to come
to him.

"Everybody eats everybody else," Kazeem sighed, and resisted
an urge to pelt the animal with a melon rind. When you came right
down to it, the cat was no different—both of them only wanted to
eat, and find a peaceful place to spend the night.

*

Kazeem spent weeks wondering when he'd stop lamenting his
old lives, and only slowly came to realize that his grief was now a
normal, everyday part of him, a low-grade kind of depression that

wasn't ever going to go away. If he had *only* lost his mother, or *only* lost his father, or *only* lost Elin and Nomar, he probably would have been better equipped to deal with his feelings, but there had been too much in too short a time, and he was honestly starting to get confused by which feelings belonged where. During those weeks life went on as it had since he'd come back, but that nagging feeling of tentativeness, of *impermanence*, continued to haunt him. He wanted, *needed* to be settled, to belong, and that need, more than anything else, pushed him irrevocably in a direction he knew was wrong.

Kazeem didn't wear the sword here. Carrying a killing blade would have been tantamount to painting a bull's-eye on his forehead. Within Zamborian city limits, only a precious few were allowed to go armed: the Wrotmar, the Caliphmen, and the army.

And a world-weary orphan didn't fit any of those categories.

Still, most everyone concealed a weapon of some sort. It was foolish to believe that one could walk the streets unprotected. Daggers, short swords, hunting knives—even sharpened spikes and lead-filled clubs hung from almost every belt, covered by vests, robes, and full length jerkins. It was a dangerous place to live, and if you didn't look out for yourself, no one else would, either. You had to provide for yourself, too, because no one was going to do *that* for you, either. So, on a warm, dry night Kazeem finally talked Hasir into burglarizing one of the shops on their alley. Kazeem knew it was dangerous, worse, that it was *wrong*, but he also knew that he couldn't go on like this. He needed to get clear of the city, straighten out his head, and find the old Wrotmar his father had often spoken of. Only then could he try to make some kind of life for himself. To do all that he needed money, and he didn't see any other way to get it.

"Are you scared?" Hasir whispered as they paused at the mouth of the alley.

Kazeem looked back. The twilight sky over the desert was dark blue, covered by violet clouds edged in pink. The sand beneath that lowering sky was a gray carpet of wavering hills and valleys, extending as far as the eye could see. To a new life, one without worries or fears…to freedom.

Kazeem clapped him on the shoulder, and tried a smile. "Always, my friend, but I never let that stop me from doing anything."

"You're just about the strangest guy I've ever met, Kazeemo."

"Thank you."

Hasir shook his head, and returned the smile. "It wasn't a compliment."

"Come on, let's get on with it."

It was almost comical to see the way they moved, so stealthily in a place where they usually came and went as if they owned it, but things were different tonight. You could feel it in the air. Change was on the wind, and they wanted to be a part of it. They crept from box to crate, from dustbin to trash barrel. They were wrapped and cloaked, wearing stolen dark colors, only their eyes showing as they crept about, scurrying like rats with a purpose.

The wind picked up, sending dust and desert sands swirling down the alley in stinging bands. It clattered against dark windows made of cheap, opaque glass, and scrapped along wood planking with a curious rushing sound. A sound like rain. Rain was rare to the area, but Kazeem remembered the sound. He remembered rocks and sand, heat, caves, the ocean, an old man with incredibly intense gray eyes, like forged and polished steel. He'd been very young, but he remembered the rain when it swept in from the coast. The sound filled him with a nostalgia he couldn't afford at the moment, and he actually found himself shaking his head.

"What's the matter?" Hasir whispered. He was just behind.

"Nothing," Kazeem lied. "Got something in my eye." He tossed his chin in the desired direction. "Hurry. I don't want to lose the cloud cover."

"Yeah, be like broad daylight without it," Hasir noted with amusement. The moon was a bare yellow sliver, and seemed impossibly far away.

Kazeem knew when he was being kidded, but didn't waste the time to say so. What Hasir didn't seem to understand was that you took every advantage you could get, because you never knew when you were going to lose one. Despite his so-far troubled youth, Hasir didn't have a clue as to how fast things could go from good to bad, from bad to worse, and then take a screaming left turn into hell, dragging you with them.

As Kazeem crept ahead, repressing a shiver, he hoped his friend never found out, either.

*

The Caliphman was a smoker, but it was a habit he had to hide. The Holy Tablets forbade tobacco, but it was the local constabulary who enforced that ban. Breaking a local ordinance was one thing, violating a law of the Kode was something else entirely, something his friends and connections wouldn't be able to protect him from. It was a habit the Caliphman had acquired from a young Turque while stationed at a border town in Argania. The Caliphman's assignment had only been three months long (he was overseeing the construction of sword blades), but it had been just long enough for the practice to become addictive. He missed Argania—there were more pleasurable things in one square mile than there was in this whole damn country, but his friend continued to ship a steady supply, and he always found the money to pay—one way or another.

He finished a cup of thick, black coffee at the closed café (the barman gave him free drinks in exchange for the armed company while he locked up for the night), and stepped out on the sand-covered cobblestones with the barman while he fumbled with the lock.

"Good night, Faldor," he told the Caliphman as he pocketed his keys. "And thank you. I always feel better having you here."

Faldor Zhan smirked, and turned away. If *he* were a skinny little dog, he'd want company, too. "That's quite all right, my friend, that's what we're here for."

The urge to smoke came on Faldor as soon as the door was closed. He watched the little man as he hurried away, and waited until he turned the corner before stepping into the alley. On duty, he never even *carried* the small canvas sack with the little drawstring. He'd roll one or two of the slim *cigs*, as the Turques called them, using the thin, parchment-like paper his Arganian friend recommended.

Zhan lit one with the sulfur matches he carried, striking it on the wall. He inhaled deeply, letting the smoke go deep into his lungs. For a brief instant, his face was a red devil's-mask in the backwash of the flame. Faldor relished the taste as the plume escaped his lips. The only thing that would have made it better was the cup of coffee he'd left behind.

It was a dark night, for which he was grateful, and Faldor took his time, one hand on his sword as he strolled through the alley, eyes on the distant sands, framed by the buildings at the end of the row. Clear glass was a luxury few could afford, especially in this part of the city; even so, drapes were drawn against the night. He checked doors as he went, the way he was supposed to, and found nothing out of place. It was exactly what he wanted, another do-nothing night on a do-nothing beat. He'd finish this row, slip out early, and head for his favorite brothel. It paid to have friends—smoking friends—in the assignment office.

*

"I'm telling you I heard something," Hasir told Kazeem as the latter pushed open the door with a soft *snick*. On the ground by his knee were various steel picks and shims. Kazeem made a face, placing them quietly and one-by-one in a small leather pouch.

"I didn't hear anything," Kazeem pushed the door open just a bit more.

"I heard a door, a window, something rattled."

"The wind." Kazeem shrugged. Come on."

"I'm not going in until I know what that sound was."

"I should have expected this," Kazeem sighed. He put away the tools, drew his sword, which he'd worn across his back for this occasion. "Tell you what. You stay and watch the alley. I'll get what we need myself, but your share just dropped to forty percent!"

He was inside before Hasir could stop him. "*Kazeem!*" he hissed, but the boy was already hidden by the shadows of the long corridor. "Fine! I'm staying put!" Hasir heard that strange rattle again, closer this time, and tried to tell himself that it was, indeed, the wind.

*

Just then, Kazeem lit the small, shielded lantern he had taken with him.

*

Faldor Zhan had finished smoking. There was really no need to go all the way to the end of the alley, after all, but then the light caught his eye, a light that didn't have any business being there. He sighed as he loosened the blade in the well-oiled sandalwood scabbard.

The clouds were thinning. The light was probably a reflection of the moon. Probably. Still, if something *was* amiss, and if anyone recalled seeing him here…

It was tiresome, really, to be so responsible, he thought as he made his way to the shop at the end of the alley.

*

Kazeem passed a window in the shop; open just a crack, it let in the dry night air. The wind howled through it, making an eerie, moaning sound, and rattling a windowpane in dire need of reglazing.

"Rabbit," Kazeem muttered, thinking about Hasir. He turned his attention to the task at hand, laying blade and lantern on a countertop near the cash box. There wasn't much in it by burglarious standards, but to him it was the world. Kazeem stuffed the leifa-notes into his shirt, filled his pockets with bronze and silver coins. His heart was pounding and his breath came in rasps. Guilt assailed him almost immediately, washing over him as he closed the lid of the teakwood box and began to move away.

The feeling worsened with every step, worse than what he'd felt when taking a life. That, he felt, had been both justified and necessary, to avenge his newfound family and to protect his own life, which surely would have been in danger had he allowed that murderous, child-killing bastard to live.

Kaidin's son told himself that this was every bit as necessary, but he knew it wasn't true. Stealing food to stay alive was one thing, but to take what someone else had *earned* simply to make his own lot easier...

Kazeem was halfway back to the cash box when he heard Hasir's insistent hiss of warning, followed by hurried footfalls and a muffled shout. Kazeem froze, knowing instinctively who had caused those rattling sounds, and wondering how he'd been dumb enough to fool himself into thinking otherwise. He blew out the lantern, watched shadows rush at him from all corners of the room. He forced himself to close his eyes for a moment as he carefully put down the lamp on the display case. He needed to get his eyes used to the dark as quickly as possible. When he opened them again, it took him a few seconds to see *any*thing, and then he was aware of moonlight-kissed shadows... and something else.

The desert breeze on his face.

Without having to look, Kazeem knew what it was. The door was still open, and Hasir was gone, but there was someone else there now. He could sense it. Remaining completely still while he searched with straining ears and wide-open eyes was one of the hardest things he had ever done. He listened the way his father had taught him: for the rustle of cloth, the scrape of steel, the creak of floorboards. The boy two-handed the sword. The snakeskin grip, halfway between the ivory above the ornate hilt and the silver wolf pommel, was cold to the touch, and yet strangely alive. There was a ridged blood-grove on each side of the shaft to add rigidity to the blade as well as to allow it to be pulled, without sticking, from whatever it got into. He recognized the notched, downward bulge at the end as an armor-piercing point. Chain mail would part like ordinary cloth at a thrust, and steel plate would be punched with a simple forward lunge. Still, it was a man's sword, too heavy and too long for his slender, boyish arms.

The reality of it was this: could he beat a grown man in a fair fight? At this point, unless he could figure out how to vanish into thin air, he didn't have much choice.

And then it came—the telltale squeak of a man's boot on a loose floorboard. Moving ever so slightly, turning just his head, Kazeem caught—not only the footfall—but also the sharp intake of breath that went with it. It was amazing how much came with it, as long as he surrendered himself to the feeling. He could hear his opponent breathing, moving, smell him, *sense* him in the dark. The Wrotmar boy stalked with the blade overhead, his knees flexed, hips close to the ground, silently. Kazeem moved this way instinctively, and managed to catch his prey off guard, his back exposed. No one was going to take Kazeem, not after what he'd been through. He would have run had he been able, but the yellow-turbaned Caliphman was between him and the door.

There was only one way out: *through* him.

*

The only thing that saved Faldor Zhan was an errant breeze. The wind blew a piece of parchment from a shelf and Faldor turned, heart pounding, just in time to see the blade descending. He got his own up just in time, pivoting on the balls of his feet, throwing one leg out to the side for stability. He had time to see that his foe was smaller, but that didn't seem to make much of a difference.

The blow rocked Faldor, crushed him to his knees, and shook him so badly that he had all he could do to keep from falling flat on his face. Pain coursed down his forearms and into his shoulders from the impact, and only long-ingrained training habits saved him. He threw himself to one side, rolled, and came up just in time to block another vicious two-handed overhead attack. The angry clash of steel on steel sent sparks winking away into the dark, and filled his ears with the harsh reality of deadly intent. Faldor was a fair swordsman, well experienced, and knew he was in the fight of his life. His foe was good, whoever he was, and strong, despite his size.

Faldor decided that chivalry wouldn't cut it, and resorted to some very nasty army tricks. Wincing from that second blow and only barely blocking a third and a fourth by dropping his elbow and flexing his arm, he reached into a pocket and took out a handful of concentrated pepper dust. Caliphmen used the hot pepper on occasion to subdue troublesome arrestees, but weren't above tossing it into the exposed eyes of a superior swordsman. Gasping for breath, chest heaving, sweat streaming from him, Faldor did so now, relishing the decidedly boyish scream of pain as the awful dust burned and temporarily blinded. Faldor got his balance back, and went on the offensive for the first time. Incredibly, his foe met every charge, blocked every thrust, parried every lunge, and deflected several overhand blows that should have driven him to the floor.

Faldor Zhan was a veteran of scores of fights, but not since his first training, years ago, had he fought with someone this skilled. This thief, whatever else he was, approached a level of personal combat that bordered on the skills of a master swordsman, an instructor, perhaps even one with Wrotmar training. Pepper dust not withstanding, Faldor knew he was in trouble. From another pocket he pulled a coil of plaited leather six feet long. Spiked metal balls were attached to one end, and Faldor shook it to arm's length. Whistling through the air, continuing to fence with this whirling little dervish, Faldor struck his foe's left leg on his third, whip-like attempt, and sucked in a harsh breath in spiteful glee as the coil wound itself around the other man's ankles. Faldor pulled hard, and his attacker went down like felled timber, striking the back of his head on the wall. He was out cold before he slumped all the way to the floor.

"Tough little bastard," Faldor Zhan said with grudging admiration as he approached, the tip of his sword on the unconscious man's chest.

The Caliphman bent warily, eyes wide. One handed, he removed the cowl. Even under dim moonlight, Faldor had no trouble realizing that his foe was only a boy, a fierce boy who could make him quite a bit of money if he turned him over to the right people.

CHAPTER SIX

"I'M TELLING YOU," Faldor told a co-worker at the precinct house, "I've never fought anyone better."

The other officer paused with a quill pen halfway to his ink well. He looked at Faldor with practiced derision. "That little bastard? Are you kidding me? He's just a kid!" He resumed work on his report.

Shackled, sitting on a bench a few feet from the lamp on the high desk, Kazeem was despondent. The light that reached him made his eyes dark and sullen. With his small chin braced on both fists, Faldor had to admit he didn't look very intimidating.

Faldor returned his attention to the deskman. "He doesn't look like much right now, I'll grant you, but you should have seen him with this in his hands!" He held up the sword with the ornate wolf's head.

"Nice. But a kid's still a kid, Faldor." He jutted his double chin. "Take a man to wield a blade like that."

"You didn't have to face him in the dark with that thing. Be glad he's chained."

"Maker-be-merciful! Faldor, you blinded him, practically bashed in his head…"

"I'm telling you, he was like a demon in that shop."

"You sure you weren't drinking something other than coffee down at Faroque's?"

Faldor gave up. Sometimes you just had to be there. "Find out who he is yet?"

"No, but good thing he's a kid. Man'd get an extra two years just for *carrying* that thing." He nodded at the wolf sword, now on the high desk. It gleamed, even under the dim lamplight. "Incidentally, you get him to tell you where he got that?"

"Nah." Faldor shook his head. "Didn't get much of anything out of him."

"No wonder." The deskman brayed laughter. "You all but broke his skull!"

"Told you," Faldor said defensively, "I had to put him down any way I could."

"Yeah, yeah, fights like a Wrotmar. I heard you the first time."

"That's *exactly* what he fights like," Faldor said slowly and more to himself than the other man.

A third man who did most of the inter-departmental paperwork in the precinct house interrupted them. He dropped a rolled parchment onto the desk, slipped a slim sheaf of papers into a three-sided box, and took another stack from a similar box on the other side of the desk. Faldor could never recall his name, but he always seemed to smell like garlic.

"You two ready for this?" He searched their eyes, looking for a reaction. "They found out who the kid is."

"Gonna make us guess?" the desk officer asked without even looking up from his paperwork.

"Nope. I don't want to wait to see the looks on your faces."

"All right, all ready," the desk officer grumbled. "We're paying attention. Who is he, the King of Ankoria?"

"Not at all. He is Kazeem, son of Kaidin, Wrotmar." The third man walked away without another word.

Faldor was tempted to say 'I told you so', to his fat co-worker, but he refrained. There'd be time enough for that, later.

And he'd tell him more than once, too.

*

"I'm sorry I had to clobber you, kid," Faldor said an hour later, "but now that I know who you are, I'm glad I did."

Kazeem had been processed, seen by a doctor. He wore a bandage on his head, and despite irrigation, his eyes were still pink. He spoke to Faldor directly for the first time.

"Need and folly often grow on the same tree."

Faldor shook his head as he unlocked the cell. The iron door swung open with a creaking sound and banged against the wall. The entire warrior class, every Wrotmar he'd ever known, talked like that. It had to be something in the bloodline.

"Uh-yeah. This is yours. Not very comfortable, but it's only for one night. Being an orphan, I guess you know you're going to the Home."

"That's my own fault," Kazeem said. He entered the cell of his own volition, and gripped the bars with both hands after the door clanged shut.

Faldor was hoping to make money from this kid; there were plenty of people who would pay a ton for someone with his skills, but he also felt sorry for him. He saw the killer in those dark eyes, but there was something sad about him, too. "You smoke?"

"Might be a good time to start, huh?" Kazeem met his eyes.

Faldor looked up and down the dark hall. Except for a couple of torches along the way, it was black as pitch. "No one else back here. Quiet night, I guess." He laid a *cig* and one match on a horizontal crossbar. "I'll be back for you in the morning, kid. Get some rest."

"Hey."

Faldor was three feet away, but the kid's voice stopped him like the hand of authority. His eyebrows went up. "Yeah?"

"My sword?"

"All personal effects go into storage at the Home. The administrator will see you get it—and anything else you had on you—when you get out." The kid's eyes were unnaturally bright. Faldor bit his lower lip. "Go on now, get some rest."

The kid took the items on the crossbar and placed them in a pocket.

When Faldor looked back, the kid was on the floor, doing push-ups.

*

The Home had cracked, white walls, and bars on the windows. There was a front yard—sparse brown grass and gravel—and a cobblestone walk that stretched from the front gate all the way up to the big house, an eighth of a mile away. The house itself was a hulking, block-like thing, three stories high and God alone knew how long. From the front gate it looked like it went on forever.

Kazeem was in the back of a wagon with four other boys. He'd been taken by Faldor and the driver at dawn, and driven around town while they picked up the other kids. Now, with the massive stone wall looming above them and the Home all gray on its hill under cloud-filled skies, Kazeem felt the first tug of panic. There was an exchange at the gatehouse, and then the guards were letting them through. One little boy, no more than seven, began to cry as soon as the gate closed behind them. Kazeem didn't blame him. Having that thing close behind you was like being buried alive.

They couldn't see much from the back of the prison van, but there was a crack in one of the boards on the right side, and if you sat just so you could make out quite a bit. There was a flower garden, and a little stand of fig trees, and what looked like a small melon patch. Each of these had a group of supervised children working in them. Several buildings were attached to the main house along the way back, hammered on as afterthoughts and serving as carpentry, blacksmith and paint shops. The wall enclosed everything like a noose.

Strangely, Kazeem felt the loss of his mother most acutely. His father, Nomar and Elin were the rawest, most recent wounds, but being motherless on this overcast day was more than poignant—it was painful. Even a boy like Kazeem—hard around the edges and all cold inside—needed a hug from time to time. It was a hard thing to bear whenever the stark reality hit him, but it was especially difficult today. To understand that there was no one there to love you, that no mother cared—these were painful enough, but to realize that such a loss was also the cause of his incarceration…well, that was the sort of thing that just might break you, if you let it.

There are peak experiences in everyone's life, moments of ultimate truth, some full of joy, some otherwise. All of these moments, however, have one thing in common: they help to define who we are. As the prison van clattered to a creaking halt by the front door, two of the other boys began to cry as well. The fourth was a year or so older than Kazeem, and berated them terribly, although he was shaking like a leaf.

"Leave them be," Kazeem said coldly, and without a trace of emotion in his voice. "They've reason enough."

One of two things could have happened to Kazeem at that moment. He could have decided he was a victim, or decided he was a survivor. Kazeem didn't understand it all, but he knew one thing for sure: being a victim was only a state of mind. If he decided, in his heart, that he was nobody's pawn, then these walls were no longer a prison—they were merely one more obstacle in a life that seemed to have more than its share of them.

The Home was big and imposing; it seemed to go on forever, blotting out the sky, but when Kazeem climbed down out of the wagon, it wasn't his first step towards incarceration; it was his first step towards freedom.

*

"Come in, my boy. Close the door behind you."

Even though the speaker was soft-spoken, Kazeem felt the panic rise again, like a hot wind in the pit of his stomach. He knew now with unquestioned certainty what a fly feels when trapped in the spider's web. Kazeem wanted his mother, his father, *anybody*—to come for him, but he also knew that no one would. As always, he was on his own.

With supreme effort, he somehow forced down the panic, squelched it with the coldness that he carried inside him like a balm.

"You are Kazeem, son of Kaidin, Wrotmar."

"I am," the boy answered without hesitation.

"Please, sit down."

As Kazeem did that, he noticed two things. The chair before the big desk was lower than the one behind it—a ploy, no doubt, to intimidate the newcomer. He also noted that the man before him was exceedingly handsome. Still, his eyes took away from that attribute, lent a sinister cast to a face that was otherwise quite pleasant.

"I am Baaka Zhinn, the administrator."

"So I was told."

There was a moment when they sized each other up. It was a rare, sunless day, the room bathed in the glow of candles and oil lamps, so neither was cast in his best light. Kazeem saw a good-looking man in his early-to-mid thirties, with the towhead, dark eyes and tanned skin of the average Zamborian. He also saw a cruel man filled with hatred and petty meanness, a person who enjoyed the suffering of others and attempted to profit by it. The strange amber flecks in the otherwise dark eyes somehow seemed to reflect that sickness.

For his part, Baaka Zhinn knew trouble when he saw it. Kazeem had a round, boyish face, high cheekbones, and wide eyes, but there was an uncommon strength in those eyes that disturbed him. This boy would grow to be a strong man, one not easily intimidated. He would question the status quo, stand apart and lend courage to others, who, left to their own devices, would have been easily managed.

The boy had fought a seasoned Caliphman and nearly beaten him. He'd survived the loss of his parents, and the family that had taken him in. He had seen his father nearly cut to ribbons before his eyes, and *still* he radiated defiance. There was also the rumor—without proof, mind you—that he was responsible for the deaths of at least three Caliphmen in connection with the questioning of the merchant Nomar and his daughter. No proof, true, but looking at his eyes, Baaka Zhinn most certainly believed he was—at the very least—capable of such things.

Baaka Zhinn had a gold mine here. Young women no one would ever miss, girls, pretty boys and strong young men he could sell into slavery or indentured mercenary work. Then there was the personal aspect of those things. He could pick and choose to satisfy any whim that took his fancy, and he didn't need some idealistic young lad with pseudo-Wrotmar training ruining a good thing. On the other hand, Kazeem was the only son of one of the most feared and respected fighters the region had ever known. He couldn't very well just do away with him. Better to find a lucrative use for him, and be done with it. Still, if the child became *too* troublesome, there would have to be a very inventive accident, one no one could question. For a moment the administrator of the Home cursed the fortune that had brought this almost priest-like young man to his door.

And then, the thing that had sustained him all along—his ability to take advantage of almost any situation—manifested itself. Why make an enemy of this rather lethal and personal weapon, when he could befriend him and wield him like a blade? Baaka Zhinn may have been overindulged in certain areas, but he maintained a very excellent physique, and was counted among Zamboor's best fencing masters. He recognized that discipline in others when he saw it. If he played his cards right, he could very well come to find that he had stumbled onto a veritable treasure.

He altered his approach without breaking stride.

"They told you who I was?"

"The man outside. The Caliphman, Faldor. He told me you run this place."

"I do the best I can." Baaka Zhinn followed Kazeem's eyes. The boy was looking at the wall behind him. The administrator turned. He'd almost forgotten the tapestry. Artfully done, it depicted a wolf pack in the highlands of Vendaria. Mountain peaks poked into gray clouds above them, while the pack ravaged a deer, blood startlingly red on virgin snow.

"You like the picture?"

"No, it's disturbing."

"And yet it has no meaning. It is only a picture."

Kazeem said nothing.

Baaka Zhinn was impressed. "You don't agree?"

"One questions why one would hang such a thing where traumatized children have to look at it."

"There is a message, no?"

"A moment ago you said it was only a picture."

Zhinn bit his lip. He'd made a mistake. He wouldn't underestimate this boy again. "Well, yes and no. It is nature's way, don't you think?" he added, turning in his seat to regard it. "The strong survive. The weak don't."

"Nature's way, certainly. Nonetheless, it is an inappropriate message for such a place."

The administrator realized immediately that the boy had put him on the defensive. He was explaining himself instead of taking charge of the interview. Almost without effort, perhaps without understanding it himself, Kazeem of Zamboria had diverted attention from himself with an adult who should have known better.

Baaka Zhinn suddenly understood why the boy had almost taken the Caliphman, and why Faldor had been so impressed with him. In fact, Faldor had even gone so far as to suggest that Kazeem might make an excellent candidate for the gladiator training camp. Zhinn thought it was too early to tell, but suspected that Faldor might be right.

"I'll tell you what, Kazeem," he said quietly, "you concentrate on getting along here, and leave the decorating to me, all right?" He made a peak with his hands and tapped his index fingers lightly against his lips. He wanted to get this just right, to get the threat across while making it sound like advice. "You've never been in an enclosed environment before. No doubt you'll have trouble adapting. If that occurs, I have several young men at my disposal that'll be only too happy to help you out." He squinted, studying the hard-looking young man before him. "Do you understand what I'm saying?"

"Perfectly," Kazeem answered without hesitation.

Baaka Zhinn took another moment staring into eyes much older than their years. He nodded, sat back in his chair, long fingers splayed on the end of each armrest. "Yes, I see that you do."

"May I go now?" Kazeem asked.

"You have somewhere else to be?" the administrator asked sharply, leaning forward again. "Perhaps you're late for an appointment?" He leveled a finger, his control failing him. "If you understand nothing else, understand this. I am the only law in this place. There are rules, *my* rules, and there are repercussions for breaking those rules. Learn them and we'll get along fine. Break them and you'll see a side of me you can do without. I've tried to be nice, to be respectful of all you've been through, and you've chosen to take that kindness as a weakness." He cleared his throat, wondering how this somber young man had managed to get so far under his skin. "I won't make that mistake again. Now get out of my sight, and take that attitude with you!"

"Yes, sir," Kazeem said in that same cold voice. "I'll do that." He stood immediately. "Thanks for the advice."

As Kazeem quietly shut the door behind him, Baaka Zhinn slumped back in his chair, disgusted with himself. The boy had bested him in every round, and, worse, they both knew it. It was as if the kid had the ability to see right through the façade to the unvarnished truth below. Something no boy his age should have been able to do. Zhinn had never really believed in the old Wrotmar legends, not before today, at any rate. The warrior class was said to have an iron will, an uncanny self-possession that was nearly inhuman. It was said that they could walk unheard, control pain, and wield unnatural physical strength. Men who had gone against them claimed that they could take control of almost any situation.

"Well, we'll see about that," he mumbled to himself.

"Smart assed little bastard," another voice said from not too far away.

"Did you hear that, Garth?" Baaka Zhinn asked in a huff. "Did you hear how he *sassed* me?"

"I heard it all, *Multan*," Garth Fegan answered, using the Ankorian word for 'master'. He closed the door to the side chamber softly behind him.

Garth Fegan was a huge, hulking sixteen-year-old boy perhaps twice the size of Kazeem. He wasn't Zamborian as the brown hair and fair skin testified, but he'd been here for most of his life and no one was quite sure exactly *what* he was. Garth had a square face, light brown eyes and amazingly large hands. Baaka Zhinn may not have known much about his origins, but he knew this much: the boy had grown from a cruel, ineffectual child to one of the best hatchet men the administrator had ever employed. He would be eligible to leave the Home in another two years, but, like most of the others, he had nowhere else to go. Garth Fegan would have made an excellent soldier, but Baaka Zhinn knew he'd make an even better bodyguard. All Zhinn had to do to retain his loyalty was toss him a bone every now and then. The poor bastard simply didn't know any better.

The administrator got up. "And what did you think?"

"I've seen his type before. Hard cases that'd rather break than bend. If you give the word, I'll gladly accommodate him."

Baaka Zhinn laid a hand on the boy's shoulder. "Just keep an eye on him for now, and tell Omar to send in the next one."

"Are you sure, *Multan?*"

Zhinn thought about that for a moment. "Yes, I'm sure," he said finally, but as Garth went out, he began to have second thoughts.

*

Kazeem was heading down the hall with the tall man called Omar. He knew he'd made a mistake with the administrator, but part of him didn't care. Let him know from the start that he couldn't be bought, bribed or bluffed. If only *half* the stories told about this place were true, then strength was the only thing he would respect.

Omar didn't say a word as he led Kazeem to his dorm room, and Kazeem didn't try to make small talk. Instead, he studied his new home, committing as much as possible to memory.

The place was dank, which threw him. Located on the edge of the desert, he'd expected dryness, not humidity. But the walls seemed to hold moisture, made the rooms and hallways musty. Kazeem didn't like the smell, but knew he'd get used to it in time—which he'd found was the key to most of life's hardships. They passed a tall boy with a mop and a bucket in one tiled gray corridor, and along another section several girls wearing long skirts, their hair hidden by wraps, attempted to scrub the yellow back into a chest high border in an otherwise black and white tile wall.

Kazeem had just decided that they kept the place pretty clean, considering, when Omar stepped on a roach with force enough to skew the gray-and-red kepi he wore. He smiled crookedly, and beckoned.

The Wrotmar boy realized he was being placed in a wing at the back of the facility, a ploy, no doubt, to degrade him, to make him walk as far as possible whenever the administrator called.

Kazeem decided he'd get more exercise that way, that it would help him to stay strong. As he'd told himself earlier that day, it was all in how you looked at it.

They passed classrooms and shops and, by the smell, what passed for a kitchen around here.

They finally reached a small hallway at the rear of the building. Omar turned left, opened a door, and held out a hand, indicating that Kazeem should enter. He was greeted by a stark room, gray walls, tile floor, cracked plaster ceiling. There were four small narrow cots, four tiny dressers, one round table and four stools in the center of the room. Except for some drawings someone had tacked above his bed and on the back of the door that was it. This was his new home.

For a moment, despair threatened to overwhelm him. The loss and the loneliness, and the pain were living things that just about drove him to his knees. They came in waves, crashing against him repeatedly, but he hung on by clenching his fists and taking a deep breath.

"Hi, I'm Imad," a brown little boy, perhaps nine-years-old and the sole occupant of the room at the moment said. "What's your name?"

"I am Kazeem," the son of Kaidin said absently and nodded at Omar's departing back. "What's with him? He doesn't talk much, does he?"

"Who, Omar?" Imad smiled grimly. "Don't let those bright green eyes fool you. He's a devil. Got his tongue ripped out for speaking against the Arganian Amir when he was a young man. Couldn't talk if he wanted to, but I don't think he'd speak to us even if he could, at least he makes you feel that way. Come on in, I'll show you where they put your clothes and stuff, although we wear the uniform most of the time." He plucked at the drab tan shirt and pants.

"Uniforms—and a guy who can't talk." Kazeem mumbled and shook his head. "Marvelous."

Imad had a quick smile and big brown eyes. Judging from the books on the shelf above his bed, they both loved to read. Kazeem liked him right off.

"So," he said, "tell me more about this place."

Imad had been folding undergarments, socks and washcloths when Kazeem arrived. He returned to this task now while Kazeem lay back on his bunk, fingers laced behind his head, staring at the ceiling. He knew from experience that he looked calm outwardly, but his stomach was in knots.

"Oh, usual drill. Same as any other place you've ever been in. As bad as most, a little worse than others if you get on the wrong side of the wrong people."

Kazeem rolled over on his side, and propped himself up on an elbow, his fist supporting his temple. "I've never been in a place like this before."

There was more than five years between them, but it was Imad who suddenly looked older. He folded his last article and put it away thoughtfully. "You'll need help then," he decided as he shut the drawer.

"Help?" Kazeem snorted. "With what?"

"Help with staying alive and out of danger," Imad told him bluntly. There was fear in his big brown eyes.

Wrotmar born, threats were something Kazeem understood, and took seriously. His dark eyes narrowed as he sat up slowly. "Explain yourself."

"Look, don't get sore, okay? I know you've been around some. We all know it. Rumor has it you even killed a couple of guys, but I thought you were a veteran, you know? Someone who understood how a place like this works. Tough guy act won't cut it in here, my friend. You fight 'em head-to-head, and they'll kill you outright and make it look like an accident. I've seen it happen. Stop it. Get that bad-assed look out of your eyes. You can't win in here. Not like that. There's too many of them and they'll keep coming at you." He shuddered involuntarily. "They'll do things to you you can't even imagine. Trust me; I've seen *that*, too."

Kazeem got up slowly. His head ached, and his shoulders felt exactly like someone had slid a steel rod through them. Imad backed away.

"You make this seem like a real dangerous place," Kazeem said on the way to the window. It looked out on a courtyard, enclosed by the very shape of the building. He wondered if the kids on the other side ever looked out at the sky like he was doing, daydreaming of freedom.

Imad breathed a sigh of relief, as if he'd narrowly escaped danger. "It is. I just hope you're smart enough to realize how things work here."

Kazeem thought about his interview with Baaka Zhinn, and nodded. "Believe me, I get the picture." He straightened, and took a deep breath. "I'm just not too impressed with it."

"Well, you'd better *get* impressed!" Imad said with more force than he'd intended. He paled as he realized to whom he was speaking. "You know, if you want to get along."

"Why start now?" Kazeem mumbled.

"Huh?"

The older boy turned from the window, where the day was drab and dark. "Nothing. Tell me about our roommates."

Imad made a face. It didn't take a genius to realize that he was afraid of them. "Zamborians like you. Same age or a little older."

"They ever bother you?" Kazeem asked intuitively.

Imad turned and began to refold a shirt that had already been folded. "No more than most."

Kazeem frowned and bit his lip, but the younger boy didn't see it. "Where are they now?"

"Kitchen and latrine duty. Three days running."

"That routine around here?"

"No, but they pissed off Garth Fegan."

"What's a Garth Fegan?"

"The administrator's enforcer. Big bastard. You'll meet him soon enough."

"Can't wait," Kazeem said dryly, then added: "Say, what happened to the other kid, you know, the one whose place I'm taking in here?" Kazeem pointed at his bunk. "He get out?"

"Yeah, he got out all right," Imad said solemnly. "*All* the way out, if you know what I mean."

Kazeem understood perfectly, and had since the first time he'd laid eyes on Baaka Zhinn.

"Say, what time do we eat around here?" Kazeem asked. "I'm starved."

Imad apparently didn't appreciate the poor attempt at humor through impertinence. He faced the larger boy and looked directly into his eyes. "Like everything else in here, Kazeem, when *they* say so."

CHAPTER SEVEN

JUDGING BY IMAD'S estimate, it must have been just before supper when Kazeem found himself at the window again. The younger boy had gone off on some pre-assigned chore, leaving Kazeem alone in the room. He tried to rest, but lying there was simply a waste of time. As the day waned, so did the storm clouds, and just before dusk, the sky grew brighter again, drawing the boy to the window with colors and light.

As the sun sank below the horizon it backlit the few remaining clouds. Shafts of bright light, like beacons from Heaven, shot down in swirling rays. The sunbeams pierced churning, multicolored clouds. Patches were stark white, aquamarine, pink, dark blue and ash. It was like viewing a beautifully lit room from a great distance on a dark and stormy night, and Kazeem wanted very much to go there.

He'd seen much in his young life, much pain, much suffering… and when he thought about it, *really* thought about it, this didn't even begin to compare. In his travels Kazeem had seen disease, hunger, homelessness and death.

And then there was the Home with all of its own attendant human pain. Children nobody wanted, children who simply had no where else to go…worst of all, kids who were actually better off in a place like this.

Kazeem hadn't prayed since the death of his father. He just couldn't see the point, and it was all so far above his comprehension that it made him dizzy just to think about it.

Kazeem watched the sunset until it was dark, and was never sure of the transition when it came—only that the blackness of night had somehow replaced those beautiful, almost angel-wrought clouds. When he blinked, took a deep breath and looked up again, the fullness of night was a black jeweler's cloth covered with brilliant, twinkling gemstones.

If the Maker of All Things has created such a vast Universe, Kazeem thought, *a thing of such splendor and immense scope, how can I be arrogant enough to believe he'd have time for the likes of me?*

Kazeem allowed himself to be overwhelmed by his emotions, something of a luxury to this point. He didn't know how many people populated this planet, but he knew it had to be a lot. Every single one of them had a personality, a life, and each one filled with hopes and dreams, fears and disillusions, goals and aspirations, trials and tribulations. What made *him* so special? What made him think that any Supreme Being would even bother with him, a thief and a killer and not even an adult yet? And what if those twinkling lights in the blackness of space represented other worlds, other beings? How, then, was the ratio changed?

Even here, on his own world, there was talk of distant lands across the Vast Expanse of sea between the Eastern Continents and the next land mass. Wise men whispered of ancient, forgotten civilizations more advanced than any now alive could even imagine, of wizards, of different races of people, of dragons and trolls and dwarves.

In light of these things, was not Kazeem's place made even less significant?

He'd prayed for guidance, for help, for the safe return of his father, for the life of his mother; he had prayed for Elin and Nomar.

All were dead. Kazeem was alone, and knew not where to turn.

What did *that* say about God?

Did He pick and chose? Did He stab an arbitrary finger down from the Heavens like a man spearing fish in a stream? Did He shout: Prosper! Suffer! Live! Die! Was everything that happened really so simple? Or was it all, as some maintained, according to some mysterious master plan?

Kazeem fervently hoped not. He wanted no part of a god that cruel, a god to whom lives and loves were only pawns in a game. Or was it something else entirely? His hand went through the window, reaching for the stars. Some said that the Westerners believed in the concept of free will, that God—*whatever* you called Him—had left us to our own devices, that He wouldn't interfere because that would break the covenant of that free will. Therefore, if you were on your own, praying to such a being was even more of a waste of time, because no one would help you—and even if He did, why you, and not the next person?

It was all very confusing, especially when every religious leader claimed righteousness. This they did, of course, while speaking disdainfully of all others.

It was easier not to believe at all.

And yet, deep inside, he *did* believe. To abstain from belief even under these circumstances was a frightening prospect.

Kazeem, therefore, tried to live his life according to the ancient texts and when he couldn't, he simply asked for the strength to do so the next time. Cut off from everything he'd ever loved, isolated, alone, knowing he was a killer and a thief, he could only hope he was forgiven, and try to salvage what was left of his soul.

And then it came to him suddenly, as he literally reached for the stars, that this, perhaps, was the true definition of faith.

The bell drew him startled from the window. He knew that it was calling them to supper, but to Kazeem, it was the wail of a tocsin, a warning, and he suddenly couldn't seem to catch his breath. He went into the hall blinking, and saw uniformed boys and girls by the score filing two-by-two like lemmings through the corridors. There were cooking smells that made his stomach rumble despite himself. Knowing it was expected of him anyway, he decided to follow. Feeling like a fool for trusting again, he rattled off a quick prayer, asking for strength. Now, as never before, he needed to believe he wasn't alone and un-thought of in the universe.

*

The other children led him to a large blue hall in the center of the main building. Two abreast, they filed silently in through the rear double doors and split off side by side at every table until each seat was taken. Kazeem wound up three-quarters of the way back, but not so far away that he couldn't see the raised dais at the head of the room. Omar stood there now with a hulking bear of a boy, and neither looked happy.

At some prearranged signal he neither saw nor understood, the children sat and began to eat. With the silence broken Kazeem felt a little better. He wasn't a particularly gregarious person, but eating in quiet solitude every night would have slowly driven him out of his mind.

At least the fare was better than he expected. On each table were huge bowls of savory *miskantofel*, a wilderness stew made with rabbit, potatoes, carrots and fresh herbs. It had thick gravy, and there were mountains of hardtack biscuits on the side. There was even fruit and cheese for dessert. Kazeem ate hugely, surprised by his own appetite. He studied their monitors while he did so, and rightly surmised that they were mainly there to keep order. He noticed other things, as well. The kids actually seemed *normal* in here, behaving as kids usually behave. There was conversation, laughter, camaraderie—quite a contrast to the mechanistic manner in which they had comported themselves in the halls. Kazeem was surprised to find the boys all mixed up with the girls, seated not in any particular pattern other than the order in which they had arrived.

He noticed two other things during that first meal: one, that no one talked to him and, two, that the monitors at the front of the room never took their eyes from him.

*

After supper Kazeem followed the other kids back out into the hall. They grew quieter as soon as they were out of the dining room, and filed away in pairs, talking softly. Kazeem found himself alone again, but that was all right. It gave him a chance to think about how he was going to get out of here. That much he was sure of. He hadn't gone through hell to end up playing the sheep now, to rot in this stink hole until *they* thought he was old enough to leave. There were bound to be opportunities soon enough. An exercise period in the yard, work details, a delivery van. Even the jailor's wagon would do.

*

If confronting Baaka Zhinn was his first mistake, Kazeem made his second while returning to his room. He relaxed and let his guard down. Because of this, he didn't see Garth Fegan watching his every move from the shadows. Kazeem was deep in thought, and Garth read his face like a book. Had Kazeem been aware, he might have been able to prevent what was to come, but when he looked back later on the whole affair, he was forced to admit that knowing exactly who your enemy is doesn't always help as much as you might think it would.

*

It was a startled gasp that pulled Kazeem from sleep. He awoke disoriented, and for a moment didn't know where he was. It took a second or two to get his bearings, and then he realized: the Home. The very name filled him with dread, tortured him with night terrors and fear of the unknown. Slanted bars of silver moonlight fell on the floor in ladder patterns from the windows. Kazeem blinked as his eyes adjusted, and heard the strange sound again.

"Who's there?" he asked before he could stop himself. Alone in the dark in a strange place, he was as much a child as the next boy.

"I said who's there?" he demanded, the uncertainty gone from his voice. He looked right, then left, his eyes more adjusted. His new roommates weren't in their beds, and Imad's bunk was in shadow.

Suddenly, without knowing how he knew, he *knew.*

As Kazeem sat up, a shape bolted left, another right. Kazeem grabbed the closest and bent him backward, a hand wrapped in long, greasy hair, exposing the throat. He was angry beyond description, and with one hand grabbed a sulfur match from the nightstand, lit it with his thumb, and touched it to the oil lamp.

Imad sat up blinking. His throat was red as if someone had been choking him.

"Look," Kazeem said, practically spitting into the face of the kid he was holding, "I don't know what usually goes on in here, but it stops now, am I clear?"

The kid in his grasp pulled away furiously, trying desperately to save face.

"Am I *clear?*" Kazeem snarled, his free hand at the exposed throat in a chokehold.

Bug-eyed, the kid stopped struggling and nodded weakly.

"You little *shit*," the other one said to Imad from across the room. "I told you to keep quiet!"

"I'm sorry, Miko," Imad said sheepishly.

"Don't you apologize to them!" Kazeem snapped. He tossed the kid he was holding onto his own bed like a rag doll, and advanced on Miko. "Who the hell do you think you are?" he asked breathlessly.

Miko was bigger than Kazeem, but he was fat, and he was scared.

Kazeem backhanded him, and the fat boy spun over onto his bed and fell backwards to the floor with a *thud*.

"Get out!" Kazeem said, jerking a thumb at the first kid. "And take *that* with you!"

"Hey, you can't—"

Kazeem bent, grabbed Miko by the windpipe with his thumb and fingers and pulled him slowly to his feet. On tiptoe, trying desperately not to choke, Miko gingerly moved wherever Kazeem wanted him to move, which was towards the door.

"But it's the middle of the night," the other one said. "Where are we supposed to go?"

"I don't care! Just go. And don't come back!"

Kazeem banged Miko's head off the wall, cracking the plaster, and would have laughed at the way they scrambled out if he wasn't so sick to his stomach.

With tears in his eyes, Kazeem went to Imad, who had pulled the sheet up to his neck.

"Don't!" he said breathlessly.

Kazeem stopped short. "Don't worry. I won't hurt you."

"You already have," Imad said. "They'll get me for this. You too."

"They won't do *shit*. I promise."

Imad shook his head. "You just don't get it, do you? You just don't understand."

Kazeem reached out and wiped the tears from Imad's cheek with a thumb. "You'd be surprised what I understand, kid." He sat on the edge of the bed, pulled the child's head closer, and rested it on his shoulder. "And I won't let them hurt you again, either."

There was an almost imperceptible shrug. "It's not like it was the first time," he whispered, as if it no longer made a difference.

Anger, panic and disgust fought for control of Kazeem. He didn't know exactly where his soul was located, but he knew that it was damaged. He could feel the ache in his chest like a red-hot coal.

"Well, it's the *last* time, Imad. You'll see."

"You can't fight them all, Kazeem. "It's just the way it is."

"Not anymore." Kazeem was about to say more, but Omar flung the door open. He entered with the big, brown haired boy, his green eyes bright. Behind them were Miko and the other boy.

"See, I *told* you!" Miko said to the well-built kid.

Kazeem wasn't stupid—he understood the inference—he just chose to ignore it. He got off the bed, and his voice was like ice. "I told you to get out."

"You don't tell *anyone* what to do," the brown haired boy said. "Not in here."

"Who the hell are you?" Kazeem asked, although he had a pretty good idea.

"He's the Trustee, you stupid *shit*," Kazeem's other roommate said. His neck was red raw from where the Wrotmar boy had held him. His voice was high and raspy.

"Shut up, Nasoh," the big kid said, his eyes never leaving Kazeem's. "I'm Garth Fegan," he said, throwing out his chest with puffed up pride. "I look after things for *Multan* Zhinn. In this place, *I* settle disputes, not you."

"Then I'm glad you're here," Kazeem said. "If there's some kind of law here, I appeal to it. I want these two kept away from him." He nodded towards Imad.

"Who cares what *you* want?" Baaka Zhinn said from the open door. He stepped inside, followed by two more teenage boys, one a wiry Zamborian, the other a fat, pimple-faced boy with a red face, a double chin and pale blue eyes. "Spinner. Abdar. Watch him."

Kazeem now faced a room full of foes. Baaka Zhinn, still tying his bed robe at the waist, moved in front of him.

"I knew you were going to be trouble the first time I laid eyes on you."

"Is it trouble to keep these two from hurting Imad?"

Baaka Zhinn crossed his arms. Part of his muscled chest was exposed. His sleeves were oversized. "Oh, why didn't you say so in the first place? What, exactly, did they do?"

Kazeem saw where this was going, but there was nothing he could do. Hands on hips, his eyes on his own bare feet, he shook his head and then looked up. "Do you really need me to draw you a picture, *Multan* Zhinn?" He turned his head slightly. "Tell him, Imad," he ordered without much hope.

"Yes, Imad," Baaka Zhinn prompted. "Do tell."

The silence that followed nearly broke Kazeem's heart.

"Imad," he said finally. "*Tell* them!"

"I really don't know *what* happened, *Multan*," Imad said in a very small voice. "Those three were fighting. The noise woke me."

"Oh, Imad," Kazeem breathed.

"Nasoh's all but had the life choked out of him," Baaka Zhinn said, moving to lift the boy's bruised chin with a finger. "Poor thing. And Miko here, well, just *look* at him. He's a wreck. I've never had a lick of trouble from either of them, Kazeem. You're in the room one night, and all hell breaks loose. What am I to think?"

"You know the truth," Kazeem told him, meeting his eyes. He, too, folded his arms across his chest. "You don't need me to tell you what to think."

For a moment, Baaka Zhinn looked like a demon. There was fire in his eyes, and Kazeem was certain he'd get violent. And then the light went out. Turning to the others he said, "Look at him, poor boy. Lost his whole family and all his friends. He's upset and his judgment's flawed. You obviously had a nightmare, Kazeem, didn't you?" The administrator stepped closer, closer still, until their noses were almost touching, until Kazeem felt his breath on his own skin. "You awoke disoriented, but it was all a mistake, *wasn't* it?"

It would have been so easy to agree, to become like them, but there are defining moments in each life, moments that decide who we are, possibly forever. This was such a moment, Kazeem realized, and he couldn't betray himself, regardless of consequences. Self respect, after all, was the mother of discipline. He met Baaka Zhinn's eyes and Omar's icy stare before shifting back to the administrator.

The silence was a living thing until Kazeem broke it. "I stand by what I've said," he declared.

"Good boy," Baaka Zhinn whispered so that no one else could hear him. He moved until his full lips were almost touching Kazeem's right ear. "To tell you the truth, I would have been disappointed by almost any other response." He stepped back, and smiled sadly. "This boy is obviously disturbed. Take him to the Time-Out room."

Kazeem had a second to wonder what *that* might be, and then they were on him.

As Imad had said, he just couldn't fight them all.

*

When Kazeem woke up, the first thing he realized was that he was on the floor. It was cold, and there was a mouse an inch from his nose. Kazeem recoiled, and the poor thing fled with a terrified squeal. He winced, and brought a hand to the lump on the back of his head. He was bleeding. There was a cut over his eyes, and he felt as if a wagon had run over him. Omar had absolutely *clobbered* him with something heavy wrapped in padded leather, and the others had kicked him as he went down.

Sitting up wasn't easy, but it was something the boy knew he had to do. Stifling a moan he got up on his knees, sat back on his legs, and took a deep breath. The room spun, but only for a moment. There wasn't much blood, which meant that the head wound wasn't serious. There was a loose flap of skin across his forehead that caused him to gasp when he touched it. The thing that *really* hurt was the back of his head, where they'd cold-cocked him. The wound over his eyes was secondary, must have been suffered when he fell. There were other aches and pains, but these were only bruises received from bare feet. And he had had worse.

Kazeem used his hands to push himself against the cold stone wall behind him, and put his head back, taking deep breaths. The throbbing subsided eventually, but not without the cost of waiting out a nasty bout of nausea. Regaining some of his wits, he bent forward and tore a strip of cloth from his right pant leg. He took a thicker strip from the left, dipped it in the water bowl on the floor by the door, and dabbed it gingerly in the long crack of the wound, dousing it with water as best he could, trying to clean it without actually touching it.

His shirt was soaked when he was finished, but he felt better, and used the other cloth as a bandage to wrap around his head. He knew it wasn't as clean as it should have been, but it was better than nothing.

On his feet, chest heaving from the effort, he reached over his head to grab the bars on the only window. It was bright. The sunlight hurt his eyes, but the breeze felt absolutely wonderful.

After a time he began to pace, getting his blood flowing. The increase in circulation warmed stiff joints and brought much needed oxygen to his foggy head. He ate the crust of bread that accompanied his water, and felt better still. The mice had been at it, but they hadn't eaten much. In fact, it seemed the best thing he had ever tasted. He sat back down, sipping water, eating bread, adding a forgotten fig wrapped in a grape leaf that had been in his pocket.

Kazeem had to admit that he felt better after that. Stronger. He longed for a bath, but settled for the same wet cloth he'd used on the cut. When he was washed, he plopped the wet clump of material on the bump at the back of his head and sat while the cool compress did its work.

"You really put your foot in it this time, didn't you?" he said to himself at length, dragging the soggy mass from the affected area.

Kazeem wanted to be angry. He'd made his life harder than it had to be—and it was probably going to get worse before it got better—but he couldn't seem to find the energy. All he'd done was stay true to himself, stand up for what was right. Perhaps the acorn hadn't fallen far from the tree, after all.

The same stubbornness had gotten his old man killed.

Kazeem's father hadn't been a man for whom religion was important, but he had imparted a certain solid spirituality to his son. The gist of which was that how one lived ones life was just as important as that life itself—was, in fact, the very same thing.

So it wasn't surprising to find that he actually felt pretty good about himself.

The cell was a cube. The dimensions weren't important, but there was room enough to exercise. The rudiments resembled an unarmed form of martial arts, but the movements themselves involved exaggerated hand and leg gestures designed to tone muscle, stretch connective tissue, and loosen tight, stiff joints. Kazeem fell easily into the rhythm, eyes focused, almost trancelike. At first the sudden exertion, controlled though it was, filled him with pain. Every muscle, every ligament and tendon cried out. The boy kept at it, softly, with round, circular swings of his arms, willing away the soreness until there was nothing left but the correct form for each movement, the measure of each form with the next, and his breathing.

When the door opened and the girl came in he stopped. Not because he was disturbed by the interruption, but because she was the most beautiful thing he'd ever seen.

He'd seen her once or twice before in the halls, but there had never been time for more than a quick glance. Now, in his heightened state, that was no longer an issue. There was bright sunlight blasting through the window in his cell, but the girl was backlit from the lamps in the corridor, as well. She was thin—like most of the kids around here, but she was well endowed, and possessed, to his eyes at least, a perfect figure. Kazeem guessed that she was at least four years older than he was, although they were roughly the same height. She was a muscular girl, with excellent arms, very pretty, with soft, sea-green eyes and short blonde hair that framed her face nicely. She had high cheekbones, a small nose and full, sensuous lips—a lovely, natural pink that complimented her olive Zamborian complexion. Such a soft, feminine girl should have been relaxed and at ease (or would have been in a normal environment), but there was a haunted look in her bright green eyes, the look of a small animal which has grown stronger through adversity and decided she liked being the hunter better than the hunted.

It was a disturbing, conflicted look, but Kazeem understood it perfectly.

"They said you were injured," she said as the guard closed the door behind her. She held up bandages, a small glass jar with blue salve, and a couple of clean washcloths. In her other hand she carried a goatskin water bag. Her uniform was similar to what the other, older girls wore, except that it was sleeveless, and that there was a tiny red crescent just above her left breast.

"I was," Kazeem confirmed after finding his voice. He was quite muscular, and physically mature for his age. He was sweating, and his bare chest was heaving from his exertions. He noticed her appraising look, and returned it; actually tried to look into her soul. He was almost fifteen; she was certainly eighteen or more. Both of them were terribly needy and each of them had grown up too fast.

"You don't look it," she said. Their eyes met, lingered, and then she bit her lip and came forward. "Sit down, you fool, and dry yourself." She tossed him a towel that she took from a shoulder bag. "It's cold in here, and your resistance is low."

Kazeem lowered himself to a sitting position right where he was, folding his legs under him. He couldn't take his eyes off that lovely face…her skin, her hair, her *lips.*

"What would you know about such things?"

She pursed her lips and shrugged. "I'm the closest thing they have to a healer in this sewer."

"Do you have a name?" he asked as she took the cap from the jar.

"Yes," she said, and offered nothing more.

Kazeem looked up, loving the fire in her green eyes. "May I know it?"

"Kalina Zamonar."

"It is a beautiful name, and suits you well," he said, studying her face and meeting her beautiful eyes. "I am Kazeem, son of Kaidin."

"I *know* who you are, you dolt. Everyone's heard of you."

"Really? I haven't been here very long."

"You didn't need all that long to knock this place on its ear."

He gave her a laugh that turned quickly to a cough. "It's kind of a knack I have."

"You don't take yourself too seriously," she asked, bending closer to look at the top of his head, "do you?"

"On the contrary. I take myself quite seriously. It is other people I take lightly."

"And you wonder why you've become so popular in such a short time." The girl dipped a finger in the jar, scooped out a small dollop of salve. She leaned even closer, and Kazeem caught her scent. It may have been due to his incarceration, but to him Kalina was the smell of freedom, of sunshine, of fresh air and wildflowers. He sighed.

"You smell good," he said without thinking.

"Take that stupid cloth off your head and turn towards the light," was her reply.

He did as she ordered, his eyes never leaving her. The girl's skin was perfect, soft, and smooth. He memorized every curve on her face, every feminine nuance, filing them away for later, when they'd be a ray of sunlight in his dark cell.

"What is that stuff?" he asked as she gently spread the salve into the head wound. He wrinkled his nose. "It smells like the woods."

"This is *baylor*. We get it from the North Country. I've never seen them, but there are dark elves, a gray-skinned people living in the hills of Vendar and on the Faylon Range. It makes cuts heal faster." She shrugged. "They trade it for cloth and things like that. It fights infection. You probably smell the pine resin."

"You know a lot for a girl."

"A girl can learn much under certain circumstances. Some of it is more useful than others." Her eyes bored into his, and with a headiness he'd never felt before, with his heart pounding in his chest, he suddenly found it hard to catch his breath.

"Have you...learned much in this place?" he asked.

"That was a good field-dressing," Kalina told him, deftly sidestepping the question, although her green eyes were aflame. "You know...for a boy."

"Have you been here long, Kalina?" he asked as she re-wrapped his head with fresh bandages.

"Forever, it seems." She closed her eyes while she put the lid back on the jar. "A long time. My father went away to the army to fight the Ankorians. He never came back. My mother died of the fever not too long after that."

"My mother, too, of the fever," he added, seizing on the connection. It was suddenly important to share a common bond.

"Were you very little at the time?" she asked softly, and something stirred in Kazeem's battered soul; he had never seen *anyone* so feminine...or so fierce.

"Five. But I remember her well."

"It's important to remember," she agreed. Kalina was examining his chest, turning him by one shoulder. "Let me see your back."

He endured her ministrations as best he could, but for the first time in his life he felt downright uncomfortable with a girl. He couldn't have described the stirrings in the pit of his stomach or the way his heart beat faster, but he knew he was having trouble keeping his hands to himself. "Tell me how you came to this place," he said to somehow regain control of his emotions.

"Same as you, I imagine." He couldn't see her, but he knew her well enough already to know that she had shrugged. "An aunt took me for a time, but my uncle began to show more interest in me. Somehow, that was my fault, so they sent me here."

"I'm sorry things have not been easy for you," he said, and meant it.

"I'm no worse off than any other girl here, Kazeem."

"Or any boy, I've learned."

"I've heard of that." She shook her head sadly. He could see her shadow on the wall as she went to one knee beside him. Her hair was in her face and it looked like silk.

He turned, and now their faces were no more than an inch apart. He longed to touch his lips to hers, *ached* for it, but was afraid in a way he'd never been before, as if too much was at stake. He could smell the sweetness of her breath, the strawberry oil in her hair, and he trembled when he shifted his eyes and saw the dovelike softness of her breasts, lying heavy just beneath the material of her shirt.

Unable to help himself, he raised a hand to the side of her face, slipped his fingers into her hair, pulled her close and touched his lips to hers. She allowed the contact for a brief time, looked down, placed a hand on his chest and pushed him away with a deep, hitching breath.

"I'm glad you're feeling better."

"How can I see you again?" he whispered.

"I'll come to you again tomorrow. It's part of my job."

"Part?"

"I also look after the little ones."

Whatever their moment had been, it was gone, and they both knew it. He shrugged his shirt back on just as the old guard pulled open the door.

"I wonder what *my* job will be?" he mused.

"Don't worry," she said quietly. "They'll let you know when it suits them."

*

"I was afraid you wouldn't come," he said the next day.

"I told you I would."

"Forgive me, please, but I've found it useful not to get my hopes up."

"I know," she agreed. "I do it myself. It keeps the pain at bay when you've been lied to."

They stood for a moment, just looking at each other. This was pleasant for a time, part of the act of discovery, of getting to know one another, but then something happened to change that, made them self-conscious, and the pleasure shifted quickly to discomfort. Neither could have explained it, but it was there nevertheless, whether they understood it or not.

"Have you been lied to, Kalina?" he asked in a husky voice he didn't even recognize. It was suddenly necessary to clear his throat.

"Sure," she answered with a look that made him feel dumb. "Hasn't everyone?"

He was surprised to find himself amused. "Lately, I thought it was just me."

"Well, you *have* caused quite a stir."

"How do you mean?"

"Sit down. Let me look at your head."

He did as he was told. "What did you mean about causing a stir? Has something happened since I've been in here?"

"Talk, only, but a lot of it." She moved closer to him, lowering her voice. He could feel her breath, warm and sweet, on his face. It took the strength from his legs and made him glad that he was sitting.

"What kind of talk?"

Kalina un-wrapped the bandage. She made a little grunt of approval. "Looks good. Healed cleanly. No sign of infection. I'm going to clean it again, and leave it open to the air." She turned his head first one way, and then the other. "Before I go I'll put a smaller covering on it. How's your back? The other bruises?"

"I'm all right." He took her wrist in his hand. The contrast of his skin against hers was electrifying. He had to think for a moment to figure out what he wanted to say. "You were going to tell me what kind of talk."

Kazeem slid his hand into hers, and held it in his lap. He was surprised to discover that her hand was as hard as his own.

Kalina looked down, and studied their hands, but made no move to disengage herself. "They're impressed. All the kids, I mean. People talk. Word gets around. You beat them, *shamed* them, and then you stood up to Zhinn, even though you knew you'd wind up in here."

"Actually, I didn't even *know* about this place."

"You're not stupid, Kazeem." She pouted, and then tried a smile. "Pigheaded, maybe, but not stupid. I'm sure you were well aware that they weren't exactly going to *reward* you."

"To be honest with you, Kalina, I didn't know *what* would happen. I only did what I had to do, would do again, to retain what I am."

"How do you manage to sound like a grown-up so much of the time?"

His heart was pounding in his chest, but he found the courage to look directly into her eyes. "How do you manage to *look* like a grown-up so much of the time?"

"You know," she whispered huskily, "I get that a lot." She put her free hand on his chest, traced the muscles there with a strong and feminine touch. "But I don't seem to mind it." She looked back into his eyes. "Coming from you."

"Do they...bother you here, Kalina?"

"I can take care of myself, Kazeem. Girls my age aren't as popular with the weirdos *we've* got. It happens." She shrugged. "But it wouldn't look good for them if half the population was walking around pregnant."

He closed his eyes, sighed, and leaned his head back against the wall as the enormity of it all hit him. He felt a tear trickle out, and ground his teeth in fury. He'd sworn that day in the desert that he was done crying—forever—and he'd meant it. "We have to get out of here. You know that, don't you?"

Kalina gently wiped away the single tear on his cheek with a thumb. "If you need to get it out, get it out," she whispered. "I'll listen, and I won't tell. Ever."

When Kazeem opened his eyes to look at her, he found something astonishing—he believed her...he actually believed he could trust her. He didn't like to talk about such things, *hadn't*, for the most part, not even with Elin, but he suddenly *wanted* Kalina to know, and before he could stop it he was telling her everything, starting with the day his mother died. He told her about the day they'd killed his father. He told her about Elin and Nomar and Hasir, about what he'd done in the desert, and about the Caliphman who had brought him here. There were tears in the words themselves, but not in his eyes. He would have welcomed the release, but it just wouldn't come.

"Dear, God, I'm so sorry," she whispered, and tenderly took him into her arms.

They were, of course, aware of each other as male and female in that cold, stark room, but all that mattered at that moment was their warmth, and their humanity.

"Now, you tell *me*," he urged, and she did. He listened to every word, but the tale itself—so much like everyone else's—didn't seem to matter as much as the need to tell it. Suddenly, he was crying, the tears hot on his cheeks, mingling with hers as each was wracked by silent, barely controlled sobs that neither wanted the guard to hear. They held each other on the brink of that particular cliff, bonding, healing, and needing. Kazeem believed then that he'd never be this close to another human being, ever again.

He would, perhaps, have cried harder if he knew just how true that would turn out to be.

*

They let him out four days later. He knew exactly how long he'd been in, down to the minute, but that didn't seem to matter once the door was open and he was standing, blinking, breathing the sweet fresh air of freedom. The short walk across the compound was like a gift.

Baaka Zhinn was there with the usual hangers-on when Kazeem arrived at the administrator's office. The master told them all to leave, and once again he found himself alone with the *Multan*, facing the wall with those terrible, ravaging wolves.

"I wanted to hear you tell me how wrong you were," Zhinn said without preamble, "how you became disoriented and confused in the dark, and attacked those other boys for no reason."

"You know that's not going to happen," Kazeem told him, folding his hands in his lap.

There was a long silence. "I can put you back in that box, you know."

"You can do that anytime you want," Kazeem told him. "Physically, you've got enough manpower to force me back in there."

"You don't think I can do it myself?"

Kazeem was wise enough not to take the bait. "That's not the issue now, is it? Physical strength? That, in and of itself, doesn't prove anything. You want to break me, make me like the rest of your little cult here. I'm telling you that's not going to happen."

"In time."

"Not in this lifetime, *Multan*." Kazeem laid a heavy emphasis on the last word.

"Why do you fight me so?" Baaka Zhinn asked suddenly, so adept at shifting emotions.

The tone of his voice brought Kazeem's head around. He'd been gazing out the window, but now found it necessary to regard the man. "I have no wish to fight you, Administrator. I only want to be left in peace."

"That can be achieved only by compliance."

"I am *Wrotmar*, born and bred. You can't use a bull to plow fields, *Multan*."

"Can't make a silk purse out of a sow's ear, either, lad, but you're only a boy, and there's time yet." He leaned forward, arms on his desk, his face dark. "We could do much, you and me."

Kazeem held his tongue. This maniac literally had the power of life and death over him.

"Do we understand one another?" Baaka Zhinn asked at length.

Kazeem nodded. It was all he dared to do.

"Good, go now. And think about all I've said. More importantly, think about what *hasn't* been said."

Kazeem went. It would be hard, if not impossible, to do anything else.

He was stopped at the door by the headmaster's voice. "And try to stay out of trouble, will you?"

CHAPTER EIGHT

KAZEEM MANAGED TO stay out of trouble for exactly one week. He went through the motions, coming and going on schedule, eating regular meals and doing his chores. The other kids left him alone for the most part, which made things easier, actually, but the silence began to wear on him after a while. People would leave the table when he arrived with his tray, stop talking when he entered a room, whisper to each other in the hall as he passed. Worst of all was the feeling of guilt they somehow managed to impart, making him feel as though he had done something wrong, if only by his steadfast non-conformance. He began to realize that 'normal' was whatever the majority said it was, and that the 'deviant' was the one who dared to be different.

Each day Kazeem hoped to see Kalina Zamonar, to speak to her, to connect with the one person alive who made him feel human. But she had no excuse to visit him, and so he had to settle for fleeting glances in the halls, a flash of her bright green eyes, a sparkle of desire and understanding, a warm smile on her sweet, soft lips.

Even little Imad, who he had befriended, ostracized him. Kazeem understood—the kid had obviously been threatened—but that didn't make it hurt any less. Miko and Nasoh also kept to themselves, which was fine with Kazeem, but he didn't like the looks they threw his way when they thought he wasn't paying attention.

After a while the solitude became part of his routine, and he grew used to it. He thought, rather philosophically, that getting used to things was the secret to everything. During that week he actually convinced himself that he could do his time without further incident; that he would someday be old enough to leave, and that would be that.

He believed it until he was sent to the storeroom for a mop and a bucket; they thought they could demean him with physical labor, but he liked to stay busy—it helped fill the terrible void of hours, by giving him something to focus on.

He was in the pantry looking for cleaning solution when he heard Miko's voice. Kazeem wasn't an eavesdropper by nature, didn't consider himself a sneak, but after all he'd been through, who could blame him? He reached up and moved a bundle of cleaning rags so he could see. Cracks in the shelving made it possible for him to see into the storage area beyond, and what he saw brought his anger back with a vengeance.

"You'll say what I tell you to say if you know what's good for you," Miko said to the little girl before him. "If you don't, I'll tell Master Zhinn that you stole Bianca's doll."

"Don't do that, Miko," she whined. "I'll get in trouble."

"Then don't tell them you saw me taking stuff out of the kitchen. It's none of your business anyway."

"But you *did* do it, Miko. I *saw* you. I'm sorry, but I just can't lie for you."

"You little punk! You lie all the time!" Miko growled, grabbed her arm roughly and raised his other hand to strike her.

Kazeem was around the shelving unit, broom handle held like a quarterstaff, before he even realized he was moving. His feet carried him as if they had a mind of their own. He swung without a word, catching the boy square on the jaw.

Miko never saw it coming. The side of his face caved in amid an explosion of blood, and he crumpled to the ground like a wet rag.

Kazeem reversed his grip on the broom handle, holding it two-handed over his head like a spear, but the second blow was unnecessary. Miko was out cold.

"Golly!" said the little girl. "You *killed* him!"

With the staff in one hand Kazeem knelt by the girl. Miko was breathing rather loudly through his nose. He turned to her, went to touch her face, but she leaned away in fear.

"Don't worry," he said gently. "I won't touch you if you don't want me to."

"Don't hurt me! I won't tell!"

"I know you won't, sweetheart," he managed softly. "And I wouldn't hurt you, even if you did." He tried a lopsided grin. "Do you know who I am?"

"You're Kazeem, silly," she said, momentarily forgetting the bloody mess at her feet. "Everyone knows *that*."

"What's *your* name?"

"Belayn." She pronounced it *Bell-ayne*.

She was precious, red haired, blue eyed, and fair skinned. She was also no more than eight. He didn't know where this poor little thing came from, but she certainly wasn't a local.

"I'll bet they call you 'Bel'."

"Hey, how did *you* know?"

"Oh, I've seen you around," he fibbed. "No, don't look at him!" He pushed bushy hair away from her cornflower blue eyes, and this time she didn't recoil. He couldn't help smiling when he noticed the cute little spattering of freckles over the bridge of her nose. She was absolutely adorable. "Hey, you're one of Kalina's kids, aren't you?"

"Yes, she's our teacher." There was a pout. "Next year I'll be too old for her group, they say."

"Don't worry about that now," he told her. "Besides, I'm sure you'll get someone just as nice."

"There's no one nicer than Kalina, and she's *beautiful!*"

"She sure is, Pumpkin."

"*Pumpkin?*" Bel giggled. "Why did you call me *that?*"

"Well," Kazeem began, and pushed back her hair again, "because of your hair and your freckles...and you're very, very cute, like a pumpkin."

"Pumpkin," Bel repeated, trying the word on as if it were a new pair of shoes. "I like that." She grinned suddenly from ear to ear.

"You're in *love* with Kalina, aren't you? That's what all the kids are saying. Is that true? Do you think you love her?"

"I think we'd better get you out of here."

"Wait!" She grabbed his wrist, panic rising in her bright blue eyes. "You know about the doll! Will you tell?"

"*Did* you take that other girl's doll, Bel?"

She looked away. "Yeah, but I only wanted to keep her a *little* while."

"Don't *you* have a dolly?"

"If I did, I wouldn't have needed to take Bianca's now, would I?" She regarded him as if he were some new subspecies of fungus. Her eyebrows went up while she waited for him to respond, and he knew then and there that they'd be friends.

"No, I guess you're right. You know you have to give her back, though?"

"I *suppose* so."

"Hey, I'll make a deal with you."

She was instantly on guard, distrust huge in her big bright eyes. The look on her face broke his heart. "What?"

"You give Bianca her doll back; do it when no one sees you so you won't get in trouble, and I'll get you a new one all for yourself."

Bel frowned darkly. "Yeah, right, where are you going to get a doll in *here?*"

"I am Kazeem." He shrugged, smiled. "I will find a way."

"And that's *all* I have to do?" she asked suspiciously.

"That's all," Kazeem said, and swallowed the lump in his throat. "I promise."

Bel threw her skinny little arms around his neck, and hugged him fiercely with a surprisingly powerful grip. Kazeem's eyes stung and he felt a tear creeping down his cheek. "Oh, thank you, Kazeem. Thank you!" She pushed herself away and touched his face. "Hey, why are you crying?"

Kazeem wiped his jaw with a shoulder. "Huh, oh, I just got something in my eye, that's all."

Bel put her hands on her bony little hips. "Good thing you don't lie much, kiddo. You're *terrible* at it!"

Kazeem smiled, took her hand, and pulled her towards the door. He knelt again, looking deep into her eyes. "And, oh, yeah, one more thing, Bel. Don't tell *anyone* I hit Miko. If you do, *I'll* be the one in trouble."

"I won't tell, Kazeem. It'll be our little secret!"

*

Kalina showed up later that night. He was mopping the meeting hall when she entered, a frown on her face.

"Are you crazy?" she asked.

"Nice to see you, too."

"You almost killed him, you know."

"She told you?"

"No, but it didn't take a genius to figure it out, Kazeem. Incidentally, where are you going to get a doll in *this* hell hole?"

"You mean like this one?" he asked, and pulled a little rag doll from one of the bundles of cleaning cloths.

"Where did you *get* that?"

"I made it." He shrugged.

"You *made* it?"

"It wasn't hard, Kalina." He held it out, and sniffed. "Would you give it to the little girl for me?"

There were tears in Kalina's eyes. She turned away and bit her lip. "You're a good boy, Kazeem. You would have been a good man. Too bad they're going to kill you."

"No one's going to kill anyone. No one knows. He never saw it coming."

"You broke his jaw in three different places."

Kazeem shrugged.

"They'll *know* it was you, you imbecile." She folded her arms under her ample breasts. "They'll make your life miserable from now on, you know that?"

"I can't do anything about that, Kalina. I can only be who I am, deal with them as they come. I learned a long time ago that I can't change anyone but myself."

"You know, I really hate you sometimes."

"I know," he answered softly. "It's one of the things you like best about me."

*

Fegan, Abdar and Spinner threatened him in the hall the next day, but it didn't amount to anything. In fact, he was sure he'd gotten the better of them.

Even if he *had* been frightened half to death.

The incident had ended up pretty much a stalemate, glaring and posturing and pushing—but that was all. Fegan tried to keep him pinned against the wall, but Kazeem faced them down bravely, doing nothing to provoke them. He silently vowed to make any confrontation look entirely their fault.

Not even Zhinn would be able to fault him for defending himself.

As it turned out Kazeem walked away without a scratch, leaving them looking like the impotent blowhards they were.

The problem now was that, by shaming them, he'd made the fight personal.

Fegan would have to save face the next time they came toe-to-toe, and it wouldn't matter who else got hurt. Kazeem liked to picture himself with no obvious weaknesses, but he now had two: Kalina and a beautiful little girl named Bel.

*

Kazeem was out in the yard, drawing water from the well. His jobs today were to water the pepper plants, weed the basil and parsley, and gather some turnips. In between these chores he was expected to pitch hay for the horses, milk the cows, shovel the manure out of the stalls and take it around back to the midden pile.

They were trying to break him, but these things only made him stronger.

While he hauled water from the north well, he faced the sky, looking up and over the wall, into the freedom beyond. It was a flawless day, the sky cornflower blue. There were no clouds, and a tangy ocean breeze was freshening, blowing east from Maranobo Bay.

The wall was old and pitted. There were cracks, loose sections where rocks had fallen, fissures choked with tenacious-looking weeds. *Handholds, toeholds* were the words his mind conjured.

"Think you can make it over?" a cultured male voice asked from behind.

Kazeem didn't have to turn to know it was the headmaster. He was, however, dismayed to have been caught so completely off guard.

"Over what, sir?" Kazeem asked without looking at the man.

Baaka Zhinn chuckled. "I really do like you, Kazeem, you remind me of me!"

Kazeem had resumed cranking the well handle. He stopped now and turned to regard the very dangerous, very sick man beside him. His voice was as cold as the well water.

"How do you figure that?"

Baaka Zhinn didn't answer right away. He turned his face to the breeze, closed his eyes, and allowed the cleansing air to ruffle his robes and his hair. The robe was the kind that tied in front. Zhinn secured the belt at his waist, allowing the peaks of bare chest muscles to show. The pectorals were broad, so toned that the fan-like ridges resembled scallop shells—evidence of the rigors of his level of training. Here was a man who kept himself in whipcord shape, not out of self-control and iron discipline—but because he enjoyed the pain.

When Baaka Zhinn opened his eyes, the boy made immediate eye contact, and held it.

"Let me put it this way: do you remember the painting in my office."

"I remember."

"There are two kinds of people in the world, Kazeem—predators and prey. You have the makings of a fine hunter, a man I can use, and perhaps make wealthy. It is one of the reasons I've put up with your little antics. I'm hoping to turn you to my way of thinking."

"What little antics?" Kazeem asked and crossed his arms.

"Oh, I don't know," Baaka Zhinn said, tracing Kazeem's cheek with the back of one finger. "Like maybe bashing in Miko's face." He came closer, his lips almost touching the boy's ear. Kazeem repressed a shudder, and held his ground, drawing a chuckle from the headmaster. "That was neat," he added, completing a circle around the orphan.

"If you think I did it, why not charge me with the crime?" Kazeem asked.

"And, what, deprive me of whatever you plan next? Perish the thought! Besides, if you decide to be, well, you know…nice to me, I'll start looking the other way when you can't seem to—oh, how can I put this?—control that horrible little temper of yours."

"How nice?" Kazeem heard himself asking.

"Come to my office anytime to find out."

The leer made Kazeem want to vomit, but he gritted his teeth enough to manage: "Not in this lifetime."

Baaka Zhinn laughed, an amusement made all the more satisfying because he had obviously gotten the reaction he expected. "You know, you're still just a child, Kazeem, but if you live—and I stress the *if*—you'll become a man of terrifying principle."

"Each of us can only be what we are, *Multan* Zhinn. I should think that much obvious to one like you."

"Men who only react to the 'obvious' don't grow old, Kazeem. I plan on being around for a while."

"That's a worthy ambition…for one who breeds enemies."

Zhinn was on him in a flash, his odd eyes full of hope, and his breath hot with passion. "Was that a threat?"

Kazeem thought it past time to play the game. He smiled and put his hands on his hips. "You know, I was just wondering whatever happened to the sword the Caliphman took from me when I arrived. The one with the wolf's head?"

"Why, it's in my office. For safekeeping. You'll get it back when you leave."

"Actually, I was hoping I could get it back before then."

"Oh, I'm afraid we don't allow our students to carry weapons."

"I wasn't talking about *carrying* it, Master Zhinn. I was talking about practicing with it."

"You want to train with me?" Baaka Zhinn asked with fire in his eyes. "No, you want to kill me, *don't* you, you murderous little bastard!"

"I hear you are a master. A…session with you—on the practice field—can only serve to improve my skills."

"I've mastered many skills, my boy. I'll train you if you've got the courage for it, and when we're better matched, we'll have a contest, you and I." He raised a finger. "Take care, though! If I win, I'll offer you a choice: death, or…loyal service to me."

"And what if *I* win?" Kazeem asked.

"See?" He tapped the boy's hard chest with a forefinger. "That's why I like you! You have wisdom, even without the knowledge and skills to back it up."

"Wisdom and knowledge aren't necessarily fruits of the same vine, headmaster. And you haven't answered my question."

"You win, I'll set you free. Those stakes high enough for you?"

"I've already told you, we can only be true to our nature."

"Excellent! Just remember what could happen to you if you lose."

"Give me the time to train properly, and I'll fight my best fight." He shrugged. "I am Kazeem. This is all I ask."

Baaka Zhinn studied him for so long that it made Kazeem uncomfortable. To the man before him he was only a piece of meat, but it was more than that…for a moment Kazeem saw doubt in the older man's eyes, and actually thought that he would try to back out.

"Finish your chores, and report to me on Firstday. The beginning of the week will usher in a new life for Kazeem of Zamboria!"

"The chance is all I ask."

"You'll get that, and more, I promise," Zhinn told him. "But remember one thing: it is said that I am here to create chaos. That's what they whisper behind my back. But it's not true. I don't cause chaos, I simply *preserve* it."

The man turned, robes twirling, and walked away laughing.

To Kazeem, it seemed the mirth of the devil.

*

Twice a year the children were required to put on a pageant of sorts. Associates of the local zoning board, the children's' commission and members of the royal house would visit. Ostensibly, this gave the outside world a good indication of the great work being done at the Home. In reality, it served to show the county officials exactly how their tax money was being spent. To the administration of the Home, this was a very necessary annoyance, as the next year's budget— not to mention work contracts—depended on it. For the kids, the three weeks prior to the show were a godsend. It wouldn't do to have children sporting bruises or sullen expressions. In short, this respite provided just about six weeks a year of feeling relatively unthreatened.

To Kazeem and Kalina it provided an opportunity to spend time together without needing to come up with an excuse beforehand.

During the same afternoon as the well incident, Kazeem found himself part of a set-design crew, using hammers and nails and other possibly lethal tools under the watchful eyes of what seemed like the entire guard staff. Kalina was on the makeshift stage in the meeting hall, leading her kids through a song they'd been working on in class. The melody was decidedly off-key, under-rehearsed, and sung by little boys and girls with shrill, squeaky chipmunk voices. To Kazeem, it sounded like a choir of angels. The singing reminded him that rays of hope could exist even in the darkest corners, and that all it took was someone like Kalina Zamonar to bring it out. The children obviously loved her—more than one actually called her 'Mama', Kazeem noted—and were not above open displays of affection.

Kalina was beautiful, with gorgeous skin, haunting green eyes, and a body just perfectly poised at the ripe threshold of young-womanhood. To Kazeem's eye she was pretty and sexy and clean and strong…and he often found it difficult not to stare when she was around. For a strong boy, a boy old beyond the number of birthdays he'd managed to survive, this incredible 'older woman' of eighteen was impossible to ignore. Still, in a way his adolescent brain couldn't put into words, seeing her with the children, reacting with them in a maternal fashion, made her all the more alluring.

Kazeem made no attempt to hide how he felt about her, but it wouldn't have made a difference anyway.

"Fancy her, do you?" a Vendarian boy named Bierdig asked as they were framing a rather large dollhouse for the play.

Kazeem kept his eyes on his work, but his voice told the story well enough. "Who *wouldn't* want her?"

"Some of us more than others, eh?" the boy asked.

"I'd be careful holding those nails, Bierdig," Kazeem warned, brandishing the hammer. "I haven't exactly had a lot of practice with this thing."

Bierdig laughed. "I *knew* it! You absolutely *drool* when you look at her!"

Bierdig was one of the few boys with whom Kazeem could be just another boy. He was tall and dark, with expressive lake water blue eyes. Kazeem thought that his mother might have been Zamborian, although his father had obviously been some wandering Westerner.

"Do I?" Kazeem sighed. "Is it that obvious?"

Bierdig's expression was playful. When he grinned, which was often, it was hard not to like him. "Here, wipe your mouth," he told Kazeem, and handed him a napkin.

"Jerk!" Kazeem laughed and swatted it away.

"She likes *you*, too. A lot. Especially the way you look after the little ones for her." The smile fled his face, whisked away like a cloud suddenly covering the sun. "Hey, have they tried to get you back yet?"

"What do you mean?" Kazeem was using a rasp to shape a peg. He looked up after several seconds of silence, and shook his head. "I don't understand."

"Rumor has it that you've been causing problems for certain people around here. Any truth to that?"

"I've heard *some* rumors," Kazeem admitted, studiously working on his peg.

"Rumor also has it that you're the one who bashed in the side of Miko's face."

"Don't believe everything you hear."

"Look, don't get sore. All I'm saying is that I wish someone like you was around when *I* first came in." He hung his head. "It's, uh, not the kind of thing you forget."

"Hey, you don't have to—"

"I know that," Bierdig said. "I just wanted to let you know what you've done for us. Hope is a strange thing. One minute it can be a terrible, awful concept, capering and dancing just out of reach. The next it's the only thing keeping you on your feet. I only wish we could be there when they come for *you*."

"What are you saying?" Kazeem studied the other boy's face intensely, all pretense of working gone.

"You didn't really think they were going to let you get away with what you've done, did you?"

Kazeem had, perhaps, fooled himself, been lulled into a false sense of safety by the passage of time, and, maybe, his coming tournament field work with *Multan* Zhinn. Still, he wanted to make sure that they were talking about the same things. "What, exactly, have I done, Bierdig?"

"You don't see it, do you?"

"See what?"

"That you've held up a mirror for them, made them see who they really are. You've *shamed* them, Kazeem, just by being *normal*. Nothing will ever be the same for them and they're not going to let you get away with it. They'll either accuse you of something to make you look exactly like *them*, or they'll get you some other way." He frowned, and pressed his lips tight in a grim, bloodless line. "Just watch your back. That's all I'm saying." This display of affection was more than Bierdig could afford at the moment. He cleared his throat. "I'll, uh, get us some more lumber."

Kalina was beside him in an instant. Kazeem stood and smiled at her. Together they watched the other boy head for the stock room.

"He's right, you know," the girl said when Bierdig was out of earshot.

As usual, Kazeem couldn't get over how pretty she was. He actually had to compose himself before he could speak. "Aw, not you, too?"

"You've upset the apple cart, Kazeem. Other kids are standing up for themselves now. That's never happened in here before. Ever. Sooner or later they'll have to give in...or make an example of you."

Kazeem usually didn't let his impatience show, but he found it easy to let his guard down around Kalina. He squeezed his eyes closed, shook his head, face tilted towards the ceiling.

"I won't live in fear, Kali, and I won't give in to their way of doing things." He faced her, hands on hips. "What would you have me do?"

"Survive; believe in a future beyond these walls; and I don't think fencing with the headmaster is the answer."

"Living and surviving are not necessarily the same, Kalina Zamonar." He sought her exquisite green eyes. "I won't exist...just to exist."

"Is fighting with him really the answer?"

"I must continue my training, Kalina. I saw no other way to accomplish this."

"Don't give me *that*, Kazeem, Son-of-Kaidin. What you *really* want is to learn his weaknesses, perhaps even find a way to 'accidentally' kill him!" She pouted, her slim hands shaking his shoulders. "But he won't fight fair and he won't be alone and if you get yourself killed I'll never speak to you again!"

She stormed away, leaving Kazeem with a startling revelation— if he lived to be a hundred, he'd never understand girls.

Bierdig arrived with an armload of wood. His eyes swept back and forth between Kalina and Kazeem.

"Everything all right?" he asked.

"Perfect," Kazeem declared.

"That's what I thought," Bierdig said cheerfully, and pointed to the twisted rasp in Kazeem's hands. "But you might want to get a new file. That one seems to have gotten itself bent in half!"

CHAPTER NINE

KAZEEM ARRIVED AT exactly the appointed time. He was unarmed, and fully expected to be beaten, but this was something he had to find out, whatever the cost.

In working robes, the headmaster greeted him amicably enough, but no amount of mirth, no smile, could hide the malice in that carefully controlled countenance. Kazeem also couldn't shake the feeling that he was being watched, recalling Kalina's warning.

Don't think about her, his mind advised. *You can't afford to lose your edge.* He steeled himself to the situation with considerable effort, and by the time the administrator had led him to the practice room, he was in control of his emotions once again.

The hall he found himself in was larger than it looked from the outside. It was not exactly a Great Hall, but wide enough and long enough for fencing.

There were practice dummies, weapons racks, and padded mats—even a small, roped-off area for boxing. The headmaster employed a variety of exercise equipment to maintain his condition. Having been at warrior camps most of his young life—at least since the fever took his mother—much of it was familiar to him: horizontal bars for chinning, rings, ropes, slant boards and free weights, but there were also deadly-looking spinning turrets, similar to the practice dummies, but with spring-loaded actions and sharp, revolving blades in place of the usual, sawn-off quarter staff poles.

"Not many surprises in here for one such as you," Baaka Zhinn said pointedly, noticing the boy's interest in the turrets.

Kazeem smiled. "Maybe, but that doesn't mean you should stop looking."

Zhinn returned the smile, one of the few genuine displays of amusement Kazeem had seen yet. Who knew, he thought, maybe the guy was human after all?

Still smiling, Zhinn disrobed. Underneath he wore close-fitting black trousers of some stretchy material foreign to Kazeem. He also wore soft-soled fencing slippers.

Zhinn was bare from the waist up, displaying an imposing physique. He wasn't the largest warrior Kazeem had ever seen, but he was certainly one of the best trained. He was tall, and impressively muscled. To Kazeem's practiced eye, there didn't appear to be an ounce of fat on the man. Veins stood out like braided ropes just beneath the skin of his arms, and individual muscles were clearly defined. Kazeem knew that this level of conditioning was more than training; it involved a strict diet in very proper balance. Zhinn affected the over-indulged fop. Clearly, he was not.

The man took a favorite sword from a rack, laid it lengthwise on a pommel horse, and retrieved another wrapped in cloth, from the shelf beneath the vertical rack.

To Kazeem's relief it was his own weapon, clean and well oiled. Whatever else Zhinn was, he understood the proper care of such things. He pulled away the wrapping delicately, and then surprised Kazeem by tossing the weapon to him. The teen caught it one-handed as it *smacked* into his palm. He loved the gleam of the blade, the feel of it in his calloused hands, the balance, the way its edge caught the light.

"You begin well," Zhinn told him. "Your reflexes are excellent."

"I never thought I would see it again," Kazeem answered, studying the workmanship of that fine, Arganian steel, studied it as lovingly as if he were gazing at Kalina.

Zhinn was on him in an instant, pressing the attack. Kazeem, who would one day be feared on three continents, gave ground quickly.

His father had taught him a duel-bladed style that he favored, but, lacking a second sword, he was easily able to convert to the more conventional, two-handed use of a relatively large weapon.

Combining his attacks, using his speed and agility, Kazeem regained the lost ground. Yellow lines painted on the floor defined the fighting alley, but Kazeem didn't use them. To gauge his progress he used his opponent's body and his position relative to landmarks in the room, especially ones that only needed to be quickly glimpsed with peripheral vision.

The boy concentrated, reacting only, using his foe's own attacks to discern weaknesses, and finding several. Zhinn depended largely on his forward thrusts, all but ignoring his backhand. He kept his right leg stiff, and lunged like a fencer, a man unused to the rigors of using a thicker, heavier blade. He favored his right hand at all times, even allowing it the dominant position in two-handed attacks. He seemed overly conscious of his own form.

Kazeem preferred substance over form.

In time, displaying patience beyond his years, Kazeem made it clear that they were evenly matched. He would never be able to beat *Multan* Zhinn with brute strength—at least not until he packed on more muscle—but by mirroring the attacker's posture, he could easily strike a balance using what attributes he did possess, mainly, speed and tenacity.

It was some while into the match—Kazeem did not measure time with much accuracy in such circumstances because his concentration was so great—that Baaka Zhinn backed off. He was sweating, chest heaving. The position of his body with hands on hips, hunched over slightly, told Kazeem that there was a stitch in his side. He lowered the point of his sword to the padded floor and leaned two-handed on the hilt. When he looked up there was a grudging smile on his face.

"My *God*," he gasped, "you're not even breathing hard." He swallowed, gulped air, and tilted his head back. "Where did you learn to counter like that?"

"My father put a sword in my hand when I was two." Kazeem employed his trademark shrug. "From five years on I spent every free moment when school wasn't in session in one Wrotmar camp or other." He cocked his head to one side, surprised by his own candor. "You pick up a thing or two."

"I guess you do! I'm surprised these…Wrotmar aren't out looking for you."

"I'd be surprised if they aren't." Another shrug. "I imagine they've been looking since they learned of Kaidin's death."

"Got too much invested in you, eh?"

"Something like that, yeah."

Zhinn held out a hand, fingers beckoning for the wolf's head sword. When Kazeem hesitated, he first put his own blade back, and then allowed the boy to put up his own.

"It infuriates me to see you so…*unworked,*" the headmaster admitted. "I'm impressed by your prowess, very much so, and I won't underestimate you again. You have a great many gifts, and if you allow me to help you polish them…you'll be a force to be reckoned with." The headmaster frowned deeply, as if he'd said too much and was now disgusted with himself. When he spoke again, his tone was harsh. "Go now to your regular duties. Come again tomorrow at the same time. You are a natural talent with much skill, but do not think that I have nothing to teach you."

Kazeem bowed, and then left, knowing how angry the headmaster was. His frustration had betrayed him at the end, yet another weakness Kazeem felt he could exploit when the time came.

He knew something else, too, something he'd have to sort out: at the very end of the match, had exhaustion not overwhelmed him, *Multan* Zhinn would have lost total control of himself. In short, his would-be instructor would most certainly have killed him had he been able to.

*

"What were you *doing*?" Fegan asked, coming out of one of the gym's many hidey-holes. "Were you toying with him? Looking for weaknesses? It looked like he had you there at the end."

Zhinn tossed aside the towel he'd been using to mop his face. "The little bastard *has* no weaknesses, you dolt! In fact, the kid played me like a fiddle! I've never seen anyone better. He's uncanny, like he was born with a sword in his hand."

"Yeah, but, if it had been real, if you'd really been trying to kill him…"

"I *was* trying to kill him, you moron, at least there at the end." He slammed his hand down on the railing near the practice dummies. "Damn it, he didn't show me a thing! Not a *tenth* of what he knows. I'm sure of it."

"I must be stupid," Garth Fegan admitted. The tall boy frowned, a perplexed look in his brown eyes. "But I still don't understand what you were trying to do."

More in control now, Zhinn smiled. "I'm not sure myself, Garth."

The boy was clearly confused. "Then why—"

"Don't crowd me now, Garth," the headmaster said and patted his cheek. "I need to think."

*

"That's *it?*" Spinner asked Garth later in the basement. "That's all he said? I need to think?"

"That's it, man. It's weird. I've never seen him like this."

"But the kid fought well?" This from Abdar, who was sitting on a crate, cleaning his nails with the tip of a makeshift boot knife. All five of them carried illegal weapons, including Miko, who was now out of the infirmary, but still bandaged. He also couldn't speak very well, but with gestures and garbled speech he was able to get his points across.

"Incredible. Better than anyone *I've* ever seen," Garth answered moodily. "I think if he'd *really* been trying, he could have killed the old man."

"All the more reason to get rid of him," Miko gurgled.

"No," Garth protested. Old Baaka's got plans for him. We hurt him; it's *us* who'll end up in the hole."

There was silence in their basement lair for a moment, a silence broken by Nasoh with evil glee. "Aw, hell, Garth, who said anything about *hurting* the kid? All we want to do is teach him a lesson."

"You didn't see him fight."

"He ain't gonna have a sword if we get him down here."

Garth was unsure, but he was on the verge now of losing leadership of the group to Nasoh. Despite his fear, despite what he'd seen, even though he knew they'd pay dearly for it, he went along.

"Well, there are *five* of us, I guess."

Garth Fegan laughed. He was top dog and intended to stay that way. If he allowed his fear to show the others would have him on his back, would be tearing out his belly, replacing him before his blood was even cold. *That's* not *going to happen,* he thought, and said out loud: "Okay, we'll show the little bastard who's boss, won't we?"

The saddest thing of all was that he was able to fool himself so easily.

Even when he didn't really believe it.

*

Two weeks passed without incident: the pageant came and went, allowing Kazeem to bond more closely with Kalina...and kiss her sweet, soft lips as often as he could.

Kazeem couldn't get over her. He'd never felt this way, not even about Elin, and found himself thinking about her constantly. Perhaps it was because he was older now, but maybe it was something else, too, something fundamental deep inside of him, something, perhaps, that she, alone, could reach.

The love he felt for her (and he had to admit that he really didn't know what love was) had an underlying sadness to it that was almost unbearable. Because of the intensity of the thing, he longed to be with her, but didn't know how to go about it. Boys and girls were housed in different wings, and the penalties for sneaking around at night were harsh.

Oh, on occasion they saw each other during the day, or spoke in the halls, but even the seating at mealtime was random, depending on filing order, and no matter how they tried to coordinate it, they hardly ever ended up at the same table. The feelings he had for her were almost overpowering, but they frustrated him because he couldn't do anything about them, at least not on a consistent basis.

Kazeem was on the roof one night, looking down on the tiny, terraced village of Tentang. He'd be severely punished if he was caught up here, but tonight he just didn't care. Part of his duties included tending the gardens, even the ones up here. So what if he wasn't allowed to do so without supervision? He was sick of rules and regulations. He missed his father and he missed Elin, who, strangely, he might never have gotten to know if his father hadn't been killed. He even missed Hasir, who was probably dead by now or in a place just like this. He sighed, walked the length of the roof to the waist-high wall, and folded his arms, leaning on the bricks.

Tentang wasn't anything special, but the people there were *free*. Standing under gray skies at the edge of the desert, it was the last refuge before that vast expanse of sun-blasted sand.

The village existed only because of irrigation. This close to the wastelands, the only fresh water was from wells and snowmelt from the Faylon Range. Terraced fields encircled the mound-like town, surrounding closely constructed stone houses, most with turf roofs and heat-blasted walls. From his vantage point Kazeem watched people come and go as dusk fell, saw children bring sheep down through the gate from the fields beyond. He saw their parents putting away garden tools, drawing water from their wells. Kazeem heard laughter, smelled dinners like his mother used to make: fish, fresh from the sea, baked with breadcrumbs and lemon; hot loaves; beans; wonderful *miskantofel* stew.

Not exactly fit for the Amir, but better than the board-of-fare served at the Home.

"Don't jump—it's not high enough."

But he did jump, startled by the voice. "You have light footfalls, Kalina Zamonar," he told her, turning from the wall and placing one hand over his heart. "You caught me off guard."

"I didn't mean to bother you, Kazeem," she said, latching the door behind her without bothering to look at it.

There was something different about her, something deliberate. She even smelled different. *Feral* was the best word for it. Wild. Ozone before a thunderstorm.

"What *did* you mean, then?" he asked, meeting her half way.

She stared at him with eyes that were bright green emeralds in the gloom. "I think you know," she said; her voice was husky; her breath sweet.

He wrapped his arms around her, drawing her close. She was at least four years older, but he was slightly taller. Their lips were pressed together before either of them knew what was happening, lightly at first, tentatively, softly, their eyes open, staring, blinking at each other and holding each other desperately.

Kalina's lips were full, pink, and the focus of much of Kazeem's imagination and attention. He'd thought about this moment for so long that he actually shook with anticipation. He took his hands from her waist and held her face; their eyes closed now, the kiss passionate. The world ceased for them, faded away until there was only each other. One of her hands was up the back of his shirt, palm down, searing, exploring; her slender girl's fingers hot and eager. Kazeem gripped her shoulders tightly, and flexed his fingers, suddenly finding it hard to breathe.

They ended up pressed against the wall of the tool shed, straining against one another. Kalina worked one hand up through his workshirt and onto the back of his neck. Her lips were on his throat.

And that's when the staircase door banged open. Eyes heavy-lidded, lips puffy, Kalina took too long to register what had happened. Kazeem reacted quicker. He had her around the back of the shed in an instant, covering her mouth with his hand even as she was asking what was wrong.

Kazeem didn't bother answering. He jutted his chin at Omar instead, who was standing in the middle of the flat roof, wispy hair blowing in the breeze as he glowered at his surroundings.

The obvious answer was to hide in the tool shed, but, being obvious, it wouldn't do. The thing to remember was that Omar was mute, not deaf, and that not much escaped his shrewd bright eyes.

"What's he doing?" Kalina whispered as they peered through cracks in the boards.

Kazeem shook his head. "*Shhhh!*" he said directly into her ear.

She shivered, and clutched his shoulders. Hard.

The huge Arganian walked towards the shed as if he'd heard something. Kazeem moved with Kalina, keeping the shed between them and the big man as he walked completely around it. Omar returned to the center of the roof, looked around, went to the wall with a puzzled expression on his broad face, and looked down. His head moved right, then left. He stroked his chin thoughtfully with thumb and forefinger. In seconds he was back at the storage shed, where he pulled the door open to peer in. They could see him through the boards, and then he was gone, clattering down the stairs.

Kalina started to speak, but with a gesture Kazeem cautioned her to wait.

"What was *that* all about?" she asked when they were sure he was gone.

"I don't know," Kazeem admitted, "but I do know he didn't make any noise coming up."

"We were a bit preoccupied," she told him, tracing a line along his jaw with one finger.

The boy was shaking his head, his blond hair swinging into his eyes. He wiped it angrily away. "No, I would have heard."

"You didn't hear *me*," she reminded him.

"Maybe. That was different." He frowned. "I don't know." Kazeem thought for a bit. "He was obviously looking for someone. I wonder if anyone *told* him to look for us."

"Maybe its part of his job, making the rounds, you know?"

"No." Kazeem shook his head. "It was too deliberate. Did you *see* him? He was definitely looking for someone. In fact, he seemed surprised that he didn't find anyone."

"Well, he's gone now," Kalina whispered. Her lips were on his neck, just under his ear.

"You take my breath away, Kalina Zamonar," he whispered back, and touched the side of her face with the back of one hand. "You know you do. But it isn't safe."

"That doesn't mean I have to be happy about it," she replied, and took his hand with one of her own.

"There will be other times, my love," he told her, and prayed that it was true.

*

Bel came to him later that night. She said she was afraid of the dark, and she held the doll he'd made for her crooked in one arm. His room was vacant now except for him, but he worried about her wandering the halls alone.

She stood outlined in the doorway after knocking tentatively, gazing in at him, backlit from shafts of yellow moonlight slanting in through the hall window.

"Kazeem, are you awake?" she whispered.

"I'm always awake," he mumbled. Kazeem bit his lip. Bel was no blossoming ingénue; she was just a scared little girl, confused by his worldly resentment.

"Huh?"

Kazeem was out of bed, taking her by the hand, shutting the door. "I said get in here."

Bel pulled the doll up and hugged her close. "Are you mad?"

"No, Bel, I'm not even awake yet."

"You're not?"

"No." Kazeem rubbed his eyes and yawned.

"But I thought you said you never sleep?"

"Never mind what I said, honey." He squatted to face her. "What is it? Why are you out of bed?"

"I'm..." She bit her lower lip, pouted, and Kazeem could almost see her mind working behind her big bright eyes. "Clara was frightened." She held out the doll to Kazeem, as if this were all the evidence she needed. "She couldn't sleep."

Instinctively, he took the doll and hugged it. "Oh, so that's it, huh? Well, what's wrong, Clara? What frightened you?"

"She got scared because the girls in the next room were fighting," Bel told him. "She's only little, and doesn't understand such things. She thought they might get her next." She gently took back the doll.

Kazeem felt a twinge of panic. "Bel, if the girls were fighting, don't you think someone might come? Won't they check the rooms and find that you're gone?"

Bel was already shaking her head, curls bouncing in the moonlight, her eyes big and round and very, very blue. "Oh, no, Kazeem. This happens a *lot*. They're older girls. They yell at each other, and then they fight. No one ever comes."

Kazeem quickly pulled on a robe. "Come on, I'll take you back. Don't worry. You'll be safe."

"Are you sure?"

"I promise."

"Will you hold my hand?"

"The whole way."

"Couldn't I just stay here with you?"

"I *can't* let you stay, Bel, it could be dangerous if someone found out."

"Couldn't I stay for just a *little* while? I'll be very quiet. Clara, too."

Kazeem slumped onto his bed, defeated, and just sat there looking at her. Letting her stay was the wrong thing to do, he knew that, but she had come to him for help.

"Bel, I—"

She came forward, the doll clutched to her, pouting. "Please, I'll even sleep on the floor. Don't you care about me anymore?"

Kazeem was stunned to find that he suddenly wanted to cry. He had to clear his throat before he could talk. "Of course I do. I'm your friend. Very much like a big brother. I love you, Bel," he said, surprised to hear it out loud. "Someday we're going to get out of here, me and you and Kalina. We'll be a family, you'll see."

"You mean like a momma and a daddy and a daughter?"

He was crying. He sniffed, pulled a sleeve across his eyes. "That's exactly what I mean, honey, yeah."

"Why are you crying?" she asked, and touched a tear on his jaw.

"Huh? Oh, I've got something in my eye. Don't worry. It's okay now."

"You *always* say that. I can stay, then?"

"Yeah, for a while, but then you have to go back, okay?" He held up the covers. She got in beside him and snuggled close. He pulled the blankets over both of them and she laid down with a heart-rending sigh.

"Go on now, try to get some sleep."

"Say goodnight to Clara." She held out the doll he'd made for her and waited while he kissed its nose.

"Good night, Clara."

Bel sighed. He pushed her hair back from her forehead, loving the way she smelled. Bel stirred something parental in him; something he hadn't even known was there. Being with her made him feel strong and capable and grown up, made him realize that it was okay to say that things were fine—even when you knew they weren't.

His eyes were closed, but tears slipped through for a few more minutes, and he did nothing to stop them. Their breathing became slow, steady. He was almost asleep when she spoke his name.

"What is it, honey?"

"Can I *really* be your little girl? Yours and Kalina's?"

He opened his eyes to study her. "You already are, sweetheart. If you want to be."

"Oh, I do, very much so."

"Well then, there you are." He closed his eyes again.

"Forever?"

"Forever, little Bel."

"Good." She pressed her head against his chest and closed her eyes, her thumb in her mouth, doll held tight.

Kazeem watched her for a while, trying to figure things out. He knew he'd have to sneak her back before they noticed she was gone, but that was later and this was now. He'd just made promises he had no way of keeping, knowing only that he wanted to care for her with the same intensity he felt for Kalina. Part of becoming a man, he realized, was in supporting someone else, caring for them, protecting them, unselfishly putting them before yourself, becoming less self-absorbed. Part of being a man, he realized, was using your own strength to nurture children—even if they weren't your own flesh and blood. *Family is as family does,* Nomar had told him often. Now he finally understood: family was not *necessarilly* a matter of blood.

Kazeem had made a promise to this precious little flower lying close to him in the dark. Forever. And forever began right now, whether he was ready for it or not.

Kazeem closed his eyes again, but it was a long time before he actually slept.

*

Kazeem remained in a kind of fog for several days after that. Despite how awful things were, no one bothered him or his little "family" and that was more than he could have hoped for. He had no idea that the hatred held against him was so well focused, or that plans were in the works that would forever set him on a path not of his own choosing. Kazeem was about to find out that we are all products of our own environment, whether we chose to believe that or not.

Kazeem was able to throw himself into his duties, growing stronger, learning more about himself with every passing day. He learned, for example, that love was a double-edged sword, and that it could cut you very deeply.

Kazeem had been assigned the stables some time ago. He enjoyed taking care of the animals, and liked the physical aspects of the job, which helped to keep him in shape. He was stacking bales of hay when Kalina found him.

"Oh, good," she said without preamble. "Katdja told me you were still here."

Kazeem was lowering a bale into its proper place on the block he was forming. "What's wrong, Kal? You're as white as a sheet."

"Just hold me," she said and stepped into his arms.

"God, you're trembling." A shiver ran through him. "Kali, are you all right?" A surge of fear ran through Kazeem. "Did somebody—"

Kalina put a finger to his lips, looking up at him and shaking her head. Her breath was sweet. "No." She shook her head again, tossing her shiny hair about her shoulders. "Nothing like that."

He waited as patiently as he could. It wasn't something he did well.

"It's Lyta," she explained after what seemed like several lifetimes. "She and Bel were playing—"

"Bel's not hurt, is she?" he interrupted.

Kalina uttered the kind of snort a person uses when she's thinking the exact same thing. "No, but that was my first reaction, too. Exactly." She studied him with intense green eyes, as if trying to make up her mind about something. She wet her lips with the tip of her tongue. "They were playing with the other kids in that little area by the gate, near the section where the fence is broken. You know, running, jumping. The cooper's horse got skittish, out of control. Lyta got trampled before anyone could grab the mare and calm her down."

"My God! Is she...is she alright?"

Kalina was shaking her head, soft blonde hair bouncing and swinging from side to side. "Right leg's broken, but it's a clean break. I did the best I could with it, Kazeem, but they've sent for a real doctor, someone who can set it properly."

"The poor kid. I hope she's not going to walk with a limp or anything." He pressed his lips into a thin, bloodless line. "All in all, though, it could have been worse."

Kalina looked down. "Lyta pushed Bel out of the way. It just as easily could have been *her*. I'm feeling guilty that I'm so relieved it wasn't."

"It's hard not to care about her, isn't it?" he asked.

"Yes, it's like she's ours. Yours and mine."

Kazeem looked at her for a long time. Of all the things she could have said, nothing could have made him feel closer to her. "I feel the same way about her. And about you."

Kali blushed. "She loves you, too, Kazeem. Ever since you made her that doll…"

"I told her we'd get out of here, Kal, the three of us, be a family."

Now she looked at *him* for a long while. "Is that what you want?" she asked in a whisper.

All he could do was nod.

It simultaneously occurred to them that they were still holding each other. Kalina embraced him even tighter, her arms pressed hard against his back.

"Bel *is* special, but I've thought a lot about someday having a baby of my own."

"I, too, would someday like a child of my own."

"With me?" She was looking at his chest. Now she lifted her eyes without moving her head.

"Yes." Kazeem hardly recognized his own voice. "With you, Kalina. No one else."

Their lips were touching slightly, softly, without pressure. Kazeem took her face in his hands, framing it, and kissed one corner of her mouth, then the other, then the tip of her nose. The girl gulped in air, her chest against his, and responded with urgency, pressing harder, her lips firm against his. Kazeem broke the contact to look in her eyes, and she arched her neck. He wanted to kiss her—be with her— but half of his mind was on who might be watching and whether or not they should even be taking a chance like this.

As their kisses became more passionate Kazeem's mind began to torture him with visions of getting caught, of being separated of Kalina being hurt because of his appalling neediness.

"Stop!" he suddenly said and grabbed both her hands.

"Why?" She closed her eyes and took a deep breath. "Did I hurt you?"

He was already shaking his head.

"No, my love, I just can't…do this. Not here." He looked around. "Not now."

She sighed and slumped to the hay and sat with her legs crossed, crying. "I know."

He sat down in front of her and after a time he just held her. He wanted her, wanted to be with her, but for now this was the best that he could do. They grew drowsy after a little while, lay back in each other arms and eventually fell asleep…and for a moment, at least, their terrible world went away.

*

"I don't think I could ever live without you," he blurted later.

The afternoon sun was slanting down across her face, turning her eyes into burning green emeralds. "I feel exactly the same way; so much so that it frightens me."

"I want to make a home with you, Kalina, see you every day, go to sleep with you beside me at night and wake up with you in the morning. Here, I'm not even alive."

Kalina smiled sadly and brushed his face with the back of one hand. Kazeem had expected amusement in the face of his admission, but got stark reality instead.

"There's great truth in what you say," she frowned. "I don't know how I can stay here now. Not after…"

"I know." He took her hand.

She sat up. He took straw from her hair. She grabbed his wrist with one hand. "You told Bel you'd get us out of here some day. Did you mean it?"

He loved the look of the sunlight on her lashes. He found it difficult to speak. "Never have I meant anything more."

"We'll go whenever you say."

Kazeem tried to forestall this, knowing it was hopeless even as he opened his mouth. "I said *someday*, Kalina Zamonar."

"*Someday* has arrived, Kazeem, Kaidin's son," she said, and stood up.

He lifted his chin to gaze up at her, nodded, and stood to match her stare. "I think maybe you are right," he agreed at length. "We just need to figure out how to do it without getting ourselves killed."

*

Baaka Zhinn was taking his "fighters" on a field trip. Garth was there, as was Kazeem, and three other boys no one bothered to introduce. Omar drove the wagon, but his real purpose for being there was clear: no one would sneak away while the headmaster was otherwise occupied. As always, Omar would watch them like hawks, his strange eyes bright and intense.

Kazeem didn't care. He was out! In the sunshine and fresh air, under open skies with a warm breeze ruffling his hair. The boy, who would one day be feared on three continents, leaned back and closed his eyes, loving the feel of the sun on his face. It was the same sun that daily hit the roof of the Home and streamed through his window, but it *felt* different out here without the gray walls to dilute it. Kazeem had recently discovered many pleasantries in life, the mysteries of young womanhood chief among them, but realized now that it could all mean so much more to a free man and his family.

It was several minutes before he realized he was missing the sights. He'd spent too much time on introspection. It was time now to just live, and *enjoy*.

Zamboor was, by and large, desert country, but there were fertile sections along the coast and in the foothills of the mountains. Here, in enriched soil fed by runoff from the Faylon Range, much of the nation's food was produced. Groves of date palms, fig trees, and melon fields encircled patches of grain, and neat rows of vegetables. Long, winding roads, pitched and rolling, competed with hayfields and round fieldstone silos for attention. Rock walls were everywhere, and from time to time peasants could be seen working in the distance. Most farmsteads were little more than huts with thatched roofs, but Kazeem could almost share their pride. Succeed or fail, they had no one standing over them. Oh, what a perfectly delicious way to live!

Before he knew it they had arrived at their destination. The other boys were out of the wagon, and Kazeem followed suit. He realized now that he hadn't been paying attention. Something was different, something was *wrong* with the other boys. It was nothing he could lay a finger on, but there was a sense of apathy about them that was appalling, a look in their eyes that reminded him of a beached shark he'd once seen in a tangle of seaweed in the sand: cold eyes, dark and dead and blank—soulless eyes.

Multan Zhinn was talking. Kazeem turned his head to regard him. He, too, had a killer's inhuman eyes, but there was nothing apathetic about *his*.

"Today, we'll take your training to the next level, gentlemen." He pointed to two of the boys Kazeem didn't know. They approached, and he handed them weapons from a velvet-lined box in the front of the wagon.

Kazeem looked about. The practice area was fenced in on one side, shaded by tall boxwood hedges on another, and shielded from the road by a neat row of cedar trees planted close together, their tops cropped so that the growth was forced to each side. It defined a long, closed-in lane, perfect for sword fighting. Plenty of room for combat maneuvers, but nowhere to hide, nowhere to run. Kazeem was reminded of stories his father had told, of gladiators forced to fight. He wondered again about the other boys, where they had come from. They were older, not quite men, but close enough. There was a ward in the Home filled with such boys, he'd been told, boys so wild they couldn't be controlled. Others told a different story: that *Multan* Zhinn kept them caged like animals, and bred them for the combat arenas; that the only way to freedom for them was in winning it the way gladiators had won it for untold years—by killing your opponents one by one. It was said that these boys would revolt one day, break out and wreak havoc, were simply biding their time.

Looking at these two, Kazeem believed it. They were solid, thick muscled and expressionless.

They were also covered with scars, he now saw, as each removed his shirt to don training harness and cestus. Kazeem looked for a long time at the lead-weighed leather straps on their hands, and then to the headmaster with disbelief. Zhinn handed each fighter a small round shield. They touched swords and, at a nod from their instructor, began to parry. The fight took on mortal tones almost instantly, as each drew blood.

It didn't take Kazeem long to figure out that this was no ordinary training match. One boy, the darker of the two, soon had the other at a disadvantage, and pressed it until his opponent was disarmed and off his feet. The dark boy reversed his grip on the sword and held it over his head, point down above his helpless foe. He paused for a fraction of a second to regard Zhinn, who shook his head slowly, almost infinitesimally, from side to side. Kazeem shivered. Had the shake been a nod, he was certain that the dark boy would have killed the other, plunging the thick-bladed short sword into his hapless victim without even changing the expression on his face. As it was he lowered the sword and offered a hand, helping him to his feet, again with the same blank expression.

"Kazeem," *Multan* Zhinn said softly, but with gravel in his voice, almost as if this sort of thing aroused him. "You're next. I think you'll make a good match for Wajda." He nodded at the dark boy.

He'll kill me the same as look at me, Kazeem thought, but bowing out wasn't an option. He was *Wrotmar*, warrior born, and would not back down from a challenge.

"As you wish, *Multan*," he said and bowed to the other boy as he took his wolf's –head saber from the box. The other boy retained his shield, but Kazeem chose a long knife instead.

Zhinn crossed his arms and nodded. "Begin," he said, and Wajda was on him like lightning. The boy came fast and furious, forcing Kazeem back on his heels. The son-of-Kaidin understood with sudden clarity that this was a fight to the death, and that only the word of the administrator could alter the inevitable outcome.

So be it, the Wrotmar boy vowed, and met the charge magnificently.

Wherever the shield crashed, trying to batter him, his long knife parried, cutting, nicking, slicing; the wolf's-head was a blur, clanging, crashing with all the fury in him. In seconds, Wajda was down, bleeding, out of breath and weaponless, fear in his wide eyes.

"So, there is some life in you after all," Kazeem said with much satisfaction.

"Finish it," Zhinn ordered.

"I *am* finished," Kazeem said without even looking at him.

"Kill him. Show us what you're made of."

"I need not prove anything to you, *Multan* Zhinn." Kazeem stepped back, lowered his weapons, and looked at the headmaster with hooded eyes. "My father was Kaidin. I am Kazeem, Wrotmar. I do not kill for sport."

"I don't think you have what it takes," Zhinn told him. "I think the stories they tell about you are false."

Kazeem shrugged. "Think what you will. The state of your thoughts is not a responsibility of mine." Kazeem could tell from the look on the man's face that he had overstepped his bounds, that none of the others would dare speak to the headmaster this way. He could tell, also, that Zhinn admired him for it.

"Would you not like to advance to our secret circle?" Baaka Zhinn asked.

"To be caged like an animal, fighting for the amusement of others, for profits I will never share?"

"I'm afraid you've gotten the wrong impression of us. Tell you what. Fight Garth. Kill him and earn your freedom. Walk away with your sword and never look back."

"And if I fail?" Kazeem found himself asking.

"You join the games."

Zhinn owned his body. Kazeem knew that. But he would not sell his soul, not for any price. He saw now that every whisper was true: that young women were sold for their bodies, that boys were recruited for the arena. Kazeem thought about killing Zhinn where he stood, and running, but where would he go? And what of Kalina, who was never far from his thoughts. What of little Bel? What would happen to *them* if he fled?

"I'll kill no one," Kazeem vowed, but Garth was on him in a split second, drawing first blood, a cut across his forehead that would leave a thin scar for life.

Furiously, putting the unchained anger of his entire existence into his attack, Kazeem defended himself. He disarmed Garth by ducking, grabbing his sword arm and pulling him forward off balance. It would have been easy to behead him, but something deep inside just wouldn't let Zhinn take his soul. He spat instead, and dropped the long knife. When Fegan's eyes followed it, Kazeem hit him with an open hand, a deadly insult among Eastern men. Kazeem had bested Garth in half the time it had taken him to put down Wajda.

"I won't kill him. He's not worth it."

Kazeem expected the worst. A rush; all of them taking him away, perhaps to the arena, where he would be given a weapon and forced to kill to stay alive, where he would never see his precious Bel or the lovely Kalina again.

Yet he would endure even that, simply to frustrate this man.

But none of that happened.

"Have it you own way," Zhinn said with a smile that was worse than anything else Kazeem could have imagined. "But don't ever say I never gave you a choice."

*

Kazeem spent the rest of the afternoon watching the others from the back of the wagon. Zhinn ignored him, but Garth glared at him whenever he could. Kazeem only got down once, to smooth a little wet clay into the wound on his forehead. He knew he had made a mistake in not killing the boy, worse, he had shamed Garth Fegan, and knew it would come back to haunt him.

Waiting for his retaliation would keep him sleepless, he knew, but at least he had kept his honor.

As they headed back to the Home through darkening fields at sunset, he hoped his honor hadn't come at a price anyone else would have to pay.

Anyone like Kalina and Bel.

*

"What was he like, Garth?" Miko asked the next day. All five of them were back in their basement lair, back in the only world where Garth Fegan felt comfortable and in control. Only one person stood in the way of that security and peace of mind, one person he'd grown to hate with a passion.

"That first day must have been a fluke," Garth lied, knowing that the others would have no way of finding out. "Kid got the stuffing knocked out of him. Hell, wait till you see the scar *I* gave him."

"I knew it!" Miko capered and rubbed his hands together. His words were still garbled, but he was more easily understood these days. "I still want to get the little bastard, though."

"Oh, we'll get him," Garth promised.

"Hey, I meant to tell you guys," Nasoh said. "He had that little girl in his room the other night."

"What little girl?" Miko asked suspiciously.

"The one you were yelling at when he slammed you."

"Son of a bitch!" Miko hissed. "And he talks about *us?* He ain't no better'n us!" He frowned, and rubbed the side of his jaw. "Wait, how do *you* know?"

Nasoh gave him a look. "Kitchen duty, brainless. I was in the corridor early. I saw him sneak her back to her dorm."

"We've got to do something about him," Miko mumbled, and shook his head.

"Yeah, but what?" Abdar asked.

Garth held up a finger. "Maybe he wouldn't like it if we paid attention to one of his little friends. Maybe, he'd even come looking for them."

"You're right, Garth," Nasoh giggled. "I'll bet he wouldn't like that at all."

*

Belayn was, in most respects, a very normal little girl. It didn't help that she had had a Western father, a mercenary from the far-off land of Arconia, and had inherited his coloring, which made her stand out from all the other kids, but she got along pretty well with most of the girls her own age. Today was no exception, but the other two girls she'd been playing with were called away, and Bel just didn't feel like going in yet. She was in a good mood, and not as vigilant as usual. It wasn't that she was unaware of how bad it was here; it was just that, if she thought about it all the time, she actually made herself sick.

Bel liked playing in the garden with her doll during freetime, the hours between the last session of the day and supper.

It was a warm and sunny spot, peaceful, but it was also, unfortunately, close to a side entrance to the basement of the main building, and Bel had no idea that she was being watched. A canvas sack was dropped over her head, a hand clapped over her mouth.

When Kalina came to call her for supper, all she found was the doll, Clara, in a dreadful heap, arms and legs in a painful-looking jumble.

*

"What do you mean, she's gone?" Kazeem asked a tearful Kalina five minutes later.

"*Gone*, Kazeem, as in *not there*. No one's *seen* her, either!"

The warrior boy shrugged. He'd been stocking mason jars in the pantry. Now he gave Kalina his full attention. "She went back to her room," he said as calmly as he could.

"No." Kalina's pretty green eyes were as wide as saucers. "I told you: no one's seen her."

Kazeem became defensive. Unable to find an answer, he took Kalina's exasperation personally. "She's in the washroom, then. By the gods, girl, this is a big place! You can't have looked everywhere already!"

"She left *Clara*, Kazeem." The blonde girl raised the doll and practically stuck it in his face. "She doesn't go anywhere without her. I'm telling you, something's happened to her!"

Kazeem was defeated. He wanted to scream, and smash all the jars, but he ended up sighing and biting his lip to keep from crying. His worst fears were coming to pass—to get to him his enemies had used someone he loved. He had no proof, but the feeling in the pit of his stomach was all the evidence he needed.

"We have to report this," he said in utter despair, his tone betraying his hopelessness.

"To *Zhinn?* You've got to be kidding."

A single tear crept from one eye. Kazeem wiped it away on a sleeve. "What else can we do? We have no other choice."

Kalina frowned, and shook her head slightly from side to side, tears welling in her own eyes. "Yeah, just like everything else around here."

Kazeem took her hand. They went without hope, but at least they went together.

CHAPTER TEN

GOING TO THE administrator was a waste of time. They'd known that from the start, but it was something that needed to be done, if only to get this out in the open. A week later, he could still hear the man's voice, see his smug smile.

"This place is a regular sieve, children. Orphans sneak out all the time, some never to be heard from again. I make prisoners of no one. If one little girl walks away because the grass looks greener on the other side, what can I do?"

Kazeem had had the discipline to keep his mouth shut; if for no other reason, he wasn't about to let this sick bastard see how upset he was.

Kalina was another story. He'd had to remove her from the room physically.

"We'll go to the Town Council," she told him later after she'd calmed down a bit, but they both knew such thinking was dangerous.

They were on their own, and likely to remain so. He also knew that the little girl hadn't just wandered off, as Zhinn had suggested. No one got out of here unless they *took* you out, feet first, if necessary. It was quite possible that they'd taken Bel, but not likely. As he exercised in his room a full week later, he did what he'd done every night since—look for logic, usually without results.

The forms of unarmed combat, the fluid movements he practiced, cleared his mind and helped him to think. With moonlight streaming in, he closed his eyes and considered. If the stories about selling kids into slavery were true—and he thought they were—then this was, indeed, something they were likely to do. But would they do it like this, so heavy-handed, snatching the girl in the yard and leaving the doll behind? He didn't think so, not when they could have done it under cover of darkness, or invented a plausible story. In a world Baaka Zhinn ruled with absolute power, it was simply not a smart way to do it. To make matters worse, no one would talk.

And there was something else, too, something that had been in the back of his mind all week and was only now just coming to the surface: the administrator had clearly been surprised by the news.

That meant that someone else was responsible, which gave Kazeem a whole new set of problems—five of them to be exact. Garth and his four little playmates: Spinner, Nasoh, Abdar and Miko. Each of them had been acting strangely. For days now they hadn't bothered him, they hadn't taunted him; they hadn't even *looked* at him. In Kazeem's mind, their guilt was underscored by their mere absence. By trying to escape his attention, they'd made themselves conspicuous.

But if it *had* been them, what did they hope to accomplish?

Kazeem finished his routine and took a towel from the bed. There was an easy answer to that, he decided as he gazed out at the stars and wiped his face.

He would ask one of them.

*

It was a cold night on the edge of that vast stretch of wasteland, and steam rose from the backs of two mares left untended in the corral. Kazeem longed to lead them into the barn, to cover them with blankets and put them in their stalls, but they would have to wait until he was through.

Sneaking from fence to hay-bale to work shed, the warrior boy breathed deeply, pausing to look up at the night sky as he took a final deep breath and steeled himself for what he had to do. The sky was clear, a solid black expanse dotted with distant, winking lights and a half moon. With not a cloud in sight, there'd be shadows; he'd have to watch that.

The horses made soft snickering noises behind him, but that wasn't the only sound. Abdar was pitching hay in the barn. Kazeem could see him clearly because of the lamp hanging on a peg near the door. The kid was sweating; huge stains under his arms, down his back and between flabby, unmanly-like breasts. His face was even redder than usual, his pale blue eyes pained. He was a fat, pimple-faced boy with a swaying belly and a double chin.

Kazeem actually felt sorry for him, but took a moment to drive that thought away. It was unwarranted, not to mention time-consuming.

It was true that Kazeem was picking on the weakest of the bunch, but he was here to get information, not practice chivalry. Kazeem fought with himself. It all boiled down to this—was he doing the right thing?

He realized suddenly that, right or not, he didn't really have any other choice, and that made it all so easy. For Kazeem, most of the rules were self-imposed, but they were still rules.

His plan was simple, but he was still taking one hell of a chance. The problem with threats was that you needed to back them up with violence. This was fine if your prey caved, but what if someone pushed the issue before telling what he knew? What if he didn't know anything? What then?

Kazeem hadn't had all that much experience in the wide world, but he knew people. He'd learned *that* much in the relatively short time he'd been alive. He looked at Abdar, really *looked* at him. There was cruelty in those pale blue eyes, and knowledge no one his age should possess. Not knowing how he knew it, only suddenly *knowing* that he knew, Kazeem grew hard inside, cold, filled with the icy certainty of hatred.

The fat little bastard knew where his little Bel was, knew, and would tell.

Either that, or Kazeem would kill him.

The realization that he could do such a thing came as no great surprise. He would crush this sick animal as easily as stepping on a scorpion, and with no additional forethought.

Kazeem didn't even know he was moving until he was out of the shadows and strolling boldly into the lamp light. His arms swinging freely at his sides, his feet seemed to carry him of their own volition, all plans of stealth forgotten. He paused in the doorway, leaned against a post, and watched as the overweight boy pitched hay.

"It's Kazeemorino," Abdar said out of the side of his mouth. He smirked at Kazeem, and paused in his work, planting the pitchfork in the hay. Abdar wiped the side of his sweaty face with bunched-up material from his sleeve, near the shoulder. "What brings *you* out? I woulda figured you was afraid of the dark."

"I'm afraid of many things," Kazeem said, making no effort to come off the post, "but the dark isn't one of them."

"Yeah, well, knowing it's half the battle, kid." Abdar grabbed the pitchfork, suddenly wary, as if something in Kazeem's tone had gotten to him. "Say, why *are* you out here? Aren't you supposed to be—"

"I had a question to ask," Kazeem said, cutting him off.

"Yeah, well, what a coincidence. I have something to tell you, too."

Kazeem's soft voice was death incarnate. He pushed himself off the post with one hand, the movement almost snakelike, and came forward with the dangerous grace he would one day be infamous for. "And what would that be?"

The pimple-faced boy was slow, but not *that* slow. He knew he was in trouble, knew, also, that there wasn't much he could do about it. His eyes darted left, right—he half turned, and then seemed to remember the pitchfork in his hands.

"You keep away from me, you freak."

"What is it you wanted to tell me?" Kazeem repeated.

"Uh, nothing. Forget it! I was just jerking you around." He laughed as Kazeem advanced, his voice a high-pitched crackle. "Pretty funny, huh?"

Kazeem could have reached out to touch him from where he stood. He nodded instead. "Uh-huh."

"Well, I, uh, gotta be going. See ya."

Kazeem moved with appalling swiftness, like a venomous snake striking. Abdar's mouth hung open as the tool was ripped from his grip and turned end over end, until the tines were upper-most.

"What's your hurry?" Kazeem asked, raising only his eyes. In a second, with what seemed blinding speed to the fat young man, Kazeem used the handle of the pitchfork to upend him, sending him heavily to the straw-covered dirt floor of the barn. Without even looking behind him, Kazeem closed the door by pushing it with the handle.

Then he spun the implement around, and held it over the young man for a moment before tossing it to one side. Abdar scuttled away on his rump, on all fours, like a fat, uncoordinated crab. His eyes were as wide as saucers.

"What do you want? Touch me and—"

"You'll what?" Kazeem interrupted. "You won't tell me where the girl is?"

He reached down, and with thumb and forefinger, using the first chokehold he'd ever been taught, Kazeem forced Abdar onto his feet, then his tiptoes, against another ceiling post.

"How did you know about the girl?" he croaked.

"I didn't," Kazeem said.

"You son of a—!"

He never got the chance to finish, as Kazeem's unnaturally strong fingers closed like a vice.

"Where is she?" he growled, and forced the boy almost completely off his feet.

"Can't...choking!" Abdar's normally ruddy face was almost purple.

"You don't know what choking is," Kazeem promised. "Not yet." He backed off, and eased up on the boy. "Now tell me where she is!"

Abdar was shaking his head slowly from side to side. "I *can't*. They'll *kill* me if

I tell."

"And I'll kill you if you don't." His fingers gripped for emphasis.

"You won't kill me," the boy tried desperately.

"Won't I?"

Abdar swallowed, which wasn't easy under the circumstances. His eyes were wide and he saw something in Kazeem's that made him a believer—he saw his own death.

"What's going to stop me, Abdar? One of your friends? The administrator? My conscience? I don't think so." The grip tightened, closed off the windpipe until his eyes bulged and his tongue lolled. "And who's going to miss one little fat kid in a stink hole like this?"

It took a moment for Abdar to find his voice, but when he did, he was suddenly cooperative.

He admitted it all to Kazeem: snatching the girl to lure him away, waiting, watching him all week. Kazeem didn't ask why. The reason was clear to him—they wanted to try and overpower him, make a present of him to the *Multan* for the gladiator games. He wanted only Bel; and he wasn't thinking clearly.

"Take me to her," Kazeem ordered, closing viselike fingers again.

"All right! All right! Don't get crazy! I'll take you!"

"I thought you might," Kazeem smiled. "And if she's been hurt... in any way... I swear to God I'll kill all five of you with my bare hands...and I don't care how long it takes!"

"No! No! I swear! We haven't touched her! Garth said not to."

Kazeem thought he had it figured out. If they were going to sell her, damaged goods were worthless.

He'd be wrong again in his life, but never *this* wrong, and never with such a high cost.

*

The real plan had been to lure him to a secluded spot, overpower and humiliate him, but after taking the girl, the truth of the matter was that none of the five had any idea of how to turn the incident to their advantage without provoking Kazeem's wrath.

Random chance, along with Kazeem's own bullheadedness, solved that for them. Instead of having to lure him to their lair, he was willing to walk in on his own.

"How the hell did you manage to get away from him, Abdar?" Garth and the others were bewildered.

The fat boy shrugged. "I told him the truth; that I didn't know where the girl was. Fact is, at that moment, I didn't. Not exactly."

The others chuckled at the word play.

"Anyway, I told him I'd find out, tell him, make sure she'd be alone when he got there."

"And he *believed* you?" Garth asked. There was concerned disbelief in his eyes.

"Well, yeah," Abdar said defensively. "Besides, what choice does he have? You know, if he wants her back?"

Garth thought about it. The kid was just thickheaded enough to do it. Trouble was, they didn't *have* the girl. The administrator came straight for them after Kazeem and that slut Kalina left his office, and demanded the kid. Baaka Zhinn was all for private enterprise, but only if *he* got the biggest piece of the pie. Last Garth knew, the little girl had been sold to a couple down on the coast. A legitimate sale, from what he understood. The folks were unable to have their own, and not quite rich enough to adopt through proper channels. Zhinn, figuring that the girl had already been reported missing, saw his chance and took it, making a good offer and turning a quick profit. The kid was better off, actually, but that didn't help them now.

"Gee, Garth," Spinner said, "what are we going to do? We ain't *got* the girl no more."

"I know that, you twit!" Garth slapped the skinny boy's hand away from his face. "And stop squeezing those damn pimples! It's disgusting!"

Nasoh was always thinking, always scheming, and he nodded slowly now. Garth wanted to hate him, but the kid kept him sharp. "So what, boys? *He* don't know we ain't got her."

"He's right," Miko added. "Just 'cause she ain't here don't mean we still can't use her to get him."

Abdar and Spinner were nodding like idiots.

"Shut up!" Garth hissed. "Let me think!"

It was perfect, actually, a lure without danger. And if he didn't do something soon, didn't best Kazeem, degrade him in some way, he would almost certainly lose control of the gang to Nasoh.

"Abdar, can you handle him one more time?"

"Sure, Garth, as long as I'm telling the kid something he wants to hear."

"Then tell him this: we're scared. He can have the girl back if he leaves us alone. Tell him to come after Seventh Bell. Tell him she's in the laundry room. It's got a heavy door and a good lock." Garth smiled. "He'll come for the girl, but *we'll* be waiting for him."

*

"Don't tell me you *believed* them, Kazeem?"

"What choice do I have, Kalina?" he asked, brushing a lock of hair from her forehead.

"Plenty. Don't go. It's a trap. Anyone can see that."

They were taking a chance being alone together in his room, but considering all that was at stake, it suddenly didn't seem like such a big deal.

Kazeem sighed, turned away, and sat down heavily on the bed.

"Don't you think I've thought of that? But what if they're telling the truth? Dear, God, Kali, I can't get her face out of my head!"

Kalina came and sat down gently beside him. The mattress straps creaked under their combined weight. She was silent for a long moment, and then she took his hand. "There's something else, Kazeem, something I haven't said until now. No one loves that little girl more than I do, not even you; but I don't feel her, in here." She touched her breast. "Not anymore. She's *gone*, Kazeem. They've taken her away. They want to get you alone, to hurt you—they're only using her name."

He was on his feet again, pacing, before she'd finished.

"You can't know that for sure, Kalina! I can't base my actions on someone else's feelings—not even yours. What if you're wrong? What happens to her then?"

"It's *already* happened to her. She's gone. I know. Don't ask me how—I just do. You're the one going on feelings...your own." He stopped and frowned at her, and she held up a hand. "I'm young. I haven't had a child of my own, but after tending to these children I know what it's like to be a mother, I understand the bond, the *connection*." She was crying suddenly, and wiped her eyes angrily to repress it. "She's *gone*, damn you, and you're a *fool* for not listening to me!"

Kazeem knelt in front of her, wrapped his arms around her, and laid his head on her lap. "It's something I have to do, Kalina."

She touched his hair. "Then I'm about to lose you, too," she whispered.

Kazeem moved his head slightly on her leg. He could feel her tears on his own cheeks as she stroked his hair. "If I live without hope, then you've already lost me."

"Do what you have to do, Kazeem. I will always love you, no matter what."

And so it was, ironically, with faith and hope and love in his heart, doing what he believed was right, that Kazeem of Zamboria took the first step towards becoming the heartless killer many would one day regard him to be.

*

Water dripped from a leaky conduit in the dark. Falling in a fetid puddle it made distant echoes, rippled under the weak light from the single lamp in that dim corridor.

Kazeem was glad to have deceived Kalina about the time and place. Not having to worry about her set his mind somewhat at ease. Abdar had told him Seven Bells, but Kazeem didn't trust him, which was why he was here early. Abdar said that the girl would be in the laundry room, but Kazeem still doubted his motive for giving her up.

Deep in his heart he knew that Kalina was right, but he didn't know what else to do.

And there was something else, too; if it *was* a trick, they were challenging him—and he wasn't about to back down, not at this stage of the game.

It was scary down here in the gloom, long shadows, dim shapes, unknown territory. There were casks and bottles and crates, barrels and baskets and packing boxes—all the detritus of running a large institution, and then some. Broken cots, mattresses, chairs and tables were stacked like cordwood, waiting to be repaired or thrown out. Little food was kept this far below the kitchens, but there were burlap sacks of grain and corn and coffee, thick enough to offer some protection from uninvited nibblers like mice.

There was the oblique stench of mildew here, of dampness, of dissipated steam and standing water. The walls oozed, were spotted with gray lichen and the white blotches of nitrites. Mixed among it all was the cleansing sharpness of antiseptic bleach, of soap powder and naphthaline.

Kazeem moved silently to the end of the corridor. He paused by a post that ran up into a header and formed another hall. The wood was wet, slimy and soft. Kazeem didn't like it. He wiped his hand on his pants and vowed not to lean on anything else. Dry rot would come next, and before they knew it, the whole thing would cave in. He shook his head and moved on.

To the right were storerooms; ahead, racks filled with lumber; to the left, the laundry. Kazeem was nervous, and made even more so by the news of yet another riot today in the east ward, where the so-called older boys were housed, where young men were being held against their will, molded for gladiatorial games in distant cities like Ankoria and Calat. Kazeem forced those thoughts away. They were dangerous and threatened his focus. He needed to concentrate, to listen for tell-tale signs, find Bel if she really was here, and return her to Kalina. He couldn't afford to be distracted. Under the circumstances, it very well might get him killed.

Kazeem approached the laundry door with caution and paused just outside. His breathing was deep and steady, and he hadn't made a sound. The door before him was oak, but it was old, warped, banded with a metal 'Z' brace and contained an opaque window. A single light burned inside.

The porcelain knob was wet, but then again the air itself seemed heavy enough to crank through the ringer. He gripped the knob, turned it and went in. Of course, there was no one there. To his left were tubular metal racks loaded with empty baskets and wooden washtubs tilted to dry. Powdered soaps stood in various tubes, jars and bottles on a shelf before him. On the other end were washboards bolted to larger tubs, a stained table and hoses hanging from conduits secured to the beams in the ceiling. These brought heated rainwater from cisterns on the roof. There were two wicked-looking ringers, a drying rack, and little else.

The whole place reeked of mold overpowered by bleach.

Now what? he wondered, and shuffled his feet, feeling foolish and stupid. He looked around again. The oil lamps were dim, but there were three of them and the shadows they courted didn't really have much room to spread out. He took a step or two to the right and noticed a small door leading to a darkened corridor or alcove beyond. It was bolted, and looked unused. He shook his head. He couldn't hear the chimes down here, but it was surely later now then seven. Kalina was right. Either it was a trap, or they were simply trying to make a fool out of him. Panic rose as he decided to get out. Bel wasn't here, nor was she likely to be. What on earth had he been thinking? He turned to go, but suddenly heard a cry that turned his bones to putty. There were the sounds of a struggle coming from that locked door, and, against his better judgment, he tossed the bolt and called out.

Kazeem was through the door before his brain had time to catch up with his feet. There was a sharp blow to the base of his skull, and he'd never seen it coming. White-hot stars exploded before his eyes, but he managed to get to his feet in time to defend himself from the second blow, which glanced off his shoulder when he turned instinctively in the dark. Kazeem fought, and fought bravely, but there were five of them and he was never going to overcome that first blow to the head, not in the time he had. Knowing what they were going to do to him gave him strength, but they beat him terribly, and in the end, all he could settle for was not allowing them the satisfaction of hearing him cry. He passed out at some point and dreamed he was falling off a cliff.

CHAPTER ELEVEN

KAZEEM WOKE UP in his room with no recollection of how he'd gotten there. Sunlight was streaming through the windows, so it was the next morning, at least. Kazeem was on his stomach, face in his pillow, his head turned slightly to the left. His eyes, cheeks and lips felt puffy, but he could see well enough.

"I see you've rejoined us," a pleasant male voice said.

It was Abul Tohla, the local holy man who oversaw the Home for the School Board. Because his head was turned towards the window, Kazeem couldn't see him, but he recognized the rich, cultured voice. Abul visited on religious holidays and sometimes on weekends for regular services. He was a strong, kind man, and had more than an inkling about what went on in here. One place like this, he'd been overheard saying outside these walls, ruined the good name of the entire system. Needless to say, he and Baaka Zhinn were not on the best of terms.

Abul Tohla came around the bed with a cool washcloth to wipe the crusted sleep from Kazeem's swollen eyes. It was unprocessed cotton, but it felt wonderful.

Kazeem tried to talk, found he couldn't, and tried to wet his lips with a tongue that was as arid as the desert. The back of his skull felt like it had been cracked open.

Abul Tohla took pity on him.

"Here, try this, lad." He placed a shallow cup near the boy's battered mouth. "Easy, son, easy."

There was a strong, soothing hand on the back of Kazeem's head, stroking, soothing. It was the kindest, most masculine thing Kazeem had ever felt. For the rest of his life he would try to model his own manly compassion on the strength in that touch.

"How long?" Kazeem managed at last, even though the words themselves hurt his throat.

"Two days ago, my boy." The priest cleared his throat. "It was I who found you." He paused, and lowered his voice carefully. "Do you know what happened to you?" His brown eyes were very direct.

Kazeem nodded, and did his best to meet that gaze. When you're hurt like *that*, you know it. Abdar had a broken hand; Spinner a badly damaged eye. Kazeem didn't know how long he'd been in that room, but he was willing to bet that those two hadn't been part of it, not with painful, debilitating injuries like that. He wet his lips, and managed to nod again. "I know who, too, but if anyone asks, I fell." He grimaced. "Hurts to breathe." *Hurts to breathe*, he thought. *God, it hurts to keep my eyes open!*

"You have three broken ribs," Tohla informed him. Your right shoulder was dislocated, but Kalina and I repaired that." The kind man sat on a stool by Kazeem's head, where he could watch him more closely, and the boy could look at him without moving too much. What Kazeem liked most about the man was that he looked you in the eye when he spoke to you. "Cuts, bruises, rope burns. Those are healing nicely." He cleared his throat. "All of it will heal, son. Flesh is, after all, only flesh."

Kazeem moved a hand that had been on the pillow by his cheek. It moved like someone else's hand. He touched his heart, and left the hand by his chest; he simply didn't have the strength to move it again.

"Ah," the kind hand was on the back of his neck again, big, strong, protecting. "Your heart, too, in time, trust me."

Almost against his will, Kazeem closed his eyes. "Trust you," he mumbled, and slept.

*

The next few days were a dreamlike blur for the warrior boy. Kalina was there, as were Abul, Imad, and other children he had befriended. Everyone, that was, except Bel.

"We can't find her," Abul told him almost a week later in answer to their ongoing conversation. He nodded to the pretty blonde girl with the big green eyes. "I'm afraid Miss Zamonar is correct. Your friend is simply not within these walls."

Kazeem was sitting up for the first time that day. He had taken clear broth and bread with fresh butter. The boy was having trouble digesting, but he could almost feel his strength returning day by day.

Kalina addressed the priest. "I tried to tell him, Abul T." A single tear coursed down her cheek. She sighed deeply. It was a gut-wrenching sound. Kalina pressed her lips firmly together, shook her head, and turned away blinking as she threw up her hands. "He didn't listen." She was crying silently.

"I've decided to have you moved. Both of you," Abul T said. "Ever since the last pageant I've had grave misgivings concerning the administration of this facility. I've begun the paperwork, and it should come through by the end of the week." He held up a hand to ward of interruptions. "I'll go over the records once you're out." He tried not to look so grim. "We'll find little Bel. One way or the other."

Kalina thanked him, moving to the gray-haired man to take his hands. They continued to talk, but Kazeem didn't hear them. All about him were flowers, hand-made cards, and trinkets from the little ones who loved him. He didn't see any of it, however. In his mind he was alone with his tormentors. But it was different this time. His inner vision showed him plans for the future, a time when he would have each of the five alone and helpless, one by one. He vowed to make each pay dearly for what they'd done, but he would never speak to anyone about it for fear of them seeing the depth of the blackness in his soul. He also knew, deep down, that he wouldn't really do the things he was contemplating.

He'd do worse.

*

"I haven't liked what I've seen the last few days," Kalina told him during the middle of the next week.

Kazeem was able to get out of bed now, and was sitting in a chair by the window. He was stronger, and the bruises were fading, but he wasn't yet back to normal, physically, and his emotional state would never be the same.

"How so?" he asked, knowing that, of all people, she was the one most likely to see through him.

"You're cold. I feel like I've lost you."

Kazeem turned his head. Looking out the window, he put his elbow on the armrest and stroked his healing, chapped lips with thumb and forefinger.

"What would you have me say, Kalina Zamonar?"

Kalina blew out an exasperated breath that actually moved the hair on her forehead. She came to him, knelt and grabbed his free hand. "Look at me, damn it! You haven't looked at me since Abul T brought you here!"

He leveled her with a look, finally meeting her gaze. "I am ashamed to look at you, my love." A single, crystal tear escaped his eye and rolled slowly down his cheek.

Kalina shook her head violently, her own tears flying across her face. "There's no shame in this, Kazeem, but that isn't it. I'm not stupid. I see death in your eyes! When I look at you, when I look in your eyes that once looked so tenderly on me, I see only death. No Kazeem. Only the instrument itself. Don't keep turning away!" She shook her head again. "Please let me make this right. Just tell me what to do!"

"You want me to hold you and kiss you, Kalina. You want me to say that everything is going to be all right. But it's *not* all right! It's never going to *be* all right! Dear God, girl, give me time to heal before you make demands of my heart!"

"I have never, ever, demanded *any*thing of you!" she growled, and pushed herself away. She put her hands on her hips and glowered at him. "You don't want to heal, you want to kill!"

"You don't know what you're talking about." He looked out the window again.

"You don't even *sound* the same anymore."

Kazeem turned back to her, waited for her to look at him, and when Kalina searched his eyes she wished she hadn't.

"I am *not* the same, Kalina. I don't believe I will ever be the same again."

*

Kalina didn't come back for two days after that, and when she did they talked about things that didn't matter. Small talk. Something they'd never engaged in before.

Kazeem continued to heal, stretching, exercising, eating well, resting and making plans, which somehow made his recovery more rapid.

Kalina told him rumors of unrest in the east ward, but he barely paid attention. What did he care if sharks chased guppies? He had his own fish to fry.

The girl left early, and didn't return the next. On the following day, the eve of the day when they were supposed to leave, Kalina crept to his room in the dark. He must have been sleeping soundly, because she had to shake him hard to wake him. He sat up abruptly, and only then did he smell the smoke. He rubbed his eyes. Most of his bruises had healed, and he was almost as limber as ever. He was instantly alert, adrenaline fueling sore muscles as he leaned forward and put a hand on her shoulder.

"Kalina! What is it? What's wrong?"

She put a finger to his lips. Only then did he realize her condition. There was only moonlight, but he could see that her face was battered and bruised. She'd been crying because he could see the dusty tracks of smoky tears on her cheeks.

"The older boys have broken out of the east wing. They've killed at least one guard, and locked up the rest. The whole place is burning.

We've got to get out of here." Then, almost as an afterthought, she said: "I brought your sword."

Kazeem gazed deeply into her lovely, bright green eyes. Despite it all he longed to touch her, but then something he saw made him shiver. Gently, he touched the scratch on her cheek, and the cut on the back of her neck, saw that her shirt was torn. Only then did he understand the price she'd paid for his steel.

"What did they *do* to you?" he asked breathlessly.

"Nothing that hasn't happened before." She looked down, her voice harsh. "I killed him, Kazeem, and it was easy." She looked surprised, but not shocked.

He touched the side of her face, knowing he would make them pay for this—all of them. "You're right," he said, swinging his legs out of bed, "we have to get out of here."

There was a far-away look in her eyes, as if she hadn't even heard him. "I'm going to kill them all someday," she promised.

The smoke was thicker, blacker. It slithered under the door and roiled along the floor like a live thing, twisting and turning and climbing the walls. Kazeem coughed, reached down, grabbed his sword and stood up.

"Are you all right?" Kalina asked, hands in midair on either side of him, unsure if she should help.

"A little dizzy, but I'm okay." He coughed again, blinked and met her eyes. "Are you armed?"

The girl reached behind her and pulled a vicious looking combat dagger from her waistband. A thin sheen of blood could still be seen in the moonlight, but she made no effort to wipe it off. "Yes." Her pants were the kind that fastened with leather cord. She put the blade of the knife between her teeth and took up the slack in her beltline. She knotted it twice, and took the blade from her bloody mouth.

"We're probably going to have to fight our way out of here," Kazeem warned her.

Kalina's eyes were blazing emeralds in the moonlight. "I wouldn't have it any other way," she told him. With a shaking finger, Kazeem wiped away the blood on her lips.

He loved the fire in her eyes, the strength in her voice even though he knew how scared she was. Despite the screams and yells coming from the halls beyond, despite the smoke and the fire now reflected outside his window, Kazeem took her in his arms and kissed her softly. He would have cried had he realized he'd be a grown man and a world-weary traveler before he'd touch those lips again.

"I love you," he whispered.

"And I love you," she replied. "From that first day on."

Kazeem reluctantly took his hands from her shoulders and went to the tiny bureau he had once shared with Imad. He took the few coins he had, his clothes (all of them fit in a tiny satchel that closed with a drawstring), a scarf and a wide-brimmed hat. He tossed it all on the bed, stuffing things into the bag. Then he went back to the bureau and came back with another scarf, pausing only to pour water from the pitcher on both.

"This is Imad's," he said, handing it to her. "Use it to cover your nose and your mouth from the smoke." Kazeem took his own plain brown scarf and wrapped it around his head. It hung down on one side under the wide-brimmed cloth hat with a plaited leather band.

He reached for the doorknob, but Kalina stopped him by grabbing his wrist.

"Wait! Check it. See if it's hot."

Her words said one thing, but her eyes said another. Kalina wasn't worried about the fire; she was worried about losing him. They both felt it as their eyes met; a sense of dread, the sudden, terrible knowledge that they might never see each other again.

"We can't stay here, Kalina." His hand joined hers, checking the door for heat. Their fingertips touched.

"I know." She pulled him close, and looked at him for a very long time. The world was going to hell all around them from the sound of it, but the two of them were like the eye of the storm. "I will always love you, Kazeem, no matter what."

The warrior boy nodded, lips pressed tightly together. Not trusting his voice he nodded again, then managed: "No matter what."

"How bad do you think it'll be?"

"Bad. This place was a powder keg waiting for a match. Stay close to me. Kill without hesitation if anyone attacks. It's the only way we'll survive."

Kalina nodded, her silky blonde hair bouncing and swishing. "I can do it…if I have you by my side, and if we find Bel…" She choked and couldn't go on.

Kazeem knew better than to comfort her at this point. There was simply no time for it, and it was dangerous. "Turn right as soon as we open the door, then left down the main hall past the kitchen and towards the administrator's office. We'll make straight for the front gate, steal the post horses if we can."

"You're not afraid?" she asked, wetting her lips. She was shaking, and her hands were trembling.

"I'm afraid. More than you'll ever know. I've just been trained not to show it." He took her by the shoulders, shook her to stop the trembling, and looked deep into her eyes. "Just go, and go fast. Try to avoid people, but if someone gets in out way, he goes down, understand? They'll kill us if we don't."

"I understand."

He shifted a hand, and felt the wall. "We've got time, I think, but not much." He hefted the sword, and gazed at the wolf's head with almost sanguineous lust in his eyes. Fire from the courtyard reflected off the highly polished steel, and cast his face in nightmare shades of red and maroon. "Right, then left. And don't stop for anything. Got it?"

Kalina grabbed his arm one last time; there was panic in her eyes, but she was fighting it. "We go together, or not at all."

"Or not at all," he promised, and opened the door.

CHAPTER TWELVE

KALINA ZAMONAR HAD already been through hell, but even she wasn't prepared for the horror on the other side of that door. Boys and girls were everywhere, scurrying like ants under magnified sunlight. Everyone was bleeding or bruised, glistening with perspiration. Not one face was free of soot.

Kalina went right, then left, just as Kazeem had ordered. The smoke was thick, but she had no real trouble seeing. Fires ranged freely up and down the halls. Kids screamed. Alarm bells rang. Every grownup they passed, from guards to cooks to groundskeepers, lay dead or dying on the stonework.

Kalina had never seen Kazeem fight before, and after the first thirty seconds wished that it had stayed that way. A big-shouldered boy with brown hair and wild blue eyes charged at her with a short sword high above his head. Kalina didn't have time to wonder why he wasn't running from the flames instead of chasing people, but she'd have time later to wonder how the hell Kazeem had moved fast enough to save her.

The blue-eyed boy was so out of control that he missed by a mile. Kazeem sidestepped the charge, chopped at the back of the boy's knees, bringing him down, and then crushed him to the floor with a blow the boy just barely blocked in time. Somehow, without Kalina understanding how he managed it, Kazeem was suddenly behind the boy. One hand pulled the boy's head back by his long, greasy hair, exposing his throat, while the other drew the sword savagely across. Kalina was sure that the young man was dead before his face struck the stone, but she gasped anyway, gawking at the sudden rush of blood, the awful, exploding *amount* of it. She, herself, had killed not an hour before, but not like *this*. It was the terrifying, appalling swiftness that got to her. The boy was literally alive one second, and dead the next. And then Kazeem was taking her hand.

"Come on!"

"There's another one!"

Kazeem tossed her against the wall and turned to meet a redheaded giant who must have been at least six and a half feet tall. He looked like no one Kalina had ever seen before. He was as thick as a barrel and had pasty white skin. Kazeem didn't waste time studying him. He blocked the redhead's clumsy lunge, and then battered him mercilessly with lightning-fast slashes that rocked the huge foe and brought him to his knees. The impact of the final blow broke the boy's sword. Kazeem spun, handle of his own sword in both hands, and decapitated the insane creature with a blood-curdling screech.

The head was still tumbling through the air in a mist of bloody froth as Kazeem grabbed her hand again without a word. She'd been afraid before. She'd been afraid earlier, afraid for her own life—but not like this. This was different. Death held her hand in a grip of steel, leading her on, and she suddenly realized that Kazeem was the most dangerous thing in here.

Baaka Zhinn had once called Kazeem a young man of terrifying principle. Kalina had never understood that—until now.

*

The whole way out it was the same. Every time they met someone, anyone they passed, Kazeem cut down like overripe wheat. Kalina lost count after a while, but was sure of one thing: some of those boys who died at Kazeem's hands, even the very wild ones from the east wing, had been running *away* from him.

But that hadn't mattered to Kazeem. Kalina hated the fact that she was afraid of him, but he didn't even seem human at the moment.

He was like some force of nature, and God help anyone who got in his way.

Hand in hand they ran through smoke filled corridors, and, after a time, they didn't see anyone else. It was like a nightmare: echoes, smoke, flames and distant screams.

And then they saw the guard, standing under the arch thirty feet away. He held a bloody sword and regarded them calmly as smoke swirled around him.

He was all that stood between them and freedom.

This particular hallway was as yet untouched by fire, but the smoke curved and eddied like a ghostly mist in the air. Earlier they'd been surrounded by chaos, flames, screaming children and a running, wailing attendant set ablaze by God alone knew what. Here, in this dim corridor, there was only silence and the promising rays of early dawn, streaking into the archway like gaps of salvation in a nightmare.

"It's Omar," Kalina whispered as the big man moved into the light.

Kazeem nodded as he moved her against the wall, safely nestled in a neat little alcove before approaching the big man with his gleaming sword held in both hands.

The bright-eyed giant smiled, showing very white teeth. He held a huge, thick bladed scimitar, twirling it in one hand as easily as if it were a baton.

"Come on, you little bastard," he said with a thick, Eastern accent. "You've gotten *this* far on your own; show me how you did it." He beckoned with the fingers of his left hand.

"So you *can* talk, you big oaf," Kazeem taunted, hiding his surprise well. "I always thought so."

"Then you're smarter than you look," the huge Arganian rumbled.

They circled each other, drawing closer. Behind him, Kazeem heard the girl gasp. He shut her out, took a deep breath, and tried to block out the shuddering in the stone beneath his feet, the far-away screams that accompanied it.

"You've proven you can talk," Kazeem said coldly, in a tone that chilled Kalina to the bone. "Now prove that you can fight. Either that, or stand aside." Kazeem twirled his own sword, swirled it around his own head, and brought it to bear once again. "Which will it be?"

"What do *you* think?" Omar growled.

Mesmerized, Kalina gaped as Kazeem seemed to dematerialize into the smoky mist, only to reappear right in front of his foe. He moved with such blinding speed that Kalina chalked it up to the smoke, a trick of the light, something. *No one can move* that *fast*, she thought, as the angry clash of steel striking steel reached her ears. The boy hadn't even given Omar the chance to blink. The big man hadn't even gotten the last word out of his mouth before Kazeem was on him, driving him back on his heels. *CLANG! CLANG! CLANG-CLANG-CLANG!* Kalina winced and fought the desire to cover her ears. She could see Omar clearly despite the smoke, his eyes wide, shock and surprise making them round.

"I hear they used you well," Omar taunted in a pitiful attempt to anger Kazeem, to make him do something foolish or cause him to lose control.

Kazeem only grunted, took a second to shake his head before pressing the attack even harder. "I expected more from you, Arganian. I expected a man's fight. Not...*this!*"

There was a flurry of activity too swift to follow, and them Omar's big sword clattered to the stone. Kalina squinted, peering through the hazy blackness. The early morning sunlight coming through the arch hurt her eyes, but she looked away from it in time to see Kazeem force Omar back against the wall, the tip of his wickedly pointed sword already bringing a bead of bright red blood to Omar's throat. The big man backed up until his wide shoulders were against the block-like stones of the arch. His arms hung at his sides, helpless, empty hands twitching.

Kazeem, God help him, was smiling.

Kalina had been worried. She'd known Omar longer, knew what the wicked Arganian was capable of, that he actually *enjoyed* hurting people.

Now, the girl actually felt sorry for him.

She heard an exchange of words between the man and the teenager, but couldn't tell what was being said. Omar went to his knees, still talking—or trying to talk—as Kazeem flicked his wrist, slashing Omar's throat from ear to ear. Shaking, panicked hands went immediately to his neck, almost as if he were choking himself, but the fountain of blood told its own story. Omar was dead even as he pitched forward, but that didn't stop Kazeem from sidestepping and running him through as he fell.

Kalina ran to her lover, but stopped several feet away, shaking, unsure, and afraid.

"What did he ask you?" she whispered.

"He asked if he could stand aside." The gleam in the teen's eyes was murderous. "I told him he'd had his chance. That they'd all had their chance."

He held out a hand, but she was suddenly afraid to take it. Kazeem turned away, glancing at the stonework stairs that lead to the courtyard and freedom. He grabbed her hand without even looking at her. "Come. It's now or never."

The rumbling under the floor was suddenly louder, deeper, as though something fundamental in the building's foundation had given way. A crack ran up the hallway, worked its way into the arch, and split the stone all along the lintel. Stone dust shifted down on them from the keystone and a billow of roiling black smoke coughed up from the crack in the floor as if from the bowels of hell. Kalina didn't know if there had been explosives stored in the subbasement, or if it was an earthquake. To tell the truth, she didn't care. All she wanted was to run.

"Now! Now!" Kalina heard him cry, but even as the words left his lips they knew it was already too late. Still, she let him lead her. His hand was dry and rough; it felt strong and sure in her own moist palm. Their eyes met, and the arch split. With the keystone cracked the rest of the structure crumbled like a set of child's blocks. The rumbling, roaring cough of it was immense. The floor tilted, leaving a gaping hole, and only the pitch of the stonework saved their lives as the arch collapsed in on itself, blocking their escape with a mighty roar. There was a billowing cloud of choking, swirling dust; a rain of small stones rattling down and then silence.

The young lovers found themselves in a tangled heap at the end of the east corridor. The floor was tilted up at a crazy angle, and they had somehow slid all the way to the end. They stood slowly, coughing, tears streaming down soot-blackened cheeks.

"What did they *do?*" Kalina whined. "Look at it! Just *look* at it! What the *hell* are we supposed to do now?"

"Are you all right?" Kazeem asked softly, but his voice still echoed. He coughed again, and his eyes watered.

"No, I'm not all right, Kazeem!" she shouted, bringing more dust down on their heads. "How the hell can I be all right when we're standing on the damn ceiling?"

"Are you hurt?" he pressed. His voice was infuriatingly patient.

Kalina remembered the young man she had just seen kill with such skill and abandon. It made his self-control much more chilling.

"No, I'm not hurt." She rubbed a sore shoulder as she spoke, and he just looked at her for a moment.

He took her hand. "We'll find another way."

Kalina gave in to him, allowing herself to be led through winding turns and passages too badly twisted to be easily recognizable. Kalina's comment about standing on the ceiling was an exaggeration, but not by much. From time to time the walls creaked and the floor groaned. Whatever the cause of such a cataclysm, it was still going on, ground settling; smoke pouring from fissures in the floor.

"Run," he said, squeezing her hand and pulling her along.

Daylight appeared unexpectedly as they rounded a corner. They were running through the smoke, hand in hand, Kazeem leading, Kalina right behind. Both of them were yelling and screaming as chunks of ceiling struck the floor, exploding, hurling shards of superheated rock in every direction.

Kalina couldn't see. The smoke and the dust were suddenly like murky water, but still those rays of sunlight pierced the swirling gloom like beacons of salvation.

The floor tilted one last time as something settled in the corridor beneath them, but before she had time to scream they were tumbling out through a gap in the broken wall, landing on grass softer and sweeter-smelling than any she'd ever known. At first, the daylight was blinding, but as they stood, choking, coughing and blinking, they saw that they were in an upper courtyard above the dreaded east wing, in a rounded garden high above the main gate. Six tiers below, twelve twisted, switched-backed sets of stairs was their only escape. Archways and trellises and stone statues lined the way, each and every one rumbling softly as the turmoil in the Home's foundation continued.

"Oh my *God*," Kalina gasped, knowing they'd have to make their way among dangerous loose rocks and crumbling archways. Halfway down, one set of stairs was completely gone. They'd have to jump when they got there, or risk going back inside.

"It's our only hope," Kazeem said and pointed to the gates far below. "There's nothing between us and freedom. Nothing but this…" He coughed, and put his sword through his belt. "But we've got to move quickly."

The slope to each side was too steep, and only the stairs made the grade navigable, but the stairs were suddenly unsafe, moving and treacherous as the hill rumbled. Steam issued from cracks in the crushed stone on either side.

"I'm afraid," Kalina said before she could stop herself.

"Me too," Kazeem admitted. He took her hand, blinking, coughing, trying to make eye contact as smoke continued to boil from the building.

Kalina looked down. It was only a matter of time before the whole facility collapsed. That would take out the lower levels, the front gate, this slope, and *them*. She nodded and started towards him, finding a nervous smile somewhere deep inside that looked more like a grimace. Hedges lined the way before them. They were running before they knew it, speed and distance giving them courage, and had almost reached the gap in the staircase when they rounded a corner and literally ran into Abdar and Miko.

*

The look on Abdar's face was almost comical as he picked himself up. There was a curse on his lips and he almost uttered it until he saw who it was.

"Oh my God!" Miko exclaimed, echoing the sentiment. He turned to his red-faced, double-chinned friend, and held his pale blue eyes with a look of lost consternation that was every bit as comical as the pimpled boy. "I told you not to come this way! I *told* you we just shoulda jumped it!"

Abdar regarded the flabby Zamborian. "You gonna be a girl all your life? There's *two* of us, you know!"

At that moment Kazeem lunged. He screamed at the top of his lungs, leaped forward and slashed first right, then left, laying Abdar's belly open almost to the backbone. The warrior boy was on one knee as he finished, and he stood slowly, a look of almost indescribable satisfaction on his face.

Kalina *wanted* to look away, but couldn't. As Abdar stood there with a look of shock and horror on his face, he began to shudder. His hands had gone instinctively to his belly, but nothing on earth could stop the flow of his intestines as they slopped out in ropey, bloody loops that splattered at his feet. He coughed once, and bright red sputum spurted from his lips. He slumped to his knees and turned to the fat Zamborian for help, but the look in his eyes revealed that he already knew that he was dead. Kazeem calmly stepped between them and kicked him in the face.

"Get out of the way," he sneered, as Abdar rolled and slid over the side of the hill. There was so much noise coming from behind them that no one heard his body strike the ground, far below.

Kalina looked over her shoulder. It wasn't just the buildings that were caving in; it was the entire set of hills they were built on. Explosives or a natural eruption, it didn't matter which. They needed to get out, and now, while they still could.

Meanwhile, Kazeem was advancing on Miko. He was silent, deadly, his eyes flat, black, like a feeding shark. The fat Zamborian with the once-broken jaw threw up his hands as if they could protect him from that razor sharp blade.

"Please, Kazeem! I can explain!" He glanced to the bloody stain where his friend had been. "You, you didn't even give him a—"

Kalina heard the swift passage of the blade through the air, and suddenly Miko was screaming. His right hand was gone, tumbling over the side of the hill. He held the bloody stump before saucer-wide eyes as Kazeem, without so much as a change of expression, cut off the other hand.

The screams were horrible, too pitiful to bear. Kalina covered her ears, but she could still hear every word.

"No! No, Kazeem, *please* don't! It wasn't me! They *made* me! Oh, God, *look* at me!"

With a single backhand motion Kazeem took one foot off at the ankle. As the boy fell, still shrieking, Kazeem leaned over him.

"I guess you won't be raping anyone else, will you?"

Kalina was crying. She had already thrown up, and was still gagging and begging Kazeem to stop, but as the mangled boy flopped away, turning over on his belly to crawl like some groping, limbless lizard, Kazeem lunged and rammed his sword into Miko's lower back, impaling him like a bug. Miko screamed even louder, an ear-piercing shriek of despair that echoed through the hills. The sound was beyond lost hope, beyond pain; it dragged what was left of Kazeem's soul to hell with it and *still* the Wrotmar wasn't through with him.

The girl could only wonder why the boy was still conscious, but all she could do was continue to yell. She begged Kazeem to stop, screamed and cried until her throat was on fire. It was enough, she reasoned, feeling her sanity slip away, wasn't it? And the very ground they stood upon cracked and hissed like a bubbling cauldron.

Kazeem didn't appear to hear her. He was down on one knee beside the impaled Miko, who continued to writhe like a worm on a hook. Kazeem reversed his grip on the sword and began twisting it back and forth savagely. The boy screamed once more and abruptly went limp. There was a sudden foul stench as his bowels emptied, and Kalina would have thrown up again had there been anything left in her stomach.

"We're still not even," Kazeem whispered, and spat on him, "but I guess that'll have to do."

He stood up, looking as calm as ever, and Kalina realized that she would be afraid of him for the rest of her life. No *normal* person could do what he'd just done. No matter what.

"*Now* we can go," Kazeem told the panic-stricken and traumatized girl, but by then, of course, it was too late.

"RUN!" Kalina screamed and took flight. The ground at her feet heaved, pitching the cobblestones in the stairs and walkways aside and tumbling over the edge of the slope. The terrified Kalina heard a great rumble far behind, but didn't need to turn to know what had happened. The Home, and the hill it rested on, had collapsed into the valley and the little village just west of here.

The gap that had brought a quick stop to Miko and Abdar came into view quickly, and Kalina came to a skidding, skipping halt, her mouth a little 'O' of despair, a tiny cry on her suddenly bloodless lips. She tottered and would have gone over the edge if Kazeem hadn't grabbed her arm. She realized then that she had been running away from him as well as the noise and the great gray plume of dust at her back.

"Don't!" she cried as he pulled her close. He had saved her life, but she was still petrified of him.

The stones tumbled into the stairwell below them, leaving a clinging, sod-and-root held bank of earth as the only bridge to the next landing. Earthworms wriggled quickly back into the bank from which they'd been disturbed. Dozens of ants and beetles joined them.

"Don't *what?*" Kazeem rasped, as she struggled in his arms.

"I don't know!" She trembled, and arched her back to put more space between them.

"We don't have *time* for this!" he snarled and started across what was left of the little land bridge, with her in tow. Earth crumbled and fell away with every step they took.

The blonde girl went, but her steps were tentative. They reached the other side and huddled in the next archway as the path they'd just crossed crumbled into the stairwell below. The roar was deafening.

"It's like a *tomb* down there!" she protested as he rounded the pylon and hurried down the next stone staircase. Kalina stopped, and put a hand to her mouth.

Kazeem skidded to a sliding halt and lost his balance when he realized that she wasn't right behind him. He used one hand to right himself, leaned on the far wall and looked up.

"Hurry!"

"I can't! I'm afraid!"

He was about to start back for her when the step he was standing on rolled beneath him. Still looking up, Kazeem craned his neck. The last he saw of Kalina Zamonar she was framed against a hole in the staircase wall, her beautiful young face set like a flawless gem in a cloudless blue background. Flaxen hair swirled in the air around her cheeks and neck, and her green eyes held...an apology.

A dust cloud obscured his vision as well as her lovely face, covered the sky and got in his eyes, making him cough violently. He fell, calling her name, retching, rolling, and found himself standing shortly in the lower courtyard without any clear idea of how he'd gotten there. He realized that he had stumbled, rolled and pitched headlong down the last of the stone steps, but nothing seemed to be broken. He turned quickly, screeching her name, and tripped over the rubble as he tried to get back into the stairwell. A tongue of flame and black smoke shot out at him, flinging him like a rag doll onto his back. By the time he got to his feet again an avalanche of rock, dust and swirling fire had blocked the collapsing stairwell. No one could have survived it, but there wasn't time to mourn her, not now. He had to get away, save himself, if only to stay alive long enough to kill the remaining three bastards who had stolen his soul.

*

Kazeem crept from a garden in a tiny village due south of where the Home had been. Riding hard, he'd come fifteen or twenty miles, but he could still see the face of the guard as he'd pulled him from the horse at the gate, pummeled him, and swung up into the saddle. He cried for Kalina; the fruit he'd stolen, along with his sword, forgotten in his lap.

The boy who would one day issue open challenges to assassination targets, work for two opposing governments at the same time, draw pay from both...and live to tell about it, sobbed like the frightened child he was. His entire world for better than a year had been one continuous trip through hell, and now, at the end, to realize that he was worse than any other monster he'd encountered, was almost more than he could bear.

While he sat there sobbing, he considered his actions this day, and grew sick to his stomach. He turned and vomited, but it didn't help. He knew he would kill again...and again...and again. Three more times, to be exact.

Nasoh and Spinner and Garth still lived. He didn't know how he knew it, but he did. Their actions—and his response to them—had cost him his soul, and this knowledge was the true start of his life's journey.

Kazeem also figured that if he was already hell-bent, at least he could go there knowing he would dedicate himself to fighting evil. If he couldn't *avoid* hell, maybe he could at least lessen his burdens there.

He had no way of knowing that he would become the most feared hired killer on three continents, or that he would take only assignments on men he truly believed should die. He *did* know that he was more afraid of what he'd become than of anything else.

The blond boy lay back in the grass with the horse grazing quietly behind him. He put a forearm over his eyes, blocking out the still-visible glow of fire from that other distant hill, blocking out, too, the pall of smoke polluting the heavens.

He knew he'd see Kali's face in his dreams for the rest of his life.

Kazeem cried for his mother; he cried for his father; he cried for Elin and Nomar and Bel and Kalina.

Most of all, he cried for himself.

CHAPTER THIRTEEN

THE OLD MAN watched the orphanage from the tiered village of Tentang. Once again, he was too late. He hung his head, refusing to look at the flames. His thin hair rustled. Even from here he could feel the heat on his face like the blush of shame. All of his preparation had been for nothing. All he could hope for now was that the boy might seek *him* out. All he could hope for now was that the boy was as tough as his father and, hopefully, a bit smarter.

The old man turned his back on the smoky hill and started for home before dawn had a chance to reclaim the sky.

He had much to do before his student arrived. *If* he arrives, he amended, and found himself biting his lip.

*

The next day was a new beginning for Kazeem of Zamboria. The sick bastards who'd ruined him were still out there, and he wouldn't rest until he'd dealt with them. Couldn't rest. Ever.

Kali's face was never far from his thoughts, and several times he almost went back to see if he could find her. There was a chance, he hoped, that she had somehow gotten out of the way, but it was too dangerous for him to entertain such thoughts at the moment, no matter how sad they continued to make him.

*

He made his way down the grassy bank to the river, his nostrils filled with balsam and pine and cedar. His skin, his hair and his *soul* reeked of blood and smoke and death, and he wanted nothing more than to at least *try* to wash away some of that stench.

Kazeem was bruised and sore. He could hardly move, but it wasn't necessarily a bad feeling, because it was a stiffness that never would have been had he not triumphed over his foes. The tears were still there, though, waiting just behind his eyes to spring forward and unravel his manhood, but he refused them, because there was still too much to do.

Something ached deep inside of him every time he thought of Kali. It was almost a physical thing, as if he was broken, and he wondered if the feeling would ever go away. He shook his head sadly. The answer to that was a simple *no*.

At the water's edge Kazeem knelt, scooped up water, and caught his reflection. His face was burdened by the stories so recently written there, a face that had braved a thousand inner storms, as well as the wind-whipped sands of the desert. It was a face reddened by blazing suns and harsh gales. It was the face of a boy who had become a survivor, a master of fieldcraft who knew how to keep his new life a secret.

No one. *No* one would ever hold him, take him, hurt him again, no matter what. Now that he was free he'd stay that way, and God help anyone who thought otherwise.

A bath was what he needed, he decided as cool water soothed him, trickled down his back, ran the length of his arms and dripped into the river. He took his sword and went in, scrubbing with white sand from the clear-bottomed bar at his feet. He left his clothes— bloody, torn and scorched—in the river, and watched them float away. There were newer ones in the saddlebags that would just fit. Physically, he felt awful, but it was nothing that wouldn't heal, given time—overworked muscles, stressed tendons, joints and ligaments abused almost to the breaking point. He felt better just being in the water, and for a while even floated on his back with his eyes half open. Food and more rest were in order, he realized as he started to drift. Get his strength back before moving on. He'd been taught by his father that a warrior did most of his healing while he slept, and when that particular, overwhelming fatigue grabbed you, the kind that wrapped around your head like a turban and tugged your eyelids closed, only sleep would do.

But he was afraid to sleep.

Kazeem was bothered by a recurring dream about an old, wizard-like man with strong, steel gray eyes and a wrinkled face. An old man who could have been fifty, who could have been a thousand: an old man with short, stone white hair and the stern glare of a desert dweller.

In the dream he felt as if he should have known him…and yet not. A strange, unsettling feeling.

"But what can I do?" he'd asked in answer to some pressing question in the dreamscape.

"Why, you can change the world," the dream wizard replied.

"But I'm only one man." A very *young*, young man, he could have added.

"One determined man can alter the world," this pinnacle of wisdom claimed.

Kazeem glanced around the dreamscape: rocks, endless sand, gray boulders. He had been here before, but when? With an effort he brought his eyes back to the old man.

"How?"

"All he need be is committed to his cause, and strong enough to see it through. If you doubt this, reflect on the course of our history… it's never, ever been a single *nation* bringing change, but a single *man*, one with a vision—for good *or* evil. In fact, that's all it's *ever* been.

"But I haven't got time for that now."

"I know, you must hunt down and kill Nasoh and Spinner and Garth. They are rabid dogs, and the world will not miss them. Come to me when you are ready."

"I can't. I can't see beyond that. I've been through too much to even *think* much farther than that."

"Listen to me, Kazeem, son of Kaidin, the measure of a man isn't in how he handles the good things in life—*any*one can do that! No, the true measure of a man is in how he handles the bad. If he holds his head up, bears his load and carries his misfortune bravely, and with dignity, only then can he truly call himself a man."

"Being a victim is not a virtue," Kazeem scoffed.

"You are only a victim if you see yourself that way. The true prison is in the mind, not around the body."

There was more. Kazeem couldn't remember any of it. He allowed, instead, the soothing waters to calm tortured limbs. Then he went back to the bank, wrapped himself in a blanket and went to lie down in his hiding place under the sandy overhang covered with long grass. He was falling asleep even as he put his head down, but one image remained in his mind as he drifted off: three, capering rabid dogs, more like hyenas, with slobbering faces he knew intimately—Nasoh, Spinner and the ring-leader, Garth.

Especially Garth.

Kazeem slept through the day, all night, and into the next dawn. He awoke, relieved himself at the river, and went to lie back down. The sun was at its midmorning station when he got back up, finding himself suddenly ravenous and with next to nothing to eat.

Drinking all the water in his goatskin helped at first, but then made his stomach feel even emptier. He got dressed, rolled up the blanket and started out. Food first, he thought. And then…other things.

Kazeem ate that night at a farmhouse just southeast of Xan Tabik, sharing a meal—and something more—with a lonely widow almost twenty years his senior. He never saw her again, and he felt badly about it for months.

Nasoh was in the next town he stopped in. He never saw Kazeem, who watched, hooded, from another table as they both ate in a small café. Nasoh left with a whore, and Kazeem killed him quietly as he slept after the woman went home. Nasoh was a nothing, a nobody, and Kazeem didn't hate him the way he hated Garth and Spinner. He was anxious to move on. He wanted to take more time with the next two, be more…deliberate, which was exactly what they deserved.

He was almost a mile out of town when he went back, found the whore Nasoh had been with, told her that he had been killed, and advised her to move on as well. He left her with a pocketful of gold coins, and got back on his horse enjoying the incredulous look on her face.

*

The dreams continued. The old man, the two men he hunted, geysering blood swirling into red mist by strong desert winds, inchoate anger, hate.

In these dreams Kazeem often asked someone in the shadows: *what is truth?* It seemed a very poignant question at those times, yet slipped from his mind during the day. The answer from the shadows was always the same.

Whatever you make it.

The world changed. *He* changed during the next couple of years, but his goal, his motivation, never varied. It was an older, leaner, more muscular Kazeem that finally stumbled across the town of Torbin Cem, the pivotal point in Kazeem's life so far. Here, in this awful, oven-like place of baking rock and red sands Kazeem planned the revenge he'd lusted after since that terrible day in the laundry—where they'd taken so much from him. Here, at Torbin Cem, he planned cold-blooded murder, with bloody torture as the vehicle of death.

Finding the two had taken longer than he had expected, but pinning down their movements now took almost no time at all. He'd become an expert at moving unseen, came and went like a ghost.

Against the night chill of the wastelands, Kazeem wore a long sealskin coat of dark gray, which hid his weapons nicely. He avoided bright colors, designs on clothes, eelskin, goat, martin or fox, which brought unwanted attention. He kept cool gray muslin for the day, and favored the headgear he'd taken from the Home: a dirt-colored scarf wrapped around his head, loose end hanging down one side of his face under the wide-brimmed drover hat with its plaited leather band. In short, day or night, he looked like a hundred others, which was exactly his intention.

*

"Should I know you?" this segment of the dream began. "I feel as if I should."

"Nothing in nature is isolated," came the cryptic reply.

"Must you always answer questions with questions?" As always, they were at the ring of boulders. It was either twilight or dawn. As always.

"Isn't a question still a reply, even, perhaps, an answer, under the proper circumstances?"

"There, you just did it again," a smug Kazeem pointed out.

"Are you ready to come home?" the known/unknown voice asked abruptly.

"I don't have one to go to. Besides, I have things to do."

"Things that will send your soul to hell."

"I've already done that," Kazeem told the shadow-man. His voice held certainty, but no fear. He had decided long ago that, from now on, *he* would be the fear.

"Have you, irrevocably?"

"Either one has, or one hasn't," Kazeem replied irritably.

"You are an expert on such matters?"

"I don't know what I am; I only know what I must do."

"Every action sets in motion another action, a whole series of actions, like a cascade of dominoes."

"As you have said, old man, nothing under God's Heaven is isolated."

"You *believe* in the Creator?"

Kazeem had to think about that for a moment. "Yes, but I do not know if *He* believe in me."

"Such arrogance!"

Kazeem shrugged.

"Today's actions will influence lives you haven't even imagined."

"Still, I must act, or have no peace."

"You'll find no peace in what you mean to do. Trust me when I say, every action has consequences, sometimes dire ones, even if we can't see them at the time."

As always, there was more. As always, Kazeem woke up with the rest slipping away. He drank some water, and went back to sleep. This time he dreamt about Kali, and when he woke again he began to cry. He felt as if something inside of him was broken, and it took at least an hour for that awful feeling to go away. He slept fitfully after that, but at least there were no more dreams.

When he got up in his rented room the next day he knew only one thing for sure: he had to act fast, because he was sure he was losing his mind.

Or, finding it, which amounted to the same thing.

*

Kazeem of Zamboria was now a man if still a young one, but he carried himself in such a way that set him apart and most people left him alone.

It wasn't his size, which was only slightly taller than average, but the way in which he moved, the cast of his eyes, the set of his jaw. Because he looked older than he was, he had easy access to bars and adult entertainment. That, by itself, wasn't any great accomplishment. These places were few and far between, especially in this territory, and, as such, were always crowded. Law in this region forbade alcohol, tobacco and prostitution, but Torbin Cem was on the border, almost in Calat, where rules were not so readily enforced. The trade was brisk, with Calatians, Vendarians and Ankorians vying with Zamborian citizens for the attention of very busy professional women. Not many local girls worked in Torbin Cem—it was too close to home—but if you looked long enough you'd find a good, old-fashioned Zamborian entrepreneur who would point you in the right direction. Still, these particular ladies-of-the-evening were very exotic; some came from as far away as Jartron-Ibek, Dacia, even Dembark. Rumor had it that a couple of the fair-skinned women came from far across the Vast Expanse, the ocean Easterners called the *Tally-fal*, from almost legendary places like Calisia, Valsack and Arconia. Seeing what each girl had to offer, he concluded that most of them, while perhaps not exactly local, were at least at home on *this* continent. People didn't travel three thousand miles to spend their evenings on their backs. Kazeem noticed something else, too, having spent much of his spare time with them—each and every one of them was looking for a way to get out of the business, even for one night, and would take an over-night encounter if it paid enough. Kazeem felt bad for them, but didn't pity them. In his own mind they weren't much different from him. Selling yourself, whatever the reason, was something he was quite familiar with.

The main room of the bar was crowded. Men slouched in chairs, held slim glasses full of pale amber liquids, mugs of warm brown beer, and cups of honey wine. The air was full of the mixed odors of roast pork, tobacco smoke, the sweat of the dancers and the mostly unwashed men in attendance. Kazeem took a seat near the door, as far from the action as he could get, and kept his back against the wall. With his hat on, with only lamps and rushlights to illuminate the place, no one would be able to tell how old he was. In fact, thanks to the near-naked dancers, who wore no more than silk and satin sashes, no one would *care*.

It took less than ten minutes for a woman to find him sitting alone in the corner as he sipped a tiny cup of strong black coffee.

"Hello, old Bear," she said. When he flashed a smile she slid onto the chair beside him and kissed his cheek. "Haven't seen you around for a while. Where you been?"

"Here and there, Saryn, here and there." Kazeem caught the barman's eye, and he sent a waiter. "Drink, my love?" Kazeem asked.

"Sure, Bear, thanks." She told the waiter what they wanted, and turned back to Kazeem. "You going out tonight?"

Going out tonight was code for *Do you want me?* but avoided the letter of the law by being just shy of out-and-out solicitation. Kazeem smiled, amused by the endearment. Bear. Bearstone. The women here had been calling him that for so long that he had actually forgotten the original false name he'd used. Why Bearstone? He wasn't sure, but he liked it.

"I *am* out, lil' darlin'," he told her as the waiter returned with honey wine for her, mineral water for him. He rather favored the Vendarian accent he affected; it made him feel randy.

Saryn slapped his upper arm playfully. "You know what I mean, silly!"

"I know *exactly* what you mean, you little vixen," he told her with a leer that was God's own truth and no lie. Saryn was a Zamborian with a light brown, very creamy complexion, big dark eyes and blonde hair that she rinsed with henna, giving it a wonderful strawberry tint. Her lips were lush and full and pink, perfectly, exquisitely shaped, and unlike a lot of the other girls she kept her teeth clean. Her figure was—well, she was twenty, thank the Maker. What more needed to be said? The only problem with being with Saryn was that the red hair made him think of Bel. He prayed to God that she didn't end up in a place like this, but at the same time he wondered why the MAKER OF ALL THINGS would even *bother* listening to the likes of him.

"So," Saryn asked, wrapping both arms around one of his and leaning into him, "do you want to get out of here or what?"

"I do," he said after a bit of a pause, "but *all* the way out, if you follow me?"

"No, I don't get it."

For a moment Kazeem couldn't get visions of Kalina and Bel out of his head. It was a pain that was almost physical, and he had to grit his teeth until it passed. Thankfully, it didn't take long, and Saryn didn't notice.

"What would it take for Paarnor to let you leave for the evening?"

Saryn raised her eyebrows. "This early? I don't know, Bear. A lot."

He pointed to his ear. "Tell me."

She pouted, sighed, rolled her eyes, and whispered a probable figure.

Kazeem allowed his head to bob playfully between his shoulders, as if considering. "Okay, you're worth it."

"Are you serious? Why?"

Kazeem found himself growing angry. He took her chin in one hand, and forced her to look up at him. "Don't ever sell yourself short, Saryn, not even over a matter such as this. Underestimating yourself is a bad habit to get into, and you'll meet enough people to do it for you. Trust me on this."

"All right, Bear," the girl said softly.

Kazeem stroked her chin with kind fingertips. Saryn closed her eyes, and sighed. "Go tell your boss I want to see him."

"All right," she breathed again.

Kazeem's heart was racing as she walked away. He hated himself for using her, but, then again, he hadn't thought much of himself *before* coming in here, either.

He bit his lip, drank his water, and tried not to think about it. Crying in a place like this didn't strike him as a particularly good idea.

Instead, he watched the show and waited for Saryn to return.

*

After funds changed hands, Paarnor released her for the night. Kazeem was known as a big spender, and always left good tips. The boss liked him, the girls loved him. He hadn't expected a problem.

"Why did you want to go out tonight?" she asked, taking his arm under the stars.

"I *am* out," he teased.

"Remind me I'm not talking to you," she giggled.

"With what *I've* got in mind, you won't need to talk." He regretted the words as soon as he said them. He'd meant to amuse, not embarrass, her. Saryn blushed fiercely. "No, really," he amended, talking fast. "I just want some company tonight. *Your* company, if you want the truth." It disturbed him to know that it *was* the truth. A relationship was something he just couldn't afford. Not now. Maybe not ever.

Saryn opened her mouth, but closed it with an almost audible snap without speaking.

"We can go to that little cafe on the other side of town, and have dinner," he suggested.

Saryn glanced at the sky. "You know, I think the market might still be open. Would you be offended if I cooked for you at home? We can go to my place. It isn't far."

Kazeem was so touched that he didn't trust himself to speak. All he could manage was a smile and a nod.

She began to rattle off her menu items. He struggled to pretend interest, knowing he was only using her, but feeling so much more. He had walked a hundred yards with one fist clenched before he realized he was doing it, and tried to relax. It was a nice soft night, not humid at all, with a gentle breeze coming from the coast. The curtains were fluttering very softly, rhythmically, invitingly in the upstairs window of the small room Saryn shared with another girl, one who would be away most or all of the night.

Kazeem carried the two grocery sacks up the stairs for her, and put them down on the table. Saryn made tea, and set about preparing the dinner. Kazeem sat nearby while she worked.

"So," she said, tossing back her hair, "what is it with you tonight?" Her head was cocked, her eyes intense. Whatever else she might have been, she wasn't stupid.

He leaned forward to take his cup from the table. "I told you," he said, and took a sip, "I wanted to be with you tonight."

"You could have *been with me* half a dozen times by now."

"I didn't mean it like that. Besides, wouldn't that have been... well, *work* to you?"

Saryn seemed to give the question a moment of serious thought. "No, not with you. You're a friend. The other stuff we share, that's something else. Not work, though. Something else."

He nodded. "I feel the same way."

Saryn paused, knife in one hand, a mushroom in the other. "I'm glad to hear that. You never talk about your feelings."

Kazeem sat back with the cup in his lap. "I don't like to talk about myself."

"So I've noticed."

Kazeem shrugged. "I've led a pretty boring life, actually."

"I, uh, somehow think that's stretching the truth."

He smiled. "You're certainly entitled to your opinion."

"And you're entitled to my thanks," she said with a catch in her voice.

He sat up straight again, cup in both hands. "Do what *you* want tonight, Saryn. You have the night off, and you don't owe me a thing."

"All right," she said quietly, and lowered her eyes demurely.

Kazeem had all but fallen asleep when she came to him. The breeze, the cooking...how he longed to stay here, love her, marry her, and wondered dumbly why he didn't do just that. Was this how it was *supposed* to be?

"Dinner's ready."

He stirred, grunting as he got up. The stress of what he planned to do, and the way he was using this girl had made him tense and sore. "Great. I think I could eat an ox."

Saryn had fixed a mushroom soup with cream and herbs, a broiled piece of fish for each of them, salad, cheesecake with local blackberries for dessert, and enough coffee to make one cup for each of them.

They talked like normal people all through dinner, and Kazeem almost forgot his grief and his guilt. He fought with himself to find another way, but sublimated those feelings, knowing he'd already gone too far. He'd chosen this path of his own free will, and now there was nowhere to go but straight ahead.

After coffee she took him to bed. She got on top, kissed him, kissed his neck, kissed his chest. She edged down the bed, kissing as she went. Her hair felt like silk. Saryn took him places he'd never been, and for the rest of his life he'd remember the breeze, the warmth of her body, the softness of her skin, and how beautiful she looked in the moonlight.

Later, lying in each other's arms, she looked up at him. "Hey, during supper you told me you had a favor to ask. What was it?" Her voice sounded so trusting and honest that he thanked God he had his eyes half closed.

For an instant, he almost called it off, but the moment passed, and he found himself speaking.

"An old friend's in town. I want to surprise him, and I could use your help."

"Sure. How?" She was up on one elbow, her hair golden in the moonlight.

"I want you to bring him someplace for me. You know, so I can surprise him."

"Where to?"

"I'll tell you tomorrow."

Saryn shrugged, laid her head on his chest and hugged him. "Okay. He a local guy?"

"No, he's only been in town about a week."

"What's his name?"

"Fegan," Kazeem said as icy coldness crept into his limbs. "Garth Fegan."

*

The ground was perfectly flat; exactly what he'd been looking for. Kazeem sat on one of the many boulders in the area, and took his lunch from the sack: an orange, a big piece of unleavened bread, a small container of long-grain rice, and a jar of honey. He pulled the drover hat down over his eyes as protection against the midday sun, and began to eat.

A ring of large red rocks encircled the little clearing of granite. The place was level, with only one or two depressions in the stone floor. It hadn't rained in weeks, so the stony hillock was hot and dry, but he'd found what he'd been seeking right away, in tiny fissures between the rock, where moss thumbed its nose at the desert heat and tiny plants clung to small patches of soil against all odds.

The fire ants beneath his feet (so named because of their color and furious bite) swarmed in and out of the earth, making two columns, very much like a human army, one column heading away, the other heading back and down into the bowels of the earth. The ants carried miniscule pieces of sand many times larger than they were, and, most interestingly, tiny chunks of flesh from a dead bird so weather-worn and desiccated that no other predator would want it. As Kazeem ate he dropped pieces of his lunch by the sides of each column: bread, rice, orange, it didn't seem to matter. Each was scooped up with equal enthusiasm. The ants took each without hesitation, then hurried off with it to do whatever it is that ants do.

Then he poured the honey near the entrance to their lair. In seconds the entire colony was out. Kazeem squatted close by, watching. They all came out for the honey, swarming like thousands of little maniacs. It didn't take long for them to clean the rocks as smooth as a dry bone, and Kazeem was convinced that, had he covered the dead bird—or anything else—with the honey, they would have stripped *that* clean in short order, too.

Before putting the top back on the honey pot, Kazeem dipped in a finger. He lowered it to where the ants could climb on, and suffered a couple of painful bites that confirmed his theory. The dead ants that he crushed between his fingers and dropped back onto the rock were consumed with equal fervor. Kazeem nodded, rubbed a small amount of baylor salve onto his wounded finger, and got up.

Working swiftly, he hammered four spikes with eyelets into cracks around the ant colony. Each was a little less than six feet away from its counterpoint, or the distance of a supine man with his arms and legs spread out. He hammered four more into the rock wall above the first four, doing so after putting his back to the wall and making sure he could see the first four spikes without any problem. He figured that both sets of spikes were no more than ten feet away from each other.

When he was finished he headed back to the rented packhorse and slowly made his way back to town.

Paarnor's was open even this early, and he went in and sat down at the bar, ordering coffee. He had only recently started to smoke—and sparingly—and lit one now.

Saryn appeared five minutes after he asked for her.

"Hi," she said, and kissed him on the cheek. "Did you want me again so soon?"

"Yes, always." He longed to take her in his arms, bring her away with him, and stop this madness.

He wanted to, but didn't. He just couldn't.

"I also came to tell you where I want to meet my friend," he managed with a smile.

*

What he planned to do should have sickened him, *would* have sickened any normal person, but a kind of madness had seized Kazeem, one in which rending, cutting or even killing was not going to be enough to satisfy him. What he wanted for his foes was *pain*, and not just any kind of pain, either. Only a pain filled with horror and loss and loathing would do—a pain that would help them to remember what they had done to others.

What they had done to *him*.

The horse bucked as he started up the slight slope towards the rocky clearing. The bound figure lying across the saddle in front of him moaned, but didn't wake. Kazeem knew he could have taken both of them in a fair fight, but he wasn't interested in a fight, he was interested in torture. Not for the first time, Kalina's face popped into his head, and he wondered what she would think of him if she knew.

His plan was simple: hide the drugged Spinner until Saryn brought Garth, then wait for her to go.

Tucking the bound and gagged Spinner into a tiny rock alcove was no problem. He slept like a log, but that wouldn't last. Exactly on time Saryn showed up with the equally useless Garth, likewise drugged, but still semiconscious and able to keep his feet with help. Kazeem thanked her, kissed her, and handed her an envelope that he made her promise not to open until she got home.

A turnip could tell that the parcel contained leifa notes, but Saryn's eyes were sad.

"I'm not going to see you again, am I?"

"I don't know," he admitted, and, for the first time, in his own voice. Other than their lovemaking, it was the most honest moment they had ever shared.

"Don't do this," she begged, holding on to him. "Whatever this is, don't do it. Leave now. With me. I'll go wherever you say, *do* whatever you say." She tried to blink back tears, but one trickled down her check. He wiped it away with a gloved finger. "Please."

"Saryn." He didn't trust his voice. "I can't. I can't let them— If you only knew..." In a moment, *he* would he crying, and that just wouldn't do. He turned to lower Garth to the stone, but Saryn pulled him to his feet with surprising strength.

"I know every time I look in your eyes, Bear. You have scars on your body, but the hurt in your eyes is worse." She softly, tenderly touched the side of his face with the backs of her fingers. In a whisper she added, "I also know this won't ease the pain."

He turned his head, took her fingers in his hand, and kissed them. It took every ounce of willpower he had not to shed a tear.

"I'll come to you when I can, Saryn."

She regarded him for a long moment, making up her mind, and then she stuffed the money in a pocket and shook her head.

"No, you won't. I'll never see *you* again. The *you* you are right now will be gone if you do this." She shook her head again. Her hair swished from side to side, and tears spilled from her lovely dark eyes. "I just hope you know what you're throwing away."

She turned her back, walking slowly, giving him every opportunity to call her, run to her, and catch her.

But he didn't. He just couldn't live while *they* lived.

Oh, he took a step forward, stumbled, bit his lip, started forward again, paused and shook his head helplessly.

And then she was gone, the echo of her horse's hooves sounding like the death toll of a tocsin. It was now or never, the chance for a normal life, but he didn't take it. He just let her go. He knew in his heart that nothing lasts forever. He had loved Bel and Kalina, and he had lost them just the same. Then he said the hell with it and started after her. He had gotten maybe six feet when Garth mumbled drunkenly. Kazeem stopped, and turned around—and then looked back at Sayrn, struggling with his conflicting emotions.

There'd be no going back to her later. He knew that, but the pull on him was stronger than he cared to admit. The urge to finish this was *overwhelming*, made his heart beat faster, took away his breath, controlled him, and made him feel like an entirely different person.

Which, he supposed, he was.

The chains for binding Garth to the wall were already in place. In his condition it was short work to secure him. The young man slumped, but a cup of cold water and a slap or two brought him around.

Next, Kazeem built a fire with cedar and balsam, got it roaring inside a ring of stones, and sat cross-legged, on a rock, waiting for Garth to realize whom he was. The sun was going down, painting the rocks red and gold and orange. The fire lit Kazeem's face from below. If he could have seen himself at that moment, it would have given him pause. He looked like a demon from hell.

"You son of a bitch!" Garth slurred and jerked the chains.

Kazeem said nothing. He sat still until Garth was struggling mightily. When he was satisfied with his level of consciousness, he went and stood, wordless, before him.

"You bastard! You lunatic! What do you want from me?"

"Do you know who I am, Garth?" Kazeem asked quietly, and, until that moment, it still could have gone either way.

"I know who you are, you freak! What're you going to do now, ream out *my* ass? Big deal. Think I never had *my* shit pushed in before? Me, *or* that little slut you love?"

When Kazeem ignored that, Garth knew he was in serious trouble.

"As long as you know who I am, Garth Fegan."

"I know you, Kazeem, son of a weakling!" His eyes hardened, and he spat, his final mistake. "You probably *enjoyed* what we did to you! Your *girlfriend* did!"

Kazeem smiled. Talking was no longer necessary, and a strange peace, born of certainty, spread through his body. "You never *were* too smart, Fegan."

Spinner was just coming to when Kazeem dragged him by the collar to the crack in the rock. The ants were not present as the sun went down, and only the fire lit the rocks, but Kazeem wasn't worried about it at the moment.

"Who's that? Hey! What are you doing?"

Kazeem staked Spinner face down over the crack. He was waking up, and the sound of Garth's voice pulled him the rest of the way.

"Garth? That you? What's going on?" He tied to get up, but the clinking chains stopped him. He could look up at Garth. They could see each other, but that was it.

"It's the weirdo," Garth answered. "Trying to scare us."

Kazeem took two small glass lamps from his pack, but did not light them. Each was filled to the top with lamp oil and tightly capped. He placed them on the ground away from the fire and reached back into his rucksack.

"What's that? What's he doing?" Spinner asked Garth in a high, squeaky voice.

"Got another one of them lamps," Garth said as Kazeem placed the honey pot by the lamps.

After that he took out some bread, sat down and began to eat, all without speaking a single word. The madness was in total control, and nothing on earth could have stopped him.

As he ate he tossed crumbs of bread down on Spinner, who was soon complaining.

"Hey! Ouch!"

"What's wrong?" Garth asked. His chains clinked. He strained to see in the dark.

"It's buggy over here," Spinner whined. "Something bit me."

They talked among themselves, ignored by Kazeem, who continued to eat. Their conversation was punctuated by an occasional complaint from Spinner.

"What's going on here, Kazeem?" Garth finally demanded.

Kazeem got up. Quite a bit of time had gone by. The fire was lower, but there was still enough light to see by.

"I'm going to ask a question," Kazeem said quietly. "You'll have one chance to answer it, and only one. If it's not the answer I want, you'll die badly. In fact, you'll wish you were never born."

"He's just messing with us," Garth said. "Don't listen to him."

Kazeem uncapped the honey, went to Spinner, squatted, and made him look up by grabbing his chin.

"Do you know what this is?" he asked. His voice was cold, dead, and quiet.

Spinner shook his head, honestly confused. Kazeem stuck a finger in the jar and then rubbed the honey across Spinner's lips.

"What's he saying?" Garth demanded.

"Pay attention, Garth," Kazeem said without looking at him. "I want you to see this. When I'm done with him, it'll be your turn."

"I ain't afraid of you!" Garth sneered, but his voice said otherwise.

"Yeah, well, you never were too bright," Kazeem replied. He looked at Garth for a moment, and then lowered his eyes to Spinner. Both boys were shaking from fear, from the cold, and from the drugs wearing off. To Spinner Kazeem whispered, "I've staked you out on an ant hill." His voice was death. Garth couldn't hear what was being said, but Spinner was suddenly screaming, vomiting, squirming frantically, and bruising his wrists on the chains.

"What's he doing?" Garth said with equal, unqualified panic. "What's happening?"

"I want to know where the girl is," Kazeem asked.

"Which one?" Spinner asked. "I'll tell you anything, I promise. Only...God...let me up. They're really biting now!"

"Either one," Kazeem said.

"I don't know who you're talking about!" Spinner yelped.

"Kalina? Bel? Where?" Kazeem asked.

"Who the hell knows?" Spinner screamed.

"Too bad," Kazeem said, and held out the jar.

"Look, I swear I would tell you if I knew. Please!"

Kazeem nodded understandingly, and then poured the honey all over him. The gooey substance, made pliable by its proximity to the heat, came out of the jar quickly.

Spinner went insane as the colony swarmed up. He threw names, locations and towns at Kazeem, who frowned and nodded.

"Too late," he said, but made mental notes to check each somewhere down the road.

Kazeem got up, and dumped what was left on Spinner's head.

"Dear God! What are you *doing* to him?" Garth screamed. He gagged, and abruptly lost his own lunch.

"Ants! They're ANTS! Everywhere!" Spinner was spitting them out. They were on his face, on his back, all over. No one had ever heard more pitiful, more panicked, pain wracked screams.

They made Kazeem feel nothing.

"Kazeem! I *told* you!" The ants were in his mouth now, eating him alive. His voice wasn't what it had been. "I told you what you wanted to know!" The last word was a gurgled screech.

"Too late," Kazeem repeated, and crossed to Garth, who was gasping for breath with his head turned away.

Without a word Kazeem took one of Garth's fingers in a hand-held pincer. There was no warning as Kazeem snipped off the tip of that finger. For an instant, Garth's scream was louder than Spinner's.

"You *look* at him," Kazeem growled, showing emotion for the first time. "You look at him the whole time. If you look away, every *time* you look away, I'll cut off something else."

Garth begged, cried and screamed as Spinner, being eaten alive, thrashed as far as the chains would allow, but he kept his eyes pinned on him. Spinner was now completely covered with red ants, a thriving, writhing mass of death. He screamed pitifully for another couple of moments, and then went silent, although his ruined body continued to shake and jerk.

"Was it worth it, Garth?" Kazeem asked softly.

"Please, Kazeem. I'm sorry I did what I did. It was wrong, but don't do *that*." His voice was raw, hoarse and weak. Pitiful sobs wracked him, and snots dripped from his nose.

Kazeem pretended to consider. "All right. Not that." He was still talking when he poured the lamp oil on Garth and set him on fire. The screams were awful, but he'd used so much oil that they didn't last long. Kazeem put everything away, and then turned back to his victims. They were both dead beyond question, but he beheaded both of them anyway and walked away into the desert, leaving their remains to the ants and the flames and the darkness.

*

Kazeem was suicidal for several weeks after that awful night. He'd never hated anyone more than he hated himself during that time, and almost ended his own life more than once. If he allowed himself to live, he would never, ever do anything like that again. Killing was one thing, but this, this had been a sickness, madness beyond description.

He didn't eat, he didn't sleep; he simply wandered from place to place in the desert, dropping from exhaustion from time to time, taking water to ease his thirst. With the madness gone, he loathed himself, and saw no reason to go on.

If not for a chance encounter during the third week, he may very well have died in the sand, food for the buzzards, and rightly so, he reckoned.

A big man, a caravan master and a teamster, found him one morning as he passed with his wagons en route to Zamboor. It was a bright, brutally hot day, and anything left out in such burning sands would surely perish.

"Whoa, lads!" He yanked on the reins, pulling back hard. His team of horses was huge, white and heavily muscled, the type once called arabeans by the locals. The mount's eyes went wide at this treatment, whining loudly as he jerked them to a halt to prevent them from running over the scarecrow lying in the trail bed.

"Will ye look at this, boys?" he called over his shoulder. "Someone drag him out of there. If he's dead, lay 'im under yon banyan trees." He nodded at an oasis fifty yards north. "If he's breathing, we just found that extra hired hand we've been looking for."

A young man with long blond, almost white hair leapt down into the burning sand, pulling his sash across his face now that he was out of the protective shade of the canopy. He bent to turn the bony figure onto its back. The blond man raised his eyebrows at the weapons the boy carried: deadly-looking sword, knives, beaded garrote, and tiny caltrops in a leather bag. He leaned closer to check for breath.

"Man's a walking arsenal," he mumbled.

"What?" the wagon master asked.

"Huh? Nothing," the blond man replied.

"Well, is he alive or not?"

Kazeem's eyes flew open. One hand went to the back of the blond man's head; the other held a razor sharp dagger to his throat.

"Oh, yeah, boss," the blond caravan guard called nervously. "He's alive, all right!"

*

Kazeem gave a false name. What it was doesn't matter. This became a way of life for him for the next several weeks, and it was probably just as well. He no longer knew who he really was anyway. Saryn had been right. The person he had been—*could* have been— was long gone. There was no mirth in his eyes, no joy, no hint of passion—only the steely-eyed gaze of a natural born killer.

It didn't take long for his new friends to realize it, either. He'd been tending the horses, and doing chores around camp for a week or so, when the burly trail boss called it a day early one afternoon.

"Well, lads, a nice soft night we have coming up, judging by the breeze. Why don't we knock off early and run into town for a bit of fun, eh?"

They drew lots to pick guards, and then the lucky ones rode off, promising to bring back potable liquids other than water. Kazeem was in their number, armed to the teeth under his gray duster, and happy to have his mind occupied for a while.

The town had a name. What it was isn't important, either. A ragtag collection of huts and buildings thrown up around what passed for a main street, conveniently close to the Caravan Route, and the trade it brought.

They stopped at the first alehouse they could find, and didn't waste time bellying up to the bar. Half an hour later they were all in their cups except for Kazeem, who only drank when he was alone, and even then, sparingly. In public he was usually content with mineral water or coffee, which was the case tonight.

Kazeem stayed sober. He never wanted to be out of control again. Most people don't share that view, however, especially at week's end, and the locals were no exception. As drunk as his companions were, the town toughs had had a *huge* head start on the mead and honeywine that afternoon. Some of them sat pleasantly enough, sitting and staring off into space. Others nodded, their backs against the chair rails, their chins on their chests. A few played cards. One of the men sat with a plump serving girl in his lap; he was trying to kiss her but was so drunk he kept missing her mouth and ended up slobbering on her chin. She laughed, and slid a hand between his legs. This seemed to wake him from his near-stupor, but did nothing to improve his aim.

There were those, of course, who played darts and games like Tumble Die, talking politics in knowing tones.

Then, of course, there were the troublemakers, recognizable in any town the world over by their shifty eyes, lack of character and loud, obnoxious mouths. One such model citizen bumped rudely into Kazeem's drinking partner for the night, none other than the blond young man who had pulled him from the sand. His name was Persham, and they had become fast friends, as young men often do.

"Excuse me, sir," Persham, always the gentleman said, even though *he* was clearly not at fault.

"Excuseyorass," the drunk slurred. "You and your big tough friends."

"Hey, what we do to you?" another of Kazeem's crew asked from the end of the bar.

"It's okay, Tibok," Persham said. "The gentleman's obviously confused us with someone else."

The drunk leaned close, his breath in Persham's face; whatever his bloodshot eyes saw, it was clearly not the reality that was there. "The sonovabitch been screwing my wife." He lurched, belched, opened and closed his eyes drunkenly.

"His old lady's been gone two years now," one of his own pals put in. "Gods! Does he go on!"

"You've got the wrong guy," Kazeem said quietly. "Why don't you let it go?"

"Let nothing go," the drunk slurred.

"And we wonder why this stuff is illegal over most of the continent," Kazeem mumbled to himself.

"What did you say?" the drunk roared threateningly. He was too close to Kazeem, and this triggered his defense mechanisms. He'd never been able to control them before, and wondered if he'd be able to now. He slipped a hand inside his duster and loosened the knife in his belt.

"I said you've got the wrong guy," Kazeem repeated.

"I know he screwed her," the drunk repeated stubbornly, and with the certainty only the true alcoholic can muster.

"Wow, I didn't even know she was puttin' out again," Tibok quipped.

Someone else moaned. "God, here we go again," and managed to get it out just before the room went crazy.

The drunk threw a punch at Persham, who brought up a hand to block it, a hand that wasn't needed. The tip of Kazeem's gleaming wolf's head saber was at the man's throat in an instant, brought there with such speed that men were still talking about it days later. This is what he'd been born to, trained for. These men may have been drunk, but they weren't stupid. They knew death when they saw Him, and gave him wide berth. Suddenly, the drunk was on his own.

"I'll say this one last time," Kazeem whispered through clenched teeth: "You have the wrong man. What do *you* say?"

The drunk moved a hand, maybe because he was shaking, maybe because he was going to try for the sword at his belt. Either way, a twitch of Kazeem's right wrist and a bead of bright red blood sprang out at the side of the man's neck, and ran the length of the razor sharp blade.

Pain has a strange way of sobering a man. The sight of blood just makes the process quicker.

"I made a mistake," the man said, backing away, hands up. "*My* mistake," he added, bumping into the bar.

Kazeem still held the sword aloft with his right arm. His left hand, holding the blade of one of his knives, flashed into the corner, where one of the man's cronies was edging closer. The knife went through his cloak, pinning him to the wall. Pivoting, Kazeem advanced.

"Pull it out," he said, nodding at his knife. The man did as he was told as Kazeem raised his sword and placed the tip just below his left eye. "Put it on the table." This the man did. They were silent for a moment, their eyes meeting, and then Kazeem asked: "We're not going to have any trouble, are we?"

The man saw a willingness to kill in the young man's eyes, an *eagerness* he had seen only once before, in a starving wolf that took sheep for almost an entire winter when he was a lad. The young man before him had the same look the wolf had had on the day the farmers finally got it—a look that said quite clearly: *do your worst; there's nothing I haven't seen, and I could care less.*

How did you scare someone like that?

"No, no trouble," the man stammered.

"Go on about your business then."

The man backed out the door as Kazeem picked up the knife. He stood in the quiet room, a blade in each hand, walking in a slow circle.

"Anyone else?"

He waited several seconds, meeting eyes that suddenly had better things to look at. Then he nodded and returned to his stool.

"Barman," he said pleasantly, "I do believe my coffee has gone cold."

*

Kazeem, son of Kaidin stopped hiding his identity after that. Whatever else he was, he'd become a man—and men didn't hide. His reputation and his destiny stemmed mostly from that night in that nameless little town, a reputation that would not only earn him an incredible living—but have his name spoken of with awe and fear and respect on three different continents. He went forth from that night as his own man, openly daring the authorities to take him back. He was still wanted, but folks didn't seem to worry about that out at the fringes. Years later he would realize that they don't much care in the center of a city, either, and that his stay at the Home may have been politically motivated.

Of course, none of that would matter much by then.

There was one other thing that happened that night that would have an impact on his life later on, and that was the studied gaze of a professional mercenary who had stopped by chance for a drink. He was a tall, lean man, with cruel, scarred features and strange amber eyes. He watched the boy with keen interest that night, marking him well, for he was always searching for new talent.

Kazeem would one day know him as Graylan Malcor.

*

The next several months saw Kazeem harden into a very dangerous but more self-disciplined young man. He would carry the emotional scars of all that he'd been through for years, but he suspected he'd carry the scars of his revenge even longer—to the grave, and beyond.

He thought about Saryn several times during that year as summer wound down into what passed for fall in that hemisphere, and once even returned to the town where she lived. He stood one night looking up at her window, but in the end, stayed away. He could bring nothing good to her life now, and would only end up using her again, trying to find forgetfulness in her arms. Along with all the other ghosts he carried on his broad shoulders was the specter of the lovely Kalina Zamonar, who had reached the meadow at the end of life's trail. Kazeem thought about her every day, including the morning when he actually met the wizard from his tormented dreams.

CHAPTER FOURTEEN

THE MARKET PLACE had not been among his favorite things since the death of his father, but one had to eat. Besides, he thought with a wry smile that masked his true feelings: what better place to meet young women?

Kazeem sat his horse near the riverbank, exactly seven leagues from the port town of Jar-ot-abuohm. He'd come far that night, riding hard, the feeling of both predator and prey strong within him. He'd had the dreams again last night, more intense than ever before. So intense, in fact, that for the first time he actually felt compelled to act on one. He had a feeling that he would, indeed, meet someone today, but he was also somehow sure that it wouldn't be a girl.

Kazeem blinked. The sunlight coming off the river was bright. A scull was making its way across the wide, shallow ford to his left, oars dripping silver droplets under the early morning sun. He caught a glimpse of the old, white-haired man being ferried across, but turned away because of the glare. Old men didn't concern him. Dreams or no dreams, the market was simply teeming with sweet young things, all, no doubt, just dying to meet him.

There was an attended hitching post just outside the farrier's shop, and Kazeem left his roan mare to rest and take water. Come to think of it, he was more than a mite thirsty himself. He smiled at the ladies as he went through the growing crowd, but only the most intrepid of girls smiled back. Not only was it considered unladylike to flirt with perfect strangers, but the awful truth of the matter was that when

Kazeem smiled that quaint little *I-could-care-less-about-anything* smile of his, he looked more than a little insane. Since Saryn, he had attracted only the most knowledgeable of women, usually much older and in search of a little excitement with a seemingly dangerous younger man. Kazeem enjoyed these encounters, but they left him feeling lonely. He wanted someone closer to his own age, someone—

"What was her name?" a gravelly voice intruded on his thoughts suddenly.

Kazeem blinked. He was sitting at an outdoor café, a steaming mug of coffee before him, with absolutely no memory of how he got there.

"Huh?" was all he could manage.

"The girl who broke your heart," the speaker explained. He was a tall, solidly built old man with steel-gray hair and a weathered face. He may have been fifty, but his strange gray eyes looked ancient, and strong.

Kazeem somehow managed to recover. He wiped his mouth on a cloth napkin while gathering his composure. "Do I know you, sir?" His question was polite; his tone was unfriendly.

The man crossed his arms. "You tell me."

"I've killed men for less," Kazeem scoffed. "Be off!"

"Is that really something you want to brag about?" the man asked, running a powerful-looking hand through his close-cropped hair.

"Look, I don't know who you are, but—"

"What if I told you I was a close friend of your father's?"

"My old man's been gone a long time."

"Maybe I knew him long ago."

"You never knew my father."

"Let's just say I'm someone your father asked to keep an eye on you."

"Great job you've done," Kazeem said sarcastically.

"Well, I'm a little late," the old man explained.

Kazeem was angry, but he was also unsettled. Something told him he *should* know this man, *had* known him long ago. Still, he was also afraid, and that made him hostile. "I'm tired of your gas, and you've worn out your welcome!"

The man rose as if to go. "I've never stayed where I'm not wanted, but hear this before I leave. I could tell you about other continents, other worlds within our own and your place in them. I could tell you that you're destined to be a man of great importance, and that that fact is known, not just to me, but to others that would not wish you well. I could tell you that there is a driving force behind all the evil that has befallen you, but I'll leave it at this before I go: consider your dreams—yes, I know all about them—and then consider my face one last time. Do you not know me, Kazeem son-of-Kaidin?"

Kazeem looked, looked deeper. Gazing into those unnatural gray eyes was like gazing into his own past: him as a young boy, his father—alive and strong, other men, all training at a camp hidden away in the mountains, a camp where men learned the way of the Wrotmar, where their leader was an old man who looked the same then as he did today, a fierce fighter and a wise philosopher they had known only as...

"Windor, is it you?" the boy gasped. "Is it *really* you?"

"It's time to come home, son," his father's mentor said gently.

Once again Kazeem's life could have gone either way, but this time he chose the right path. Unable to help it, he began to cry like a baby, but with the old man's arm around his shoulder he didn't seem to care, in fact, no one even noticed.

On their way out, after Kazeem regained some semblance of control, the wizard-like old man spoke again.

"You never did tell me her name."

"Who?" Kazeem asked, and sniffed. He swung one leg over the roan.

"The girl who broke your heart."

Kazeem tugged on the reins, looking out at the desert as the tears started again. "She didn't exactly break my heart, Windor. She died." He wanted to say more, wanted to blame himself, but he bit his lip. It was a waste of time, and it wasn't going to do anyone any good.

Windor's eyes bored into his, unblinking in the brutal, unrelenting glare of that hot, pre-noon sun. "Amounts to the same thing, doesn't it?"

Kazeem wanted to admit that that was one way to look at it, but he just couldn't do it. Not today. Too much burdened his soul as it was. "If we have work to do, old man, let's get to it. It helps me not to think."

"Then that'll be the first thing we change," Windor said with a grin as he grabbed the reins. "A warrior who doesn't think isn't much of a threat."

They started out, but Kazeem wasn't listening. He was thinking about Kalina, about how he'd basically left her to die. He shook his head, and wiped his tears away on his shoulders as he held the reins, first one, and then the other. He'd never know for sure if she'd lived or died, or what had happened to her after the collapse of that awful stairwell. And he knew he would wonder about it for the rest of his life, regardless of what Windor had to teach him.

*

At almost the exact same instant in which Kazeem was beginning his apprenticeship, a beautiful young blonde woman was beginning one of her own. The men on the hill watching her through a spyglass couldn't have known this, though. All they knew was how strong and attractive she was, with fair skin, full lips and gorgeous, sea green eyes. All they knew was that they had been hunting the men who were now hunting *her*.

The thing was, she was watching, too, waiting as the slaver's caravan bounced over the hard trail cutting through the barren steppes of Eastern Vendar like a scar. Dust told the story in this mountain country, but cold winds sweeping down quickly cleared the air. Steam rose from the packhorses' wide backs, their hooves kicking clods of dirt. The girl was currently unseen by the main body of the caravan as she hid behind a huge cedar, her horse's head wreathed in morning mist, but the scouts knew where she was, and were closing in fast.

The first mountain man lowered the spyglass and turned to his companion, who was older by several years. "What do you think, Sarth?"

The older man pulled off a glove with his teeth and scratched the stubble on his chin with curled fingertips. "I think, Ineer, that she's in trouble." He pointed. "She's been seen."

"I think so, too. Should we help her?" Ineer was young and brash. The girl was luscious. Naturally, he wanted to help her.

"Wait. Give it a minute. Let's see what happens."

The younger man nodded, but he wasn't happy about it. "Can we at least get closer?" There was honest concern on the younger man's wide face, and compassion, as well.

Sarth was a brutal, efficient fighter, but he was not without feelings. He grabbed the back of the young man's upper arm. "Of course. But be careful."

The girl was good. She had natural instincts, but she was inexperienced and hadn't yet seen the scouts. The thing was, she had gotten off the trail when she'd heard the caravan coming, but she was impatient now, ignorant of the ways of range scouts, and that was what had gotten her in trouble.

Both scouts had lost her for a moment, but picked her up again as she attempted to move around some bushes. Her horse was rigged for silence, with every buckle padded, and she was trying to keep the foliage between herself and the passing column. As she edged out, one of the scouts broke off and rode high, climbing the bank behind her. The other dropped back, knowing her attention would be riveted on the larger body. As she watched them pass, he lagged, and after they'd gone, he rode straight at her, coming from an angle on the other side of the trail. He used the same foliage she'd picked as a screen, and with her attention elsewhere, she never saw him coming. He took her blindside, leaping off his horse and knocking her to the ground with a thud and a big puff of dust. He got up first, attempting to yell to his partner, but she kicked him flush in the face, getting some nose and mouth. He grunted and went flat on his back, blood staining the front of his robes. By this time the girl was on her own feet, a wicked-looking dagger in her right hand.

The girl swiped right then left, the handle firm in her palm, blade facing down, sharp edge out. The mountain men took this in from their screen, a moss-covered clump of gray boulders. They shook their heads and looked at each other. Whatever else she was, the blonde girl was a born knife fighter.

The scout was back on his heels, too winded to call for help, too busy to take his eyes from her. Twice now she had only just missed opening his midsection; once she had even sliced through his clothing, drawling a razor thin line of beaded blood.

"She'll *kill* him," Ineer whispered with respect.

"Don't forget the other bastard," Sarth cautioned. He jutted his chin at the second scout, who had dismounted and was making his way through the cedar trees with a long knife in his hand.

"Should we help?" Ineer asked urgently.

Sarth put a hand on his shoulder, restraining him. "Wait."

"But you know what they'll do to her!"

"Wait."

The young man bit his tongue. Meanwhile the scout had fought for some breathing room and had gotten his own knife out. He and the girl circled each other, talking in breathless hisses. Sarth and Ineer were still too far away to hear what was being said, but they could imagine well enough.

"Can we at least get a little closer, just in case?" Ineer complained.

"Aye," Sarth agreed. "That much we can do. But be careful, we don't want to bring that whole column back down on us."

Ineer kept one eye glued to the girl on the way down. She was good with that knife, and very brave; her face was a mask as she fought, but there was no way she was going to outmuscle two grown men once they got their hands on her. This would only end one way unless he and Sarth did something about it, and they had to do it quickly, before the scouts were missed.

The girl was holding her own, keeping her attacker at bay, so Sarth and Ineer took their time, keeping silent, but when the second scout took her by surprise, grabbing her from behind and pinning her arms, they broke cover and ran, hoping their approach was lost in the chaos.

Ending up with a handful of more-than-ample breast surprised and delighted scout number two. "Hey, she's a girl!" he called to his friend.

"You think?" the first one said sarcastically. He was out of breath and nicked in several places. Needless to say, he was embarrassed and not too happy. He backhanded the girl without another word, cutting her lip. She sagged in the other one's arms, but got her feet under her as soon as he started to get too free with his hands.

"Nice one, too!" the second scout exclaimed, holding both breasts now. The first one violently ripped open her shirt.

"Let's take a closer look!" the other one said, and forced her to the ground with his friend's help. They had her naked in seconds; her thrashing only helped their efforts, and while the second held her the first got on top of her and pinned her down.

"Me first. I'm the one she tried to gut!"

"Just don't take too long!"

"Look at her!" the first commanded. "Just *look* at her! How long do you think it'll take?" He laughed as he said this, and pried her legs apart. She fought, but the two of them were too strong for her.

"Gods! She's beautiful!" the second scout exclaimed. A thin thread of drool actually escaped one corner of his mouth. "Hurry up. We can make it last the next time. Come on, come on, I can't wait!"

"Afraid you're going to have to," a gruff voice said from behind just as the girl began to scream.

The words were accompanied by action, as a club-wielding Ineer hit the man over the head. The weapon was a knobkerrie, favored by the *urlkin*, the dark elves, and Ineer was not gentle. The man's skull cracked like an eggshell, and he dropped sideways like a stone, dead before he hit the ground.

The first scout was getting to his feet when Sarth pulled him back, yanking by long, greasy hair, and slit his throat with a dagger, all in one motion. The scout's chest and belly were suddenly, shockingly covered in blood. Sarth tossed him aside contemptuously.

As naked as the day she was born, the girl regained her knife and got behind a tree where she could watch both of them.

"We're not going to hurt you," Sarth explained.

"Couldn't wait your turn?" the girl asked between choked sobs.

She was so beautiful, so voluptuous, that Sarth had to force himself to look away before he could speak again. "They'll have heard you scream, and they'll miss their scouts. They'll send out a search party shortly, trust me."

The girl looked at the dead bodies, and that seemed to help her make up her mind. "I'll trust you long enough to get my clothes." She brandished the bloody knife. "Back up!"

"Look, we're not *with* them," Ineer tried to explain.

"I'm on my way to join the Judge's band," she told them. "So don't interfere with me, or you'll pay for it!"

Sarth and Ineer shared an amused look. "Would it help if we turned our backs while you dressed?" Sarth asked.

"Would it help *you* if our circumstances were reversed?" she asked with a plea in her voice, sobs hitching her words.

"Turn around, Ineer," Sarth ordered.

Ineer hadn't stopped staring, and he wasn't looking at the knife, either. "I'll try."

"Turn around!" he snapped. Then to her, "Go on, get those clothes on."

"Will you look?" she asked like a child.

"We'll respect you, young lady," Sarth promised, "but your beauty is such that it won't be easy."

She dashed out, got her clothes, and ran back behind the tree. To their credit, neither man looked while she got dressed.

"Hurry now," Sarth urged when she was through. "Go get your horse. We haven't much time."

Ineer had moved back towards the boulders. "I hear them already," he warned.

They took the horses and led them into the cedar grove just as the first caravan guard produced a cloud of dust on the trail. With no choice, the girl trusted them enough to allow them to lead her to a back trail screened by more boulders.

"Why do you seek the Judge?" Ineer asked.

"To join his band. He needs good fighters, I hear, and I would help in his cause." She lowered her eyes. "I am an orphan, with nowhere else to go." She looked up again, suddenly defiant. "Who are you?"

"I am Sarth. This is Ineer. We, also, serve the Judge, and will take you to him if you wish."

The girl thought about it for a long time as they rode. It was either them or the caravan, though, and she decided to trust them, for the moment. "I'll follow," she agreed, "from a safe distance."

"Good enough." Sarth nodded. "I would ask your name, though. One as fierce as you, I would make a friend."

The girl hesitated one last time as the first riders entered the clearing far below and found the bodies. There was a shout, but the trio was high above them now.

At this point the girl had a choice: distrust and face this country alone, trust and be a part of something good for the first time in her life. There was risk, but she had learned that life, itself, was a risk. Since everybody she had ever loved had left her, the decision wasn't hard to make.

"I am Kalina," she told them with pride in her beautiful, sea green eyes. "Kalina Zamonar of Zamboria!"

CHAPTER FIFTEEN

WHEN SHALAH'S HARSH cry shook him out of his reverie, Kazeem was grateful enough to reward her. Not only had her unruly braying brought him back into the present and away from those painful memories, but she had also kept him from knocking himself out on a low-hanging branch.

Camping in desert country was never a pleasant experience for him; one baked during the day and froze at night. An oasis like this was always a haven, providing water and shade and, sometimes, food—but one also ran the risk of confrontation with other travelers.

Kazeem blinked. He opened his eyes and squeezed them shut. Hard. He'd traveled far, unfeeling of the desert heat, but the cost had been high; he was so emotional that he felt as if he'd actually relived the past several years.

The young warrior slid off the dromedary's back. It was easy with cramped legs—Shalah stood eighty inches high at the shoulder. He found a treat for her in a bag, which was gobbled in seconds. He fed her while she brayed for more, that elongated and unique face of hers almost human, and making him laugh. When she was settled he spread a blanket for himself and sat down with water and dates to watch the sun set.

Kazeem had trained long and hard with Windor, but today had been the hardest thing he'd ever done. Reliving those boyhood moments had been torture, but so was living with the fact that his father's killers had gone unpunished. When you added Nomar and

Elin to the mix, and the unshakable feeling that Baaka Zhinn was still out there…it was almost more than he could stand. Kazeem knew that Windor would never forgive him for leaving his training unfinished, but there wasn't anything he could do about that now.

That nervous, anxious feeling was back, and he took a deep breath in an unsuccessful attempt to fight through it. Unbidden thoughts of Kalina made tears spring to his eyes, but when he turned his mind from her with great effort, all he did was dredge up images of his parents and Bel…and what those sick bastards had done to him in the Home. Worse than anything, were his own actions afterward. He knew that he was setting himself on that very same path again, but if he was ever going to have a life, he needed to put all of this behind him, no matter what it took.

He also knew that his actions might get him killed, but that didn't scare him anymore. He was more afraid of living, and if he died, his worries would be over.

Not for the first time, he considered suicide, but that was a coward's way out. He was sobbing, his eyes filled with hot tears, furious with himself and with Windor for not telling him the truth about his father. Pushing everything from his mind, he wiped his eyes on a sleeve and set about making camp. Two thoughts and two thoughts only kept him from choking as he ate: one, that he had known about his father on some subconscious level all along; two, that he hadn't been ready to deal with it until now.

Kazeem finished eating, and stored the unused portions. He had no immediate plans beyond sleep, so, grabbing a blanket, did just that as the first stars appeared on the horizon.

*

Shalah didn't wake him the next morning, but then there wasn't any need. Usually, she poked and prodded and stuck her foam-flecked muzzle into his sleeping face, looking for breakfast.

But that was only when someone else hadn't already fed her.

In Kazeem's defense, he was physically and emotionally exhausted, but that didn't keep him from berating himself for days.

It also didn't keep him from leaping to his feet with a sword in each hand as soon as he realized he wasn't alone.

"Easy, lad, easy! I mean no harm!"

The speaker was a big man with a wide, tanned face and dark hair. His blue eyes and broad accent identified him as a Westerner.

Kazeem didn't press the attack, but he didn't put up his swords, either.

"Who are you!" he demanded.

The big man sat cross-legged on the other side of the sandy clearing. He put his hands on his knees and narrowed his eyes.

"I'm not sure I like your tone, son."

"I'm not your son," Kazeem snapped, perhaps a bit too quickly.

"You're not very friendly, either."

Kazeem looked at him for a moment, measuring the man.

"I don't take kindly to strangers waltzing uninvited into my camp!"

The man frowned, raised an eyebrow, and crossed his arms across a very broad chest. "Camp? Let me tell you something, kid. I staggered in here after midnight, my horse all but done in and me not much better. I saw you sleeping there and went to sleep myself. When I woke up I fed the animals—yours, included—and then you wake up and raise a blade to me!" He stood up, and put his hands on his hips. "It's a big desert, and this is the only fresh water around. If you own the bloody place, why don't you put up a sign?"

Kazeem frowned, but only to keep from laughing at the outburst. The big man wore simple workman's clothes. His horse was a draft animal and he led a pack mule. This was no warrior, no spy serving his enemies.

"Wait!" he called as the man was reaching for his horse. "You caught me off guard, and it threw me. I've, uh, spent a bad night, and I'd rather not have you judging me badly after caring for my mount. Stay and break bread with me?"

"I've little enough to eat, lad, apart from dry rations and stock feed."

"You misunderstand. I am fortunate enough to have food. Nothing special, but plenty."

"I accept," the man said after a long moment. "My name is Ned. Ned Maywood. Everyone calls me Woody".

"Woody", Kazeem said, trying the name and finding that he liked it. "Please, sit down."

The blue-eyed man did as he was asked, grunting as he returned to his mat. Kazeem didn't wonder. If asked, he would have placed Ned's weight at twenty-stone or better. He pulled a small stoccado from a boot and began to clean his nails with it.

"Mind a personal question?" he asked as Kazeem prepared their meal.

"Ask away." Kazeem was running a cold camp, but he had meal and goat's milk, cheese and bread and a lot of jerky. There were plenty of dates in the grove, and all the fresh water he could carry. He pulled a couple of goatskin bags out of his pack so he wouldn't forget to take some.

"You fight with two swords." This wasn't a question, Kazeem noted, and it made him distrust Ned Maywood all over again.

"What about it?" Kazeem managed with no emotion, as he handed over his one extra wooden bowl.

"Thanks. I, uh, only ask because they don't fight that way where I come from, except for the rangers."

"Rangers?"

"Everfel. Elite fighters who patrol the northern borders of my country."

"I have heard something of them," Kazeem said respectfully. "They count elves and dwarves and Gedendron warriors among their allies. They fight trolls and goblins and Calisians."

"You know much about my people," Ned said as he ate.

Kazeem took a moment to collect his thoughts, hiding this uncertainty with the act of chewing. He realized that he might have been tricked into giving away too much, that the kind of knowledge he possessed wasn't usually privy to teenage boys.

"I love tales of adventure," Kazeem said. "Quests and such. My father often read to me when I was younger."

"I just thought you might be a fighter, someone with formal training. I know a man who's looking for payroll guards. He pays well, and pays me for good leads." Woody smiled. "Everybody makes money."

Kazeem didn't take the bait. "Actually, I'm on my way to the capitol. I'm seeking an old friend. Perhaps you've heard of him, or know where I can find him?"

"He a mercenary? A caravan or body guard?"

Perhaps even an assassin, Kazeem thought. "Most likely," he said. "I haven't seen him in quite some time."

"What's his name?"

"Hasir, of Zamboor."

Ned Maywood shook his head. "Doesn't ring a bell, but a lot of these guys don't use their real names." He shrugged. "My friend might know of him," he added as he broke off a piece of bread. "I'm going into the city myself. Why not travel together?"

"Good idea," Kazeem agreed. This man *could* have slit his throat as he slept. It'd be better to find out more about him. "Two heads are better than one."

"Not always, kid. Not even usually, but you go ahead and think that way if it makes you feel better."

*

They rode together for three days, and at the end of that time Kazeem would have called him a friend had he been capable of trusting anyone. Ned was likable enough, with his boisterous ways and roguish good looks. He even looked the part in eastern style clothes, when he bound his head in red velvet, his wild blue eyes sparkling above that bushy black beard.

Still, Kazeem didn't trust him; more importantly, he felt it was a good idea *not* to trust him. The truth was he'd been hurt too many times, and wasn't willing to take chances. It was easier to play it safe.

They arrived in Zamboria's Outer Ring at noon on the third day, and went right to the market pavilion. Kazeem insisted they care for the animals first, and after they were watered and fed, the men saw to themselves. After half a week of cold camp rations it was good to get a hot meal: lamb and rice and steamed vegetables for Kazeem, rabbit stew with potatoes for Woody. They ate more than was good for them, and sat back with dazed expressions when they were through.

"I do believe I was wasting away," Woody said with a sigh.

"My old aunt used to say that a man wasn't really a man unless he had a little beef on him," Kazeem joked.

"Then I must be quite a man," Ned announced, patting his not-inconsiderable paunch with both hands.

They laughed, and Kazeem looked around. The pavilion was crowded, with throngs of people queuing up to order food, finding tables, eating, talking and enjoying the warm but strong-handed touch of the desert breeze.

"So, where's this friend of yours?" Kazeem asked.

"Be here any minute. He comes to the market every day, looking for men who want work."

"He does this *every* day?" Kazeem wasn't able to hide his surprise. "How big is his outfit?"

Woody was shaking his head. "It isn't all for him. He's...kind of an agent."

"And where does Ned Maywood fit in?"

"I already told you, I get a finder's fee."

"Isn't that what *he* gets—as the agent?"

"No, he gets the actual commission from the hiring party. I get a small piece of his action, half on starting the job, half if the candidate lasts more than sixty days."

"Looks like everyone makes money," Kazeem said, and meant it. By playing "dumb", he'd gotten far more information than he would have otherwise. Also, he'd actually heard of such outfits before, all perfectly legit. Around here, you didn't move *anything* on a caravan without a full guard contingent. Smart owners knew that professionals fought much better than men conscripted against their will, as they were able to see each assignment objectively. In fact, the arrangement was perfect for him, exactly what he needed to find Hasir, who, in turn, would help him track down everyone else he was looking for. Kazeem didn't like to think of an old friend as a means to an end, but he was too far along this particular path to turn back now. He honestly wanted to see Hasir again, but he had to be practical, too. The truth of the matter was that everyone used everybody else.

"That's the general idea. Ah, there he is now." Ned waved him over. "One thing. I'll introduce him, and I'll do most of the talking. Don't ask personal questions, and for God's sake don't put him on the spot if you catch him in a lie. These guys bullshit so much their back teeth are stained. Probably don't even remember their real names anymore."

"I think I can handle it," Kazeem promised, but as the man approached, he was suddenly unsure. There was something about him, something familiar about the strange amber eyes, something he should have been able to put a finger on…and couldn't.

"Ah, Graylan," Ned Maywood said, getting up to clasp hands. Kazeem noted the old, imperial-style shake, forearms gripped, shoulders pulled in close.

"Maywood, good to see you again!"

"Keeping out of trouble, I hope?"

"There's no making money without trouble, Woody." The mercenary's face grew serious for a moment, revealing a brief glimpse of the true personality, but it was gone so quickly Kazeem wondered if such fierceness had ever really been there.

They released each other. Kazeem noted fingerprints, like brands, on the big man's arm. Ned unconsciously rubbed the sore spot where his friend had clasped him. On the other man's skin there was no mark at all.

"What have you got for me today?"

"Good things, Graylan. To start, here is Kazeem, of Zamboor. Kazeem, Graylan Malcor."

The man offered his hand, and Kazeem took it without hesitation. Graylan Malcor was a tall man, and Kazeem had to look up to meet his stare, but he more than made up for his shorter stature with the intensity of his gaze.

Graylan Malcor was lean and hard, like rawhide left too long in the sun. He wasn't bulky like Ned, but his muscles were like rocks and there wasn't an ounce of fat on him. The mercenary leader may have been fifty—the lines on his face told *that* tale—but his body was young, and his eyes strangely non-human. His voice, when he finally spoke to Kazeem, was the sound of gravel tumbling in a streambed.

"Kazeem...of *many* places, I think."

"Have we met before?" Kazeem asked, and then realized that it was more basic than that—it was simply one born killer recognizing another.

Or was it?

Graylan Malcor pursed his thin lips, warbled his head back and forth. "No, I don't think so, but I keep my ear to the ground and I hear things. Might you be looking for work? I could get you fair wages." He looked Kazeem up and down. "More than fair, I think."

Not having met before was an out-and-out lie, Kazeem decided suddenly. He didn't know how or when they had met, but there had been recognition in the man's eyes for an instant, and in that instant, a spark of respect.

"I'm looking for work, yes. Who isn't these days? But I'm also looking for a friend."

"Usually, when men say this to me, they are really looking for someone they want to harm, perhaps even to kill."

There was a smile on Malcor's face as he attempted to let go, but Kazeem didn't return it—nor did he release the other's arm.

"With all due respect, I would not need you—or anyone else—if I wanted to kill someone."

Malcor pulled his arm away, wincing, but he recovered quickly. "A true soldier of fortune, then. What's your friend's name?"

Kazeem saw a look of horror pass over Ned's face like a storm cloud, but he ignored it and answered the question.

"Hasir, from this city. He would be my age and height."

"Ah, Hasir! Curly hair, cleft chin."

"That's him!"

"I know him well. Got him his first posting, in fact. His current assignment is the gold shipment from Dashmir." Malcor glanced at the position of the sun. "The Great Wheel turns for you, my young friend. You are in luck. They should arrive by day's end. But I warn you! They go out two days hence, so you won't have much time to catch up."

"I don't suppose they could use an extra hand on that next shipment?" Kazeem asked.

Malcor smirked; he'd obviously been expecting that. "On that run, they can use all the help they can get!"

*

"You dirty sack of dung!" Kazeem called out as the team of guarded wagons clattered to a stop on the dusty main street. "You dishonored my sister!"

Every guard on the wagon turned (and they all had guilty expressions), but it was Hasir, recognizing Kazeem instantly, who spoke first.

"She would've needed to *have* some honor in the first place!" he called back. The dimple-faced young man with the cleft chin leapt down into the dusty street, sword in hand, desert breeze whipping his cloak about.

"Die, you dog!" Kazeem said, and drew his own steel. The other guards watched with their mouths hanging open.

They closed with raised weapons, circled each other...and burst out laughing. Kazeem looked around. There hadn't been much in the way of foot traffic to begin with, but what there was disappeared quickly. This made them laugh even harder. They hugged and thumped each other on the back.

It was an odd moment. Happy and somehow sad at the same time. They pushed each other to arm's length, and looked at one another. The sun was just going down. A dog sniffed around a dustbin at the mouth of the alley. A few crows pecked at spilled grain. The other guards jumped down with smiles on their faces, shaking their heads. Two old women in shawls stood talking quietly with folded arms, oblivious to anything else. There was no one else around. Kazeem somehow knew that this was an important occasion in his life, and he doubted that he would ever forget it.

"Looks like you scared 'em all off!" He laughed.

"*Me?*" Hasir threw a mock punch. "That ugly face of yours should be outlawed!"

"It, uh, actually has been," Kazeem told him, and they were laughing again, the solemn moment was gone, and it was as if the years in between had fallen away.

"Ah, Kazeem! It's good to see you, my friend. After that night in the alley…well, I was afraid you'd come to a bad end."

"It hasn't been easy these last years," Kazeem admitted, coming as close to complaining as he ever did.

"Tell me," the boy with the cleft chin prompted. There was deep concern in his eyes.

"Not here." Kazeem glanced at the setting sun, which was now a small, burning half circle in the west. "Let's get out of the street and get something to drink." He clapped a callused hand on his friend's shoulder. "And I'll wager *you've* got one or two tales, eh?"

"One or two," Hasir said, and although he was grinning, there was sadness in his eyes.

*

"I've *heard* things about you," Hasir confided in a low voice.

They were on their third drink, and even though the liquor on the Outer Ring was at least thirty percent water, they were still boys, after all, and unused to what the local teamsters called "coffin varnish".

"Yeah," Kazeem asked with grave sincerity, "just what have you heard?"

"I've heard you've *killed* a man." Hasir took a drink. He licked his lips. "More than one. A lot."

Kazeem lit a cigarette, and blew out a plume of smoke. He shrugged, and took his time with the reply. "I guess I've had one or two hard choices to make."

"So it's true, then, what they say of you?"

Kazeem let his eyes wander around the tent before speaking. There was a cool breeze coming from an open flap, and he briefly turned his face towards it. He wore a turban and robes, and the beginnings of a sparse beard peppered his cheeks, but he was still technically wanted for questioning, and didn't relish the prospect of losing his freedom. Again. "What is it, exactly, that they say, friend Hasir?"

"That you fight with the skill of a professional, a *Wrotmar*, like your father!"

Kazeem, never one to do things by half measures, nevertheless felt it would have been pretentious to say so. He nodded instead, looking much older than his seventeen years. He drew his lips into a thin white line.

"Killing is no glorious thing, Hasir." He suddenly felt as sober as a judge. "It is…distasteful, to say the least. You do it when you have to, like anything else, and if you let your emotions overcome you in the heat of battle, you may find yourself forgetting where your best interests lie. It's never something you want to talk about, especially the ones you've coldly planned ahead of time."

Hasir's eyes grew wide. He didn't have Kazeem's discipline, or even the uncanny ability to kind of just *slide* back into sobriety, but he wasn't stupid, drinks or not. He knew when it was time to shut his mouth.

"Let us talk then of pleasant things, of our reunion, our new jobs—working together at last! Let us speak of women and the wonders of the open road!"

Kazeem had caught the eye of one of the house girls. She was stunning, and he knew it would cost him, but at this point in his life he preferred the freedom found in professional arrangements. He winked at the doe-eyed girl, nodding with his chin to indicate that she should bring along a friend.

"For tonight, Hasir, let us stick to women. The road will still be there tomorrow."

"Very early tomorrow," Hasir corrected.

"But I thought…Ned told me two days hence."

Hasir was already shaking his head. "That's Malcor talking. It's standard procedure. We never let anyone know when we're *really* leaving. Too much money involved." He shook his head with the certainty of the drunk and near-drunk. "Too dangerous."

The girls arrived just then. They were eighteen or so, luscious and available. What more need be said concerning young men?

"Are you saying you'd rather not, Hasir?" Kazeem teased. "You'd rather save your strength for tomorrow?"

"If we stay awake and active all night, Kaz, 'tomorrow' will never get here; it'll just be part of today."

Kazeem raised his eyebrows as the girls led them to their tent, but he didn't say anything. He was too busy staring at the backside of the girl before him as she walked, and he wouldn't have known how to respond to such profound wisdom in the first place.

"Which one do you want?" Hasir whispered, leaning close and breathing alcohol in his face.

"Does it matter, my brother?" Kazeem asked, pushed him in and closed the tent flap.

*

"Oh, my God, my head hurts!" Hasir said miserably, early the next morning.

They hadn't been able to stay 'up' all night, in any capacity. Too much to drink. Each of them fell asleep after only one brief encounter, and awoke just before daybreak.

Now, as the wagon bounced them over ruts in the main street obviously put there to torture them, they were paying for it all a second time.

"Just turn that thing off," Kazeem commiserated, clasping a hand to his eyes to block out the sun.

The boys rode in the lead wagon, with Malcor himself driving.

"Here!" he barked, and handed them a flask. "A little hair o' the dog that bit you!"

Hasir took the bottle happily, and up-ended it. He swallowed a healthy amount, looked for a moment like he might vomit, took a deep breath, belched and cried: "Better!" as they went over another bump. Tears sprang up in his eyes, but he no longer looked sick to his stomach.

Kazeem eyed the bottle with distrust, but thought about how bad he already felt, and decided to risk it. The whiskey went down like ball lightning, rolled around in his gut, threatened to come back up—burning all the way—and then settled. He gasped, handed the flask back to Malcor, and grinned crookedly.

"I'll be a son-of-a-bitch, it works!"

"You'll sleep tonight," Graylan Malcor said knowingly. "For now, keep sharp. We get bush-whacked, you'll think your hangover was a picnic!"

He went back to his driving without another word.

Kazeem used the time to think about what he was doing. Hasir would put two and two together before long, but what did that really matter? He needed money right now, and the security of a solid position. That he was using his friend, not to mention his new employer, to find men he planned to kill—those were thoughts for another day. The reality was here, now. He was a caravan guard, and he'd be the best one he could be.

It was hot, and the day dragged. By the afternoon, it was a hard-won struggle just to keep their eyes open. The sun was just setting when Graylan called it a day, and it couldn't have come a moment too soon.

The caravan usually started out around four of the clock, long before cock's-crow, which meant dinner was at half-part six, bed at eight. But the sun was still visible as a small, burnt umber crescent on the horizon when Hasir and Kazeem dragged out their blankets and crawled under a wagon. They were asleep in minutes, foregoing supper, remaining, as always, under the watchful eye of Graylan Malcor.

*

Hasir and Kazeem slept straight through the night, ate hugely in the morning, and were able to retake their mounts.

"Give me the open road anytime!" Hasir announced. His horse, fresh from being un-ridden the day before, pawed impatiently at the ground.

Kazeem was also glad to be mounted again. Riding in one of the wagons hadn't been his idea of fun. "That goes double for me!" he proclaimed, pulling the cinch tight on his saddle.

Graylan Malcor came around the corner of the chuck wagon, a cup of strong black coffee in his hand. He always seemed to show up when you least expected him, his strange eyes intense. Rumor had it that he had elven blood, and that explanation was as good as any as far as Kazeem was concerned. His way of always knowing what was happening was uncanny and he *did* look like some kind of a half-breed.

"Feeling your oats this morning, eh, boys?" he asked as he sipped the rancid-smelling brew.

"We're raring to go," Kazeem told him, and tipped the brim of his hat.

"What he said," added Hasir with a good-natured grin.

Malcor kind of fell back and leaned on the nearest wagon while he drank. He was dressed in western style clothes, trousers, and work shirt, boots and drover coat. There was a sword at his hip, and a knife in his belt.

"Well, I'm certainly glad to hear that, especially after yesterday." He smiled, but there was no warmth in it. "Hell, I ought to dock the both of you a day's pay!"

Hasir took the ribbing seriously. "Hey, we showed up!"

"Barely."

Kazeem was mounted by this time, and perhaps a little better at dealing with people. "We'll make it up today, boss. Just say the word."

"Bet your ass you will!" Malcor came off the wagon, deliberately poured the remaining coffee out in a steady stream, and approached the mounted teenagers. "Point men, both of you. Get going now. You're burnin' daylight!"

Hasir was impressed. It was an honor to ride 'point', to lead the way, and it showed all the other guards that the big man trusted you. Kazeem took a different view.

Point men may have been held in high esteem, but they were also the most vulnerable. This was no honor he was bestowing; it was Malcor's way of kicking them in the ass. *Think twice before you mess up again, boys,* he was saying. *I'm the guy who makes all the assignments, so you don't want to get on my bad side!"*

Kazeem's gaze just happened to pass over the rangy man while he thought this, and Malcor picked that exact same moment to look up at him and smile. It wouldn't be the last time the teen winced and wondered if his mind was being read.

It also wouldn't be the last time he wished he had stayed with Windor.

"Come on, you knucklehead," he told Hasir, and plucked at his shirt. "Like the man says, we're burnin' daylightl"

"What daylight?" Hasir glanced at the sky to the east. It was early to begin with, and overcast, with fog rolling out of the valley to the north.

Kazeem grinned and tugged on the reins. "Anything special we should watch for, boss?" he asked Graylan Malcor.

All levity vanished from the man's face. "Everything. Everyone. And I'll tell you something else, too: someone tries to take you, they'll try to take *us*, too." He jerked a thumb over his shoulder. "This ain't no candy we're hauling. Show no mercy if someone takes you on...and don't expect any in return!"

*

"Don't mind him," Hasir said a few minutes later. The trail ran out before them like a long brown ribbon winding through foggy hills. "He's just trying to keep us on our toes."

Kazeem didn't know about that, but he was smart enough to keep his mouth shut. Most of the time it was better to simply let people think whatever they wanted to think. What *you* thought wasn't really what they wanted to hear.

"He did seem concerned, though," Kazeem insisted, keeping the talk at a level where Hasir was comfortable. He glanced at the slowly-brightening sky, at the rim rock above them, and at the slowly dissipating fog. "Do you think he's worried about the shipment?"

"He's worried about *every* shipment, Kazemo. There's a lot of money in those wagons."

"I know *that*, stupid! I meant *today*. He was acting kind of funny, as if he expected something bad to happen."

Hasir chewed jerky, and replied sagely. "It's his job to expect something. Malcor always says, 'expect the unexpected.'"

Kazeem was sure that Malcor couldn't take credit for *that* pearl of wisdom, either, but again, he let it go. "I suppose that's good advice."

Hasir kept talking, but Kazeem wasn't listening. Something was wrong. He could feel it without knowing exactly what it was. And then it occurred to him that a successful ambush would take you on several fronts at once, not just take out the scouts, which might improve your odds, but still not guarantee you the prize. But it was more than that. It was these damn canyon walls, the fog, that knowing *smirk* on Malcor's face when he'd sent them out here alone. Kazeem had heard that the man always played several angles towards the middle, but was he double-dealing here, and if so, what did he stand to gain?

"Damn you, Kaz, you ain't even listening to me!"

"Quiet!"

"Quiet, my ass!" Hasir snapped indignantly. "You pay attention to me when—"

Kazeem reached behind him and clapped a hand over Hasir's mouth. His grip was hard, and his eyes were serious. He jerked his chin towards the defile up ahead, then nodded and tilted his head at the canyon wall, at the spot where it bent like a dogleg and turned west. Hasir didn't have a clue as to what was going on, but he knew enough to keep his mouth shut. He pulled Kazeem's hand away and mouthed the words: *What is it?*

Kazeem shook his head, raised a finger to his lips, and kept riding. Hasir frowned, but reluctantly followed. The horses' hoofs were steady—they hadn't broken their slow stride all this time—and the constant *clip-clop-clip* didn't betray anything amiss.

The breeze was fresh. Blowing from the west it should have carried the scent of cedar and moss-covered rocks. Instead, it carried the unmistakable smell of overworked horseflesh.

Hasir watched his friend with interest, confusion and more than a little awe. In years to come Kazeem would be famous for knowing things he had no earthly business knowing, but even now that singular ability was uncanny. Even on the night he'd been taken there'd been signs, and only the treachery of middle age had been able to defeat his youth and skill.

To sum it up, Hasir didn't *need* to understand it; if Kazeem sensed something amiss, that was good enough for him. The boys slipped weapons from scabbards, and rode with steel in plain sight. Fog continued to swirl around them, while the sun continued trying to break through the cloud cover. The combination made for a weird sort of half-light, where man and beast wore sepia, and the weapons displayed a dull gleam, closer to pewter than the brilliance usually associated with fine Arganian steel. Echoes rolled back eerily from canyon walls and the occasional arroyo; these pitched off into the darkness like crooked hallways. Now, in addition to strange horses, Kazeem smelled the odor of unwashed clothes, the scent of men several days on the road.

They came without warning, but the boys were ready for them. Kazeem because of his senses, Hasir because he was a born soldier who followed orders.

There were six of them, all on horseback. Two charged from the arroyo on the left, effectively blindsiding them, two from the cover of boulders slightly behind, riding hard as soon as the boys passed. The other two came straight at them, weapons drawn, battle cries on their lips.

Movement caught Kazeem's eyes. There were at least half a dozen more on the ridge above. Against the struggling, cloud-choked light, and riding in the fog, they were outlined as ghostly silhouettes. Kazeem took a quick count, but that was all he had time for.

The others were upon them, and they hadn't come for tea.

Hasir had seen combat before, as he was sure Kazeem had. In fact, if even *half* of the stories they told about him were true, then he was certainly the most dangerous thing in this valley. Still, fighting was one thing—being charged at by armored men on horseback was quite another. It was terrifying, and anyone who claimed differently was a liar.

The raiders rode straight ahead, screaming as they came. As they closed, Hasir gasped when he realized what they were. These were no common highwaymen; their surcoats and sigils identified them as Ankorian Guard, warriors under the direct command of the Warlord Slagja. This was a political faction, in contention with the rightful government. That meant they wanted the gold to continue their raids—and wouldn't leave anyone behind to tell the tale.

"Kazeem!" he shouted and started to explain, but the other boy shook his head. It was clear from the look on his face that he already knew what they were…and didn't care. He nodded, indicating that Hasir should watch his back, and then he pulled leather and brought his stallion to a dust-throwing halt.

The first raider was almost on top of him, but Kazeem was ready. He reached over his shoulder and drew the second sword he carried lashed to his back. The sword came clear with a satisfying rasping sound, gleaming in that weird, shimmering half-light. As the

Ankorian approached, the boy made an 'x' with his weapons crossed before him; there was a single spark, brilliant in the near-gloom, and the high, clear ring of steel meeting steel. Kazeem bent his wrists down and in, and twisted sideways in the saddle. The raider's scimitar was ripped from his grasp, leaving him empty handed as he passed. Not understanding how it had happened, he was still game enough to pull a knife and wheel around, pulling hard on the reins and charging with the blade high above his head.

He leapt from his mount with the intention of taking Kazeem to the canyon floor, but the boy leaned low, his face in the horse's mane, and whispered. The stallion jerked, and somehow the Ankorian went face-first into the rock wall beyond. He slid down the stone, rolled over in a cloud of dust, and lay still. Kazeem gave him as much thought as a swatted fly, and turned just in time to meet the second rider. Kazeem again used both blades, one batting the other's down and away, the other slashing at the unprotected neck of the Ankorian as he twisted and tried to backhand his foe. The move widened the only chink in his armor, and he was falling, his hand maroon at his throat. Kazeem looked for the other two, but three of his own men had ridden hard to engage them in the arroyo. They fought at the mouth to that dark corridor, and Kazeem suddenly found himself alone.

And then he realized that Hasir wasn't where he thought he would be.

When Kazeem turned, he fully expected his friend to be in trouble, but one Ankorian was already down, thrown from his horse, and Hasir was taking on a second in mounted swordplay. The boy would have done all right, given time, but time was something they didn't have. Luck alone had disabled the first rider, and Kazeem didn't believe in turning up his nose at that particular lady. The Wrotmar tossed a knife; he did this so swiftly, and with so much force, that the hilt of the blade made a dull *thud* as it embedded itself in the man's head. Kazeem simply seemed to flick his arm sideways, and then the knife, with brutal suddenness, was protruding from the eye slot of the man's helmet. His right hand went strangely over the top of his head; as if he were attempting to scratch his back, and then he was falling out of the saddle.

For an instant there was only labored breathing. Then the telltale sounds of swordplay intruded, and Hasir was suddenly furious.

"You son of a bitch!" he yelled at Kazeem.

"You're welcome."

"I could have handled him!"

"He got dusted," Kazeem said, indicating Hasir's first attacker, "by pure luck, and you know it. Besides, we're going to have company."

Hasir saw the ridge riders heading down, and nodded. "Where the hell *they* come from?"

"Been up there all along," Kazeem told him. "Looking for a way down, I should think. Come on," he added, "you can yell at me later."

"Don't wanna yell at you," Hasir mumbled, more to himself than to anybody else. "I just want you to be wrong once in a while."

They rode hard, leaning forward over wind-whipped manes. Nothing mattered now except warning the others, but Kazeem feared that attackers working the backtrail might already have taken the wagons. The men behind them gave chase, and for several heartbeats the world was reduced to the labored, gasping breathing of their mounts, and the thunderous echoes of desperate hooves.

Hasir was the first to see the caravan, because Kazeem was looking over his shoulder, but the shout from his friend brought his head around.

"They're running straight at us!" Hasir cried, his words snatched away by the wind. "And coming hard!"

Kazeem nodded. He was chewing the flesh inside his lower lip. "Someone's *behind* them!" he yelled back.

Well, so much for warning them. Kazeem and Hasir could see what was happening. Hell, the dust cloud was probably visible for half a mile, even with the fog, but, more importantly, could the lead teams see them? Knowledge was a double-edged sword. If you couldn't do anything with it, what good was it?

"Pull up!" Kazeem yelled suddenly, and did just that.

Hasir followed suit, yanking the reins savagely. "Now what?"

Kazeem beckoned with one finger. "They're going to have to shoot at the men *behind* us. We're in their line of fire!"

Hasir's eyes went wide. As if to underscore Kazeem's concern, a crossbow quarrel *thwacked* off a stone four feet from his head.

The fog and the dust had made the day dim. Kazeem used it to their advantage, pulling the horses around a column of red stone. The horses didn't want to go; they were tired and hot and choking from the dust, but they pulled hard on the reins to get them under cover.

"You got a plan?" Hasir yelled above the din.

"Yeah, live to see the sun come up tomorrow!"

The boys peered through the fog. To the left of their cover, the teamsters thundered towards them with enemy riders in tow. To their right—back the way they had come—were the six ridge riders. It should have been hard—but not impossible, Kazeem cautioned himself—for them to have been observed as they took cover. Now the question was: how to put their position to good use? They had one longbow between them, and swords for combat, useless at the moment. What else?

Kazeem looked around. He hated the idea of sitting here while the rest of the men were under attack, but there didn't seem to be much he could do about it. Then his eyes settled on the coiled rope on Hasir's saddle, and his eyes lit up. He took the heavy, braided cord and sat up straight, holding one end out to his friend.

"Tie this to that stone over there!"

Hasir frowned. "Are you serious?"

"Just do it before I lose my nerve."

Hasir looked like he wanted to smile, but didn't indulge himself. With grudging admiration he said, "It's your funeral, man!"

"Maybe. Just tie it tight!"

"Long as I don't have to *hold* it," Hasir growled as he jumped down. "All set," he yelled as soon as he was done, and leapt back into the saddle.

"See ya!" Kazeem said, yelled, "*Hee*-up!" at his horse, and hit it on the rump with the coil of rope.

"Sure you will," Hasir mumbled, and shrugged the bow off his shoulder.

Kazeem darted out. He was a pale streak, a ghost through the dust, a gust of wind that stirred and eddied, and then he was all the way across the ravine. Despite their proximity, Hasir doubted that the ridge riders could have seen him. Hell, even if they had, they were going too fast to do anything about it. The boy rubbed his chin on a shoulder, shrugged his shirt back into place, and put a clothyard shaft to the string. The arrow was a full thirty-six inches long, wickedly pointed and expertly feathered for hunting at long distances. Working with Kazeem had taught him that it was better to act fast than be caught with your thumb up your ass. Kazeem may have been more than a little bit crazy, but he was as close to family as Hasir got. He sighted down the length of the shaft and picked a moving target. Timing was everything, though—too soon and he'd screw it up, too late, and he might as well have stayed home.

The wagons were closer, thundering along with tortured wheels churning furiously. Lathered horses labored with their heads pumping up and down, and the men driving pelted them mercilessly with pebbles from the jokey box. Mounted men riding in a swirling dust chased them, yelling and screaming at the top of their lungs. Hasir didn't have a clue as to what Malcor was doing, but he'd never known him to run blindly. He *did* know that they'd all be in his lap shortly, and he doubted if the caravan could make out the ridge riders in all this dust. The fear swelled in him again, but by then the riders were abreast, and Kazeem was in motion.

As the ridge riders came upon the sandstone pillars, Kazeem pulled the rope tight, whipping it up out of the dust, wrapped it three times around a thin slab of rock, made a quick half-hitch, and got the hell out of the way.

The rope was as taut as a guy wire, and took the lead rider an inch above his collarbone. The rope, combined with his speed, took his head off. The decapitated body flipped backwards out of the saddle, and landed in the path of the on-coming riders. The others were going too fast to avoid them. In seconds, all six of them were rolling forward in a bloody mass of hoofs and arms and legs—all of this before the severed and visored head, eyes wide, had even tumbled to the ground. When the wounded and dazed survivors tried to get up, Hasir shot them. Penetrating heavy leather armor wasn't easy, but cloth-yard shafts aren't ordinary arrows, and neither were arrowheads designed for big game.

The Ankorians dropped like stones, twitched once or twice, and lay still.

Kazeem had ridden part of the way out of his hiding place, swords drawn, but it wasn't necessary. He put one blade away, and the boys shared a look. They had done much in their short time together, but this is the first time they had ever killed as a team. Their eyes met across the gulf, tearful because of the dust, but there wasn't anything resembling emotion. They nodded to one another and turned towards the wagons. Each had the presence of mind to cut the rope, and did so at the same time; it seemed to leap into the air of its own accord, and then it settled to the ground.

The wagons were a few yards away, but the crossbow men held their fire. When Malcor saw who it was, he shouted.

"You two all right?"

Both boys nodded; Hasir indicated with his chin that he should look behind him.

Malcor took a quick glance over his shoulder, and took in the dead bodies. A pale light gleamed in his strange, almost elvish eyes.

"So much for bottling us in. Good work, lads." He peered around the side of the wagon. "Good a place as any to make a stand," he added, and leapt down. He drew steel. "Time to earn your pay, boys. Get us out of this, and you all get a bonus. Fail...and I'll see you in hell."

He looked like he wanted to say more, but there wasn't time.

The raiders were cautious, but they still came hard. They slowed down when they saw the dead bodies, but it was more out of curiosity than fear. Their leader held up a hand, bringing their pace to a slow trot. Another movement a few seconds later brought the troop to a dead stop. He sat his horse and looked straight at Graylan Malcor. The man on his right looked from one canyon wall to the other.

"You know what we want," the first man said. The man on his right brought his eyes down from the wall and fixed them on the men standing before them.

Graylan Malcor stepped forward, a cruel-looking scimitar with a wicked cutting edge in his hand. He twirled it once, turned his head and spat. "All you have to do is take it."

The Ankorian lifted his visor, revealing eyes as black as pitch. "We take it, you die."

Malcor smiled. "Dying's nothing compared to what the people we work for would do to us if we gave in without a fight." He spat again. "You going to fight, or just sit there all day?"

The Ankorian soldier was suddenly at a loss. His information, coupled with the way they'd run, had prepared him only for frightened rabbits, not wolves that would fight to the death. He glanced at his men, first right, then left, counting heads until he realized how he looked. He didn't know how many guards were hidden among the wagons, but he was pretty sure he had them outnumbered.

Still, he didn't like the look in Malcor's eyes.

He sat back in the saddle, crossed his arms and pretended to be reasonable. While everyone was watching *him*, Kazeem quietly slipped a longbow from the wagon and held it by his side.

"There's no need for this," the leader said; he was trying to be a friend giving sage advice, his arms open, palms up. "I'll tell you what: give us half, keep the rest for yourselves. No one will know."

"*I'll* know," Malcor said. His voice was a low growl through clenched teeth.

The Ankorians didn't know what to do. Their leader had lost his nerve, and they were directionless without him.

"Did you come here to steal, or talk us to death?" a clear, unwavering voice asked.

Malcor turned slightly, unsurprised that the speaker was Kazeem. He turned back, and tilted his head towards the teen. "Like the lad said. Take what you want, or stop wasting our time."

For a moment it could have gone either way. Slagja's warriors may have been feared on the lower end of the continent, but they were far from awe-inspiring here. They were young men far from home for perhaps the first time. They had been sent on a mission, not of glory, but of theft, and it clearly rubbed them the wrong way. To make matters worse, their leader had gone soft. This wasn't what they'd signed on for, and you could see it in their eyes.

Hasir doubted that anyone else heard it, but Kazeem mumbled, *"This is what we were running from?"*

The arrow was flying even as he spoke, and the cloth-yard shaft struck the leader in the throat. The sound of the impact was a terrible wet *thud*. There was an explosion of red sputum, blood and saliva, and then the lead man fell sideways out of the saddle. His men watched in horror as he landed in a puff of dust, with one of his boots still wobbling in the stirrup.

The Ankorians probably would have run, but Kazeem made an obscene gesture. Fear changed to anger in their eyes as they charged, but they'd been goaded, and they weren't thinking clearly.

Hasir watched all of this in a kind of fog. He'd seen fighting before—seen it up close—had engaged in combat himself, but never, never in his life had he *ever* seen anything like Kazeem. His friend with the blond hair and the stormy dark eyes went into battle with a willingness that was alarming. Men fell before him like wheat, arms and hands and legs severed at weak points in their armor. His blades flashed, hacking, slicing hammering, until he was alone amid a circle of dead and dying bodies. His own men backed off to watch him finish off the last few. When it was over, Kazeem and Malcor eyed each other through the dust. Their faces were expressionless, but it was their eyes that bothered Hasir. He'd once watched from a distance as two timber wolves fought over a carcass, tearing it in half and gulping torn strips without taking their eyes from each other.

Kazeem and Malcor reminded him of that, but at least the damn wolves hadn't looked so goddamned pleased with themselves.

*

They left the canyon, found a hill, took the wagons up and placed guards on the ridge above. Malcor had been running cold camps—dried beef, cashews, bread and water—but tonight he ordered the cook to build a fire and fed them properly. The dead men would buy them a night's peace. Several travelers, including a drummer, a horse wrangler and a tinker, had already come upon them. News would travel fast, and their reputation—already larger than life—would grow. The boss was indeed magnanimous, and allowed them each two flagons of ale.

When everyone had eaten they sat around the fire savoring their ale.

"Look at those poor bastards." Hasir motioned with his cup at the guards on the ridge above. These members of their caravan were seen in outline against the quickly-darkening sky.

Kazeem took a drink. "I hate to tell you, but they ate before we did."

The statement seemed to deflate Hasir. He'd been enjoying the fact that he might have been special—even if it *was* only for a little while.

Kazeem finished his ale, wiped his cup with a soft cloth, and put it away. "You want to feel bad for someone..." He looked up with bright eyes. "Feel bad for those dead soldiers."

"I didn't see *you* showing 'em much sympathy when you were down there!" Hasir said defensively.

"That wasn't the right time for it."

"Oh, but it is now?"

Kazeem folded his arms, and looked up at the stars. "Yes," he said, "I believe it is."

That thoughtful affirmation completely deflated Hasir. "You're a strange young man, Kazeem, anyone ever tell you that?"

Kazeem reached out and gently touched his friend on the arm. "Why don't you say what's really on your mind?"

That made it Hasir's turn to grow pensive. He finished his ale with much less gusto than he'd been looking for, put the cup down and licked his lips. He, too, folded his arms.

"All right, I will. I've known you since we were kids, Kaz." He looked right, then left, but no one seemed to be listening. "And tonight I find out you're not who I thought you were."

There was roasted lamb on a spit by the fire. Kazeem took a piece, popped it in his mouth, chewed, and licked his fingertips. He responded while he was still swallowing. "Okay, if I'm not me, who am I?"

"That's not what I meant." Hasir wore an expression that would have been called a 'pout' if he were even just a couple of years younger. "I heard stories about you, Kazeem. We all have." He waved his arm to indicate the camp. "Word is, you wiped out half the guards breaking out of the Home, and hunted down five other inmates you ran afoul of."

The firelight was reflected in Kazeem's eyes, but they were cold, cold. "So?"

"There's even a rumor you went to finish your Wrotmar training." Hasir leaned forward, his voice low. "Someone told me you took Baaka Zhinn in a fair fight."

"All of this…" Kazeem waved a hand. "You already knew." He cleared his throat while tearing another piece of meat from the rack. "Before today."

"Well, maybe I didn't want to believe it." Hasir looked into the dying embers of the fire, suddenly ashamed without really knowing why.

"Didn't want to believe what—that Kazeem is a killer? Are we so unlike, friend Hasir?"

"I think maybe we are, Kazeem," Hasir said in a hoarse whisper.

"You have killed," Kazeem informed him. He paused, and chewed thoughtfully. "I have killed." He shrugged. "How is it not the same?"

"I love you like a brother," Hasir said carefully, "and would not insult you or make you an enemy, but I think today could have been handled differently. You say to feel badly about those men, and yet you were the one who did the killing." Hasir found the courage to turn and look his friend in the eyes. "Most of those soldiers were our age. Most would have walked away."

"You are correct. Most."

"Then why did you let that first arrow fly?"

"Well, someone had to," Kazeem answered with a smile.

"You make a *joke* of it?"

"No." The smile dropped from his face as if a cold wind had blown it away. "I only did what was necessary."

"They wanted to *talk* their way out of it. You didn't give them that chance."

"I did not create that situation, Hasir—I only took it to its logical conclusion." Kazeem squinted, and his eyes became twin points of shining black ice in the night. "Those soldiers—and let us not fool ourselves into thinking them otherwise—stalked and attacked us. Only when we showed a willingness for battle—and not a moment before—did they think twice about slaughtering every last one of us. Peace is maintained only through the aggressive use of force, Haisr. Talking reveals weakness. No, make no mistake, they would have killed us had they been able, and were only following the path of least resistance. They didn't have the stomach for battle once they saw our resolve, but if we had shown anything less than a total willingness to die for what we believed in, *we'd* be the ones lying out there." He gestured with his thumb.

"You seem so sure of yourself." Hasir frowned and looked away, blinking rapidly.

Kazeem relaxed, and the frost slipped from his tone. "One kills only when one has to, Hasir. That is not a bad thing, and will allow you a normal life—if you are smart enough to embrace it. I, too, love you like a brother, and have no wish to anger you. You are a fierce fighter, when motivated, and a brave and loyal comrade, but I do not know if killing for money—and that is what we do—is the proper life for you."

"How would *you* know what's proper for me?" Hasir snapped. "You were gone for *years*. You have no knowledge of me, or what I'm capable of!" He hit his own chest with a fist. "I'm as worthy as the next man!"

"No doubt," Kazeem said softly, and stood up. "I am sorry," he added, and bowed slightly. "It was not my intention to upset you."

"Then just what *was* your intention?" Hasir asked, glaring up at him.

The lines on Kazeem's face deepened. For a moment, despite the strength he usually projected, it was the face of an old man. "My intention was to help you save your soul, before it is too late, because I was less than honest with you earlier. Death *is* a joke, but, perhaps, not the ultimate joke. I have looked over the brink and into the abyss, my friend. I know what awaits *me* when I reach the end of my road. I would have spared you that—if I could have, but I guess that's something you'll have to figure out for yourself. Maybe that's the way it should be. Goodnight, my brother," he added, and went to find his bed.

Hasir sat alone, but not unobserved. Graylan Malcor stood in the shadows, watching Kazeem's retreating back with thoughtful eyes. *A killer with a conscience*, he thought, *was a very dangerous man to have around.*

Even if he *did* have his uses.

*

The gold shipment was delivered safely, and on time, to Cronon. Needless to say, no one else even *looked* at them on the last leg of their journey. As tradition held, the men headed to the nearest bars and brothels. This far from the capital, the morals they'd been bred with failed, and human nature reasserted itself. Being healthy young men, they were quickly occupied, and just as quickly parted from their pay. Kazeem found himself on the main street with Hasir. They had gotten along for the past few days by diplomatically avoiding their differences, but it hadn't been easy.

"So, my friend," Hasir said, draping an arm about Kazeem's shoulders, "what shall we do tonight? Wine? Women? Song?"

"Why not all three?"

Lamps were being lit. Vendors with pushcarts were just closing down for the night. Taverns and alehouses were just coming alive. At the end of the street, the sun was sinking into the distant Faylon Range like a giant red ball.

"And lose all our pay?" Hasir asked with mock concern.

"But isn't that what it's for?"

"Yeah, but it isn't all that much to begin with," Hasir lamented, looking in his pocket.

"Enough, I think, to suit our needs," Kazeem told him with a huge smile.

"And, what, my good friend, do *you* need the most?" Hasir asked, as a young woman walked by and grinned at them. Hasir blushed and turned his head to look at her.

Kazeem had to pull Hasir along by one arm to keep him moving in a straight line. In fact, he actually had to say his name three times to get him to turn around.

Kazeem didn't blame him. In Cronon, anything went. It was an odd mixture of cultures, a place of immense diversity. A territory they'd been taught to think of as a citadel of sin. Where they came from, women wore shapeless clothes and covered their hair. They'd been brought up to regard sexuality as inherently evil, never mind the hypocritical stance on alcohol. This kind of thinking had created an awful conflict within them, and only being on the road had taught them that there was more than way of looking at the world.

"I don't know what *I* need, my brother, but I can clearly see what *you* need!"

"And what is that?" Hasir asked. He was still trying to walk backwards to look at the girl.

"Why, The Maker of All Thing's most glorious creation: woman!"

They laughed, and went on down the street arm in arm, as if they'd *already* been drinking. Young women of every race, creed, size and shape were to be seen, and the young men were like boys in a candy shop. As they were entering a public house at the end of one side street, a tall, bearded man wearing a tarboosh and turban was creating quite a stir by a fruit cart.

"Come on," Hasir urged, tugging Kazeem's sleeve when the latter hesitated on the steps, turning to watch the spectacle. "Let us tend to our own business."

Patrons were coming and going from the tavern. Hasir and Kazeem were like rocks in a stream, with people flowing around them.

"Kaz!" Hasir said more urgently, as a group of Caliphmen had to go around them to get in, and favored them with stern looks for the inconvenience. Kazeem was bumped twice, but it didn't even register. "We're blocking the entrance!"

Kazeem of Zamboor made a vague patting gesture in midair. "A moment," he said, and went back down the steps and into the street.

As they had noticed earlier, Cronon was a town of infinite diversity. A little girl with reddish hair and blue eyes seemed to have galvanized Kazeem, and Hasir couldn't figure out why.

The tall man with the gray muslin robes and the turban was a pushcart vendor, and he had the little girl by the arm. She was perhaps ten years of age, very pretty in an exotic-looking way, and cowered by the tall man's harsh words. They couldn't hear exactly what was being said, but body language and angry tones conveyed enough. Kazeem went further into the street and only avoided being run down by a mule team when Hasir tugged him out of the way. When questioned, Kazeem mumbled something about a bell.

"What bells?" Hasir asked, but Kazeem was gone, crossing the street in large, angry steps. As Hasir watched, nonplussed, his friend strode up to the merchant and spun him violently around.

"Leave the child alone!"

"Oh, my God of gods," Hasir whispered, and sprinted across the street.

"This does not concern you!" the merchant snapped back.

"Maybe not," Kazeem promised, "but it will most certainly concern *you* if you do not release that child!"

His voice was like ice, and Hasir realized he'd never seen his friend this angry. Not even in battle. Hasir flat out ran the rest of the way.

"What is it? What's wrong?"

The merchant was less sure of himself with two armed men accosting him. "She stole from me!" he accused.

"This iddy-bitty little girl?" Hasir asked in confusion. "What in God's name could she steal that would make you so upset?"

"Fruit!" the turbaned man shouted.

"*Fruit?*" Hasir mumbled with raised eyebrows. "You raised *this* kind of ruckus over a piece of *fruit?*"

"Not one, but two!" He reached for the girl, but Kazeem slapped his hand away. "There is a pear! She hides it!"

Kazeem's voice scared Hasir, scared him badly. It was the voice Death would use when He came calling. "Perhaps you sought something other than fruit if you were trying to look in her clothing?" Kazeem moved so close to the man that their noses almost touched. His hand rested on the hilt of one sword, and Hasir saw...that it was trembling.

"I will call the law," the merchant said in a shaking voice.

Hasir looked over his shoulder. Malcor could get them out of most any jam, but with the fire burning in Kazeem there'd be more than simple trouble. If the man cried out, the Caliphmen in the tavern would respond. Hasir did not know for sure what would happen then, but he knew that he did not want to be here when it did. Nervously, stubbornly, he held his ground.

"I was hungry," the little girl wailed. "I'm sorry." The only reason she had not backed away was that the man still held her wrist.

"Release that girl," Kazeem said softly. There was a terrible note of finality in his tone. "I won't ask you again."

The merchant did as he was told. For the first time, Kazeem turned his attention to the child. He squatted on haunches to speak to her eye to eye. Hasir searched for the emotion controlling his friend, and was surprised to see that it was...regret. Further, he was terribly let down. There was a look of painful disappointment on his face, as if he had expected someone else.

"Are you still hungry, child?" he asked in the gentlest tones Hasir had ever heard.

"No," the girl lied. She still had some pear in her mouth, was afraid to swallow.

Kazeem touched her cheek softly with the back of one finger. "Have no fear," he told her. "Take what you want." He got her a sack and handed it to her. She accepted it with trembling hands.

"I *will* call the law," the vendor repeated.

Kazeem stood up, grabbed the man's wrist, turned his hand over and slammed a gold coin into his palm. Without a doubt it was more than he had earned all week. "*Caliphs* are no law," Kazeem hissed, "and neither are you." His eyes were moist, but they were the tears of restrained passion, not fear. "The only true law belongs to a prince not of this world, and does not consider the whims of men. You will see it for yourself as you leave this life, but go now, while you can, while my patience lasts, or you may see this law before the sun sets."

"What about my cart?" the man blubbered.

"Come back later," Kazeem ordered, and deliberately turned his back. His eyes were like blazing coals, and the heat of battle was already in his cheeks. Hasir honestly believed that if he touched his friend at that moment, he would burn his fingers. Hasir just shook his head, and the man left.

The girl was still standing there trembling, the canvas sack in her skinny little hands.

"Here, child," Kazeem said, taking it from her. He quickly filled it, but stopped just short of making it too heavy. He asked the girl what she liked, but she only mumbled that her mother liked grapes and that her baby sister loved figs and dates. He handed her the sack when it was full, and tucked a coin into her palm. "Go now, young miss, and feed your family." He was down on his haunches again, looking into her eyes.

"Thank you," she whispered.

"You are welcome, my little desert rose."

The girl wet her lips, started to speak, and then stopped with tears in her eyes.

"Tell me what you have to say," Kazeem said gently.

She hesitated, then blurted it out. "My mother says that my father was a soldier, a man from across the Great Expanse, from another land far to the west. He talked of beings of great power who do the bidding of the Maker of All Things."

"Angels," Kazeem said patiently, softly. "The Arconians call them 'Angels'. It is part of their...religion."

The little girl looked at the sack in her tiny, pear-sticky hands, then back up at Kazeem. Tears had carved twin streaks on her dusty cheeks, and her mouth smelled of pear juice. "Are *you* an angel?" she whispered, with her eyes as wide as saucers.

Kazeem laughed, but Hasir didn't much care for the sound of it. It was the laugh of a man who has seriously considered ending his own life on more than one occasion.

"No, child. I am only...Kazeem. A man."

"I'll remember your name, Kazeem, and what you've done."

"Good. Now, do *you* have a name, sweet flower?"

"Yes."

Kazeem smiled. "May I know it?"

"They call me Elizabess. I am told it is a Western name."

"It is a *beautiful* name, and I, too, shall remember."

And then, without warning, the little girl dropped the sack and threw her pitifully thin arms around Kazeem's neck, hugging him with such fierceness that Hasir was not surprised to see the tears fall from Kazeem's eyes.

While no one was looking, Hasir dropped a few more coins into the sack and stood back up.

Kazeem patted the girl's back, suddenly uncomfortable with his own tears. "Go now, Elizabess. Tend to your family."

The girl turned, bolted, came back for the sack, grabbed Kazeem's hand and kissed it before backing slowly away. She paused at the mouth of the alley when Kazeem called her name. She turned, and for a moment Hasir did not know how it would turn out. As far as Kazeem went: he had known right off that she hadn't been Bel...and yet, he hadn't been able to stop himself.

They stood that way for a moment, the young man and the child, looking at one another, connecting in a way Hasir couldn't comprehend.

And then Kazeem took a pear from the cart and tossed it to her. She caught it with one hand.

"I don't think you got to finish the last one," he said and turned around abruptly, as if he were suddenly in pain. It took Hasir several heartbeats before he realized that Kazeem was halfway down the block. The little girl was still standing there; bottom lip trembling like she'd lost her best friend.

"Hey, Kaz, wait up!" Hasir called. He turned back to offer the child a last smile, but she had vanished into the growing twilight as if she'd never really been there.

"What was *that* all about?" Hasir asked when he caught up.

"Ghosts," Kazeem said, and wouldn't say another word because he was trying not to cry.

*

They were in a pub at the end of the road before Kazeem would talk again and even then not until they took their drinks and moved onto the patio at the rear, finding seats at the very back, in a section protected by mosquito netting.

"Feel like talking now?" Hasir said carefully, taking a sip of some almond-based liqueur he couldn't even pronounce. "Think he ever came back for the pushcart?" Hasir added nervously when Kazeem didn't answer. He held the small glass at arm's length, looking at it, trying to decided if he liked it or not.

"I think he watched us the whole time," Kazeem said flatly. "I think he was back before anyone else even had a *chance* to come near it." Kazeem threw back his glass, drank the hot liquor called *annish* by the locals, and motioned for the serving girl while he still had a mouthful.

"What was that all about, anyway?" Hasir asked. "You didn't even *know* that kid, and yet…"

"I was ready to kill for her? Is *that* what you were going to say?"

"Well, yeah."

Kazeem looked at him for a long time, lids half closed. "I did not include you in my actions," Kazeem said after their drinks had been refreshed.

"I don't deserve that shit," Hasir said coldly.

Suddenly, Kazeem laughed, and Hasir knew that it was somehow all right. "No. I don't suppose you do. I'm sorry." He sipped his drink, and actually seemed more interested in moving it around the table than consuming it. "At first I thought she was someone else, a little girl Kalina and I would have taken as our own in a perfect world. After that..." A shrug. "I was just...angry. To begrudge a starving child food..." He shook his head.

"Gods, I thought you were actually going to take her home!"

"I *have* no home, Hasir, other than the road, and even if I had, I could not help all of them."

"Is that your mission in life," Hasir asked softly, "to save the children of the world?"

"Oh, if only someone could," Kazeem said so seriously that the smile jumped off Hasir's face and fled. "But I'm not the man for the job. My heart is too full of hate, and my anger just barely under control." He took a small sip, thumbed condensation from the glass, and looked up. "Anyone can *cause* pain, my friend." He raised a finger. "But to alleviate it, ah, that would indeed take a special kind of man."

"I would hear more of Kalina, if you would," Hasir told him quietly.

"Let us eat," Kazeem said, wobbling slightly in his chair, "and I will tell you the whole story, from the night I was taken from you, until today. How will that be? Then you will know better how to judge, hmmm?"

Hasir knew that Kazeem was as close to intoxicated as he ever got. He also knew how quickly his friend could reassert control. "I am no judge," was all he could think to say, "but I would hear your tale regardless."

"It is well that you are not." Kazeem leaned forward with his arms on the table, and his eyes burned deeply into Hasir's. "If you were, I would surely rest on the ax man's block at daybreak!"

*

Hasir listened to the story with a disturbing mixture of horror and fascination. The revenge Kazeem had exacted from the boys who had (Hasir couldn't say the word, not even to himself) *wronged* Kazeem was stomach turning. Add that to how badly Kazeem still wanted the men responsible for his father's death, not to mention the Caliphmen who had gotten away after killing Nomar and Elin, and it became clear that Kazeem was very possibly the most dangerous man in the East. And as if *that* weren't enough, Kazeem also wanted the head of Baaka Zhinn—whom he blamed for Kalina's death. He was so full of hate, so seething with anger, that Hasir wondered how he functioned at all.

"But Zhinn is a powerful man!" Hasir warned in a low voice.

"He is scum!" Kazeem said in a voice every bit as quiet, and tossed back what was left in his glass.

"He was appointed superintendent after the Home was destroyed. You cannot just murder a man like that in cold blood! Not unless you really *do* want to end up on the headman's block!"

"Murder is only one definition of killing, Hasir, and while it is true that I may not be able to dispose of him the way I see fit, this is still the East, and it is in my rights to be granted a chance at justice."

"A challenge of honor," Hasir said, understanding.

Kazeem grinned, the roast duck arrived, and all talk of killing—at least for a little while—stopped. They ate well; there was plenty of meat as well as potatoes and vegetables, roasted to what seemed like perfection to young men who usually lived on cold rations.

Kazeem ate quite a bit of unleavened bread with his, and drank an entire carafe of water—something he didn't usually do unless they were sure of the local well. The boys made small talk during the meal, and it was the better part of an hour before they returned to their topic.

"I can understand you wanting the men responsible for your father's death," Hasir said shortly and wiped his mouth. "I respect that, and I will stay out of it. As for Nomar and Elin, I would stand by you if you would have me."

"Thank you, but you have, I think, more to say."

"You think correctly. This business with Baaka Zhinn is madness. You will get yourself killed!"

"Not if I issue a fair and open challenge. You know our laws. Under such circumstances, not even his immediate family can legally retaliate after the Call to Combat has been accepted."

"The operative word here is 'legally'."

Kazeem's smile was huge. "Will I not have my friend Hasir to watch my back?"

"Always. But what if he doesn't accept?"

Kazeem was already shaking his head. "He'd rather die."

Hasir nodded. "Okay, but ask yourself this: is he really responsible for Kalina's death, or was it simply an accident?"

Kazeem was hunched forward, elbows on the table, hands flat. Now he sat back, sighed, and allowed his shoulders to sink. "If you mean, Hasir, do I blame him for the collapsed stairwell, no, but there are…other reasons." He looked like he wanted to say more, stopped himself, licked his lips and turned away, blinking rapidly.

Hasir knew when to stop pushing, and felt saddened at the loss of the man Kazeem could have been. There was a capacity for love and compassion in his friend, all but buried now that would only manifest itself in extreme cases involving factors he could relate to.

"How are you going to do it?"

"I have no immediate plans," Kazeem assured him. "I've secured a good position, and—"

"You can work on your reputation in the meantime; make him sweat a little bit."

Kazeem grinned, tilted his head, and took a sip from the glass the serving girl had just put down.

Hasir was relieved, but tried not to show it. "How about your plans for tonight?" "Tonight, my friend, we will seek the company of fine women, to comfort ourselves in our troubles." He finished his drink in one gulp by throwing his head back.

"I'm powerful glad to hear that," Hasir admitted. "All this talk about death has given me great need for the comfort of fine women!"

*

The rest of that fall went by quickly, and passed into what was considered winter in that latitude. The 'rainy season', as it was called, consisted of a handful of cloudy days and maybe half-a-dozen when rain actually fell. The rest of the time the temperature remained in a range where it wasn't actively *uncomfortable*, so no one complained about the lack of moisture. It wasn't like the local growers counted on it. They had long ago taken to irrigating their fields.

During that fine fall, as the skies churned orange and pink and dusky purple, as cedars darkened and the few deciduous trees showed a splash of color, Kazeem 'worked' on the reputation Hasir had alluded to.

There were several more missions, some like the first, some not, but Kazeem earned further distinction in each and every one of them. He started fights, never backed down, and fought with reckless abandon—as if he were actually *trying* to get himself killed. It didn't seem to matter if he was working as a freight guard, delivering the mail, fighting a small border skirmish or acting as someone's bodyguard. Wherever Kazeem went, whatever he did, the job got done and only the Maker of All Things could help anyone who got in his way. His fierce reputation was, of course, a double-edged sword. The tougher, the *faster*, he was reported to be, the more young toughs came out of the woodwork to challenge him. This, however, didn't last long, as challenger after challenger fell. In a very short time, the word was out—whatever you wanted done, hire Malcor and insist on Kazeem of Zamboor.

For a while, Hasir was able to believe that enough time had gone by for Kazeem to forget about Baaka Zhinn. Kazeem was earning so many bonuses on top of his regular pay, that the only man in the whole outfit making more was the owner—and not by much. To Hasir's way of thinking, Kazeem now had everything a man could want. He had the respect of powerful men, the attention of beautiful women, anything he wanted. He was well on his way to becoming rich. Why then, would he want to toss it all away on an uncertainty? Hasir couldn't see any logical reason, but, then again, he didn't know his friend as well as he thought he did. On the outside Kazeem appeared fit and well adjusted, even happy. He was tall for a Zamborian, good-looking and highly skilled. He always seemed well rested and relaxed. How he felt, however, was a different story. Inside, the true Kazeem was a bundle of raw nerves, a bomb set on a trip wire. He was nervous and shaky and hyper-vigilant. In his mind no one wanted him, no one loved him, and those who *had* were now dead. He was alone, and a target, always and everywhere expecting that knife in the back, that midnight assassin. Kazeem didn't stand on *terra firma* like the rest of his comrades; he stood on the uncertain edge of a great and dangerous precipice, one ready to crumble under his weight at any awful second. There was no place he felt comfortable, not even in a house of worship. He *tried* to pray, but was afraid the Maker would strike him down for such blasphemy.

What then, was left to live for?

When Hasir looked at his friend, he saw another human being. When Kazeem looked at himself, he saw an automaton with carefully monitored feelings. The passion of revenge was all he lived for, and the only thing that motivated him to even get out of bed in the morning. But so much time had passed, and Kazeem looked so *normal*, that Hasir dared to think that maybe, just maybe, the poison of revenge had run its course.

They had just passed the holiday the Westerners called *Michaelmas*. In the Outer Rim there was more diversity, and folks were less intolerant of other ways. It was an Eastern holiday, too, and what matter if some called it one thing, others another? It was a festive, holy time, a time for brotherhood and goodwill. Several very different religions went about their business, but it wasn't business as usual. No one looked down their nose at another, and no one had any trouble accepting an offer of peace from another, no matter *what* he called it. It was a warm, friendly time, even if it was the coldest month of the year.

So to say that it came as a surprise to Hasir to find his friend harboring ill will, was a shock, to say the least.

They were walking one morning in the marketplace on the day before a holy day. The ground was covered in hoarfrost, and crunched underfoot. Breath plumed in the air like tiny, frosted clouds, and a scant covering of grainy snow had fallen the night before. Several boys with too much time on their hands had scraped up what little there was of the stuff, and were pelting each other with snowballs, but the snow was so dry that the projectiles broke apart before they reached their targets. Hasir stopped by a water trough, broke the thin crust of gray ice, and waved the boys over. He proceeded to teach them how to make ice balls, using water and hard packed snow.

As he and Kazeem pushed on, howls of pain and delight testified to his success.

"Is that what you consider your good deed for the day," Kazeem asked dryly, "instructing young miscreants in the art of missile making?"

"I like to do what I can to help today's youth," Hasir managed with an absolutely straight face.

"Very civic minded," Kazeem said, and then they both cracked up.

People were coming and going in their best clothes, heading for temples and churches and mosques. Others milled about, sipping coffee or hot cider purchased from pushcart vendors. There was a cat standing by a jumble of barrels beside the cooper's shop, with a perfectly indignant expression on his face, as if waiting for someone who was late. There was a cedar grove to the east, a stone wall to the west. Except for the beverage vendors and a couple of fruit carts, no one else had even set up shop yet.

"What was it you wanted down here so early?" Hasir asked with a yawn and raised eyebrows.

"Nothing in particular," Kazeem lied badly. His eyes betrayed his off-hand manner, darting swiftly from place to place with disconcerting thoroughness. Kazeem looked like a hunting hawk. One that hadn't eaten in days. "I just thought we might get out, have breakfast. You know, see what the day has in store for us."

Hasir nodded. They could have done *that* at their hotel. Their wages were such that they only stayed in the finest establishments. They could have had breakfast—and anything else they'd wanted—in bed.

"I still think it's too early to be up and about." He rubbed his hands together and blew on them. "Too cold, too."

Kazeem inclined his head. "Go back and knock somebody's eye out with those kids. That'll warm you up in a hurry."

"I, uh, probably shouldn't have shown them that, huh?" he asked with a wince, as a smallish boy took a hit in the back of the head.

Kazeem shrugged. "I've spent time up north, but they might never see snow again. Let them enjoy it while it lasts."

"It *is* kind of weird, even for this time of year, isn't it?"

Kazeem nodded slightly. He was silent for a moment, and his boots seemed loud on the gravel. "Some have said that a great sorcerer plays at controlling the elements, far to the north. Maybe he's bored. Maybe the weather's unnatural."

Hasir had heard such stories. *Dar-Marion, Slagja, Agar-Hoyt* and *Conner-Seth* were talked about in whispers among those more inclined to the occult. The legends said that some of these beings had passed beyond, but that others still walked among us. The sorcerers were the keepers of time and had seen whole civilizations rise and fall. Hasir had even heard that they had fought side by side with humans in great wars, eons past, that they employed immense engines of destruction, and weapons that were biological in nature, and that elves and dwarves and trolls, Gedendrons and urlkin and the mutants called "goblins" had never even existed before one conflagration referred to as the *Great Holocaust*. Hasir didn't buy it. How could chemicals and such be responsible for half the world's population? It was ridiculous. Still, the whole idea made him uneasy, and he didn't like Kazeem discussing it with such derision. Hasir believed that Kazeem would spit in the eye of the devil himself and, despite their friendship, it made him afraid.

"Damn it, Kazeem, must you joke about everything?"

"Who says I was joking?"

"That smirk on your face."

Kazeem was still searching the growing crowd in a way that only intensified Hasir's apprehension. "This?" Kazeem indicated his own face with a finger. "That's just the way I look at the world."

Hasir was about to reply, but an awful tension suddenly filled the air. The hint of ozone and the crackle of power in the air during a thunderstorm came to mind.

And when he saw them an instant later, Kazeem was already heading their way.

"*Maker be merciful*," Hasir whispered, and hurried after his friend.

The others had made it through the cedars, seen them, and were coming straight at them. Hasir half walked, half ran to get in front of Kazeem. He backpedaled, his palms on his chest.

"Are you hungry?" he asked, unable to slow him down. "*I'm* hungry. There's a new tavern down on—"

"This is not your concern, Hasir," Kazeem informed him, and pushed past, boots crunching on hard-packed gravel.

"The hell it isn't, you pompous ass!" Kazeem spared him a brief look, and Hasir took encouragement. "You knew he'd be here! You *knew* it! Didn't you?"

"I may have heard something about it."

"And yet you let me come along!

"You would not have stayed behind, Hasir. *You* appointed yourself my keeper, not I."

Hasir stopped and dug in his heels. He shifted when Kazeem shifted, making it clear that Kazeem would have to knock him down if he wanted to get by.

"You have lived without this for a very long time, Kazeem." His tone was stern, yet caring, but Kazeem didn't even notice. His eyes were leveled over his shoulder at Baaka Zhinn and the five young men with him.

"You have fame, Kazeem. Money. Women and respect. More respect than *that*," he inclined his head, "will ever have. Listen to me," he added as the others reached the road and were waiting only for a wagon to pass. "They're not worth it. *He's* not worth it." Hasir wasn't even making a dent, and he knew it. He took a chance and grabbed Kazeem by the shoulders. "I *know* what happened to you. Becoming like them won't change that. It's not worth your soul."

The six men were crossing the street. Kazeem shifted his eyes long enough to look at Hasir. "It is far too late, my friend, to worry about my soul."

Hasir could see all of it slipping away, but his friend's eyes were still on him, and that was a good sign. "I don't believe that. What's done in battle, in the raw heat of anger, is not the same as planning a death in cold blood!"

Baaka Zhinn and the others were at the near curb, and starting over. Hasir dropped his voice. "I am your friend, and I love you. Trust me. Let this go."

Kazeem's shoulders slumped slightly, and some semblance of control crept back into his eyes. He started to say something, but by then—Baaka Zhinn was upon them.

"Ah, look who is here," he said over his shoulders to the young men. He did this by cocking his head, but without taking his eyes from Kazeem. "Let me introduce Graylan Malcor's celebrated pit bull, Kazeem of Zamboria."

Hasir held his breath. Baaka Zhinn had never done anything to Kazeem, but *causing* it amounted to the same thing. This was something that had been destined to happen, and he was a fool to think otherwise. He'd have more luck trying to change the course of a river.

But again Kazeem surprised him. He looked at the youngsters one by one, with absolutely no expression on his face. Then he turned his attention calmly back to their master. His tone gave away nothing.

"A pleasure to make your acquaintance," he said mildly. The boys stopped snickering when he spoke, but they weren't sure now whether to be angry or complimented. They settled for a collective look of boredom, each copying the studied nonchalance on the next one's face. "*Multan*," Kazeem continued, "you are looking well. I trust your health is good?"

"Never better," Zhinn said with a step forward. He had been hoping to turn the encounter into something to strengthen his own position, and once more this pup had outclassed him. "And any time you doubt it, all you need do is find me."

The expression on Kazeem's face—which was none at all—didn't change. As Zhinn himself had noted more than once, the young Wrotmar was a man of terrible conviction and almost unnatural control.

In a voice that didn't match his icy stare, Kazeem said, "That's a gracious invitation, *Multan*. Thank you. Rest assured, when the time is right, I'll know exactly where to look for you."

The smooth, good-looking face of the man before him almost broke itself into fragments of screaming rage, and then, he, too, regained control.

"When the time is right, I'll be at your service. Until then, I'll look forward to seeing you."

"As will I."

They continued to stare at each other, but the superintendent couldn't hold the young man's eyes for long. He jerked his head, and stepped around Kazeem. The others followed like lemmings.

"That went well," Hasir said.

"Come on," Kazeem said. I believe I owe you breakfast."

"You actually owe me about ten years of my life, Kaz, but I'll take a full belly as partial payment." He let out a breath, causing Kazeem to laugh and wrap an arm around him.

"Filling your belly is certainly something I can accomplish without causing you further distress. I think." He held his friend's neck in the crook of his elbow, rubbing his knuckles briskly on the top of his head as they walked.

Hasir took the ribbing that went along with it good-naturedly, but as they rounded a bend and spotted a good place to eat, Hasir glanced back. Baaka Zhinn stood alone in the street at the top of the hill. The sun was blazing all around him, a fitting allusion to the man's hatred.

Hasir realized sadly—and with more than a hint of panic—that he hadn't prevented anything.

He'd only put it off for another day.

CHAPTER SIXTEEN

BAAKA ZHINN DIDN'T look very handsome at the moment. His hair stuck up in several places, his face was red and contorted from screaming, and he had just thrown a good sized vase through a lovely stain glass window. All of his attendants had fled, leaving him alone. He was grateful for this once he caught a glimpse of himself in the ornate hall mirror, but had to stifle an urge to smash that, too.

He was a mess: robe open, face blotchy, hair disheveled, but at least he felt a little better. There was a basin and pitcher on the sideboard. He poured some, washed his face, and smoothed down his hair. While he was toweling off he began to laugh, easily, at first, then with abandon. Finally, with tears streaming down his face, he sat on a chair and took stock of his position. Not for the first time he wondered if he was more than a little bit insane. Instead of sobering him, the thought brought another gale of laughter. He wiped his face again and stood up.

This new appointment, these new quarters, were far superior to anything he had had at the Home. In every measurable sense, he was better off than he had been. Still, there were times when he would have given anything to go back to the old days, to go back to who he'd been. An administrator: that much hadn't changed, but at the Home he'd been so much more; he'd been almost a god, with every whim attended, with the power of life and death over everyone around him. Now he was no more than a public servant, at least on the surface, and it would take years, *years* to build another organization like the one he'd had. All of this, he told himself, could be laid at the feet of one man: Kazeem of bloody Zamboor and his damnable Wrotmar ways; a boy who never should have even survived his first month, had brought him to ruin, had killed professional soldiers with the same ease with which he'd dispatched the boys from the Home. And speaking of *them*, good gods! He'd seen the reports: bodies mutilated beyond recognition, identifiable by personal affects only. Burned, eaten, hacked to pieces, and probably all of them taken with that same damned calm expression on his face!

Well it wasn't going to happen to *him*, not without a fight!

Multan Zhinn had regained some measure of control. He paused by the only artifact he'd managed to salvage after the destruction of the Home. It was the painting of the wolf pack. The frame had been ruined beyond repair, and the edges of the painting itself singed, but the damage had been reasonably even, trimable and reframable; it wasn't as big as it had been, but it was every bit as *poignant*.

The administrator was calmed by the scene above his desk, wolves hunting in the wilderness, and finally felt that he could stand up without leaning. He took his hands off the desktop and nodded, looking up…and then it came to him. There were two ways to handle this. He could kill Kazeem outright (or have it done), or he could try to bring him back into the fold, use him for all he was worth, and *then* have him done away with. The second option was much more agreeable, and would serve his purpose just the same.

The only thing he had to do was figure out how to go about it. After thinking for a while with his feet up on the desk, Baaka Zhinn actually smiled. When you took the time to think things through, a viable answer usually presented itself.

Like anyone else, Kazeem had weaknesses, something he couldn't say 'no' to; someone he cared for. Some men were easy—wine or women or coin of the realm tempted them. Kazeem would take a little more effort than that, but Zhinn thought he had just the thing. He thought he knew exactly who to use for leverage, and exactly how much to apply.

Baaka Zhinn's smile widened, showing his teeth. It would have pleased him to know that he resembled one of the wolves in his painting.

*

As on so many other nights, Kazeem saw the ants every time he closed his eyes. He heard the screams, and he sat bolt upright in bed, as if he'd been pulled violently by the wrists. Water didn't help, relieving himself didn't help, and looking out the window didn't help. What he'd done was awful and cowardly and worse than anything the creatures he'd dispatched had done to *him*. Instead of getting rid of them forever, he'd *become* them, and it made his skin crawl. He shook his head and hugged himself and walked back and forth, sick to his stomach and hoping it would pass.

Kazeem was well aware of what he'd done. More importantly, he was aware of *why*, but it still seemed like it had been another person who did those awful things, not him. The person he was now would never even entertain the *thought* of torture. Kazeem possessed a good soul, but he was guilty of vile deeds, and it sickened him to think of what he'd done. Still, when he closed his eyes he could feel them on him, *hurting* him, using and humiliating him. He could hear their laughter and their jokes, and that made him even sicker. None of this had been his doing, but that knowledge wasn't any comfort. He'd given back more than he'd gotten, a hundred times more, but instead of feeling satisfaction, all he felt was shame.

To make matters worse, he'd transferred all of his anger—*all* of it—to his foes, did so to this day every time he fought, not only what had been forced on him, personally, but the fury he still carried from the deaths of all those he'd ever cared about. It didn't matter if they deserved it or not, they got all of it, all at once, every time, multiplied beyond counting by his own pain.

And, yet, where had it gotten him?

In the back of his mind there'd always been the hope of returning to Windor, but now he'd have to admit the truth: revenge had not cleansed him, it had insidiously turned him into the things he hated.

And even now, as long as Baaka Zhinn was alive and well and capering in the streets, Kazeem could never be free. He knew he'd have to deal with him eventually, and only admitting that helped him relax enough to go back to bed.

He'd learned long ago that the truth was like that, whether you liked it or not.

The thing was, he would execute Baaka Zhinn, not with hate, but with precision, and because it was necessary. He would do away with him like he would a rapid dog, and with not one ounce more emotion than that.

And then he could get on with his life—such as it was.

Kazeem slept eventually, listening to the soft and steady breathing of the older woman beside him. Her body was warm and soft, full of curves, and she nestled close to him in her sleep. Kazeem took comfort from her presence, and hoped he could remember her name in the morning. There were no dreams this time, at least none he could recall, and the calmness of self-deceit crept over him like a blanket.

In later years Kazeem would not be able to lie to himself, not even for the desperately needed oblivion of sleep. Tonight, however, was different. If he could convince himself that he was mature and well adjusted, if he could convince himself that these things were necessary, then he could rest without that awful pressure in his chest.

The wind came softly into the room, stirring the drapes, lifting them into the air like the myriad ghosts who haunted the corridors of Kazeem's tormented mind.

He awoke sometime later, alert and restless. The girl stirred beside him, and he found her mouth, kissed her and took her; she complied, but she was sleepy. She sighed when he was through, laid her head on his chest, and went back to sleep almost immediately. Kazeem tried to find sleep again, but it was useless, and he knew it. He contented himself with laying there, his strong hand stroking the

girl's soft and silky hair. He had no way of knowing that he would
have trouble sleeping for the rest of his life, and as he would on so
many future occasions, he watched the sun come up, amazed that he
had actually lived to see another day.

*

Hasir kept a close watch on his friend for the next several weeks,
but the extra attention turned out to be unnecessary.

They saw Baaka Zhinn on occasion, going about his business in
the square. They never spoke, only nodded to one another.

"I glad you two have learned to get along," Hasir said to Kazeem
one morning when they were between assignments.

"I'm sorry?" was the reply from Kazeem, who was looking over
his shoulder at Baaka Zhinn and his entourage.

"I said I'm glad you've let this go."

Kazeem smiled that crooked little smile of his. "Have I?"

They stopped at a pushcart where Kazeem bought some dates.
He continued walking, eating them without a word.

"But I don't understand…" Hasir began.

"You're amazed that we can co-exist without violence."

"Well, yeah."

"That doesn't mean we've learned to get along. It just means that
each of us knows where our bread is buttered. He is an influential
person. My personal feelings about him don't change that. On the
other hand, I, too, have become something of a public figure. Neither
can challenge the other without a damned good reason, and even then
it might end up in the courts. We hate each other, and leave it at that.
Of course, if an opportunity presented itself…"

"I do believe, friend Kazeem, that you are the most calculating
son-of-a-bitch I've ever known."

"Why, thank you, Hasir."

"It wasn't exactly a compliment, Kaz."

Kazeem offered him a date. "Sure it was. You just aren't mature
enough to realize it."

"What do *you* know about maturity?" Hasir said, and instantly regretted it. Kazeem may have been young, but he had an elder's way of looking at things.

"Oh, I may have seen one or two things you've been lucky enough to avoid," Kazeem said mildly. "You have very strong opinions about how things *should* be, Hasir, but the truth of the matter is far more complex. *Nothing* is what it seems on the surface. Nothing...and no one." He held up a finger. "Make no mistake, Baaka Zhinn would not hesitate to kill me if he could."

"And I take it the reverse is also true?"

"Absolutely."

"I know you hate him, Kaz, but what did *you* do to him? What started this?"

Kazeem sighed. "He couldn't control me. In addition to that, my conduct held up a mirror that reflected his own behavior, and he didn't like what he saw. Don't ask me to explain why. I can't. The fact of the matter remains that he measured himself against me, and found himself wanting."

"That's *it?*"

"Isn't it enough? Others saw the way I lived and began to stand up for themselves as well. To a man like him that makes me a very dangerous animal."

"But we aren't animals, K!"

"Oh, but we are! We are vicious and self-serving creatures." He waved a hand that took in the whole city. "There is only a thin veneer of civility separating us from the beasts. They, at least, have the excuse of not knowing any better. Conversely, that's what makes us, flawed, perhaps even evil."

"By the gods, K, how do you figure *that?*"

"Stop!"

"What?"

"I said 'stop'. What were you just doing?"

"Huh?" Hasir looked confused. He blinked and shook his head. "I was listening to *you*."

Kazeem reached out, grabbed him by the top of the head, and turned his face thirty degrees. "You were looking at that girl."

"So what?"

"She's beautiful, isn't she?"

Hasir took a better look. "Well, yeah, but she's younger than I thought."

"Yes, she is young, but almost a woman, too. Old enough, no?"

"Old enough for what?"

"Don't play at coyness. I am trying to improve your education. Can you look at me—look me in the eyes—and honestly say that a part of you—if only for a moment—didn't want her, regardless of consequences?"

"Every man feels that way, Kaz," Hasir said defensively. His face was turning red. "We are attracted to the feminine. We are attracted to…to…the energy, and the youth."

"Why not go then, and take her…on the spot?"

"*Kazeem!*"

"I am serious. You eat when you hunger, drink when you thirst. Is this somehow different?"

"Hell, yes!"

"How? If the Maker has anything better, surely He kept it for Himself."

"Kazeem, I might *want* to—if only for a moment, as you said—but I wouldn't. Ever!"

"Why not?" The question was sudden, brutal. It hung there between them like something tangible.

"Because it would be *wrong.*"

"Because you *believe* it to be wrong, Hasir. There is a difference. Not because someone told you, not because it is the law, but because you, yourself, *believe* it to be wrong. It is the same as stealing, no? Taking what does not belong to you, treating a person like a thing. You, being a reasonable person, would not even *entertain* such thoughts. Baaka Zhinn would not hesitate to take what he wanted. Only the law stops him, the fear of punishment, of public opinion. If we *were* animals, we would protect our females with aggressive force.

But we are 'civilized', and so the law does this for us. Otherwise, we'd be killing each other constantly. If you think I exaggerate, think what that girl's father would do to you if he knew what was in your heart—even for that moment. Do you understand?"

"I understand what you're getting at, but not how it applies to what you were *saying*. I mean, you just told me we *were* animals."

Kazeem paused. He ate the last of his fruit, wiped his hand absently on the front of his shirt, and made a face. It was the look of someone who has changed his mind and changed it back again. "We are, but we're flawed. We hide behind that thin veneer of civility I told you about; we use the law like a shield. We're animals, but we're not honest about it. Something in us makes us feel shame when we act naturally."

"You're talking about our souls, Kazeem."

Kazeem shrugged. "You said that people are not animals. I endeavored to prove you wrong. As a man, your natural inclination is to be attracted to and seek out young females, and be willing to kill other males that would seek out yours. It is ingrained in our behavior—part of us, the part we struggle to control, if only because we fear the consequences of doing otherwise. If this were not true, we would not need the law; we are brought up in a lie, Hasir, being told to ignore or control every natural impulse the Maker gave us, being told that those instincts are wrong. We need the law, simply because not all of us can live within that lie—otherwise, we would have no crime. Do you see?" He paused again, and waited until Hasir was looking directly in his eyes. "The law, that thin veneer of false civility I speak of, keeps us from acting naturally—otherwise, Baaka Zhinn and I would have killed one another long ago."

Hasir was shaking his head. "I need ale, and lots of it, if we're going to continue this conversation. You mock the law, but we'd live in chaos without it. Don't you see that?"

Kazeem smiled tolerantly. "It is the lie that makes you think that we are not already living in chaos."

*

They got drunk, but for two days Hasir worried mightily about the mental state of his friend. In the end he came to the conclusion that Kazeem was a sane as anyone else, maybe saner, and maybe *that* made him crazy, simply because he wasn't like everyone else. The more Hasir thought about it the more he became convinced that Kazeem was just more honest than most people, and the more he thought about *that*, the more he drank, so he stopped doing it.

Walking home alone one evening, Hasir considered the fact that, sane or not, Kazeem could go off without warning. Hasir had seen it firsthand more than once. In short, Kazeem was scary, and there were times when Hasir honestly wished they'd never met. Still, Kazeem was the closest thing he had to family, and he worried about him.

Hasir was deep in thought, hands in his pockets, and not as alert as he should have been. Unlike most people, Hasir relished the colder weather. It made him feel alive and relaxed. The streets were nearly deserted at this time of night, but Hasir was no stranger to them, and he was well armed. His way took him down back roads and narrow alleys, through a relatively unsafe section of town. Prudence didn't cross his mind. This was the quickest way home, and no one would dare attack a member of Graylan Malcor's cartel, especially under the light of a very full moon! He went past an abandoned building, turned the corner, and got shoved, hard, into a wall. The blow dazed him, and with his hands in his pockets he couldn't even brace himself. Rough hands jerked his vest down over his arms, effectively pinning them to his sides, and someone else slammed his head against the wall. He had time to marvel how bright the stars were, and found room for one quick thought before he blacked out: maybe Kazeem wasn't crazy after all!

*

The caller came just after midnight. There was a sharp rap on the door, bringing Kazeem to his feet. He reached under the bed for his sword and padded barefoot to the door. He was clad only in soft cotton trousers, tied at the waist, but the sword held an elegance all its own.

Kazeem moved to one side of the door, blade shoulder high, two hands on the hilt, ready to decapitate the first man through.

After a moment, the door opened; someone was standing there.

Kazeem's grip tightened on the sword. His shoulder muscles flexed, and a thin bead of sweat crawled down one side of his face. He waited, not moving, controlling his breathing, until the boy made his way into the apartment, allowing the door to close behind him. Kazeem kept still, wanting to see if the boy was alone. He didn't hear anything, but that didn't mean that there weren't five other men just outside.

The boy turned, went to the bed, called his name, shrugged, and checked the pantry. He was maybe fourteen, and Kazeem recognized him instantly as one of Baaka Zhinn's flunkies. He was dressed in dark, balloon-like trousers, tan blouse, yellow sash. A laborer on the city patrol payroll. The boy looked right, then left, and shrugged again. He started out and was just reaching for the doorknob when a shadow detached itself from the wall and cut him off. The shadow didn't just move, it simply *was*. One moment the way was clear, the next it was blocked. He opened his mouth to protest, but the gleaming blade at his throat made him think better of it.

"Are you alone?" Kazeem whispered; his voice was the sound of raindrops freezing slowly into icicles.

The boy instinctively raised a hand to his throat, but Kazeem flicked his wrist ever so slightly, bringing a bright bead of blood to the surface. "Did I say you could move?"

The boy shook his head, but he did it very carefully. "I am alone. I've come to deliver a message."

Kazeem moved around him, blade still at his throat. He maneuvered the boy away from the door, changed the position of his hands, and forced him into the center of the room. When he had him under the full light of them moon, Kazeem smiled.

"Big surprise there." Kazeem continued to circle until he was directly behind the intruder. The point of his sword rested on the back of his neck. "I'll bet I even know who sent you."

"I can't say."

Kazeem raised an eyebrow. "Am I supposed to guess?"

"The message is: do you remember the wolves?"

Kazeem remembered the painting in Baaka Zhinn's office vividly. He ground his teeth together. "The rest of it?"

"He wants to see you."

"When?"

"Now, tonight. I'll take you."

"What's he want?"

The kid licked his lips. He was nervous, but keeping his head. "I honestly don't know. He only said that a friend of yours was a guest, and that if you *didn't* come, that friend would no longer be considered a guest, and no longer under his protection."

Kazeem sighed. "Tell him I'll be there presently, but not with you."

The kid started to protest, but the angle of the blade shifted again. Kazeem moved around to face him and raised his eyebrows.

Whatever else the kid was, he wasn't stupid. "I'll tell him to expect you."

"You do that, and one other thing."

"As you wish."

"Tell him I'll be more direct than he's been if his 'guest' has been mistreated."

"Hey, that's almost exactly what he said you'd say!"

Kazeem frowned, and shook his head. "Get out. And shut the door behind you."

As the boy exited, Kazeem sighed explosively, dropped the tip of his blade to the carpet, abruptly kicked over a chair, and stood there fuming.

An image of Kalina swam into his mind, followed by one of Bel, Elin, his father... "No!" he hissed, and snatched a shirt off a peg. "Not *this* time, damnit!" With laces tied, he draped his boots around his neck, buckled on his sword, and dropped out the window.

The stars had never been brighter.

*

Kazeem knew the city like the back of his hand. He moved off into the shadows without a sound, his face a mask of barely-controlled rage. Slow and steady breathing calmed him, and after a while he wore no expression at all. In later years friend and foe alike would marvel at the way Kazeem simply materialized whenever he wanted, like magic, and disappear the same way. The truth was more mundane; his stealth was a result of living in a dysfunctional world as a child, of having to go softly to avoid trouble. He had been told that children should be seen and not heard, and at a tender age he'd understood that it was better to be un*seen*, rather than unheard.

In short order he found himself in the alley behind the superintendent's quarters. His travel time was half what it would have been by the main road, and he had met no one. To his right were the administrative offices, to his left a garden. Latticework was covered with creeping grape vines, tomatoes and basil. There were olive trees, too, but they were on the other side.

He was up and over the fence, into the garden and running crouched between rows of staked tomatoes and pole beans as soon as clouds scudded in front of the moon. By the time the shadow of that cloudbank had passed, he was on the back porch of the building, climbing a drainpipe to the second floor. There was a balcony, a glass door, but it was unlocked. He was inside in seconds, flat against the wall in total darkness, waiting for his eyes to adjust. The trip from the alley had taken less than a minute.

While his eyes got used to the light, he listened to the voices in the next room.

"What do you *mean*, he wouldn't come with you?" Baaka Zhinn demanded. "When I give an order, I expect it to be obeyed!"

"Yes, *Multan*, but he had a sword." The boy put a palm to his neck, and brought it forth bloody. "He, uh, told me to tell you he'd make this personal if our guest was harmed."

Baaka Zhinn laughed. "Now you see why I love the lad!"

Hasir was tied waist, feet and hands to a large chair in the center of the room. "If you wanted to see Kazeem," he said petulantly, "all you had to do was invite him."

"Ah, but this is more fun, isn't it, boys?"

The door burst open suddenly, and the guard tumbled into the room. He'd been disarmed, and his lip was bloodied. He rolled to a violent stop against Baaka Zhinn's heavy cherry wood chair, and bounced back into the center of the room, near Hasir, where he sat up with a dazed expression on his bruised face.

"My friend's right," Kazeem said from the doorway. "All you had to do was ask."

There was stunned silence for a moment, and then a surprising reaction: laughter. Baaka Zhinn held out a hand, and two of the eight young men in the room grudgingly slapped money into his palm.

"I'm afraid I read you like a book, Kazeem," Zhinn said as he put away the bills.

Kazeem frowned at this childish display, but didn't dignify it with a response. He went to Hasir and cut his bonds. "What's this all about, *Multan*?" he asked as he pulled Hasir to his feet.

"I just wanted to see how quickly you would come," Baaka Zhinn said companionably. "You know, for sport. It was quite entertaining."

As always, Zhinn's voice was reasonable and pleasant, belying the capering insanity behind his eyes.

Kazeem approached him, still holding his sword. The boys tensed, but a gesture from their master prevented them from trying anything foolish.

"I warned you once before about playing games with me," Kazeem said softly.

Hasir marveled at Kazeem's composure, knew that only a flexed muscle stood between Baaka Zhinn and death.

"The only people that don't like to play games are the ones who aren't good at them," Baaka Zhinn declared. When this was met with stony silence, he sat back in his chair. "Oh, all right." He held up thumb and forefinger, barely apart. "There *is* one tiny little matter."

"I thought there might be."

Baaka Zhinn's eyes narrowed. The tip of his tongue poked through dry lips to moisten them. "Would you think more kindly of me if I was able to reunite you with an old friend?"

Kazeem smiled, but there was absolutely no humanity in it. "With very few exceptions," he began quietly, "most of my old friends...are no longer with us." His icy tone tore at Hasir's heart.

"Most, but not all," Zhinn said.

"You're starting to boor me now," Kazeem told him disgustedly.

"There was a girl," the former administrator said, and tormented his listener by pausing to sip his tea. "Someone you were quite close to, I'm told."

The change in Kazeem startled Hasir. For the first time since they'd been children, his friend became animated. There was passion and hope, tempered with horror on his face for an instant. Then, with tremendous effort, he regained control of himself. "Are you telling me that Kalina Zamonar lives?"

"Her? No." Baaka Zhinn's face showed honest confusion for a moment. It was the one and only time Hasir ever saw sincerity there. "Well, I don't know, actually. We never recovered her body." He pursed his lips. "She very well may have gotten away."

"Or she may be buried under tons of rubble," Hasir interjected. He was rubbing a sore wrist, but he had already strapped his sword belt back on. "Forgive me, my friend, but I would not see you suffer false hope."

Without looking at him, Kazeem put an arm over Hasir's chest and held up a palm, a gesture demanding silence, but Baaka Zhinn was already speaking again.

"Nor I." He leaned forward and put both elbows on the desk, looking straight up into Kazeem's eyes. "I'm talking about the little one. Belayn."

This was the last thing Kazeem had expected him to say, and his guard was down. "She lives?" he asked. To Hasir, his voice sounded shaky and weak.

"Right here," Zhinn told him. "In the city."

"Out!" Kazeem barked, and the force of his command was such that even Baaka Zhinn's troupe obeyed. "Leave me with your master!"

When they'd gone, Kazeem turned around. The paneled room, with its books, tapestries and paintings, looked very large to Hasir now that the boys were gone. "You, too, Hasir, I would talk to *Multan* Zhinn alone."

Hasir struggled mightily to keep the disappointment off his face. "As you wish, my friend. But I'll not leave you. If you need me, call. I'll be right outside the door."

"Thank you," Kazeem managed. There was moisture in his eyes. "If you're lying..." Kazeem said as soon as the door was closed.

"You know I'm not," Zhinn said softly, and sat back again. He folded his hands in his lap.

"Where is she?" Kazeem asked. He closed his eyes for an instant, and took a deep breath. He was trembling, and the knuckles of his right hand where he gripped the sword were white. His head was still turned, as he did not trust himself to look at his nemesis. In his present state, he might skewer him on the spot. "Tell, me, while I still have patience."

"Your patience dried up and blew away long before you got here, but I wouldn't have sent for you if I didn't want to tell you. Surely," he added with, slow, measured tones, "even someone with your limited intelligence should be able to see that."

Kazeem retained that iron will, turning to face him now that he felt more in control of his emotions. Still, he did not speak.

"Excellent," Baaka Zhinn said and slapped his hands down on the armrests as he got up. "I envy your discipline."

"Your opinion of my temperament," Kazeem said through clenched teeth, "means nothing to me."

"Fair enough." The older man kept coming until they were nose to nose. "I don't care what you think of *me*, either."

Kazeem knew it was a tactical error, but he was so distraught he couldn't help himself. "Where is she?"

"Not so fast." Zhinn held up a finger as he began to pace back and forth. "First, we must negotiate a price."

Kazeem crossed his arms to hide the fact that his hands were shaking. He was still holding his wolf's head saber. "I have become quite wealthy this past year," he allowed. "But I will not pay you without proof that the girl lives."

"Who said anything about coin of the realm? I said there was a *price*. I said nothing about money. As to proof, I will provide the girl's whereabouts and allow you to retrieve her before payment is due." He paused by his painting, leaned against the wall with his hands in the pockets of his robe, and waited with raised eyebrows for Kazeem's reaction.

Kazeem allowed a disgusted expression to surface on his face. He actually put away his sword and flopped onto one of Baaka Zhinn's chairs. He rubbed his forehead and eyes with the palm of one hand. "I can't *wait* to hear what you want."

"Nothing you can't afford," Zhinn assured him, and pushed himself off the wall without removing his hands from his pockets. "I'll require a service from you." He pursed his lips to hint that it wouldn't be anything arduous. "Shouldn't take more than an hour of your time, all together."

"If you want to hire an assassin," Kazeem protested and pushed himself out of the chair, "talk to *Multan* Malcor. I won't do your dirty work. Not to earn your lies." He started for the door.

"No, nothing like that!" Zhinn tried, but Kazeem kept on going. Then he played his trump card, blurting out his information and freezing Kazeem in his tracks. "She's at Ula bin Jaglyyn's!"

"What do you want of me?" Kazeem asked without turning, his blood on fire, and his eyes on his boots.

"Why, I want you to fight me in public," Baaka Zhinn said with a laugh, "and I want you to let me win!"

Kazeem nodded after a long moment, unable to look up. He didn't know what else to do. If Bel lived, he had to get her out of there. Bin Jaglyyn's was a whorehouse.

*

The door banged open, slammed off the wall, cracked the plaster and swung to. In the space of those scant seconds Hasir saw his friend explode from Zhinn's office and storm down the hall. Behind them, Baaka Zhinn was laughing hysterically.

"Kazeem! Hey, Kazeem!" Hasir called, hurrying after him. His head was whipping back and forth between his friend and the startled hangers-on, who were now flooding the office. "What is it? What's wrong?" When Kazeem didn't answer, he shouted his name.

"When we're outside!" Kazeem hissed through clenched teeth.

Hasir was a smart lad. He shut his mouth and followed in silence.

Kazeem stalked the length of the hall, pounded down the stairs, knocked the doorman over, and sent clouds of dust into the air when he jumped the last few steps into the street.

He turned left and headed downtown.

"Kazeem! Kazeem! What happened? Where are we going?"

Kazeem stopped, ground his teeth, looked at him, shook his head in frustration and started walking again.

"*What?*" Hasir begged.

"Do you remember the little girl I spoke of?" Kazeem asked. "The redhead?"

Hasir was hurrying to keep up. He was panting and out of breath, trying to walk and ask questions at the same time and wondering why his friend was crying. "The one you and Kalina hoped to adopt?"

"That's her." Kazeem wiped his eyes on his sleeve and started walking even faster. "She's at Madame Jaglyyn's, in the Outer Rim, according to that son-of-a-bitch back there!" He stabbed a thumb over one shoulder.

"God of gods!" Hasir exploded. "Let's get her out of there!"

Kazeem was only capable of nodding.

They hurried on in silence through deserted streets, seeing no one, finding their way by moonlight and occasional street lamps. The 'cold' season was almost at an end, and it would have been pleasurable to pass through the green and fragrant darkness of the olive groves at the city line, but neither of them noticed. They continued on in angry silence, and, in that angry silence, finally reached their destination.

Kazeem was no longer crying, but his eyes were red and he looked more than a little insane.

"Hold on now," Hasir said at last. "It's the middle of the night, and Madame Jaglyyn, despite her occupation, is not without influence in the City Council Chambers."

"You mean *because* of her occupation!" Kazeem corrected.

Hasir looked exasperated. He touched Kazeem on the shoulder. "All I'm saying is, let's use our heads. Incidentally, why did Baaka Zhinn tell you this? What's he looking for?"

"He wants me to challenge him."

Hasir grabbed Kazeem's arm as he started up the steps. "What will you do?"

"I will accommodate him, but not in the way he thinks." Seeing Hasir's confusion, Kazeem patted his arm. "Come, I will explain later."

"You can bet on that," Hasir mumbled under his breath.

*

The inside of Madame Jaglyyn's was posh, decorated in a style far beyond the means of all but the wealthiest in Zamboria. The front hall was open, as client's came and went at all hours, but the house was quiet and dim at the moment.

The hallway before them was adorned with colorful tapestries that lent an extravagant air to the place, and helped keep it warm at night, when desert winds grew cold. Hasir wrinkled his nose at the stale odor of perfume, of tobacco and blinked rapidly, as the hall was illuminated by rushlights only.

"Now what?" Hasir asked.

There was a huge bald man with shoulders like an ox. He sat before an empty desk on a high bench at the far end of the hall, regarding them in expectant silence.

"Let's ask," Kazeem said and started down.

"Careful, my friend," Hasir said softly. "This gentleman does not appear to be refined."

"Can I help you boys?" the man asked, his voice a deep bass rumble that seemed to come from the bowels of the earth.

"We're looking for a girl," Kazeem informed him.

"Isn't everyone?" The big man looked them up and down. He wore a sleeveless jerkin, and his hairy arms were bare. The muscles were huge, and most of his skin was covered with tattoos. To Hasir, he looked like a gorilla he had once seen in a cage at El Mator. "But you two aren't going to find what you're looking for." He folded his arms and pursed his lips. "Not in here."

Kazeem was less than two feet away. All that separated them was the desk. He, too, folded his arms. "Now why is that?"

The bald man looked at them again. "Well...just look at you." Kazeem and Hasir were wearing only plain workman's garb; to make matters worse, they both looked like they'd been through the mill. "Place's too expensive for the likes of you. Where's a couple of kids like you going to come up with enough to cover an appointment in a classy joint like this? Besides, you look too young to me."

Hasir had seen this particular look in Kazeem's eyes before. He hadn't liked it then, and he sure didn't like it now. "Funny you should mention that."

"Oh, why's that?"

"Because that's just what we're looking for. A young girl. A *real* young girl, if you know what I mean?" Kazeem added with a wink.

The bald man stood up. "Who sent you here, you little bastard?" He leaned forward on the desk, massive arms resting on his knuckles.

"No one. Like I told you, we're looking for a girl." He smiled hugely, confusing the big man, but Hasir had seen it all before.

"All you're gonna find here is trouble, sonny," the bald man said. Hasir suspected he was an outworlder, possibly a displaced Westerner, and from the look on his face he wasn't too happy with his lot in life, *or* Kazeem's expression.

Kazeem disarmed him by pulling a small bag of gold from a pouch on his belt. "Let's not be hasty," he said, jingling the coins. "You give me what I want; I'll give you what you want. I go away. You stay here. Everybody's happy."

The man was a player. He'd been down this road before. "You don't have enough in that bag to make me risk my job, boy."

Like magic, a second bag appeared in Kazeem's fist. The man hesitated, then asked, "What else you got, kid?"

"Aw, come on," Kazeem said disarmingly, "don't be greedy. At least hear me out. Find out what I want."

"What *do* you want?" Despite his claimed disinterest, he couldn't take his eyes from the coins.

Kazeem feigned impatience. He rolled his eyes good-naturedly, as if he were jokingly chastising an old friend. "I already *told* you: we're looking for a girl. A *particular* girl, in fact." He handed over the first bag.

"Yeah, who exactly?" the man asked, taking the bag, pulling open the drawstring and looking inside.

"Gorgeous little girl. She'd be...what? Close to ten now, I guess, maybe eleven. Red hair, *flawless* skin, eyes like cornflowers."

The bald man dropped the bag as if it were hot. "We ain't got no little kids in here." He folded his arms again. "Madame J runs an honest house, strictly by the book. Only kids *ever* come in here are the ones she hires as maids."

The second bag clinked onto the desk. "Maybe you just forgot about her." He nodded at the gold. "Does that refresh your memory?"

The man licked his lips nervously. There was a lot of money in those bags. "What do you want with her, assuming she was here, I mean?"

"I'm, uh, her brother. I've come to take her home."

The expression on the big man's face hardened. He had made up his mind, and Hasir was pretty sure how.

"You ain't no brother to no redhead." He pushed the bags across the desk with the back of one hand, as if they were dirty. He leaned on his knuckles again. "I don't know what kind of scam you're running, kid, but I think you should go now."

"Your loss," Kazeem said softly and shrugged. He took the bags back one by one, and secured them in his pouch. Then he looked up with a huge smile, as if there were no hard feelings. He was still smiling when his right fist chopped down on the back of the bald man's left elbow. The blow was so forceful that it broke one of the desk legs as well as the big man's arm. He went down heavily, with Kazeem on his back.

Hasir had trouble believing that anyone could move that quickly—and he had just seen it with his own eyes. One second Kazeem was on this side of the table, facing the man, the next he was behind him, pulling his arm up and back at an unnatural angle. The already broken arm was as pliable as putty under Kazeem's strong hands. When the man cried out, the Wrotmar covered his mouth with one hand, but kept constant pressure on the elbow.

"I'm only going to say this once, you son-of-a-bitch," Kazeem hissed, "so pay real good attention. In a moment, I will release the pressure on your arm. You will get up with me, and take me to the child. If you fight, if you yell, if you struggle or call out or try to get away, I will snap your arm off and beat you to death with it!" He growled the last few words, and applied awful pressure. "Do you understand?" When the bald man didn't reply Kazeem pulled back on the broken elbow even harder; blood spurted from the break in the skin. The man grunted in pain, but the calloused hand covering his mouth was like a vise. "Nod if you understand."

The man was in incredible pain, but he wasn't dim-witted. He nodded, breathing hard, sweat pouring from him in rivers. When the pressure didn't let up, he grunted again, and nodded in an exaggerated fashion.

"There will be no warning, no second chance," Kazeem promised, "so think hard before you act." He removed one hand so the man could speak, but immediately gripped the wrist below the broken elbow for a better grip. "I'm going to let you up now."

"Don't cripple me," the man begged. "I've got a family!"

"He's *got a family*," Hasir said incredulously.

Kazeem threw Hasir a look. Sweat was pouring down his face from his exertions. "You can chastise him later."

Hasir frowned, then nodded. "What do you want me to do?"

"Go ahead of us, open the doors, check it out…"

"You got that."

"Where to?" Kazeem asked. The big man was shaky, but to his credit he was standing on his own.

"That way," the bald man nodded at a staircase in the rear. "Second floor, first door on the right."

The big man was too agonized to speak further, but led them down the hall, up the stairs and halted before the first door on the right. He was gasping, swaying; blood and sweat poured from him. "In there," he managed.

"What else will we find behind that door?" Kazeem asked.

"It's no trick, kid, I swear."

"If it is, you'll be dead before you hit the floor."

"She's in there. That's where Madame J keeps the cleaners. You know, the maids."

"*The maids,*" Hasir said in disgust.

"Let me go now," the man begged. "I haven't done *anything* to you."

"What will happen to you when they find you helped us?"

Fear mingled with the pain in his eyes. This was something he hadn't considered. He shook his head. "I don't know."

"You'll think of something," Kazeem said, and handed him to Hasir. "Hold him, Hasir. If he's telling the truth, let him go, if he isn't, slit his throat!"

*

The face on the pillow was that of an angel—fair skin, soft features, strawberry blonde hair. Her hands seemed tiny, clasped together as they were at her cheeks. Kazeem stood for a moment, shaking, thinking that his heart would burst, and then he pulled back the drapes. With pale moonlight spilling in, he was sure.

"Bel," he whispered, unable to stop the tears. "Wake up, Bel, it's me."

The little girl opened her bright blue eyes.

"I'm dreaming again," she breathed, and closed her eyes.

"You're not dreaming, daughter." He sat on the bed and touched her cheek. "I've come to take you home." He stood back up and pulled back the comforter, but the girl didn't stir.

"Dream," she sighed as her eyelids fluttered. "*Nice* dream." The last two words were slow and drawn out. As she spoke, her long lashes touched her cheeks.

"What's wrong?" Hasir hissed from the doorway.

"I don't know, Kazeem said, and scooped Bel up in his arms. "Bring that big oaf in here."

Hasir brought in the doorman and pushed him into a chair. "Don't move," he ordered. He put away the knife and drew his sword.

Kazeem stood with Bel in his arms. She was dead weight, and seemed heavier than she should have been. He'd wrapped her in a blanket, but one arm hung lifeless, and her hair fell in a gorgeous fan beneath her head. "What's wrong with her?" he growled.

The doorman frowned, and indicated the table with his chin. "Poppy seed elixir. Tastes sweet." He shook his head, bit down on the pain, and cradled the injured arm with the other. "Something in it makes 'em sleepy. So they can't run away. MJ's orders."

Hasir looked at the bald man, went to the table, lifted the vial and held it up to the moonlight. The syrup was gone. Only a splash of color remained at the bottom. Hasir took out the stopper, smelled it, replaced the cork and tossed the vial onto the bed. "I've heard about this stuff. She'll be like this till morning."

"Then let's let her be like this somewhere else," Kazeem said and headed for the door.

"Guess it just wasn't my day," the doorman moaned.

Hasir spared a moment to watch Kazeem exit; when he was through the door, Hasir walked over to the chair. "I'd say it was the luckiest day of your life, whether you know it or not!"

*

"How do you think she is?" Kazeem asked nervously. He was literally wringing his hands.

Despite Hasir's wide experience in the world, there were certain areas where he still required education. To him, one sleeping child looked very much like another. He yawned, got up and bent over the couch for a better look.

"Breathing's okay. Good color." He shrugged. "No bruises or anything."

"I can see that much for myself!" Kazeem snapped irritably. Hasir didn't blame him. They'd been up all night. Kazeem flopped onto a chair and yawned himself. Beyond the drapes a dove-gray sky with pink swirls was just beginning to replace the darkness. He rubbed his face. "We got any coffee?"

"Yeah." Hasir straightened up. "I'll even make it if you stop being such a bear."

"I'm sorry, Hasir." Tears seeped from his eyes again, and he wiped them angrily away. He put his head down, and started to sob. Hasir hesitated, went over, and touched his shoulder. Kazeem stopped, took his hand, and looked up. "I'm so happy to see her, but I'm a mess, too. Sorry."

Hasir patted his shoulder and looked away; he was surprised to find that he, too, was crying. "No need." He sniffed and went to get the coffee started.

"I never expected to see her again," Kazeem added, and sat forward with his hands clasped between his knees. "I just can't help thinking that Kalina should be here."

"She can't stay here," Hasir said after a pause. He stuck his head out of the pantry. There was a jar of ground coffee in on hand and a spoon in the other. "In the apartment, I mean. Who's going to watch her while we're on the road?"

Kazeem covered his face with both hands. "Hell," he mumbled, "I never even thought of that."

Hasir ducked back into the pantry, put the jar away and then rejoined his friend. He sat across from him with a tired grunt. "The coffee'll be ready in a minute; we'll have some, and you can tell me the whole story."

Kazeem made a face. "If you really want to hear it."

"Don't be an ass! Of course I want to hear it!"

"After I tossed everyone out," Kazeem said slowly and yawned again, "*Multan* Zhinn told me about Bel... and what he wanted." A nervous hand ran through his short blond hair. "There were tears in my eyes, Hasir. I couldn't help it."

They could hear the coffee percolating, and it smelled good, too. Hasir got up, went into the pantry and came back with cups in one hand and the steaming pot in the other. "I can guess the rest. An open challenge; you get Bel if you agree to let him win—if he doesn't kill you—and he gets boasting rights. Close?"

"Better than close."

Hasir poured coffee. Drank some. It was too hot, so he put it down. Kazeem took his cup but didn't raise it. He sat with his hands wrapped around it, steam curling into his face.

"What are you going to do?" Hasir asked at length.

Kazeem's eyes blazed. "He underestimated me, Hasir. I don't like that. I'll fight him, just like he wants...and then I'm going to do something he won't expect."

"What's that?"

"I'm going to kill the son-of-a-bitch!"

*

They were on their third cup when Bel woke up. She opened her eyes, yawned, stretched and sat up. She looked around, licked her lips, swallowed...and bolted for the door.

Tired as he was, Kazeem caught her by the arm. She twisted, and he held her by the waist. He couldn't believe how strong she was, and she fought like a tiger. "Bel!" he cried. "PUMPKIN! It's *me!* Kazeem!"

Bel stopped struggling, and he let her go. She turned around and looked up at him. "*OhmyGod!*" she gasped. "I thought I was dreaming!" Sobbing, she touched his face. Instantly, tears welled up in his eyes. "Kazeem? Is it you? Dear, *God*, is it really *you?*"

"It's me, Pumpkin," he managed around the lump in his throat.

Bel didn't have any words after that, only wracking sobs. She sank to the carpet right on the spot, all the strength gone from her tired little body.

Kazeem dropped to his knees, pulled her off the floor, and hugged her. He was crying as hard as she was.

Being unable to hide his own tears, Hasir kindly went back to the pantry to see about putting together a meal.

*

After they'd eaten, Bel said she was tired. They put her to bed, but she wouldn't let them leave. They sat in armchairs, one on either side of her, and in five minutes exhaustion overtook them.

*

It was Bel who did the cooking this time, and, ultimately, that was what woke them. It was halfpart the dinner hour, judging by the shadows on the wall, but they had all needed the rest.

"Smells like she cooks better'n you," Hasir said and sniffed appreciably.

"Everyone cooks better than me," Kazeem joked, even though it wasn't true.

"Have you thought about what we're going to do with her?"

"Yeah, I was going to ask you about that after we ate."

"Me?" Hasir was at the basin washing his face. He grabbed a towel. "What can *I* do?"

"Well, not *you*, exactly, that girl you're seeing..."

"Aw, hell Kaz!" Hasir threw the towel into a corner. "Don't put me in the middle like that!"

Kazeem held a finger to his lips pleadingly.

"All right! All right!" Hasir said in a lower voice. "I'll ask her."

"Thank you. It's just that I don't know anyone, well, you know, respectable, but your friend, Mariam, comes from a good family."

"Stop it!" Hasir begged, but he couldn't keep the grin from his face. "I'll do it. But you owe me. You owe me large!"

"Always." Kazeem got up and hugged him. "Thanks. You're the best."

Hasir pushed him away. "Yeah, yeah, I've heard it before."

Kazeem grew quiet.

"When do you want to tell her?" Hasir asked.

"Now. Tonight." He rubbed his palms together. "As soon as I get up the courage."

Hasir went to a peg on the wall and pulled down a cloak.

"Where are you going?" Kazeem asked, panicked now at the thought of having to break such news to the child alone.

"Relax," Hasir assured him. "I'm only going to Mariam's. It'll be easier on all of us if she's *here*." He paused to buckle on his weapons. "Trust me, Mariam's a good kid. Once she sees that adorable little face and those pouty little lips…"

"Thank you again, Hasir. Uh, when you talk to her, make sure her father understands that I'll pay room and board, that all we want is to place her in a safe home."

Hasir was holding up a hand. "I'll tell her, but I don't think money's going to be an issue."

"I just want to do the right thing, H…I just wish I knew what the hell that was."

*

Bel would have none of it. She took a fit, screaming and crying. Kazeem was her only family now that Kalina was gone, she said, and if they parted, they'd never see each other again, she was sure. Kazeem countered by saying he couldn't work, go out on the road, and leave her alone, and Bel demanded to know why. She'd been alone all this time already, and couldn't Mariam just kind of look in on her, here in the apartment?

"Because one day I might not make it home!" Kazeem snapped in frustration.

Bel wasn't impressed. "Well, who told you to be a bloody mercenary anyway?" she demanded with her bottom lip stuck out. "You're smart. You can do anything you want!"

Mariam and Hasir had remained quietly attentive. This wasn't their fight, but they were too involved to leave.

"I can't help who I am, Bel," Kazeem said, dropping to his knees and facing her.

Bel stood her ground, looking much older than she really was. Her bright blue eyes were suddenly as cold as a mountain lake. "Neither can I."

"I can't take you with me, Belayn. It's impossible. A soldier's camp is no place for a girl, even if it *was* allowed."

She threw her arms around his neck. "I won't let you go anywhere without me, Kazeem! You're all I have. I *love* you. I won't lose you again! I won't!"

Kazeem hadn't heard those three words too often in his young life, and they were all the more powerful for that reason. He could face any man alive, but this little girl, with her honest wisdom, had defeated him. Love wasn't something to turn away from, not for work, not for money, not for anything. This child offered him the one thing his violent life needed, a sense of family, a *connection*, a purpose other than killing. Still, how would he care for her? How would he make a living? Would he meet some woman, settle down, become a farmer? They'd *all* be miserable. He was what he was. That left only middle ground, and the fact that Bel couldn't be denied. She was as fierce as he was in her own way, and it was this thought that helped him make up his mind. "All right, Pumpkin. You win. We'll find a compromise, somehow, you and I."

He pushed her to arm's length. "But there are things I must attend to first, and if I fail, you must go with Mariam, because there won't *be* anyone else. Do you understand?"

"You won't fail, Kazeem, you never do. You made Clara for me, remember?" She threw her strong, slender, little girl's arms around his neck again. "I love you!"

Kazeem looked helplessly over her shoulder at Mariam and Hasir, and held Bel as close as he could. He was crying again, but he just couldn't seem to help it.

*

"What are you going to do?" Hasir asked the next day on the way to Baaka Zhinn's office.

"I've got a plan of sorts, H, but you'll forgive me if I don't talk about it till the challenge is over."

"You want to focus. I understand."

"That's part of it. I don't mean to keep you in the dark, not after all you've done, but I just want to take this one step at a time. I'll tell you everything as soon as I put this behind me."

They walked in silence for a while until Hasir could take it no longer. "Kazeem, why would Zhinn take this chance with you? And what does he hope to gain by beating you? He's beaten many men, and frankly, most of them had been around a lot longer than you. Will beating such a young and relatively inexperienced fighter add so much to his reputation?"

Kazeem laughed. "Haven't you figured it out? This is about control; it's about humiliation. He doesn't want a challenge. He doesn't even want a fight. You're right. He doesn't want to defeat some kid in a duel. He wants to kill me, H, with impunity, under the full protection of the law. His mistake is his arrogance, in his underestimation of me. I got Bel; I got what I wanted. Now I'll deal with the dirty bastard and be done with it, one way or the other."

"You think you can take him?" Hasir asked after a respectable silence.

"Anything can happen," Kazeem answered cryptically.

There had been no need to play act, to dramatize the event. These two hated each other, and everyone knew it. Kazeem had issued the challenge publicly the day before at the City Council Chamber, officially, and with absolutely no emotion whatsoever, stating for the record that this was a private affair that had no other viable solution. Each had agreed to fight until first blood, but of course such agreements were meaningless. Men died all the time in these duels. Where the heat of action was concerned, self-control was always the first casualty.

"There he is," Hasir whispered as Baaka Zhinn, in robes and sandals, his head wrapped in red cloth, his curved sword at his side, descended the Administration Center's steps. There were at least twelve teenage boys behind him. Kazeem shook his head in disgust.

"Why in God's name did you agree to fight him *here?*" Hasir asked.

Kazeem looked sideways at his friend. "I am the one who issued the challenge, Hasir. What difference does it make?"

"It gives him a tactical advantage, and you know it," Hasir stated baldly.

Kazeem shrugged. "Not much I can do about it now."

"Think again," Hasir told him and pointed. Coming down the dusty road were Graylan Malcor and at least a dozen of his men.

"This your doing?" Kazeem asked.

"I couldn't very well let you come here on your own now, could I?"

"You are my friend," Kazeem managed. He didn't trust his voice further at the moment.

"Thank you for coming," Kazeem said and took Graylan's forearm in a handclasp.

"Are you kidding me?" Malcor asked in that curiously western way of his. "I wouldn't miss this for the world!"

"Thanks all the same," Kazeem told him. "It means a lot."

Malcor was still holding his arm. He leaned closer and said out of the side of his mouth: "I'll say it does. You knock this clown on his ass, it makes me look real good, kid. Don't forget, you work for *me.*" He pulled Kazeem closer and said in his ear: "The boys are pulling for you. They've all got money riding on this."

Baaka Zhinn approached them. Malcor released Kazeem, so he could face his opponent. The two groups eyed each other nervously.

"You come to hold the boy's hand?" Zhinn asked.

"This 'boy's' gonna kick your ass, Zhinn," Malcor told him with genuine glee in his strange amber eyes.

"You think so?" Zhinn asked, moving in till they were nose to nose. "When I'm done with him, maybe I'll come for *you*."

Malcor laughed in his face. "If there's anything *left* of you when the kid's through, I'll be right here, cupcake."

"Maybe we should cut to the chase and do it here and now?" Baaka Zhinn suggested.

"Maybe we should at that," Graylan Malcor agreed, his Western vernacular more pronounced, now that he was angry.

"You should," Kazeem said in a tone that brooked no argument, "but *I'm* the one who issued the challenge."

Zhinn stared at his hated rival for a long, heated moment. "I'll see you later."

"No you won't," Malcor told him. "When Kaz is done with you, you won't be seeing anybody."

When Baaka Zhinn moved off to prepare, Malcor turned to his star employee. "Do the rest of us a favor and drop this jerk!"

The men took turns slapping him on the back, offering encouragement, and then moved off to form the circle. Only Hasir remained.

"You up for this?" he asked.

Kazeem took off his shirt, and then his boots. Despite the chill in the air, he was already sweating.

"Always." He wanted to smile, to comment on how much Malcor's Western slang was rubbing off on all of them, but he didn't. He needed to concentrate. "You and Mariam…take care of Bel if—"

"Don't give it another thought."

Their eyes met. "Is there anything else I can do for you?" Hasir asked. He held Kazeem's footwear with two fingers; the shirt was draped over his forearm.

"Pray."

Hasir laughed, but it was strained. "I thought you didn't believe in God?"

"No." Kazeem smiled and clapped him on the shoulder. "I never said that. I only said that maybe *He* doesn't believe in *me*."

Kazeem turned from him, drew his sword from the scabbard, and knelt. He faced the sun, and held the blade horizontally before him, the grip in his right hand, the tip resting on his left forearm, cutting edge towards the heavens.

Father, I haven't led a good life, he prayed, *and I will accept punishment for my sins, gladly, but do not let me fall today. I beg you, do not let this child suffer further on my account.*

Kazeem stood and faced his opponent. Stripped to the waist, Baaka Zhinn stood ready, curved sword in one hand, the tip of the blade resting in the palm of the other. His magnificent physique looked chiseled in the bright morning sun. He was bigger, thicker than Kazeem, but he hadn't had a Wrotmar's training. Kazeem stared at him, memorizing every line, every chiseled plane; he recalled their former encounters, and he remembered all the lessons Windor and his father had taught him.

"You have challenged me," Baaka Zhinn said, "and I will have my satisfaction."

Kazeem wouldn't play that game. He knew the truth; they both did. "Come and get it then."

The combatants circled each other carefully. Kazeem twirled his sword, and raised it with both hands to a ready position above his right shoulder. For all his talk, Baaka Zhinn took Kazeem as a very serious threat. The men around them cheered, catcalled, jostled. Money changed hands. Kazeem shut them out. He remembered an evening not so very long ago, one near the end of his days at Windor's desert retreat. The sun had been in his eyes, then, too, and sweat had covered his torso. There had been a fierce exchange of swordplay, ending with Windor knocking the blade from his bloodless hand. It hadn't happened because of the brilliant fighter Windor was, it had happened because of his own lack of focus. Kazeem didn't mind losing—not deep down in his warrior's heart—but he would take the bitter disappointment of *self*-defeat to the grave.

Therefore, Kazeem reduced Baaka Zhinn to his essence, which was malice, and took in every detail, every subtle leaning, every muscle, until he knew exactly what Zhinn was doing—even as he himself, knew it. Kazeem had been taught, and rightly so, that personal combat was as much in the mind as in the body—more so, in fact—and the best way to frustrate a bold fighter like Zhinn, was to mock him, match him move for move, like a mirror, until he got tired of it and tried something stupid.

"Clever," Baaka Zhinn breathed when they separated, "but I'd hoped for more from you."

"You'll get more," Kazeem said. Such was his concentration that he had barely felt the blows or heard the angry clash of steel on steel. Baaka Zhinn was winded; he transferred the sword to his left hand and shook the right.

"You've gotten stronger," he said with tutorial authority, as if he were an impressed mentor who had been momentarily surprised by an over-zealous pupil.

Kazeem knew better. "I am the same," he taunted. "*You* are weaker."

The strategy worked. Zhinn charged him, yelling his displeasure. Kazeem sidestepped him easily, raking his cheek. A razor thin line of blood appeared instantly. The blood was proof. Kazeem had drawn first, and the blow just as easily could have taken his head.

And they all knew it.

"First blood!" someone yelled from the crowd. "Kazeem has struck first!"

"Yield!" Graylan Malcor called with hands cupped to his mouth.

"I am the wronged party!" Baaka Zhinn screamed back. He clutched his bloody face and leveled his sword at Kazeem.

"*Liar!*" he hissed.

"Go on now," Kazeem said and actually straightened up. The point of his weapon dipped. "Tell them. Tell them what I lied about."

Baaka Zhinn's scream was pure rage. He ran at Kazeem like a berserk amateur, completely out of control, and, like an amateur, he was struck down.

Zhinn got up slowly. It took him a moment to realize that Kazeem had hit him with an open left hand, had slapped him hard enough to dump him on his ass. The men—including some of his own—laughed. Zhinn looked up, wiped the blood from his lip with a free hand, looked at it and smiled. "All right, you little bastard," he said as he caught his breath, "let's see you do that again."

Kazeem knew that, from this point on, it would be a different fight, one that would end only when one of them was dead.

"I *trusted* you," he whispered when they closed.

Kazeem pushed him away. "What do *you* know about trust?"

Baaka Zhinn was in control again, and that made him dangerous.

"Do you remember the wolves?" he asked as they resumed. The wildness was gone from his eyes, replaced by an awful sense of purpose.

"I remember hearing that lone wolves are easy prey," Kazeem said softly, deceptively, then attacked. He went high, went low, went for the midsection for a clean, swift kill, but Baaka Zhinn was ready every time. Where Kazeem had found it easy to penetrate his defenses only moments before, he was now frustrated. He lost his patience after several futile attempts, and received a slash across one shoulder for his eagerness.

Well, he thought, *I won't do* that *again.* The wound was on his left arm and not deep, but he couldn't take too many like that and hope to win, not against someone with Baaka Zhinn's experience.

Getting cut puts you into shock. You had to fight it off. Kazeem did so now, gritting his teeth and focusing on the task at hand.

"Will you yield?" the older man asked quietly, and without any hope in his eyes.

"This'll only end one way," Kazeem said calculatingly, and forced a smile. "I think you know that."

Baaka Zhinn slapped at Kazeem's sword. It was more defiance than an attack, and for one brief moment Kazeem saw a glimmer of fear in his eyes. "You can still walk away. You know what I want."

"I don't give a damn about what you want." He struck back, striking the blade of Zhinn's sword with equal defiance. Then he deliberately turned his head and spat. "You don't walk away from this one!"

"We'll see about that," *Multan* Zhinn said and went immediately, furiously, on the offensive.

The attack was so sudden, so focused, and so fierce, that Kazeem was on his heels in an instant, forced into mere defense simply to keep himself from being sliced to bloody ribbons. For what seemed a lifetime he barely managed to keep his footing, and suffered several nicks from savage blows barely blocked in time. At the end of it he lost his balance and fell flat on his back. He was dazed for an instant with the sun in his eyes, and only managed to escape Zhinn's stabbing, two-handed thrust by rolling to one side. Zhinn hacked at him again, this time with the cutting edge of the huge, curved sword, forcing Kazeem to continue his dizzying roll. When Kazeem got his feet under him at last, springing sideways onto his haunches, Baaka Zhinn chopped at him again. Kazeem lost his balance again, fell to one knee, planted his sword tip first in the ground, blocked the blow and kicked the administrator full in the face. They both fell down, and while the older man scrambled to get up, swinging wildly at an opponent who wasn't even there, Kazeem got slowly to his feet. He was bleeding from a dozen cuts and slashes, but Zhinn didn't look any better. They stood, facing each other, gasping for breath. The right side of Zhinn's face bore the clear outline of Kazeem's open palm. Above it, the eye was beginning to blacken, and was already half-closed.

There was no talking this time. No one had the breath for it. There were catcalls from the crowd, but Kazeem shut them out. His whole world at this moment was the man before him, and no one else even existed.

Bent at the waist with his hands on his thighs, Baaka Zhinn looked up at him and smiled. "Not bad, kid, not half bad." He licked his split lip.

"I'm just getting started," Kazeem managed, and congratulated himself on being able to do so without gasping.

Zhinn nodded, his smirk one of grudging admiration. "Show me."

They straightened, began to circle again, and tried desperately to catch their breath. Both were worn out. Neither wanted to make a mistake now. Yells of derision intruded from those gathered, and with even greater effort than before, Kazeem shut them out.

Baaka Zhinn slapped at his sword half-heartedly, but Kazeem didn't take the bait. There was too much treachery in the man, and Kazeem was trying to concentrate, seeking to tap those deep reserves of strength that the study of any martial art provides—the ability to overcome the body with the strength of the mind.

Zhinn hacked, Kazeem parried. They went on like this for a while, feeling each other out, catching their breath, and that's when Kazeem decided to try something. He lunged in, missing by a wide margin, and deliberately presented his unprotected back. He was ready with a backhand, confident that he could deflect a stab in time, but he wanted to gauge an honest reaction. *Multan* Zhinn, exhausted and seeing his chance, went for it. He tried a straight-arm thrust directed at Kazeem's exposed left kidney, and took a savage backhand blow from Kazeem between neck and shoulder. Kazeem spun, leapt, tilted like an acrobat, and slashed a second time, knocking the blade from Baaka Zhinn's hand. Kazeem shifted his grip and swung two-handed, doing his level best to decapitate the man, but his old nemesis, grievously wounded though he was, still had a few tricks left. On his hands and knees, with Kazeem above him and about to deliver a deathblow, he tossed a handful of sand into the young man's face. The crowd howled in protest, but the damage was already done. With irritating grains of stinging sand in his eyes, Kazeem was effectively blinded. He staggered back while Baaka Zhinn scrambled for his weapon. With magnificent willpower, he didn't raise his hands to his face. He blinked rapidly, keeping his blade before him, and prayed that his vision would clear. The men watching this spectacle continued to voice their displeasure, but as everyone knew, there were no rules in a blood feud.

The wind was in Kazeem's face, and he used it to his advantage. Baaka Zhinn reeked of stale sweat and the over-indulgence of red meat in his diet. There was the coppery odor of blood, as well as the man's awful breath.

Kazeem's eyesight returned slowly as tears sluiced away the sand, but his vision was blurry. That left his ears, his sense of smell, and the sensation of movement around him. He stood stock-still, all available senses heightened and focused. Craftily, Baaka Zhinn held his ground. For several long moments they stayed that way, circling slowly, but the longer they did that, the more Kazeem's eyes improved. Baaka Zhinn knew this and decided to toy with him—for the sheer savage amusement of it—as well as to test Kazeem's vision. The older man moved right, feigned left, and went to the right again. Kazeem stood like a statue using only his ears, and slashed to the right when wind kissed his cheek. There was the clang of steel and a surprised grunt to reward him, as well as the crowd's reaction.

Instead of shutting them out again, this time he listened. They were shouting directions, instruction and encouragement. True, he wouldn't know which voice to trust, wouldn't be able to pick friend from foe in the din, but it was better than nothing. He would put the two streams of information together, and extrapolate. Under the circumstances it was the best he could hope for. Between the yelling, his own best judgment and his blurred vision, Kazeem managed to hold his own. Baaka Zhinn became increasingly frustrated during this time, and his clumsy attempts showed it. Somewhere during this freak show Kazeem's eyes snapped back into focus. He played it down, not giving it away until he was sure he had him cold. Then, with wicked deliberation, he disarmed Zhinn as Windor had taught, twisting his wrist in the air and catching the hilt of his opponent's sword. As the weapon flew off to the side, Baaka Zhinn lunged at it, and received a kick in the chin for his trouble. Choking, he tried again, only to find Kazeem's foot pressing the blade into the sand.

Kazeem's wolf's head flashed in the sun, the tip of the cruel steel stopping just shy of his windpipe. Kazeem wanted him dead—he had no illusions about leaving him alive to cause further mischief down the road—but he wanted him talking, so that he would be revealed for what he was.

"Tell them how the challenge came to be," Kazeem said, drawing a thin bead of blood. "Tell them!" he growled for emphasis.

Kazeem had expected defiance, a lunge for his own weapon, anything but the frustrated, terrified tears that actually came. "Please don't kill me, Kazeem," he cried. "I don't *want* to die!"

"Tell them about Bel."

Baaka Zhinn was on all fours. He was beaten, bleeding and exhausted, humiliated, defeated by a blinded teenager.

"I *made* him issue the challenge!" this sorry excuse for a man cried out. He sat back on his haunches, and then fell forward to his knees,

"Tell them *why*," Kazeem insisted.

Zhinn bit his lip, a trace of his former insolence gleaming in his eyes. Kazeem lifted the blade with the merest flick of the wrist, like a man tossing a bone to a dog. Baaka Zhinn's right ear fell neatly into his lap. He screamed, and clutched the bloody thing, stifling himself only when Kazeem's blade rested on his manhood with a significant pause. "*Tell* them."

"I did it!" Baaka Zhinn cried. "I told him where to find the girl, the one he wanted to adopt!" Tears streamed down his face, mingled with blood, dripped from his chin. "I told him…I told him, if he let me win…I would help him get her back. Please don't hurt me anymore, Kazeem," he pleaded, his pride completely ruined.

Kazeem sighed. Letting him live was a mistake, but this was a chance to atone for his sins, wasn't it? To show mercy? To, perhaps, shorten his own time in hell? Besides, what would it prove to strike down such a pathetic specimen? Every man here acknowledged and respected his prowess in battle. The one sure way to shock them would be to show compassion. Such an act might even things out a bit between him and God, and, at the same time, it would show the world what he truly thought: Baaka Zhinn was nothing.

Kazeem bit his lip. This was among the hardest things he'd ever done. With great effort he refrained from doing further damage. With even greater control, he showed absolutely no discomfort, restraining himself from the simple human actions of rubbing his eyes or using a forearm to remove blood from the slash over his eyes.

"Do you yield?" Kazeem asked. His voice was rock steady.

"I do! I yield to the better man!" Baaka Zhinn broke into sobs. He clutched the severed ear to his chest like a bloody doll, crying like a child.

An odd subspecies of empathy was born in Kazeem. He took a deep breath, and found the air he took in the sweetest in long memory. He hated with a passion the poor excuse for a human being lying in the dust at his feet, but if he could summon enough mercy for *this*, then he could surely accomplish *anything*. And while it might not make up for previous sins, it was a good, solid first step towards redemption.

"This man yields!" Kazeem said in a loud, clear voice. "I will allow him to leave the field."

As tradition demanded, he deliberately turned his back. The men cheered him, chanting his name. Even Baaka Zhinn's entourage recognized a man who fought with integrity, strength and courage. They had no respect for Baaka Zhinn, whether they worked for him or not.

They had even less when he got up with hate blazing in his eyes, and took a knife from a sheath strapped to his leg.

Kazeem couldn't see him with his back turned. He couldn't even hear the warnings the crowd shouted over the din of the others who were still cheering. To make matters worse, even though Kazeem's eyes had improved, they weren't at a hundred percent. He couldn't distinguish between those applauding and those trying to warn him. Baaka Zhinn lurched forward, fell to one knee in the sand, but got up quickly for one so battered and bloody. He stumbled, but closed the gap between him and Kazeem.

And no one was close enough to do a damn thing about it.

The ring of men was closing again. That was the first thing Kazeem noticed. Coming to greet him was one thing, but closing in with something approaching panic in their voices was something else entirely.

And it could mean only one thing.

Kazeem didn't even turn. There was no need to match the stare of his own bloodshot eyes with the hatred burning in Baaka Zhinn. Kazeem could *feel* that heat, and rather than frighten him, if filled him with cold and deliberate fury. Working with Windor had taught him many things, including techniques for reading opponents. The process wasn't anything he could have explained, but that didn't make it any less effective.

The hate-infested creature behind him was dead. Kazeem willed it, made it a reality in his own mind.

The ring of men was closer now, so he didn't have much time. In his mind's eye he saw Baaka Zhinn raise the dagger over his head. He'd be on Kazeem in three steps, intending to plunge the killing thing into his unprotected back. The wolf's head saber was still in Kazeem's right hand, the blade up and resting on his left shoulder. Without even slowing down, Kazeem held that sword before him, and gripped it with both hands, turning the weapon so that its savage, piercing tip faced his own midsection. Kazeem kept walking. From the rear he appeared calm and composed. Without turning, without even looking, without hesitating or drawing a breath, the Wrotmar abruptly fell to one knee, planted himself in the sand, and drove the blade backwards with every ounce of strength he possessed, under his right arm. The cutting tip caught the treacherous Zhinn full in the sternum, splitting him apart like a butchered fowl, and the blade, with all of Kazeem's fury behind it, exploded through the back of the administrator's ribcage. Zhinn shuddered, impaled, breathless—but he was still alive and aware of what was happening to him. With his back still toward the older man, Kazeem gave the blade a savage twist. He turned without letting go of the weapon, and kicked Zhinn away. There was the horrible screech of steel on bone, a gasp of utter despair, and then silence. Baaka Zhinn fell backwards, landing flat on his back in a puff of dusty sand. His head bounced once, dead eyes staring at the sky, and then he was still.

The knife he had intended to dishonor himself with was still in his hand.

Other than to pull the blade out, Kazeem had never even looked at him. He turned back towards the crowd, his face a blank slate, and walked away. The men roared.

"What did I tell you?" Graylan Malcor exclaimed, slapping the back of a fellow gambler. "Ain't he the best you ever saw?"

Everyone agreed. Only Hasir saw the tears in his friend's eyes as he handed him a water skin and a soft cloth. Kazeem's eyes had been tearing all along, but not all of it was due to the sand.

CHAPTER SEVENTEEN

"LOOK AT THIS! Just *look* at it!" Graylan Malcor looked like a miser from one of the old fairy tales. Coins and bills were stacked neatly on the high desk before him, already counted and waiting to be put away. And just like a miser from one of the old lost tales, he actually rubbed his hands together. The palms made a dry, rasping sound.

Akim watched him and chuckled. He was a tall, lanky Zamborian, and had been with Malcor almost from the beginning. He was currently assigned as a Route Master, a job he loved because he got a decent piece of the pie. "You usually don't laugh like this unless you been laid." He leaned back in his chair, grinning hugely.

The building was many things to Malcor's operation: storeroom, warehouse, office, armory, stables and garage, among other things. It had a raised platform at one end, ringed by cedar rails, like a ship's deck, and was called, appropriately enough by the men, 'the dock'. Malcor used it when he wanted to do paperwork and keep an eye on things at the same time, but the huge room was empty for the moment except for the two of them.

"Women aren't everything, Akim. Money is."

Akim laughed again, harder, more honestly. He was smart, but not overly ambitious—a useful combination to a man like Malcor. Akim actually *liked* his boss, but he really didn't trust him; *that* would have been stupid. Men who trusted Malcor ended up one of two ways: serving at his pleasure for shit pay, or dead. Akim didn't relish either prospect.

"I'm telling you, this Kazeem kid's a goldmine!" Malcor waved at the coins as Akim let the chair legs hit the floor.

"Just take good care of him; we don't want to lose a kid who can fight like that." He got up and started putting the money in the safe.

"What, me kill the goose that laid the golden egg?" Malcor looked pained. "I'm crazy, Akim, not stupid." He laced his fingertips behind his head and leaned back in his chair. "In fact, I just heard about these gladiator games they got going up in Vendar. Men, women...regular bloodbath, but, God, they make a *ton* of money up there!" Then he shook his head. "Nah, why take the chance with a kid like that?"

Akim nodded, carefully considering how to bring this up. The east was only one corner of the world. There were trolls and dark elves (*urlkin* to the Westerners), wizards, witches, Gedendron warriors and a place called Arconia that they said had as many trees as Zamboria had grains of sand. Akim was still relatively young. He wanted to see this wide world. There were places to go; there was money to be made, and women to win.

But not if Malcor wasn't careful.

Akim thought again how to broach the subject. He hadn't done well the last time. Still, bad timing or not, it had to be dealt with before Graylan got them both killed.

"Speaking of Kazeem," he began, trying very hard to make it sound like an off-hand comment, "have you given any thought to his next assignment?"

Malcor let his chair slam to the floor. He was suddenly in a bad mood, and didn't bother to hide it.

Akim stood and faced him. "We can be rid of him and that troublesome Hasir all at the same time if we play this right."

"Damn it, Akim, we've already been through all this! I want him close, where I can keep an eye on him!"

"Boss, the kid finds out, he's gonna kill you. Twice."

Malcor sighed explosively, turning his head away at the same time. Akim knew he had him on the ropes now, and pressed his advantage.

"If you send them to Calat, like we talked about, we can keep them on the payroll without tipping them off, and have them safely out of the way, both at the same time." He raised a finger. "And, with *your* contacts, you can keep and eye on him from here."

Malcor frowned. "I'm not sure I want to part with him just yet, Akim."

"Well *get* sure!" Akim took a step closer—a dangerous thing to do with a man like Graylan—but he had to get through to him, he just had to. "That kid ever finds out you…"

"Don't even *think* it!" Malcor hissed, and threw up his hands. He took a step away, shook his head, and turned back, meeting his subaltern's stare, those strange amber orbs bright and intense. Almost…inhuman. It was the thing Akim hated most about working for him. That stare. Those eyes.

"Get one thing straight, Akim; I ain't the one who did it. I'm a businessman, not a bloody politician!"

"Won't matter one bit to that kid, Graylan. I think you know that."

"But I'm just one guy!" Malcor actually whined. "And I'm not even the one who actually did it!"

"Won't matter one tiny little bit to that kid, Graylan," Akim stressed, hammering home the point. "He'll go through the whole damn government and every mercenary in the country if he has to." Akim leveled a finger. "Starting with you."

Graylan Malcor found his chair, leaned back, and frowned. He steepled his fingers in his lap, studying the ceiling. "Calat?" he mumbled after a minute.

"Calat," Akim confirmed. "Either that, or you have to kill him now, yourself, before he finds out. There's no third way."

When Malcor didn't reply, Akim raised his voice.

"For the *Maker's* sake, Malcor! Did you see what he *did* to Zhinn?"

Malcor nodded and sighed. "Kill him. Easier said than done." He let the chair legs bang to the floor again. "Get him in here. Get 'em both in here, in fact, but not together. Set something up for tomorrow."

"I'll handle it," Akim promised. "Trust me, Graylan; this is the best way to handle it."

"No, the *best* way would be to whack the son-of-a-bitch, but I'm afraid he'd go through all my men in a week! Hell, I can see it now: we'd have 'em stacked outside the door like cordwood!"

"Well, hell, boss," Akim asked, managing to keep a straight face, "why don't you do it yourself?"

"I already told you: I may be more than a little bit crazy, but I ain't stupid. You want the truth, though; I've actually grown quite fond of the little bastard."

Akim nodded, but kept his mouth shut. He made a mental note, maybe useful, maybe not. Still, in all the years he'd known him, this was the first time he had ever seen fear in Graylan Malcor's strange amber eyes.

*

"You wanted to see me?"

Kazeem stood at attention in the boss's office. He was razor sharp, as keen as his weapons. A born soldier. Malcor reminded himself of just how careful he needed to be.

"Yes, I did, Kazeem. Please sit down. Is this a good time for you?"

Kazeem actually smiled, but to Malcor, it looked as if it hurt. "These days, one time is as good as another."

"Well, I wouldn't want to inconvenience you. I know you're still trying to find a foster home for your, uh, daughter. We can reschedule, if you like."

Malcor was behind his desk, eyes warm for the first time in Kazeem's memory. Kazeem was seated in a comfortable chair on the other side of the desk. Usually, one stood in Malcor's office. He was either being promoted or being asked to do something. Perhaps the two went hand in hand. He looked around. "No, this is fine. I've already made arrangements."

They had decided that the best place for Bel was with Windor. He'd bring her to his old mentor before his next assignment. Women were rare, but not unheard of, in the Wrotmar class. It was better than what awaited her here in the city, and he could visit her regularly.

"Really? Good."

There was a silence that was more uncomfortable than it should have been.

"I'll just need a few days before my next assignment to see to her needs," Kazeem said finally.

"That's fine," Malcor said, perhaps a bit too quickly. "Take whatever time you need."

"Thank you," Kazeem said. He was more than a little bewildered at this royal treatment.

"But speaking of your next assignment," Malcor said, and took a sheaf of papers, a scroll and a map from the shelf behind him.

This oughta be good, Kazeem thought.

"Speaking of your next assignment," Malcor repeated, "it's customary for me to reward good work—"

"Thank you," Kazeem interrupted, "but I don't need—"

"Please." Malcor held up a hand. "I wasn't finished."

Kazeem sat back. It wouldn't hurt to be polite. He knew he was too impatient, and that was something he needed to work on, especially with people that had been good to him. "Sorry."

"It's the policy of this company, and my personal philosophy, to provide incentives. Not only does this reward excellence, but it also gives inexperienced men something to shoot for. As young as you are, there's a fresh new crop coming along behind you. I want them to see how Graylan Malcor treats his people. I'll get better performance in the long run, so you'll actually be doing me a favor by accepting."

"What, uh, exactly, is it that I'll be accepting?"

"I'll get to that in a moment."

Longest-winded bastard I've ever heard, Kazeem thought, and forced himself to pay attention.

"Despite the fact that he died like a dog," Graylan Malcor was saying, "Baaka Zhinn was one of the best swordsmen south of Vendar. You put him down, and you put him down *hard*; you also work for me. Those are the facts. You made me look good. Which, of course, is my whole point. When one of my men screws up, he makes the whole outfit look bad. I've got to reprimand him. With equal deliberation it's just as important to reward those who bring us to good light. Today, that's you. In fact, it's been you for a long time now." He retrieved his papers and began to arrange them on the table between them

Finally, Kazeem thought. Platitudes were lost on him. He knew exactly what he was and what he was worth. The taking of human lives was not a thing to be proud of. In Kazeem's estimation it was a flaw, a weakness, an expression of fear. A truly strong man would be able to find and employ peaceful solutions. Kazeem was still young enough to be naive about such things, and just jaded enough to be too hard on himself, especially after what he'd been through.

"This is not a pretty business," Malcor went on, as if he were reading Kazeem's mind, "but it's business, nonetheless, our bread and butter. Only the strong survive—in the literal as well as the fiscal sense. Winners earn the accolades and the high priced jobs. Losers get tossed on the slagheap. There's also a widely shared impression that it takes fire to fight fire. If we were asked, for example, to rid a town of vandals, rapists and thieves, we would not send castrated altar boys. Likewise, when we are hired for guardwork, our employers have the right to expect only the best in exchange for their money."

Kazeem managed to keep his mouth shut, but it wasn't easy.

"I have a client," Malcor went on, "a *potential* client, I should say, a very rich, very influential potential client, one that could put us at the top of the list when it comes to the higher paying jobs." Malcor sat back, folded his hands and looked at Kazeem. Kazeem forced himself to keep his eyes off the maps. "This man has several things troubling him at the moment. He is fighting a war on two fronts, financing one out of his own pocket. To make matters worse, he has some beautiful daughters and no sons. The rebel leader behind his troubles has threatened the lives of those daughters, has in fact, already made two failed attempts to take their lives, once with armed men, later with catapults and fire arrows. Needless to say, this greatly annoyed and displeased our potential client. He is seeking a man deadly enough, skilled enough, and smart enough, to keep his children alive, and he is seeking a man who can remain detached and professional. In short, a man capable of keeping his hands off the girls, the youngest of whom, is, uh, quite active, if you know what I mean?"

Kazeem had been on the circuit long enough to know whom the players were. Such stories fairly raged in the public alehouses and Outer Rim tents. "And has the Calipha of Calat been told to expect me?"

Graylan Malcor let his chair slam to the floor. "One does not *tell* the Calipha anything. One *asks*, politely, if one wants to keep one's head."

Kazeem had had all he could stomach of polite talk. He'd picked up most of his Western slang from Malcor, and found this sudden attention to Eastern sensibilities annoying. "Cut me some slack, Graylan," Kazeem said, employing one of those colloquialisms. "You got the wrong man for the job. Keep the girls safe? Sure, I can do that; keep my hands off them? That I can't promise you."

Malcor's eyes narrowed dangerously. "Are you saying you're not professional enough to maintain proper discipline?"

Kazeem sighed. "We've been friends far too long for you to pull outraged rank at this stage of the game, Graylan." Kazeem leaned forward, tilting the maps and taking a quick look. "We're talking about one of the most beautiful and intriguing women in the world here. Not to mention one of the richest. I get around. I hear things. Jordana Liefkin is tall, with lustrous brown hair, green eyes and flawless, olive-hued skin. She is worldly and voluptuous and has a body any queen on this continent would *die* for. She's seduced statesmen and princes, ministers and Kings. One prin*cess* that I know of and probably half the castle guards." He sat back. "There's even a rumor that she's to blame for the war. All of this just shy of her nineteenth birthday, and you want me, of all people, to sleep in the same room with her!"

Malcor struggled hard to maintain a professional distance, didn't make it, and laughed heartily.

"It's a good thing I like you, kid." He closed his eyes, raised his brows, and looked at Kazeem with a sigh. "Hell, maybe that's *why* I like you, because you're so damned irreverent. Now, back to business. As long as you work for me, you go where I assign you. I tried to be nice, because of all you've been through, but you wouldn't have any of that. Now, I want you in Calat. Do you still work for me, or do I have to send Hasir?"

"*Hasir?* God, man, you want to start *another* war? Sending *him* to Calat would be like sending a hungry little boy to a candy shop!"

Malcor was suddenly playing hardball, and it showed in his eyes. "You haven't answered the question."

"I still work for you," Kazeem said evenly. "Just give me a week or so to set Bel straight, and I'm your man."

"You can have the week, but do it on the way. And take Hasir with you."

"You want me to take Hasir *with* me?"

"I want you two to keep an eye on each other, starting dawn tomorrow. Now get out of here and let me get to work!"

As Kazeem left the building, he couldn't help thinking how lucky he was. Not many people were fortunate enough to have an employer like Graylan Malcor.

CHAPTER EIGHTEEN

THE SUN WAS just climbing into the foothills of the Faylon Range as the two men and the little girl set out. The town fell quickly behind them, replaced first by the village of Anatoba, by the shabby huts of Rifton and, finally, by the tents of the Outer Rim. A short part of the journey took them past irrigated fields of olive trees and date palms. After that, a sparse brake of cedar and, then, without almost any transition, they were in the desert. The trio left what passed for a road and coaxed the horses onto the sand. It was windy and their tracks were soon filled, leaving no trace that they had passed. Their mounts were well-trained arabeans, used to the heat, but Kazeem set a moderate pace so as not to overheat them. Even Bel's pony didn't seem to mind.

"Take it easy!" he had told Hasir early on, *"you bake that animal you won't ride double with me!"*

Hasir made an obscene gesture, grimaced when Bel caught him doing it, and burst out laughing. The mood was infectious. As soon as Bel started, Kazeem joined in. If there was a man alive immune to her giggle, Kazeem wanted to meet him. It was good to be on the road again, and all of them felt the same about it. Bel sensed mainly freedom from the boys, a wanderlust neither of them would ever outgrow. It was different for her. Remaining in the city would have meant death for her, worse than death; it would have meant the demise of her spirit, and, very possibly, the loss of her soul. Bel was well aware, even at her age, how hard this choice would turn out to be, but it was her decision as much as his and that made all the difference.

The horses had been picked with care. They were lean, sure-footed and strong. The trio made good time and was resting in the shade of an oasis before mid-morning. They had covered many miles, and would remain here in the shade until late afternoon.

"We're going to travel mostly in the evenings from now on, Pumpkin," Kazeem told her as they ate. "Takes some time to get used to, but it'll be cooler. Better for the horses, better for us."

"That's okay," Bel answered without realizing how Kazeem would take it, "I'm used to being up all night." She smiled sweetly, absentmindedly wiping her mouth on a sleeve. "Can I play under the palm trees?"

Kazeem couldn't find his voice. He nodded, forced a horrible-looking smile, and accepted a kiss on the cheek.

"Little hot for that sort of thing, isn't it" Hasir asked as she scooped up her dolls: two handmade beauties Mariam had bought for her. Kazeem vowed to make her another one himself, to replace Clara, the one he had made for her a lifetime ago.

"Let her be," Kazeem said. His voice was thick.

Hasir looked quickly at his friend. "What's with you?"

Again Kazeem had trouble getting past that lump in his throat. "She took a blanket. She's in the shade. She'll sleep when she's tired."

"That isn't what I asked," Hasir told him.

"I just feel so *bad* for her, H. And guilty, too."

Hasir raised an eyebrow. He looked up from where he was sitting, one hand before his eyes because of the sun. "Why?"

"Because of everything that's happened to her. Because I wasn't around to stop it. I might not know what's right anymore, but I damn well know *wrong* when I see it."

"Listen to yourself! *That's* your fault, too? No one is *that* guilty, Kaz! In fact, you exaggerate your own importance."

"I can't sand it, H." Kazeem looked down at the sand. "When I look in those pretty blue eyes…when I looked in them *before*, I saw a little girl's eyes, wide open and hopeful, now I see…a knowledge that shouldn't be there. It makes me so angry I could strangle someone. She knows things she wasn't ready to know, Hasir, and there isn't a damn thing I can do about it."

Hasir was silent for so long that Kazeem finally turned to meet his eyes. When they did, Hasir said, "You killed the man who ran the Home, the man truly responsible for what's happened to her." In a lower voice he added, "You've killed a lot of people, K, do you feel any better yet?"

"I'm just worried about her, that's all." He sat back down and started eating again.

"Will you take some advice from an old friend?" Hasir asked.

"Sure, what?" Kazeem asked as he chewed a piece of bread.

"Let the past *be* the past." Hasir held up a hand, halting Kazeem's protests. "I know what you are, what you were trained to be; more importantly, I know *who* you are.

You've made revenge a way of life and all it's done is eat away at you. You've punished those responsible for your pain at the Home; you've done away with Baaka Zhinn. The Maker alone knows what else you've done. But the thing is, it's time to let it go. I know you want the men behind your father's death, and those who took Elin and Nomar from you…but where will it stop? When will you find time to live?"

"To set things right—that *is* my life."

"That isn't life, K…it's death. Death waiting to happen. Don't you see that?"

"I appreciate what you say," Kazeem acknowledged with a deep sigh, "but how can I exist, knowing I allow murderous bastards to do the same? How can I live with myself, knowing they're still out there, hurting, killing others?"

"It's a large world, *Wrotmar*," Hasir said softly. "A *very* large world. A man could waste his entire life seeking killers in such a place."

The wind seemed to blow clouds over their heads. Grains of sand made them wince, but the breeze was cool, blessedly so. Kazeem glanced at Bel; she was far enough away; she probably couldn't hear what they were saying. She'd pinned one blanket to a date palm to make a little tent for herself. It made Kazeem smile.

"Is it a waste if one has a purpose?" he asked, and returned his attention to Hasir.

Hasir shook his head, and thought about that while he finished his bread. "Purpose...or revenge? You tell me, are they necessarily one in the same?"

"I don't want to argue with you, H, and I love you for what you're doing. You've been like a brother to me, and you've never steered me wrong, whether I've agreed with you or not. Let us not even speak of it again. Chances are I'll never be able to find the rest of them anyway."

"That's probably best, now that you've got Bel to consider."

"She knows what I do, but no details, not even who we work for."

Hasir was nodding again. "That's probably best, as well."

They were silent while they finished their meal. The clouds moved on, replaced by an unrelenting sun, a great, yellow, baleful orb that had every intention of baking them to death.

Kazeem swallowed a mouthful of water. "We'd better get some rest," he said, and broke out the bedrolls. He walked languidly across the hot sand to Bel's side. "Here," he said, "take this. It's time we got some sleep."

"Can I sleep in my tent?"

Kazeem was arranging a 'bed' of palm fronds and blankets. The sand was soft enough, but it was too hot to lie down on it without insulation. He answered without looking at her. "Uh-huh."

"With my dollies, too?"

"Sure. They need sleep, too."

She giggled as she lay down. "You're *silly.*"

"Snuggle in now."

Bel didn't hesitate to make use of the makeshift little nest. Watching her, Kazeem felt a pressure in his chest that he couldn't have explained. Later on in his life, he would know it as the love a father feels for his child, but right this moment, all he knew was that he'd do anything to protect her. Here she was safe from the sun and sand, and safe from the world. As long as there was breath in his lungs, she always would be.

Kazeem put his bedroll on some palm fronds and sat down on the sand beside her. The saw grass rustled under the gentle, but steady assault of the wind. There was a hint of honeysuckle in the air, even though there was none in sight. He yawned.

"Will you tell me a story, like when I was little?" She popped a thumb into her mouth, reverting just a little, which warmed his heart. A *start* towards normalcy, anyway. Maybe Hasir was right; maybe there'd be an end of it—for all three of them—if he *made* one.

"Of course I will, Pumpkin," he promised, and reached out to touch her hair. The girl allowed a sigh of contentment and closed her eyes.

"It's soooo good to be together again," she said around her thumb and took his left hand with her own.

She'd made him smile. She always had. "Yes, honey. Yes it is, isn't it?"

"Kazeem?"

"Yes, baby?"

"Will Windor let me stay with him, for sure?"

His touch soothed her forehead. "Women are rare, but not unheard of, in the Wrotmar. You will find a home with him until I return, although I still wonder if you wouldn't have been better off with Mariam."

"No." There was an adamant shake of her head, the certainty with which only children can apply to most any situation. "With you...or your family. That means Windor."

"Sleep now, there's no need for worries. Not anymore."

"Are you sure?"

"Yeah," he said gently. "Why wouldn't I be?"

Bel was silent.

"Why *wouldn't* I be, Pumpkin?" he asked again softly, and tucked a lock of hair behind her left ear.

"I'm just afraid you'll forget your job, maybe even forget about me."

"That could never happen," he promised. "Ever."

"Even if you go off looking for bad men?" she asked, and took her thumb from her mouth. At that moment, in that instant, her face grew harder, more mature; he knew then that she would someday be a formidable fighter, and an absolutely devastating young woman. In that instant he pitied any man fool enough to fall in love with such a fearsome creature.

His eyes narrowed, trying to match her stare. "Did you overhear us talking?"

She shrugged, and put her thumb back in her mouth.

"Tell the truth now."

The corners of her eyes crinkled, and she looked like a little girl once more. She took out her thumb again, spread her hands in an, '*I couldn't help it!*' gesture, and allowed a corner of her mouth to turn up. "Well, yeah, a little…I guess."

"You guess," he said, and tried unsuccessfully to look angry.

Bel made a face. "When the wind was right."

"I'm not 'going off' anywhere, my one true love. You are like my daughter, and have been from the start. When my work is done, I will return to you. Besides, our friend Hasir has said that there are too many bad men, and that I should focus instead on the good ones."

"Do you promise?"

"I've said so."

"Say it again!"

He thought once more of that as yet unknown young man somewhere off in her future, and couldn't help but feel bad for him. "I promise."

"Good! Now my story!"

He only had to think for a moment; she had her favorites, after all. "Ah, I've got one. Once upon a time…" he began, and closed his eyes as the cooling breezes from the coast wrapped around them like loving arms.

*

When he was finished, and thought her asleep, he lay down and stretched out beside her. The wind had died, and the sand was still very warm beneath them, in spite of the palm fronds, but with the shade above them, it was as comfortable as it ever got in the desert. He sighed and stretched his legs, amazed at how tired he suddenly seemed to be. He was almost asleep when she called his name, and answered with his eyes closed.

"Hmmmm? What is it, honey?"

"I'm glad you'll be with me again soon, after your work, and won't be off chasing bad men."

"I told you not to worry about that anymore, didn't I? Now go to sleep." He rolled to face her and brushed a lock of hair out of her face. "Besides, I wouldn't even know where to look for the men who killed my father, wouldn't even know where to *start*."

"I'm glad to hear that. I was afraid that, if you found out, you'd leave me."

He closed his eyes again. "I won't leave you, sweetheart." A moment later, his eyes were open again, his heart was pounding, and his fatigue was gone like a dream from another life. He was filled, suddenly, with an awful, purposeful energy. "Belayn, my daughter," he asked carefully, softly, staring into those big blue eyes, "how do you suppose I'd find out?"

"I don't know," she answered, much too quickly.

"Do you know something I should know, child?"

She bit her lower lip, and then started to pout. He hated that, it turned him into jelly, but he forced himself to remain steadfast, and waited her out.

"If I did, if I told you, would you leave me? Forever?"

"I've told you I won't, and you know I don't lie, but it isn't right to withhold information from those you love, simply because you don't want them to do something."

"I *had* heard *some* things, from men...you know, at Madam J's," she began.

God, please don't let her tell me about that, he prayed. *I don't think my heart could stand it!*

"There were two of them one night," she began, and Kazeem clenched his teeth, forcing himself to remain calm, motionless. It was among the hardest things he'd ever do, but somehow, he managed.

"Go on," he said quietly, with incredible willpower.

"They were City officials—I know 'cause I heard them talking. Then they started talking about *you*, that's when I first knew you'd come for me. In fact, it was just *before* you came for me, a day or two, I *think*..."

He wanted to scream, but somehow didn't.

"...you know, talking about the challenge and all? I was in the parlor, and they didn't know I was there. They were waiting for two of the older girls, and I had just finished cleaning but I didn't want them to know that I was there, so I hid behind the curtain." That hard, awful look came over her face again like a shadow. "Sometimes," she said, "they're not *nice*."

Kazeem was like ice inside, ice encasing a raging fire. He was sure that, if he moved, even a little, he'd explode.

"Anyway, they were talking about the big fight coming up between you and *Multan* Zhinn, how the betting was going, odds, you know. Then one of them said it was ironic that you were fighting Baaka Zhinn over trifles—I didn't know what a trifle was, so I looked it up later." She stopped and asked him, "Do you know what a trifle is?"

He nodded, realizing that he wasn't even breathing. Thoughts of what might have happened to her in there, combined with thoughts about his father, threatened to overwhelm him.

"Anyway, they said that it was ironic because the man who had your father killed—the man who was *behind* it—was the word they used, was right here in the city."

The tent fluttered, and for a moment there was the scent of honeysuckle on the air again. He glanced at Hasir, who appeared to be sleeping.

"Did you hear them mention a name?" he asked so softly that he didn't recognize his own voice.

"Yup."

Again he wanted to scream and somehow didn't.

"Do you remember it, sweetheart?"

"Yeah, I remembered it because it was a funny name, like a color." She looked up at him. "Someone named Gray-something Malcor. That mean anything to you?"

Here ends WARRIOR, being Book One of <u>The Faylon Range Trilogy</u>; the story will be continued in Book Two, NOMAD and concluded in Book Three, ASSASSIN.

ABOUT THE AUTHOR

Jaysen Christopher is the author of numerous articles on social justice and human rights published under a variety of pen-names. A martial artist and former investigative consultant he lives in Massachusetts with his wife Susan. He is also the author of The Broken Heroes series, and The Kaylyn Vale Mysteries.

jaysenchristopher.wordpress.com

Printed in the United States
By Bookmasters